Be there at the beginning:

Charlie Hernández and the League of Shadows

CHARLIE HERNÁNDEZ&
THE CASTLE OF BONES

RYAN CALEJO

Aladdin

New York ✦ London ✦ Toronto ✦ Sydney ✦ New Delhi

ALADDIN

An imprint of Simon & Schuster Children's Publishing Division
1230 Avenue of the Americas, New York, New York 10020
First Aladdin hardcover edition November 2019
Text copyright © 2019 by Ryan Calejo
Jacket illustration copyright © 2019 by Manuel Sumberac
All rights reserved, including the right of reproduction in whole or in part in any form.
ALADDIN and related logo are registered trademarks of Simon & Schuster, Inc.
For information about special discounts for bulk purchases, please contact
Simon & Schuster Special Sales at 1-866-506-1949 or business@simonandschuster.com.
The Simon & Schuster Speakers Bureau can bring authors to your live event.
For more information or to book an event, contact the Simon & Schuster Speakers Bureau
at 1-866-248-3049 or visit our website at www.simonspeakers.com.
Jacket designed by Karin Paprocki
Interior designed by Hilary Zarycky
The text of this book was set in Adobe Jenson Pro.
Manufactured in the United States of America 1019 FFG
2 4 6 8 10 9 7 5 3 1
Library of Congress Cataloging-in-Publication Data
Names: Calejo, Ryan, author.
Title: Charlie Hernández & the castle of bones / Ryan Calejo.
Other titles: Charlie Hernández and the castle of bones
Description: First Aladdin hardcover edition. | New York : Aladdin, 2019. | Summary: "When Queen Joanna is kidnapped, Charlie and Violet set out across South America to find her and discover a conspiracy to raise the dead"—Provided by publisher.
Identifiers: LCCN 2019011849 (print) | LCCN 2019016419 (eBook) |
ISBN 9781534426634 (eBook) | ISBN 9781534426610 (hardback)
Subjects: | CYAC: Shapeshifting—Fiction. | Folklore—Latin America—Fiction. | Secret societies—Fiction. | Good and evil—Fiction. | Kidnapping—Fiction. | Kings, queens, rulers, etc.—Fiction. | Hispanic Americans—Fiction. | BISAC: JUVENILE FICTION / People & Places / United States / Hispanic & Latino. |
JUVENILE FICTION / Fantasy & Magic.
Classification: LCC PZ7.1.C312 (eBook) | LCC PZ7.1.C312 Cd 2019 (print) |
DDC [Fic]—dc23
LC record available at https://lccn.loc.gov/2019011849

To every teacher and librarian
who ever put a book in my hands—
thank you

When the dead walk the earth,
the living run in fear.

CHARLIE HERNÁNDEZ &
THE CASTLE OF BONES

CHAPTER ONE

I t was raining frogs. That's the first thing I noticed when we stepped through la bruja's mirror. Fat ones, green ones, black ones. They tumbled from the sky, bounced off the road, clunked off mailboxes. They croaked and chirped and peeped. They hopped through the tall grass like punch-drunk boxers.

One plopped down on the toe of my sneaker, glared up at me with its bulging, beady eyes, and said, "Rrriiiibbbbbiiitt!"

I stared at it for a moment, frowning, then squinted up at the dark churning clouds from where the slimy amphibians were falling in bunches. In *knots*.

My name is Charlie Hernández, and over the last few months, my life had been all kinds of freaky; I'd grown horns, sprouted feathers, teleported from South Florida to northwest Spain, made a quick stop in the Land of the Dead, and even faced off against one of the most famous and feared brujas in all of human history—but *raining frogs . . . ?* Yeah, that was new for me.

"Estamos aquí," said the witch queen, her green eyes blazing in the gloom.

I looked around. We were standing on the side of a narrow dirt track, smack-dab in the middle of . . . well, *nowhere.* A huge, grassy field spread out before us, flanked by walls of thick forest. Pines, maybe. The air was cold. The sky was dark, choked with storm clouds. Thunder rumbled in the distance.

"Where exactly *is* here . . . ?" I asked, but la bruja didn't answer.

Violet said, "And what's up with the *frogs?*" but she didn't answer that, either.

Maybe thirty yards ahead of us a strip of yellow crime-scene tape had been stretched across the field, from end to end, looped around the trunks of the nearest trees. A crowd of curious people was pressing up against the tape, shouting questions as a dozen or so police officers tried to keep them from busting through. There were even more people wandering aimlessly around; these were dodging the falling croakers while snapping pictures of the sky or recording the whole thing on their smartphones.

A couple of little kids in denim overalls were trying to catch the frogs as they fell. I watched one of them catch a plummeting toad in her front pocket, then start cheering and jumping all over the place like she'd just won the Super Bowl. Honestly, if I'd been about seven years younger and wearing overalls, I would've totally jumped in for a round or two. Looked pretty fun, actually.

Past the main crowd, more police officers were hauling heavy wooden barricades out of the backs of police vans, their flashing lights turning the woods red then blue, red then blue.

"Do not leave my side," Queen Joanna warned us. "And speak to no one. We cannot be seen, ¿me entienden?"

As we started across the field, the wind kicked up, shrieking through the trees and slinging the amphibians sideways now. I dodged one the size of a Frisbee, then wrapped my arms around myself, wondering where the heck we were and what the heck we were doing here; thanks to the police cruisers (which had the word "policía" and not "police" emblazoned across the driver-side doors), I knew we weren't in Miami anymore, but that was about it. And that wasn't exactly a whole lot to go on.

"Are they gonna let us through?" Violet asked as we approached the barricade, but again Joanna didn't answer; she simply touched one pale, ringed finger to the golden brooch pinned to the front of her dress (it looked like some sort of butterfly, maybe—or a giant moth) and whispered,

"Vuela," which means "fly," and the pin's wings suddenly beat to life.

It rose silently into the air, a golden blur in the night, and then flew out ahead of us, floating lazily over to where the large crowd was pressing against the police tape. Leaving dusty, glittery trails, the pin began to fly circles above everyone's heads, and next thing I knew, all fifty or so people—cops included—were staring up at it, some pointing and smiling, others giggling with childlike wonder in their eyes.

They were all so mesmerized by it, in fact, that not one of them even glanced our way as we ducked under the ribbon of yellow tape and marched right past them, following the rhythmic swish of the witch queen's cape.

Yep, Joanna was awesome like that. . . .

We'd made it maybe fifteen yards when a fat, bumpy, squishy toad plopped down on the top of my head and just sort of sat there like a warty green hat.

Glancing up at la bruja, I said, "So, about the frogs . . . ?"

"The dark magia in the atmosphere has begun to warp nature," she replied quickly. And pretty casually, too—like she'd just said, *Hey, your shoes are untied.* Or, *Hey, you dropped your pencil.*

Personally, it was my opinion that whenever the words "dark" and "magic" came together in a sentence, the entire situation should be taken a bit more seriously. But, hey, that was just me.

"So not a good sign then, huh?"

The queen stayed quiet, but the frog on my head said, "Riibbbbbiiittt," then hopped off, and I had to resist the urge to try to catch it in my pocket.

Up ahead, where the field curved out of sight, a man and woman in white lab coats strode into view, walking this way. They were carrying walkie-talkies and yelling into them in a language that was almost familiar. Portuguese, maybe?

"¡Escóndanse!" Joanna whispered, and we did exactly that, ducking out of sight and vanishing into the dark woods. Leaves crunched and branches made shifting patterns against the sky as we zigzagged through the trees, leaping logs and rocks. "Do not slow!" she ordered, and Violet and I weren't about to argue. Joanna, also known as the Witch Queen of Toledo, was one of the most powerful brujas on the face of the planet. Not only that, but she was the leader of the League of Shadows, which was sort of like a superhero team-up of the most legendary mythological beings—or sombras—in all of Hispanic mythology. The first time we'd met, she'd fed me worms, then tried to drown me (and basically *succeeded!*) But, surprisingly, it had all been for my own good, so I wasn't holding a grudge. She had dark auburn hair, long dark nails, and even darker lashes framing her glowing emerald eyes. When you topped that off with the golden crown she liked to wear and her elaborate, tiered gown the color of a midnight sky, she might as well have had a big neon sign over her head that read: SUPERNATURAL ROYALTY COMING THROUGH.

As we hurried through the woods, Violet shot me an uneasy look, and finally I couldn't take it anymore—I opened my mouth to ask Joanna where she was taking us and what in the Land of the Living we were doing here, but as we emerged from the trees, the words died on my lips.

My jaw dropped open. My toes seemed to hook themselves into the ground.

Before us, rising up almost as tall as the great trees that flanked the field, stood the most terrible thing I had ever seen—a thing so mind-bogglingly *awful*, my suddenly panicking brain could hardly make sense of it.

CHAPTER TWO

When I was nine years old, my parents took me on a trip to Spain. It was in early October, during the Concurs de Castells celebration, which is basically this huge festival where people get together to create these awesome body towers. Think cheerleader pyramids, but with a *whole* lot more people climbing all over each other, trying to see which team can build the tallest, most complex tower, or "castell." In Catalonia it was a centuries-old tradition, something everyone looked forward to all year. And *this* looked a lot like *that* . . . except a *nightmare* version.

This tower stood at least thirty feet high and was made up of the lifeless, shriveled-up carcasses of at least fifty milk cows. Most had been stacked flat on their bellies, one on top of another, but some were lying upside down, their bony, hoofed legs sticking straight up to support the ones above. There was also a whole mess of bones, big ones, picked clean of any flesh—spines and femurs and hip bones—which seemed to act like a kind of glue, holding the whole thing together. The air was heavy with rotting smells and hummed with the buzzing of flies. Everywhere I looked it was all slack jaws, bulging purple eyes, and the saggy black-and-white folds of dried-up cowhide.

It's a castle of bones, I thought dazedly. And even with my head spinning and my pulse thudding wildly in my ears, I was *positive* about one thing: This wasn't just a random stack of dead cows—no, this was something else, something dark and sinister and otherworldly.

And even more terrifying, it was *alive. . . .*

I could feel its presence like a physical force—like greedy, invisible fingers reaching out from deep within the bony pile, fingers that would grab me if they could—that would hurt me. Would hurt all of us.

"Oh my God," Violet breathed, staring up at it, shaking her head. "What is that *thing . . . ?*"

"The abomination you see before you, niños," said the witch, "has been called many different things by many different peoples. But it is most widely known as a castell."

I blinked, not sure I'd heard her right. "Hold up. You mean, like, *castell* castell? Like, the festival of *people pyramids?*"

"That festival began as a celebration of the day the earth was liberated from these ancient altars of dark magic. It is, in fact, its genesis." Sweat had broken out all over the queen's face. She wiped it with the back of one hand and stared down at me with eyes that seemed to swim in their sockets. Her cheeks were all red and blotchy. She looked tired—no, she looked *exhausted*. "We haven't seen one in many, many years . . . and . . . this one here in Portugal has many worried, for . . . for they are without question an omen of a rising evil."

As she spoke, the wind gusted, tugging at our clothes, and I was pelted by a hailstorm of frogs the size of quarters. One somehow managed to drop down the front of my shirt, and I had to shake it free.

Beside me, the witch queen made an odd, hacking, wheezing sound, as though she was having trouble getting air into her lungs, then began to back away from the terrible pile of bones. "Excuse me a moment . . . I . . . Perdónenme."

"Are you okay?" Violet asked her.

"I'm fine . . . no te preocupes por mi."

"Can we, um, *look around* . . . ?"

"Sí, sí, cómo no. That is why I brought you both."

As Joanna headed farther up the field, away from the castell, Violet began walking slow circles around the castle of cow corpses, looking it up and down with squinted eyes like some crime-scene detective on a TV show. Had this been anyone else, I probably would've laughed and told them to get real. But this wasn't just anyone; this was Violet Rey—or Ultra Violet, as I liked to call her.

Violet wasn't a Morphling like me, but she didn't need any special powers. Mostly because she wasn't your typical middle school student. Take a peek into her backpack and you'll find a pair of military-grade wire cutters, an extra-large can of pepper spray, and a professional forensics kit all tucked neatly beside her Hello Kitty pencil case and pom-poms.

Besides being the captain of both the debate team and the cheerleading squad, Violet was editor in chief of our school's newspaper (the *Leon Gazette*) and there wasn't much she wouldn't do to get a story. Including blackmail. Trust me, I would know. Violet was as tenacious as she was pretty, pretty as she was smart, and so smart she was practically a genius. Cool part was V wasn't one of those people who are all into themselves, either. She was caring, sensitive, *unbelievably* brave, and sometimes even motivational in an army drill sergeant sort of way.

In second grade she'd convinced me that I possessed the inner strength to do the monkey bars backward and using only three fingers. So I'd given it a shot, banged my head on the edge of the slide, spent the rest of that day in the nurse's office, and have been madly in love with Violet ever since.

She might not have been old enough to operate a motor vehicle, but the girl already had detective skills on par with Sherlock Holmes and it was mostly thanks to those skills that I was still alive. So I was happy to stand back and let her do her thing. Currently, Violet was wearing her cheerleading uniform—sneakers, white skirt, crisp white top with gray and blue stripes down both arms. Not exactly the ideal attire for going all CSI on a pile of dead cows, but somehow she made it work.

"Charlie, what kind of sombras could have done something like this?" she asked me, squatting down beside the castell.

I racked my brain. "Um, Dips, I guess. Those are vampire dogs. Obviously, a chupacabra, too . . . They're probably big and hungry enough."

"Check these out." Violet lifted a fold of skin at the base of a dead cow's neck, revealing a pair of marks—no, *holes*.

"How'd you see that?" I asked, stunned. It was like the girl had X-ray vision or something.

"I see everything, Charlie. It's my gift." She sank even lower into a squat, her face now less than three inches from the cow's.

"Ew, c'mon, V . . . stop touching it. It's *dead*."

"It's just a cow, Charlie."

"I know, but it's gross. . . ." And if I'd thought *that* was nasty, she then took her other hand and stuck two fingers into the holes in the cow's neck! There was this sick, sticky, squishy sound, and I nearly barfed on the spot.

"Definitely puncture wounds," she said. "About six inches deep." She jammed her fingers in deeper. A nasty yellowish pus gushed up out of the holes. "Make that *eight*."

"Please"—I burped, tasting this morning's breakfast (pork rinds and a chicken-and-egg empanada) in the back of my throat—"stop." Last thing I wanted was to barf all over the coolest girl in the world, but she sure wasn't making it easy on me.

Finally, Violet pulled her fingers out of the cow. She wiped them on the front of her uniform, staining it blood red and pus yellow.

Yuck and double yuck. "I think I'm gonna puke," I admitted.

V ignored me. "You think a chupacabra could've sucked this many animals dry? I mean, these things got slurped like—*like milkshakes!*"

I sighed.

"What's wrong?"

"I think you just ruined milkshakes for me. Like, *forever*."

She rolled her eyes. "Charlie, I'm being serious. . . . Could a chupacabra have done this?"

"Yeah, I mean, I don't know . . . maybe a pack of them?"

"And are they known to pile up their prey like this?"

"Nah, I've never heard of anything like this. . . ." And I was pretty sure I wasn't the only one either.

"Huh." Violet was down on one knee now, searching around the stinky, blood-spattered, fly-infested base of the castell as frogs hopped and croaked around us; this girl must've been an ER doctor in a past life, because she certainly didn't have any problem with blood or guts. Now, for the record, I wasn't squeamish or anything. Heck, just last summer I'd eaten an *entire* dung beetle on a dare. Okay, so maybe I hadn't *actually* eaten a dung beetle, but I *had* almost touched its nasty, armored insect legs to the tip of my tongue. And that had to count for something, right? Anyway, I had to draw the line on nastiness somewhere, and shriveled-up cow carcasses seemed like a mighty fine place to draw it.

"Oh, c'mon, V, get up. . . . That's *sooooo* nasty." I couldn't even watch anymore. Seriously.

"Interesting." She held up a hunk of wood—no, something else.

I squinted. "Is that—*a chancleta?*"

"Actually, they're called *clogs.* That's what the Dutch call them, anyway." She paused for a second, thinking. "Looks like Cinderella lost her slipper at the ball. . . . We should show this to Joanna. C'mon."

The Witch Queen of Toledo had been standing in the middle of the field, maybe thirty yards from the castell, staring up at the dark sky, which was still pouring frogs. Now she turned, and I saw surprise flicker in her eyes. "You two are still here?" she asked, sounding baffled.

"We, uh, never left . . . ," I couldn't help pointing out. *Geez, what's up with her?*

Violet held out the clog. "We found this near the castell," she said, and Joanna smiled weakly.

"That's very nice, mi vida."

"No, I mean—don't you think it's *odd?* Look at it. This thing's gotta be at least a hundred years old. And cows aren't exactly known for their footwear."

La bruja nodded like she got Violet's point, but her glowing green gaze had already drifted past her. "Odd, sí . . . but we have bigger problems."

I turned, trying to see what she was looking at. "Like what?"

"We're being watched."

"By who?" Violet asked.

The witch queen's voice dropped to a low whisper that told me I wasn't going to like the answer. "*Minairons.*"

CHAPTER THREE

A moment later a strange sound filled the air. It sounded like bees . . . a swarm of angry bees.

Violet glanced around, confused. "What the heck is that?" she breathed.

And suddenly the minairons took flight. Against the starless night sky, only their tiny elven silhouettes were visible. They began to mass together, hundreds of them— *thousands* of them—a shapeless buzzing glob rising higher and higher into the air.

"But there's nothing to worry about, right?" I shot a panicky look back at Joanna. "I mean, minairons are builder elves. They—they're, like, super friendly, *right?*"

Even as I spoke these words, the mass began to form a shape—first a head, then arms, and then wide, muscular shoulders. Whoa, it was like watching a million tiny pixels come together to form a single massive image. Except this image was in constant motion, which made it all the more awesome.

"Um, what are they doing?" Violet asked, sounding a little worried as the newly formed "arm" reached down and picked up one of the boulders that littered the field.

And what it looked like was a) they wanted to play catch or b) they weren't anywhere *near* as friendly as I'd thought.

Joanna hardly had time to say "Get behind me, niños," before the minairons made it very clear that "b" was the right answer and hurled the boulder at us.

"BUT I THOUGHT THEY WERE *SUPER FRIENDLY!*" I shrieked. Thankfully, the queen wasn't as caught up in the whole minairons-being-sweethearts thing as I was. She stepped forward without the slightest hesitation and raised a hand toward the incoming rock. A beam of bright light exploded out of the center of her palm, crackling through the air like a bolt of lightning and cleaving the stone straight down the middle. The two smoking halves, their insides now glowing molten red, plopped harmlessly to the muddy ground, rolling past us on either side and leaving trails of charred grass in their wakes.

But she wasn't done yet. Clearly in pwning mode, Joanna unleashed another blast of energy—this one a shaft of dazzling green light—and another total bull's-eye, piercing the heart of the minairon mass like a flaming arrow. Instantly the enormous shape dissolved, the teeny-tiny elves scattering, shrieking in terror and surprise. Their buzzing grew even louder, deeper, becoming a snarl of anger.

"¡Corran!" Joanna shouted. "Into the trees!"

We ran. My feet flew over the muddy, uneven ground, my heart playing the bongo drums on my rib cage. The funny part was just a couple of weeks ago I didn't believe things like minairons actually existed. I didn't believe in witches, either, or acalicas, or calacas, La Llorona, El Sombrerón, or even La Cuca—none of those creepy old myths. Sure, I'd grown up hearing all the stories. My abuelita was totally obsessed with stuff like that. She loved legends and myths and folklore and had spent her life traveling the globe, collecting tales from all over the Spanish- and Portuguese-speaking world. And I'm not gonna lie—she'd gotten me pretty into them too. In fact, I knew most of the stories by heart. But I never *believed* in them. Not even a little. Which was what made the fact that I was once again running for my life from one of those "made-up" legends *so* sick.

Throwing a terrified glance over my shoulder, I saw that the minairons had already regrouped: They were swarming around the base of an ancient oak near the center of the field, and as I watched, they took the shape of a giant hand, huge brawny fingers closing around the tree's thick trunk.

A split second later, there was a loud *crack!* and an avalanche of dirt came raining down as they ripped the massive tree right out of the ground, gnarled roots and all.

Man, those things were strong!

"HERE THEY COME!" I shouted as the so-very-*unfriendly* minairons surged across the field after us, lifting the oak high into the air. Its huge shadow fell over us. I barely had time to yell "WATCH OUT!" before the colossal tree came screaming down at us.

In the same instant, Joanna whirled, removing her silky red scarf and whipping it in the direction of the minairons with a shriek. Honestly, I wasn't sure what I expected to happen, but it certainly wasn't what *did* happen. Suddenly, with the sound of air rushing into a huge, empty space, the oak caught fire. Tongues of reddish-purple flames licked up the trunk, setting the branches ablaze, and almost immediately the minairon hand disbanded, releasing the burning tree.

"¡DALE!" the queen ordered. "We may be able to outrun them yet!" Only I wasn't so sure about that, because just then another swarm of minairons (they seemed to be coming from everywhere: from inside fallen logs, under rocks—even out of the ground itself!) had joined up with the others, and together they had begun to rearrange themselves into another shape—I could see eyes forming . . . a crooked nose . . . something like an open, snarling mouth: It was the humongous face of a furious minairon! For an instant, an image of my tombstone flashed before my eyes: CHARLIE HERNÁNDEZ—FIFTH

AND FINAL MORPHLING—CAUSE OF DEATH? KILLED BY THE TEENY, TINIEST, MOST ITTY-BITTY ELVES KNOWN TO MAN.

I could already hear abuelas across the world telling the story and their grandchildren laughing their little heads off.

Nah, not this Morphling . . .

I gritted my teeth. Ran harder, faster. The world around me blurred. The frenzied, buzzing sound of the minairons began to fade. I started to believe that we could actually outrun those things, that we could make it. Just maybe.

But then I noticed something strange: Not only had the minairon's buzzing faded—so had any sound of Violet and the queen.

Confused, I looked around and realized I'd pulled way out ahead of them—like, *way* out ahead. Almost thirty yards. But—*how . . . ?*

Then, as my eyes drifted down to my legs, I got my answer: My legs weren't my legs anymore! Well, they were still *my* legs, but they certainly weren't *human* legs. They were almost twice as thick and covered with sleek, black-and-yellow-spotted fur.

Which could only mean one thing—

I morphed jaguar legs . . . JAGUAR LEGS!

I almost couldn't wrap my brain around it. I mean, sure, being a Morphling, manifesting something like jaguar legs was nothing to tweet home about. In fact, in some of the legends my abuela had told me, I'd heard of Morphlings who had manifested puma paws, porcupine quills, and gills—all at the same time! But for me this was a pretty huge deal, because I hadn't manifested so much as *a zit* in almost *a week* now . . . not since I'd battled La Cuca in the kitchen of that little house on Giralda. And to say the rest of La Liga was concerned about my total lack of morphing ability would be, like, the understatement of the *millennium*. Joanna had actually been planning on calling some kind of emergency gathering of sombras (a Convención, I think it was called), hoping that when the scattered clans saw that the League had found another Morphling, more would join us in the fight against La Mano Peluda, which was basically a cabal of evil sombras trying to expand their dominion from the Land of the Dead into our world. But she'd had to ditch those plans, because since my morphing abilities were apparently on perma-pause, none of the other sombras were going to believe that I was *actually* a Morphling. Yet here I was, manifesting *jaguar legs* out of the blue, without even trying to! Talk about total irony.

Unfortunately, though, I didn't even make it another five steps on my awesome new legs before they began to change back, slimming out before my eyes, losing all the beautiful fur and rippling bands of muscles. All of a sudden my human legs couldn't keep up with the speed I'd built up with my kitty ones, and I went sprawling, face-first, onto the damp, squishy ground.

Dazed—feeling like I'd been sucker punched by Oscar

De La Hoya—I pushed unsteadily up to my knees. The world had gone completely silent around me. My thoughts were running through my brain at half speed, like thick syrup creeping down a windowpane.

Glancing back, I saw the giant angry faces of minairons bearing down on me, maybe half a soccer field away. Closer, a voice was calling my name.

I blinked. Slowly. My eyelids felt sticky, heavy. And then came: "CHAAARRRLLIIIEEE!" The voice was everywhere—for that instant it *was* everything, my *entire world*—and then I felt hands hooking underneath my armpits, felt them lifting me to my feet and pulling me forward.

"Charlie, c'mon!" It was Violet. "You have to move! We have to move!"

And that was enough to snap me back to reality. Instantly, as if someone had hit x2 on a Blu-ray player, the world came rushing back in a flood of sound and movement: the sizzling crackle of Joanna's energy blasts, the dark trees blurring past, the deafening buzzing of twenty thousand or so furious minairons. And all I could think was, *We're about to get totally owned.*

"GO," I shouted. "GO, GO, GO!"

But it was too late. Just as we reached the edge of the woods, the mass of minairons crashed over us like a mighty tidal wave.

CHAPTER FOUR

It was like a bee attack, only much, *much* worse, because these things had teeth and claws and tiny little daggers carved out of splinters, and they used all of it to dish out as much pain as humanly—or, in their case, *elfishly*—possible. One jammed something sharp into the side of my neck. Another two landed high on my cheek and yanked out a bunch of my eyelashes. I cried out, trying to squash them under my palms, but slapping my own face felt pretty bad too, and it was essentially useless; for every two or three I turned to jam, another *fifty* were assaulting me somewhere else on my body! Beside me, Violet wasn't doing much better. She kept shouting, "They're everywhere! *Everywhere!*" as she tore madly at her hair, trying to fend off the vicious little elves. But there were simply too many. She shrieked and dropped to one knee as another buzzing swarm slammed into her from the side.

"VIOLET!" Ignoring the pain lighting up my entire body, I started toward her but tripped as a cloud of minairons stabbed me in the shin with a branch.

My left knee buckled, and I fell sideways onto the ground, covering my face, crying out for Joanna.

Just when I thought it was all over, a gust of freezing-cold air roared through the woods, and suddenly the entire forest seemed to come alive. The earth quaked. The soil churned and boiled. Thick vines exploded out of the ground all around us, stretching high into the sky, like long, crooked fingers, and then began to slice through the air like whips. A few of the minairons managed to dodge their attacks, but most weren't so lucky, and those were sent screaming end over end into the stormy sky. A heartbeat later more vines— these thinner and leafier—broke through the soil and began to encircle us. They wound around us like coils, stacking one on top of another until they closed over us like a protective, leafy cocoon.

Next thing I knew, the top section began to unravel itself, opening up like a blossoming flower, and (this part I could hardly believe even though I was watching it happen with my own two eyes) Madremonte, the great protector of nature herself, descended on a nest of writhing, twisting roots.

CHAPTER FIVE

Her hair was a wild jumble of vines, which coiled halfway down her back, squirming like angry snakes as it changed color from harsh reds to pale yellows to tree-trunk brown. Her skin was a deep, rich green that was almost black. Madremonte's name basically translates to "Mother Mountain," which has a warm, friendly vibe to it, but I'd always thought of her as an *angry* mountain because she hadn't exactly been my biggest fan when we'd first met. Still, was I glad to see her? You betcha!

"Madremonte!" I heard Joanna shout, surprised. "¿Qué haces aquí?"

"I had to see the castell for myself," she replied coolly, stepping off the roots. As her feet touched down upon the earth, it was as if the soil itself responded to her, gathering itself into soft mounds under her feet to cushion her steps, which I had to admit was pretty neat. "And fortunately for you three."

"You can say that again!" I shook off a dozen or so minairons still clinging to the tops of my socks and stomped them into the ground.

"Get los niños to safety. I bring news from the south, and I'm afraid very little of it is good."

Her bright yellow eyes met Joanna's. "Can you manage brinco?"

The queen thought for a moment before shaking her head. "Not with both of them."

Madremonte's gaze did not leave her face. The strips of moss and small blooming flowers that grew wild over her body blew in the wind. "The presence of the castell weighs heavily upon you, does it not?"

"Like an iron yoke," Joanna answered, sounding out of breath.

"Llévate el niño. I'll take the girl." Madremonte held her hand out toward Violet. "Vamos."

"Hold up," I said, making a time-out sign with my hands. "You travel *through* roots. Is that even *safe* for her?"

"Quite safe," Joanna replied quickly, motioning for me to move closer. Then she wrapped an arm around my head, her fingers sliding over my face to cover my eyes. An instant later I felt the ground itself yanked out from under my feet, and I knew that when I opened my eyes again, I wasn't going to see Portugal.

CHAPTER SIX

When Joanna removed her fingers, we were standing on the sidewalk of a quiet, tree-lined neighborhood. Artificial cobwebs covered the front door and windows of the house across the street. Cardboard cutouts—skeletons, broomsticks, and bats—hung from the edge of their neighbor's roof. There was a CROCODILE CROSSING warning by the canal across the street, and at the corner I could see a wall of palms with their trunks painted white. Translation: We were back in South Florida. Right near my new house.

My *old* house, the one La Cuca had burned down the day she'd kidnapped my parents, wasn't far from here. Maybe five or six blocks down the street, and every time we drove past it on the way to school or to the grocery store and I saw the charred, crumbling walls and the scorched lawn, I'd feel this awful stab of sadness right in the middle of my chest. But our new place wasn't too bad, I guess. It had been recently built and there were a bunch of mango and avocado trees in the backyard, which was cool. Anyway, truth is, I would've been happy in *any* house. I was just glad to have my parents back.

"¿Estás bien?" Queen Joanna asked me. "Are you hurt?"

I rubbed at an ache in the side of my neck. "Nah, I'm good. . . ."

La bruja studied me closely. In the glow of a nearby lamppost, her eyes glittered like jewels. It was hard not to stare at them. Finally she said, "You are very fortunate to have made it out of those woods alive . . . we *both* are."

You can say that again, I thought. "But—why'd the minairons *attack us?*"

"We were trampling on their homes. The field was full of Saint-John's-wort, and it goes without saying that minairons can be extremely territorial this time of year. Fue mi culpa. I should have realized it sooner." She slipped a hand into her sleeve and brought out a small glass vial. Inside, still buzzing angrily about and pounding on the glass with its teeny-tiny fists, was one of the flower elves; she'd managed to capture one. "Perhaps it can tell us who built the castell. Although I doubt whoever it was would have been careless enough to leave witnesses . . . even one as *tiny* as this."

As we started down the street, Joanna slipped the vial back into her sleeve and said, "Charlie, I want to speak openly with you, if that's all right?" When I nodded, she drew in a deep breath and continued in a low, troubled voice. "The time of peace treaties and allegiances, I fear, has come to its inevitable end. La Liga will soon pass away, and in its place there will be chaos. *Anarchy*. A darkness is descending upon this world, Charlie—no, is already *here*—and I do not believe we possess the strength, or, in some instances, the will to stand against it." She shut her eyes briefly. "Even now La Mano Peluda schemes in secret, plotting our demise. Which is why you must know everything that *we* know, why you must see everything that *we* see, for it is *you* they want most."

"So that's why you took us to see the castell?"

"Sí. The construction of that *abomination* has set into motion a series of otherworldly events—a doomsday clock, if you will—which will tick and tock until its time runs out or *ours* does."

She hesitated, lifting her eyes toward the sky, and for a moment the moonlight glinted off her crown, casting her features in a pale yellowish light. After a moment, she said, "When I was younger—*much* younger, in fact—I thought that with a large enough army I could force peace upon this world. That I could save lives with swords and shields.

This is, of course, not true. You cannot *force* people to live in peace or you yourself will become the very tyranny you sought to liberate them from." Glancing back at me, she shook her head, as if she wasn't sure what she wanted to say—or maybe just wasn't sure *how* to say it. "The world has changed much since my youth," she went on, "yet the nature of evil has largely remained the same. I find that quite interesting, don't you?"

I nodded, not sure what else to do.

Joanna sighed. "Aye, Charlie, there is so much I want to tell you, but the time is not yet right. . . . I know I haven't been myself lately, and for that I apologize. I find myself of two minds, warring against my own nature. The old saying is true: To wear the crown is to bear its full weight. Yet I have learned in the times of greatest testing to look to it for guidance. So that is the advice I now offer you: When you've come to the end of your path and can go no farther—*look to the crown.*"

Trying to seem like we were on the same page or whatever, I just kept nodding along. But the truth was I still didn't have the *slightest* clue what she was talking about.

Suddenly—and with startling speed—Joanna gripped my shoulders firmly in both hands and whispered, "You are the last of five, the fifth and the final. *You*, Carlito, are the only one who stands between La Mano Peluda and the soul of this world. . . . ¿Me entiendes?"

That I understood. "Yes."

Joanna studied my face for a quiet moment before saying, "Sí, sí . . . I perceive that you do, yet I fear I lay too heavy a burden on you, that perhaps you are not ready. However, it is not upon the ready that great tasks are laid, but merely upon the willing." She paused for a moment, her glowing eyes looking deeply into mine. "Are you willing, Charlie? Will you fight for the soul of this world? Will you fight for those who cannot fight for themselves?"

"I mean, yeah . . . but my manifestations—"

"They *will* come. . . . You'll get stronger; I have no doubt about that. *Cero.*"

"Well then, yeah, of course I'll fight."

Joanna gave a firm nod. "Alas, your time has come."

Behind us, a great gusting wind kicked up. It screamed down the block, shaking the trees and sending leaves skittering along the sidewalk. Shielding my face, I turned to glance back. And when I turned around again, the witch was gone.

CHAPTER SEVEN

"CARLITO ERNESTO HERNÁNDEZ, WHERE HAVE YOU BEEN?" my mother shouted the moment I stepped foot through the door. "Sí, sí, acaba de entrar por la puerta," she said into the phone, then slammed it back into its cradle and stormed out of the kitchen, clutching a saltshaker in the shape of a curly-tailed puerquito in one hand, her dark eyes narrowed in a dangerous sort of way. First thing that worried me—she was using my full name, which, in my experience, usually meant trouble. Second thing, she was saying it in Spanish, which *always* meant double trouble.

"Do you have ANY IDEA what you've put your father and me through today?" she yelled at me. "Tu papá was waiting for you in his car for almost *two hours*. Joanna said you were going to be TEN MINUTES!" Lynda Hernández—or as I called her, *Mom*—came from a big family of Cuban immigrants. Like my grandma, my mom was one of the most caring and loving people you could ever hope to meet. But *unlike* my grandma, she had fiery salsa moves, fiery reddish hair, and a fiery Latin temper to match. My mom taught Spanish at my school (and sometimes dance, when the school had the money to offer it), and even though all her students loved her, they knew she was not a teacher you could mess with. Unless, of course, you wanted to spend the year scraping globs of bubble gum off the bottom of desks.

"You *know* you're supposed to call us if you're going somewhere with her!" she continued, wagging the saltshaker at me now and flinging salt all over the place. "That was the deal. We have to know where you are—AT *ALL TIMES!*"

Something hissed and popped behind her. She ignored it. Another thing about my mom—when she gets nervous, she cooks. Some people pace, some people call a friend—my mom bakes, broils, and roasts her fears away. Through the door into the kitchen, I could see at least three different stainless-steel pots bubbling away on the stove top. The oven had been set to 350. The microwave was on full blast, and somewhere in the background I could hear the whir and whine of the blender. I smelled arroz con pollo (my mom's famous chicken and rice), croquetas, which are basically bread-crumb-fried ham meatballs, and the citrusy, tangy scent of mojo sauce. It was all starting to make me kind of hungry.

My mom, meanwhile, hadn't even paused to take a breath. "I tried texting Violet; she never answered back. We had no idea if you were hurt, if something terrible had happened. How were we supposed to find you? Who were we supposed to call?" Her wide brown eyes slid down to my arms, my legs—and for a second I thought they were going to pop out of her head Saturday-morning-cartoon style. "¡DIOS MÍO, YOU'RE ALL SCRATCHED UP!" she cried.

And since I knew this was only going to get worse the more bumps and bruises she spotted, I decided to make my move.

"Mom—"

"¡No lo creo! I take my eyes off of you for one minute— UN MINUTICO—and look what happens! You're a mess! No, you're BLEEDING!"

"Mom—"

"And your HAIR! You look like you went rolling down the side of una montaña! Except there AREN'T any mountains in Miami! What are all those leaves and bits of—"

"Mom!"

She glared at me. "What?"

"I'm okay . . . ," I said, and that seemed to stop her.

Closing her eyes, she reached out and pulled me into a tight hug, her long hair falling over my face like a curtain. "You know that's the only thing that matters to me . . . ," she whispered into my ear. "The *only* thing."

"I know," I said, and thought about how nice it was to have parents who worried about you. Even if sometimes they worried *too* much.

A small laugh escaped her as she gave me another squeeze. "I was driving your poor father crazy trying to find you. . . . ¡Lo tenia *loco!*" She held me for a moment longer, then pulled back to look at me. "So where were you?"

She'd asked it all nice and innocent-like, but I knew my mom well enough to know it was a front; she was still in full-on interrogation mode, which meant that I had to watch my step. And closely. Like walking-through-a-field-of-bear-traps closely. So I decided to play dumb. I was good at that.

"Uh, I was with Joanna," I said. "You knew that."

"Yes, I know. But that doesn't answer my question. I asked, *where* were you?"

"We . . . went for a walk" was the first (and only) thing that popped into my head, so I tried it. Lame, for sure, but I pretty much sucked at lying.

Her eyes narrowed in an *I know something's up* sort of way. "So you went for a walk with Joanna and came back looking like you got beat up by a gang of angry cacti?"

Actually, it was more like a gang of angry flower elves, but she wasn't too far off. "Well, uh, *no* . . . I played some . . . *tackle football* with Violet after." Why couldn't they teach Fibbing 101 at school to help kids like me out?

Thankfully, before I could come up with any other ridiculous excuses, the front door swung open, and my dad came in carrying a silver cross that was almost as tall as he was.

The instant his eyes found mine, I saw relief spread across his face, and he let out a long, low sigh. "Ay, gracias a Dios, you're okay. . . ."

Now, just to be clear, my dad wasn't one of those people who likes to dress all matchy-matchy and stuff, but today he was decked out in head-to-toe Hurricanes gear: green baseball cap, green and orange football T-shirt, orange and gray sweats. My dad had been a University of Miami sports fan ever since he moved here and now he worked for the school as an animal geneticist. Crazy thing was when he told certain people that he was a legit scientist, they'd give him this funny look as if his thick Spanish accent (which I thought was awesome) and his dark honey-colored skin somehow disqualified him from being "a smart person." It sort of sucked that there were people who'd make judgments like that just based on how someone looks or talks, but whatever. My dad was Mexican on his mother's side and Portuguese on his father's, but rooted for the Costa Rican team during the World Cup because Costa Rica was known to have the highest density of biodiversity of any country in the entire world. Yeah, my dad always used stuff like that to pick his favorite teams. Go figure. Anyway, he was tall, about six foot two with thick black hair and dark brown eyes that shouted, "Latino and proud!" All my mom's friends thought that he looked like a telenovela star, which I guess was cool because pretty much everyone told me I was his spitting image.

"Dad? Seriously?" I arched a brow, staring at the ginormous cross he was carrying. "You couldn't have found a bigger one?"

He sighed. "It's your mother. . . . She's making me take it with me *everywhere* I go."

"Ay, sí, *I'm* the crazy one!" My mom, who was still holding the pig-shaped saltshaker, shook it first over one shoulder, then the other, sending salt racing across the tile floor. "Sure!"

Under normal circumstances, I might've found my parents' behavior a little bit . . . well . . . *kooky*. But I couldn't blame them—I'd probably be acting a bit kooky myself if I'd been turned into a little kid's plaything by some bloodthirsty bruja.

My dad kissed me on my head as he set the cross down on the sofa. I heard the springs squeak under its weight. "You gave us a scare today, Charlie," he said, ruffling my hair. "That's for sure."

"So how long should we ground him for?" my mom asked with a sly smirk.

My dad grinned. "I believe eighteen's the legal limit."

My mother wrapped an arm around my shoulder and gave me another squeeze. "You heard your father. Eighteen it is. Now go wash up and get ready for dinner. ¡Tienes que alimentarte porque estás *bien* flaco!"

CHAPTER EIGHT

Dinner with my parents was usually great; my mom was an amazing cook, and my dad always had some interesting animal-related facts or jokes to tell us. There was usually a lot of laughing and talking to each other about our day and stuff like that, but today just wasn't the same; I wasn't sure if it was because I'd almost died at the teeny-tiny hands of arguably the teeny-tiniest sombras on the face of the planet, or the fact that I couldn't get the image of that gruesome castell out of my mind, but I could barely muster a smile for my dad's jokes, and I hardly touched my plate of arroz con pollo, which was my mom's specialty and probably my favorite food in the entire world. My mom, of course—being my mom—figured out pretty quick something was up. She started asking me all sorts of questions, like *What happened today with Joanna? Where did she take you? What'd you see?* And a whole bunch of other questions I really didn't want to answer. Mostly because I didn't want to worry her, but also because I had a whole bunch of my *own* questions racing through my head, like *Why did one of those castell things show up now, after so many years? Who built it? And why did it seem to have such a negative effect on Joanna?*

Problem was, no matter how many times I asked myself those questions, I couldn't come up with any answers. And that bothered me. It *scared* me. Fortunately, I happened to be best friends with a girl who wouldn't quit until she'd gotten a few, and she called me just as I was helping my dad wash the dishes.

"It's all wrong, Charlie," she nearly shouted in my ear when I picked up the phone. "The minairon attack. The castell. Everything! And I'm pretty sure Joanna is keeping secrets from us."

"I got that feeling too . . . ," I admitted, sitting down in the kitchen.

I could hear Violet rummaging around in a drawer. "Anyway, the second I got home, I pulled out a few of my mom's vintage-shoe-collector books and started researching the clog. Turns out, I was right. It's old. And by old I mean, like, early *1600s.*"

"Whoa."

"Yeah, and just to be sure, I snapped a picture and sent

it to one of the appraisers my parents sometimes use, and she totally agrees—in fact, she says she's never seen grain patterns like that before, which means the species of tree that was used to make the clog doesn't even *exist* anymore."

"Double whoa."

"Exactly. So I have to ask myself: What was a four-hundred-year-old shoe made from extinct wood doing in the middle of a field in Portugal?"

Good question. "And let me guess—you have a theory?"

"Working on one, but first I wanna go back to the Provencia. I wanna see if Joanna has any books about those castell things, and I want her to take another look at the clog. My gut's telling me it's important."

And since her gut was usually right, it was time to get the parentals involved.

CHAPTER NINE

y mom agreed to drive us. I didn't say much—just told her we'd left some stuff back at the monastery, and she was more than happy to play chaperone. I hated lying to my parents (and not just because I sucked at it), but in this case the truth wasn't going to help.

It was almost eight o'clock, and the moon was a big silver disk glowing above the rows of palms that bordered Dixie Highway when my mom pulled her SUV into the dark parking lot in front of the church. She told us she'd wait for us here, and Violet and I hopped out and started through the high iron gate, the broad green leaves of the banyan trees crisscrossing over us to form a leafy canopy.

The first time we tried to sneak into this place, back when we'd thought it was just an old Spanish monastery in North Miami Beach, I'd almost been made dinner by some psycho shape-shifting sorcerer (aka a nahual) they'd hired to work security. Later, we learned this place was actually a Provencia—an ancient, warded stronghold used by La Liga and its allies. Since then V and I had probably visited here at least half a dozen times and usually hung out in the gardens or in the massive library with all its ancient scrolls and a ceiling mosaic that showed the map of the world as they knew it in the early 1400s.

"Let's talk to Joanna first," Violet said. "Show her the clog again and then go from there."

"Sounds like a plan," I said, and it did—

Except that the moment we walked through the tall, arched doors leading into Joanna's study, our plan crumbled like week-old cookies.

Queen Jo's study, which to me had always felt like some fancy Spanish museum (you know, the sort of place you'd visit on a school field trip and wouldn't be allowed to touch anything) now looked like a total *war zone*.

There were huge, smoldering craters in the marble walls big enough to drive a semi through. Jagged cracks zigzagged their way across the domed glass ceiling, and the slimy green guts of plant life were splattered all over the furniture and floors like bugs on a windshield. I could see muddy handprints on the tile; they made faint tracks over the thick red-and-gold carpets, as though someone had been dragging themselves across the room. Weird thing was, they'd only been using one hand—the tracks all appeared to be right-handed. In the center of the room, the queen's colossal wooden desk had been overturned. Papers and postcards and small leather-bound notebooks—all stamped with old-school wax seals—were strewn everywhere. Every single drawer had been ripped out, their contents scattered carelessly about.

On the other side of the room, the beautiful oak bookcases had been toppled over; books littered the floor, their covers torn off, pages shredded. Even the paintings had been pulled down. A few were lying on the carpet near the wall with their backs peeled away like an onion skin.

The only thing that appeared to have been left undamaged was El Espejo de Viaje—the magical, body-length mirror we'd stepped through earlier today to get to Portugal.

"What the . . . ?" Violet's words died on her lips, and the ones inside my brain didn't get much farther. Slowly, careful not to step on anything, we picked our way to the center of the room, where Violet lowered herself into a crouch, peering around. Her shocked expression was already gone, replaced by her trademark look of concentration.

"What are you doing?" I whispered.

But she ignored me, her blue eyes scanning the room. Yep, she was in full Sherlock mode.

"V? *Hello . . . ?*"

"There was a struggle," she said after a pause so long that I didn't think she'd heard me.

I blinked. "A *what?*"

"A fight. . . . Check out the hand and claw marks on the desk."

I hadn't noticed those: more muddy prints, along with a few deep, curving scratches in the wood.

"They're on some of the handles of the drawers, too." Violet stood up and went over to the desk, stepping carefully around a pile of charred, smoking stuff. "Looks like they were fighting over something . . . ," she said. "Something in one of the drawers." Squatting down, she peered into the huge piece of overturned furniture, then narrowed her eyes, gazing around as if she were trying to see into the past. "Here—*right* here—is where the would-be thief stood. . . ."

"The who?" I honestly had no idea what she was talking about, and I started to get the feeling she wasn't talking so much to me as to herself.

"Scuff marks on the tiles indicate a sudden powerful transfer of weight, which makes it pretty obvious that they were the ones who flipped the desk." She pointed at the floor in front of her, and I could almost make out the outline of footprints on the pinkish tiles. "Joanna, most likely standing on the other side at this point, would've had to jump back to avoid it"—her eyes tracked along the ground, following something I couldn't see—"but . . . she *stumbled*. Hit her back against that wall." I could see a vertical, almost shoulder-width crack in the marble. V passed a hand over it as she said, "Then, as Joanna struggled to find her balance, the thief tried to *end her*." Violet's fingers traced the charred rim of the still-smoldering crater in the wall; it was just a foot or two to the left of the crack. "But Joanna obviously dodged it or there would be an extremely well-dressed corpse with a smoking hole in it right about *here*."

"But there isn't," I said, "so that's good, right?"

"That's *very* good. But . . ." Violet cleared away the blackened remains of some old scroll with her foot, uncovering a small wooden box. It reminded me of one of those fancy boxes people use to keep expensive family heirlooms and stuff, lacquered on all six sides and polished to a rich coppery shine. "*Interesting*."

"What is that?" I whispered, still trying to catch up.

"Maybe what they were fighting over. . . ." There was some kind of fancy combination lock on the box, but Violet didn't bother with it. Carefully she thumbed the latch, flipped it open . . . and her lips bent into a frown.

"It's empty," I said, not understanding.

"That's because they weren't fighting over *the box*; they

were fighting over whatever was *inside* the box...."

"So the thief or whoever got it, then? Left the box behind."

Violet was shaking her head as she gazed slowly around. "No, I don't think they did get it...."

"What? Why not?"

"First off, the little combination lock on the box had been opened. I doubt a thief would've wasted time trying to figure it out here; they would've just taken the box with them, messed with the combination later. Second, check out the craters in the walls...."

I shrugged. "What about them?"

"Well, they're not just on the wall behind the desk; they run along that entire side."

"So?"

"So that means Joanna was still scrambling around and they were still trying to hit her with those blasts or whatever."

"Which means she probably still had whatever they were after...," I said, finally starting to see the same movie that was playing in Violet's head.

"Exactly." Violet's footsteps echoed softly on the marble floor as she edged her way around the craters, and I followed, placing my feet exactly where she had. She paused near the entrance to the widest and most ornate of the three hallways, where a large hunk was missing from the top of the golden archway, as if something huge had taken a bite out of it. "They almost got her *here* . . . and that's when she finally dropped whatever it was they were fighting over."

"How do you know?"

She pointed at the floor where there was a slight indent in one of the tiles; but it could've been made by anything.

"Okay, then what?" I said.

"Well, then they took it from her." Violet paused for a moment, thinking. "Unless . . ."

"Unless *what?*"

"Unless Joanna had a moment—just *a second*, really—to hide it. . . ." Dropping down onto her hands and knees, she peered into what looked like a small mousehole at the base of the archway. She pressed her left cheek flat against the floor . . . and suddenly her eyes lit up. With all the excitement of a little kid on Christmas, she reached into the hole with the tips of her fingers and brought out what looked like—

"*An egg?*" Violet said, sounding about as confused as I felt. But that was exactly what it looked like—a big, shiny, yellow egg. Even weirder, as she held it between her thumb and index finger, the egg seemed to glow faintly. Like a cocuyo. Or a half-drained glowstick.

I honestly didn't get it. Actually saying I didn't get it would be like saying the earth is big. It didn't quite do my level of not-getting-it justice. "Is that what they were fighting over? Why? I mean, *why?*"

"It's solid *gold*, Charlie. . . . I can think of about *a hundred million* reasons why someone would want this."

"Okay, so gimme one."

She gave me a sideways look. "I'm talking about money, Charlie. Cash."

Oh. Duh. Knew that.

Violet thought for a second, then said, "Quick! Hand me the box."

The box. Right. I hustled over to it, snatched it up like I was running the line drill in PE, then brought it back to her and watched with silent fascination as she placed the golden egg into the small scoop in the soft velvet lining of the box. It was a *perfect* fit.

Violet's eyes grinned up at mine. "We have a match."

CHAPTER TEN

I was about to open my mouth to tell Violet that what she'd done was probably the most amazing thing I'd ever seen *in my life* when a soft rattling sound came from somewhere nearby. Violet and I froze, staring at each other for a moment in silent panic, like we'd been caught passing answers during a pop quiz.

Then, slipping the egg into her backpack, she whispered, "What was that?"

"No idea." My eyes scanned the room, trying to pinpoint the source of the sound. "I think it came from the desk."

Violet nodded. And we both crept not so silently toward the huge piece of overturned furniture, our feet crunching plaster and chunks of charred marble like a couple of half-panicky, completely *un*-stealthy ninjas.

When we reached it, I bent down, peering into one of the empty drawer compartments. There was another low, crackling rattle, and in the shadows deep inside the desk, I spotted a slim glass tube lying on its side.

"What is that?" V whispered into my ear.

Shaking my head, I cautiously reached one hand into the hole. And as my fingers closed around the tube, I remembered that this was what Joanna had used to capture one of the minairons that had attacked us in Portugal.

And the flower elf was still in there!

"Is that what I think it is?" Violet hissed.

"Yep." There was a soft *pop!* as I yanked the plastic stopper out.

"Isn't it . . . *dangerous?*"

"Shouldn't be. It's all alone." I swirled the tube gently, but the tiny elf wouldn't wake—it didn't even flinch.

V frowned. "Is it—*dead?*"

"Might've just died. ¡Apúrate! Get me . . . get me some *water and dirt!*"

Violet was off and running almost before I had finished talking, and next thing I knew she was back, holding some sort of fancy teacup in one hand and a scoop of dirt in the other. "Here," she said, dumping the dirt on the floor next to me. "Fresh from the garden."

"Thanks." I gathered it up with my other hand, shaping it into a nice fluffy mound, then poured the tiny elf onto it. Next I dipped my fingertips into the teacup and sprinkled the minairon a few times. Just to be clear, I had no idea if any of this would actually revive the thing, but I knew that they came from plants, so I figured what works for a plant might work for a plant elf. King of logic, that's me.

Seconds passed—nothing. I felt dumber with each one that went by. I started to panic, wondered how CPR would work on something this tiny (especially the mouth-to-mouth part), and right as I was about to dip my fingers into the water again and try another sprinkling, the minairon suddenly sucked in a harsh, choking breath. It sprang to its feet, looking wildly around, and shouted, "AAAAAAYYYYYY!"

Violet and I jumped back in surprise. Man, that thing could yell! "Hey, you okay?" I asked it.

The elf gagged, coughed, and gagged some more, shaking its bald little head. I guess the answer was no. "Perdona, pero tienen caras *muy* grandes—me asustaron." Its voice, thin and high pitched, reminded me of a teakettle.

"What'd it say?" Violet wanted to know.

"That we have very big faces and we scared it."

V didn't take too kindly to that. Her eyes narrowed into thin slits. "Well, tell it that it has a very small, very *blue* face and that it scared *us*."

The minairon buzzed angrily, batting its tiny, translucent wings. "I speak English, you know!"

"*Good!* Then start talking. What happened here?"

"Why you ask me? I was a prisoner! I was trapped in *a tube*, in *that drawer*, in *that desk*, in THIS ROOM—when I should be free in the forest, BUILDING!"

"So you didn't hear anything?" I asked.

"Who *cares* what I hear?" it screeched back. Then it began jumping up and down on its tiny pink toes. *"What should I build? What should I build? What should I build?"*

"Uh, what's it doing?" V sounded confused—and a little worried.

"It wants us to give it a task. That's what they live for."

"Okay, how about this?" Violet said to the elf. "We'll give *you* a task if *you* tell *us* what happened here. Deal?"

The minairon stopped bouncing, considered that a second, then sighed and threw its tiny bluish hands above its tiny bluish head, as if to say, *Ugh, humans can be SO annoying.* "Deal, deal!"

"So what'd you hear?"

The elf closed its eyes for a moment, as if trying to recall as much as possible. "First I hear a door open," it said in a voice so small that Violet and I had to lean forward, almost poking it with our noses, to hear. "Then it close. And then—*an argument*. . . . But it start off friendly-like. Two sombras"—it held up two miniature fingers—"no, three. Only two talked, though—and they were arguing over . . . over an *egg*!" Violet and I looked at each other. The

minairon continued, "Then . . . then they started to fight—
BOOM, BAM, POP! That big stupid desk flies up. Then
CRASH! I go flippy-flip! And then . . . I hear this *strange*
humming sound."

"What kind of humming sound?" I asked.

The elf looked at me like I was one peanut short of
a SNICKERS. "What you mean, 'what kind of humming
sound?' A *HUMMING* sound!"

"Go on," Violet said.

"Then . . . they all go away from the desk, a couple
steps . . . and then they all gone. *Poof!*"

Violet's face fell. "Is that . . . it? I mean, did you hear the
door open again? Did they leave through the front?"

The minairon's shoulders went up and down like it
didn't have the slightest clue.

"And you don't remember anything else? Maybe something they said?"

The elf was shaking its head. "No . . . oh, one say they
gonna take the other to *a cave*! Sí, that I remember!"

"A cave?" Violet's eyes met mine, hopeful but guarded.
"I mean, that's *something*. . . ."

I turned back to the elf, who was staring eagerly up
at us with eyes that were startlingly bright. "Uh, did they
maybe happen to mention where that cave was?"

"No . . . no, they don't mention."

I felt my heart begin to sink. That wasn't nearly enough info to work with. Not even for the great Violet Rey. Heck, there were caves all over the world. And it wasn't like we could search them one by one. We'd both be celebrating our 120th birthdays before we even made it out of Central America. Just when I started to think it was time to come up with plan B, the minairon batted its tiny wings and said, "But . . . maybe I hear something like Lapa se Sasso."

The words rang a bell. "Wait. What did you say?"

"Lapa se Sasso? No, that wasn't it. . . . Maybe, Lapa du Papo? No . . ."

"Lapa do Santo?" I threw out, and the fairy's itty-bitty eyes lit up like sparklers.

"Sí, sí! That's the one!"

And just like that, I knew where they had taken Joanna.

V gripped my arm. "Charlie, what is that?"

"It's this famous cave in Brazil!" I explained, barely able to contain my excitement. "Southern Brazil. It's a place of sacrifice." But why would whoever kidnapped Joanna take her to a place like that? They couldn't be planning to *sacrifice her*, could they . . . ? And if they were, who were they planning on sacrificing her *to*?

"Charlie, you're a genius!" V shouted, and without even pausing to think it through, she leaned forward and planted this huge kiss right on my cheek!

And then we both just sort of froze, staring off in opposite directions.

The spot on my cheek where her lips had touched felt like it had been splashed with burning-hot lava, and for some reason I didn't know where to put my hands. Violet, meanwhile, was staring across the room, staring hard like she'd spotted something really, really interesting, though there wasn't much over there except for a smoking crater in the wall.

"Oye, HELLO?" the minairon screeched up at us. "What just happened . . . ? What's wrong with *you two*? You going to give me a task now or *what*? Oye . . . can anyone HEAR me?"

Violet still hadn't looked back at me but said, "We should probably . . . go."

I had to swallow this huge lump in my throat before I was finally able to answer. I managed "Uh-huh," but all I could think was *AWKWARD!*

"WHAT ABOUT MY TASK?" shrieked the minairon.

"Right," I said. "And you . . . build us a nice sculpture out of all this mess."

"What kind of sculpture?" the elf asked inquisitively.

"Uh, builder's choice."

CHAPTER ELEVEN

On our way out of the study, Violet thought that it might be a good idea to search the Provencia, see if there was anyone else here, any witnesses. So we started with the bigger brick buildings, peering in through the stained-glass windows and iron gates, then moved on to the courtyards beyond the gardens, making a quick stop by the Chapter House with its white stone columns, archways, and shadowy alcoves. Fifteen minutes later we'd made it all the way back around to Joanna's study, and by that point, it had become pretty obvious that there was no one else here.

My mom was still waiting for us in the parking lot. Seeing us coming, she rolled down the passenger-side window and said, "What took you guys so long? I was about to go looking for you."

"It's Queen Joanna!" I shouted, sprinting up to the car.

I was panting, barely able to breathe. "Someone . . . we don't know who . . . someone . . ."

"Attacked the monastery!" Violet finished. "The queen's been kidnapped!"

"*What?*" My mother's eyes went wide with shock.

"They took her!" I shouted between breaths. "She's gone!"

"Get in the car!" my mom screamed, slapping blindly at the buttons on the side of her door, making all the locks pop open at once. "¡Apúrense!"

The moment our butts hit the seats, my mom punched the start button on the dashboard, and the SUV's engine roared to life. Then she went into total stunt-driver mode, slamming the car into reverse while simultaneously stamping on the accelerator, and we shot backward out of the parking lot and onto the empty street, peeling out.

"Mom, what are you DOING?" I yelled over the revving engine.

"Getting you away from here," she said. "That's what."

Violet and I had to hold on to our seat belts (we hadn't even gotten a chance to strap in yet) as my mom weaved wildly through the traffic, honking her horn, whipping by other moving cars as if they were standing still.

"Mom, we have to help Joanna! They're taking her to Brazil! We have to do something!"

"How do you know they're taking her to Brazil?" she

asked, glancing briefly at the rearview mirror. Her fingers were tight around the steering wheel, her knuckles white.

"A minairon told us! What are we going to do?"

But my mom ignored me. She swerved us in front of one car and then another as horns blared and people rolled down their windows to shout things she wouldn't want me repeating.

"Mrs. Hernández, Charlie's right," Violet said. "From what I've heard, we have about a ninety-six-hour window from the time someone is kidnapped to find them. Then things just get a lot harder."

How do you know that? I mouthed.

Taken, *the movie,* she mouthed back.

Right. Anyway . . ."Mom, we need to do something!"

"Mrs. Hernández, maybe we should turn around."

"Mom, we can't just do noth—"

"ENOUGH!" my mom burst out. It was so sudden and unexpected that Violet and I went stiff in our seats. "BOTH OF YOU—JUST STOP IT, OKAY? I am NOT turning this car around, and NO ONE'S going back to help *anyone.* Am I understood?"

"Mrs. Hernández—"

"But, Mom—"

"No! No *buts!* I am your mother and it's *my job* to protect you. And that's precisely what I'm going to do! End.

Of. Discussion. ¿Me oíste?" My mom looked up to glare at me in the rearview mirror, and I knew her well enough (and I knew *that look* well enough) to know that when she said the conversation was over, that's exactly what it was.

CHAPTER TWELVE

The second we got home after dropping Violet off, my mom stormed in through the front door, and the first thing she did was set the alarm. Then (with the help of my dad, who, by the way, was so caught off guard by everything that his expression was basically what I'd expect to see from someone who has accidentally walked into a ballroom party . . . *naked*) she ran around the house, putting the entire place on *extreme* lockdown. They locked all the outside doors; they closed and locked every single window, including the two tiny ones in the attic and the one in my dad's office, which he never opened; they unplugged the garage door's motor, so it couldn't be controlled via remote. They maneuvered all the furniture around, positioning the tables, couches, and chairs to form mini blockades. Then, as if all that wasn't enough, they glued pieces of Cuban bread to the ceiling in the kitchen, the living room, and all the bedrooms; sprinkled sugar on both the love seats; placed glasses of tap water on top of the fridge; and positioned upside-down brooms behind all the inside doors (and an extra upside-down baseball bat behind the door in my room). Then my mom grabbed every single potted cactus she owned—and she owned *a lot* of cacti—and began strategically positioning them in front of every window in the house. And when she ran out of cacti, she used her aloe vera plants, which she owned a bunch of too. By the time they were finished, our house looked like it had been decorated by some insane horticulturist with a serious gluten issue. Obviously, I knew what they were doing; I'd heard enough myths and superstitions from my abuela to understand that they were trying to ward the house against pretty much every evil sombra known to man. And *why* they were doing it was also pretty obvious—my mom figured now that La Mano Peluda had gotten Joanna, I was next. Scary part was, she was probably right. Still, did I think they'd gone WAY overboard? Duh. But then again, I'd never been turned into a four-inch-tall doll by some psycho bruja.

At around eleven, my mom told me to go upstairs and get ready for bed. More like *ordered* it. And since I wasn't about to argue with someone who had spent almost half an hour gluing bread to the ceiling, that was exactly what I did.

After brushing my teeth and changing into my pj's, I

jumped into bed, closed my eyes, and tried to make sense of the questions racing through my brain.

And the first one was pretty big: Who'd kidnapped Joanna? And why? I mean, I was sure she had a ton of enemies—probably every single sombra that had sworn their allegiance to La Mano Peluda—so I guessed what I was really wondering was who (or more like *what*) was actually powerful enough to kidnap *the Witch Queen of Toledo?*

Another thing: Provencias were, like, the most protected places in the *entire world*. They were charmed and spelled and warded and filled with all sorts of powerful objects designed to keep evil out. So how exactly had it gotten *in?* And why had everyone suddenly abandoned the place?

Then there was that golden *egg*. . . . Was it worth a *gazillion* dollars like Violet said? Probably. But I couldn't see mythological beings fighting over something because it was valuable. Most sombras didn't even care about money. They didn't use it. Which meant there had to be more to it than that. But *what?* What was so special about that egg? Why had Joanna been fighting so desperately to keep it out of her kidnappers' hands? And why did her kidnappers want it so badly?

Sighing, I pulled the sheets over my face, starting to feel a little overwhelmed. A lot overwhelmed, actually. We needed answers. Needed them *badly* . . . No, what we needed was *help*.

My mind flashed to El Justo Juez, to El Cadejo—arguably two of the most powerful and legendary sombras of all time. El Justo Juez is, like, *the king* of Salvadoran folklore, the headless horseman who roams the night, hunting criminals and outlaws; and El Cadejo, who takes the form of a huge white dog, is *literally* the divinely appointed guardian of the human race. They'd each saved my life on multiple occasions and were two of the cleverest sombras I'd ever met; they would know what to do. They'd know how to help Joanna. But the question was, *where* were they? And what were they up to? I hadn't seen either one in *days*.

Definitely not the best time to go pulling a disappearing act, guys. . . .

Honestly, I don't think they could have picked a *worse* time. Rolling over, I buried my face in my pillow, trying to slow my racing mind. And surprisingly, I managed to fall asleep for a bit. Though it wasn't long before a sound had me snapping awake.

I lay perfectly still in the pitch-dark room, listening—and heard it again.

A soft *thump.*

Or was it—*a footstep?*

With my heart slamming against my ribs with the force a jackhammer, I reached slowly out for the lamp on my bedside table—

And that was when my bedroom window flew open!

My breath stopped. My heart stopped. Every cell in my body went absolutely *glacial* as a figure appeared, silhouetted against the night sky. I was too terrified to run. Too terrified to even open my mouth to scream! But somehow my fingers found the light switch.

The lamp snapped on, flooding the room with light—

And what I saw next nearly sent me tumbling out of bed!

CHAPTER THIRTEEN

"V IOLET, what the *HECK*?" I rasped. ¡Santo cielos! She'd scared the albóndigas out of me!

"Were you sleeping?" she asked almost innocently, poking her head in through the window.

Tossing my covers aside, I jumped to my feet. "Was I *sleeping*? Of course I was SLEEPING! That's what people do in a bedroom!"

She giggled, then waved her hand like she wanted to shut me up. "*Shhhhhhh!* You're going to get us caught!"

"Get *you* caught, you mean. I'm not doing anything where *getting caught* would be a problem!"

"Not yet, you're not." Violet grinned at me. My stomach did some kind of weird fluttery thing. Then she pulled herself through the window and into my room in one smooth, practiced motion. If I had to guess, I'd say she'd done that exact same move *a thousand* or so times through *a thousand* or so windows all across Greater Miami-Dade County. It worried me, to say the least.

"And how'd you unlock my window from the outside? Huh?" I'd literally watched my mom double-check the latch.

"Skills, Charlie . . . mad skills."

My heart still a runaway locomotive in my chest, I rushed over to the window and looked down—no ladder. Which meant she'd scaled the side of my house using nothing but the flimsy old rain gutter and raw grip strength. Not bad.

"What are you even *doing* here?" I whisper-shouted. Though maybe I shouldn't have been so surprised; this was, after all, typical Violet, wasn't it? For her, rules weren't made to be broken—they were made to be ignored, trampled on, and, in most cases, simply *obliterated*.

"I'm here to bust *you out*."

"Hey, in case you haven't noticed, this isn't a prison! I don't *need* busting . . ." I trailed off, watching as she quietly dumped the contents of my book bag onto the floor, opened my dresser, and began rummaging through it for T-shirts and shorts, which she quickly stuffed into said book bag.

Before I could ask what in the world she was doing, she said, in a breezy sort of way, "Why is there a hunk of bread glued to your ceiling?"

I glanced up—and nearly passed out from embarrassment. My mom had apparently used an *extra-large* piece for my room. You could've made a Subway party sub out of that thing.

Kill me now.

"Get the midnight munchies much?" I heard Violet ask as she giggled to herself.

"No, I don't get the midnight munchies . . . ," I hissed. "And forget the bread! It's not even bread. It's *art*. You know, the modern kind? Anyway, the real question is, what are *you* doing *now*?"

"Helping you pack. I bought us two tickets to Brazil. Used my mom's traveler's rewards card, so I scored a pretty sweet deal. Our ride is waiting for us in the driveway."

My eyes bugged. "Are you *insane?* My mom clearly told me not to leave this room. Which, in other words, means *I can't leave my room!*"

"Charlie, you defeated one of the scariest, most evil witches in the entire world, and you're scared of your *mommy?*"

"Scared? More like *terrified*. Have you ever watched a Dolphins game with that woman? *Especially* one where they blow a big lead?"

Rolling her eyes, she continued rummaging around in my dresser. "You still wearing cartoon underwear, huh?"

"*What?* Those aren't mine." I felt my ears turning pink.

"Charlie, they're in *your* drawer. . . ." Then, digging a little deeper: "Oh my gosh, you have the complete Power Rangers set!" She glanced back at me with eyes so blue they seemed to sparkle in the glow of my night lamp.

"I don't wear those, okay? They're collectibles! Now put them back!"

She pulled out another pair. My favorite pair too. "You even have Tommy the Green Ranger! I had such a crush on him," she said with her trademark million-megawatt smile. I tried not to look directly at it.

"Would you please stay out of there?" I snatched at my underwear, but she was too quick, so I gave up and just shut my dresser drawer instead.

V's playful expression faded, and she turned serious. "Charlie, we *have to* find Joanna. And we have to find her *now.* You know this. So why are you wasting time?"

"Look, of course I know that, but you heard my mom. She said *no.* In fact, I have a feeling she might not let me leave the house. Like, ever again."

"Charlie, if we don't help Joanna, pretty soon you might not *have* a house. No one might. La Mano Peluda is up to something. I mean, you saw that *thing* in Portugal. We *have* to save the queen!" She paused. "Listen to me—I sound like I'm British, but you know what I mean."

The worst part about this conversation was that I knew she was right. . . . Violet usually was.

I sighed. "Then give me my lucky pair of Green Ranger underwear, 'cause we're gonna need it."

CHAPTER FOURTEEN

I couldn't believe it, but there was a very blue, very *familiar* minivan parked in my driveway. I slid open the side door, and *big surprise*, there were Alvin Campbell and Sam Rodriguez, my two best and, besides Violet, only friends. Alvin, Sam, and me had started our own Latin rock band—we called ourselves Los Chicharrones—and about a week ago we'd even almost gotten to play in front of a *huge* television audience on a Spanish talent show. It would've definitely been our biggest gig to date (we usually played "solo gigs," meaning we only played in front of one person—that being Sam's *uncle*, and mostly because he happened to live smack-dab in the middle of our jam studio—i.e., Sam's *garage*), but I'd kind of messed that all up for us while running around Miami with Violet trying to figure out why I was sprouting feathers and horns and what had happened to my parents. The guys both claimed they'd forgiven me, but I wasn't sure I bought it—sometimes I still caught them flinging corn kernels at me during lunch.

"Your carriage awaits, my good sir," Alvin said, jerking his head so that his mop of curly orange hair flipped back out of his eyes. His Dwyane Wade bobblehead doll grinned at me from the dashboard.

"So glad we got to meet one last time before your funeral," I told him. "'Cause your mom's gonna *kill* you when she finds out. . . ."

"I know," he said, "but Violet calls me up, and I'm all, *OMG it's Violet Rey*, and she's, like, calling *me*! I mean, how do you turn down Violet Rey? She's *Violet Rey*!"

"If that's going to be your excuse, you might as well save your mom the trouble."

"Dude, *no girl* has ever called me before. What was I *supposed* to do?"

"*Dang*, good point," I said, rolling my eyes. "What about you, Sam?"

"No girl's ever called me, either, hermano." He grinned at me.

Nice. Dumb and dumber. "Great going, guys."

CHAPTER FIFTEEN

To say Alvin was a bad driver would be an insult to bad drivers everywhere. Fortunately, this was Miami, and no one followed the traffic laws, so we didn't really stick out as we ran red lights and stop signs, swerved in and out of our lane without signaling, almost hit a light post, and threw in the occasional illegal U-turn. I had no idea how we made it to Miami Beach alive (or without being stopped by a cop), but twenty minutes later we'd pulled into the dark, tree-lined parking lot in front of the Provencia. The digital clock on the dash read 3:55 a.m.

"You two wait here," Violet said to the guys. "We'll be in and out."

Alvin grabbed my arm. "Dude, hold up. I was going to give you this when we got to the airport, but I don't wanna forget." He dug around in the glove compartment and brought out what looked like—*a pink dog collar?*

I frowned. "What is that?"

"Sort of like a good-luck charm."

"Isn't that your *dog's* collar?"

"Not anymore, dude. Sissy's been dead for almost a year now."

I gave him an annoyed look. "I know that, Al. *Thank you.* So you're giving me your *dead dog's* collar . . . ?"

"Damn straight I am," he said with a proud grin. "Sissy was a champ! Plus, it's waterproof, fireproof, shock resistant. It's even got GPS tracking. It's basically a G-Shock for dogs."

Was he for real? "Al, I don't bark. I'm not wearing that."

"Dude, why not? It's a choker. It's totally punk. Punk is in nowadays."

Sam was nodding his head. "Punk is in, hermano. . . ."

"They're right," Violet agreed half-heartedly. "Punk's definitely trending."

Trending? Seriously? "Fine. Then *you guys* wear it."

"C'mon, man," Alvin said. "Put it on. For me."

"What? No. *Why do you want me to wear that?*"

"Because I gotta know you're gonna be safe, man!" Alvin's expression suddenly turned serious, earnest. His voice was low as he said, "Look, I know there's a whole lot of freaky stuff going on in the world, and I don't ask you to tell me about it or whatever—you know I already get panic attacks just thinking about putting a demo together—but you're my best friend, and I don't want to have to sit around wondering if you're safe or not, man. God forbid anything bad happens, at least I'll know I gave you something that *maybe* could've helped. The police can track this thing, dude." He turned the collar around. "And see this button? You press it, and it's like an emergency signal. Help will be on its way before you know it."

"That's almost touching," Violet said. "Weird, but touching."

Alvin held the collar out to me. "Do it for me, dude?"

I sniffed it. "Smells like flea-and-tick shampoo."

"Oh, gimme a break. . . ." Violet snatched the collar, attached it to one of her necklaces, then slung it around my neck. "There. Everyone happy?"

I gave it another sniff. "Not really," I admitted.

CHAPTER SIXTEEN

Not so surprisingly, Joanna's study still looked like a war zone when we walked in. In fact, it looked even *worse* now that the smoke had mostly cleared from the air, and this huge, twelve-foot-tall, cobbled-together sculpture of a grinning minairon doing a sort of Superman pose—chest out, hands on hips—now dominated the room. Guess that last one was my fault, though.

"What are we doing here, anyway?" I asked Violet.

"Saw a few things last time that we should probably take with us...." She went behind Joanna's desk, kicked aside some papers, and picked up an old-looking map. Its edges had been charred a little and there were few pencil-size holes in the middle, but otherwise it was in good shape. "It's a map of Brazil," she said, blowing off some of the ash. "Might come in handy."

"Smart," I said. Hey, I'd never been to Brazil, so anything that was going to help us get around was more than welcome. "You're almost starting to make me feel better about this. *Almost.* Anything else?"

"Yeah, I saw this awesome steel compass somewhere around here, and one of those old-school navigational thingamajigs with the . . ." Her voice trailed off, her gaze moving toward the hallway with the golden archway. "Wait, wait, wait."

"What? What's wrong?"

"Those tracks . . ."

Glancing around, I said, "You mean the ones that are literally *everywhere* . . . ?" And they were. I didn't think there was a single patch of floor that didn't have prints on it.

"The ones leading to the mirror," she said.

I shook my head. To El Espejo? I was pretty sure those had been there yesterday. "What about them?"

Violet thought for a sec. "Do you remember how the minairon told us that it heard a door open before the talking started?"

"Yeah, so?"

"Do you *also* remember how it never mentioned hearing a door open again when all the talking stopped and everyone left?"

I sort of did. But hold up— "Are you saying that whoever kidnapped Joanna is still . . . *in here?*"

Violet rolled her eyes. "Of course not. What I'm *saying*

is that they must've used the *mirror* to leave! That's why the minairon never heard another door."

Huh. I hadn't thought of that. But it did make sense. I mean, what faster way to leave the scene of a crime than through a magical teleporting mirror?

"We're going to have to do the same thing," V said. She had *that* look on her face now—the one that said she was going to try to make me do something we both knew we shouldn't.

"Come again?"

"Charlie, we have to use El Espejo! We have to stay right on their heels. It's our best chance of tracking them. Maybe our *only* chance."

"But, V, we don't even know how to operate that thing!"

She hesitated, then said, "Maybe we don't have to," and hustled over to the mirror.

When I came up beside her, she pointed at the designs along its hammered silver edges. Last time we'd used it, the designs had looked like a series of interconnected rooster heads and little three-towered castles. Now the polished silver showed an intricate alternating pattern of full-bodied jaguars and stars.

"See?" Violet said. "The images are different. The mirror's already been prepared. It probably keeps the last destination until someone changes it, and since they were the last ones through it, the destination hasn't changed." When I didn't say anything, she gripped my shoulders, looking me right in the eyes. "Charlie, we *have to* risk it. It's our best shot!"

I sighed, and apparently she took that as me agreeing, because she said, "Gimme thirty secs," and in *exactly* thirty secs returned with our backpacks and a big mischievous grin on her face. Tossing me my backpack, she said, "Told the guys we found alternative means of transportation."

Alternative. Yeah, that was one way of putting it. "But hold on! What if it's a trap, huh? What if—what if the mirror drops us in the middle of . . . of the *Sahara desert*? Or in the center of an exploding star in a galaxy far, far away?" Okay, so that last one was a bit far-fetched, but didn't she realize how *dangerous* this was?

"That's a lot of what-ifs, Charlie."

"You do realize we've never done this without witch supervision before, right?"

"That's what makes it so exciting!" she said, practically bouncing up and down on her toes. She folded up the map of Brazil and tucked it into her backpack alongside the golden egg we'd found and all her spare clothes.

"You're certifiable," I said.

Ignoring me, Violet turned to El Espejo and, in a sort of singsong voice, chanted, "Mirror, mirror on the wall, who's the *scarediest* of them all?" and then smirked at me.

I glared back. "That's not funny. And that's also not at all how that thing works."

Her smirk stretched into a full-blown grin. "I know. Just always wanted to say something like that to a magical mirror. . . ." And then she started toward El Espejo. I saw its shiny, flawless surface begin to ripple and glisten at her touch. A dazzling reddish-golden light shone out, washing all the color out of Violet's face and hair, and a moment later, the mirror's glow had become so fierce it seemed to throw the rest of the room into deep shadow.

I could feel an icy breeze blowing off of it and heard myself swallow.

"Ladies first," V said, beaming.

CHAPTER SEVENTEEN

The instant we stepped through the rectangle of shimmering light, the world around us changed: The polished marble floors and tall arched ceilings suddenly vanished, replaced by blue sky, rocky red earth, and a thick canopy of leafy green trees. Birds chirped, and colorful flower vines wound their way around branches thicker than telephone poles, while peat and moss grew over the dark roots that jutted out of the jungle floor. The air was thick—I mean, like, *sauna* thick—and alive with the low, constant hum of jungle sounds. As I looked around, a snort of laughter just bubbled out of me. I mean, this was *incredible*! A second ago we had been standing inside a monastery in North Miami Beach, and the next we were in the middle of the deepest, densest, most *wild* jungle I'd ever seen!

"Toto, I've got a feeling we're not in So-Fla anymore," Violet said.

I blinked around, grinning like a maniac. "I'm sooooo gonna get grounded."

There was a winding barely there path down one side of the mountain. It was pretty steep—*dangerously* steep, actually—but we didn't exactly have a whole lot of options. So we followed it, sort of half stumbling, half butt-crawling our way past knots of thorny bushes and knee-high weeds, over soccer-ball-size holes in the ground, our ankles twisting and our knees buckling, until we finally—*thankfully*—reached the Lapa do Santo cave. . . . At least I was pretty sure this was it.

We squatted behind a scrub of thorny bushes, eyes locked on the entrance of the cave as a sudden gust of wind blew through the jungle. It howled between the trees, shaking the branches and making leaves rain down.

"Doesn't look like anyone's home," I said, staring up at the massive stony cliff looming over us; it looked like the wild side of some huge blood-soaked mountain.

Violet's eyes hadn't left the cave's mouth. "No, it doesn't." The mouth was a rocky almost-V shape carved right into the reddish-orangey limestone. It must've been close to thirty feet high but probably only eight or nine feet wide, with all the clusters of gray stalactites seeming to ooze from the rock like giant frozen tears. The most surprising part, I guess, was the fact that the entrance to the cave didn't look anything like a skeleton's mouth; in the only tale my abuela had ever told me about Lapa do Santo, it mentioned how in order to enter the cave, the priests would have to walk through La Boca de la Calavera—or, the Mouth of the Skull. That was supposedly the price that had to be paid before anyone could enter the altar room, which was where the priests performed their most sacred rituals. I also remembered something about blood running up the walls so high you could swim in it, and now that I was standing here, seeing this place for the first time—*specifically* those high, coppery-red limestone walls—I finally understood where those legends had come from.

With everything I knew about the place—with everything I knew that had gone on inside—just the thought of approaching it (not to mention the thought of actually *entering* it) was enough to make me shiver even in the fierce jungle heat.

"You really think Joanna's in there?" I whispered, but it came out sounding more like a hope than what I actually thought.

"I don't know," Violet said. "But if she is, that means whoever captured her is too."

Well, that wasn't reassuring. More like, *terrifying*. "So what's the plan?"

"Still working on that."

High up in the trees, a bird began to caw loudly. Somewhere close by, another bird called back.

They didn't sound awfully friendly.

"You better work faster," I told her.

CHAPTER EIGHTEEN

Unlike the entrance, the inside of the cave was mostly smooth limestone, which had been cut into angles and planes by natural forces (time and erosion) and other not-so-natural ones (i.e., explorers and archaeologists). Masses of grayish blobby formations dangled from the ceilings, while others ran sideways up the stony walls and reminded me of the ancient chewed-up globs of bubble gum stuck to the underside of school desks. Even though it was around six or seven in the morning Brazil time and the hot tropical sun was already up and bright, the sunlight couldn't seem to penetrate the darkness inside the cave.

Violet's cell phone, with her flashlight app, helped a little, but not much.

With our ears on high alert and our eyes scanning the shadows for any tiny movement, we crept cautiously inside, pausing every few steps just to be safe. It didn't seem like some kind of trap (emphasis on *seem*) so we kept going, tiptoeing along one wall, Violet hardly making any noise at all, me trying to resist the urge to whisper, "Be vewy vewy quiet, we're hunting for *wabbits!*" (I have a bad habit of saying silly things when I get nervous.)

"So what was this place?" Violet whispered, waving her phone over the rocky walls, painting them with wedges of bluish light.

Sidestepping one of the shallow holes in the ground where archaeologists had unearthed ancient remains, I said, "Sort of like a ritualistic burial site. It was used for, like, hundreds of years by local warlords and sorcerers and stuff."

I thought I heard Violet swallow, though it might've been me. "What kinda things did they do in here?" she whispered.

"Body mutilation, decapitation . . . cannibalism—you know, all that fun stuff."

"So not just your friendly neighborhood cemetery then, huh?"

"More like, part cemetery, part *torture chamber.*"

Maybe twenty yards in, the cave opened up, widening to about the size of a baseball diamond but also seeming to dead-end. I didn't see anything that would make me think someone had recently been here. *Guess no one was home, after all. . . .*

Digging into her pocket, Violet brought out a mini Maglite flashlight and handed it to me. "As Cap McCaw would say, 'Time to spread out and see what turns up, my dear.'"

I had to do a double take. "You've had that the *whole time?*"

"Yeah, but it's super low on battery; only use it when you need to."

"It's pitch-black in here . . . ," I pointed out. "I'm gonna need to *a lot.*"

While Violet slowly picked her way over to the far wall, ducking under a low-hanging section of ceiling, I snapped on the flashlight and wagged the beam around, squinting. The harsh white glow stung my eyes a little but did a heck of a lot better job of illuminating this place than Violet's phone. And now I could see that this was *definitely* where the cave dead-ended; I couldn't pick out any passageways in the walls—no corridors leading deeper in.

As I followed the curve of the wall, tracking the flashlight beam along its craggy base, I heard Violet say, "Very funny, Charlie."

I glanced back; she was maybe ten yards down the cave. "What?"

Shaking her head, she turned—and then froze, staring at me. "Wait. How'd you do that?"

"Do *what?*"

"Tug on my backpack from way over there . . ."

"I didn't tug on anything," I said, and she gave me a *Yeah, right* sort of smile.

"Course you didn't. . . . It was probably the ghost of a decapitated warlord, right?" She paused, sniffing lightly at the air. "And what the heck is that *smell* . . . ?"

I didn't have the slightest clue what she was talking about—and didn't smell anything, either—so I went back to inspecting the walls, and a couple of seconds later I felt the tiniest of tugs on *my* backpack. I grinned in the dark. "Yeah, *very* funny, V . . . I like the way you set it up, talking about ghosts and stuff, but I'm not a Shaggy Rogers. You can't get me that e—"

I broke off, catching a whiff of something just *awful* in the still, stale air. Man, it smelled like something had died in here, then been eaten by something else, and then that something else had died too! I'd barely gotten my shirt over my nose when I heard Violet yell, "Charlie, come look at this!"

I turned, saw she was still about ten yards down the cave, squinting at the wall. And I felt my face screw up. "Wait. How did you—"

"Charlie, get *over here!*"

Holding my breath, I rushed over, trying not to trip over the shallow holes.

"Tell me you see that . . . ," she said, holding her phone out, illuminating a large, sort of oval shape on the rock wall.

Thing was, at first, *I didn't.* All I saw was wall and light and a tiny fat worm wriggling its way out of a crack in the rock. But then my eyes began to adjust and there it was: a life-size skeleton head, seeming to grin at us right out of the rock! "Looks like a . . . *calavera* . . . but it doesn't seem like anyone—"

"Carved it? No. I don't think anyone did. . . . It's just—"

"*There.*"

And like a flash, I remembered that legend about Lapa do Santo again, how it claimed that to enter it—to *truly* enter the cave—you had to walk through the mouth of the skull. "That's it," I breathed.

"What's it?"

"That's our way in."

Violet's brow furrowed in confusion. "We *are* in, Charlie . . . *aren't we?*"

"Maybe not." I crouched down, pressed the heel of my hand against the center of the skull's open, grinning mouth.

For a split second nothing happened—

Then, with a faint grinding sound that was barely

audible over the steady *wham-wham-wham* of my heart, the rectangle of the stony mouth slid smoothly back into the wall and disappeared.

Violet's wide, shocked eyes found my wider and even more shocked ones. For a moment neither one of us said anything. Neither of us even *blinked*. But once we'd finally accepted what had just happened, we craned our necks to peer into the slot . . . and immediately the ground began to tremble under our feet.

CHAPTER NINETEEN

I had time to think, *¡DIOS MÍO! AN EARTHQUAKE!* (which, for a kid from Miami, is just about the scariest kind of natural disaster, because we never experience those) before a deep, jagged crack tore across the ground like a fault line. Violet and I stumbled backward, nearly tripping over each other as a huge rocky triangle rose out of that crack, shedding clumps of dirt and blocking our way out. Our *only* way out.

"CHARLIE!" Violet shrieked; she was pointing at something behind me, and I whirled around to see gallons of some sort of red, syrupy liquid (*blood . . . it had to be BLOOD!*) spilling out of the gap where the skull's mouth used to be.

But the blood wasn't just pouring from the skull's mouth; no, it looked like the walls were bleeding too! Streaks of dark reddish liquid were running down the limestone like sticky sweat. As I watched, too frightened to blink, think, or even puke (it was super gross!), the blood began to pool on the ground, flowing rapidly along the base of the walls. And the smell . . . ? Man, it was like sticking your head in a bag full of moldy pennies!

Just when I thought things couldn't get any worse, I spotted the glassy oval eyes of scaly reptiles peeking out of the bloody pools—*seripentes*!

"Snakes! I hate snakes!" I shouted.

V gripped my arm. "Take a chill pill there, Indy! They don't look poisonous to me."

"How can you tell?"

"Haven't you heard the snake rhyme? 'Red touches yellow, you're a dead fellow. Red touches black, you're all right, Jack.'"

"My dad's an animal geneticist—the snake rhyme is on our fridge! But—news flash—it only applies to snake species found in NORTH AMERICA!"

"Oh." Violet didn't seem too happy to learn that. "Okay, well, anyway, there's not a whole lot of them swimming around here, so unless the blood starts to rise or something else crazy happens I don't think we're in any serious danger."

And, as if on cue (because, why not, right?) the blood started to rise. . . .

I glared at her. "You had to say that, didn't you?"

Terrified, holding on to each other, V and I scrambled away from the wall, retreating to the center of the cave with the blood already lapping at our sneakers. It was rising fast . . . rising like the tide!

And it's going to keep *on rising!* I thought with a flash of horror. *Rising and rising until we're drowning in it— drowning in blood!*

But no sooner had that terrible thought crossed my mind than the flow of blood began to slow—first the rush of it spewing from the skeleton face's mouth slowed to a trickle; then the droplets streaking down the walls seemed to run dry.

The ground began to rumble under our feet again, and there was a wet, sucking, slurping sound like water swirling down a half-clogged drain.

"WHAT'S HAPPENING?" Violet yelled.

"NO IDEA! BUT IT DOESN'T SOUND HEALTHY!" I glanced down to see streams of tiny bubbles drifting up through the bloody pools at our feet.

Then, just as quickly as they had begun to rise, the pools of blood receded into rows of small circular openings that had appeared in the ground.

And when they had completely drained away, we got another huge surprise: Not only had the stony triangle that was blocking our way out sunk back into the ground, but there was now a large half-moon-shaped hole— some sort of passageway—descending into the cave floor directly in front of the still-grinning face of the calavera. Through the gloom, I could see the top of an ancient spiral staircase twisting down into darkness, the narrow stony steps leading—*where* . . . ?

Honestly, I wasn't even sure I *wanted* to know.

"Guess you were right . . ." Violet clutched my arm tightly as she leaned forward to peer into the passageway, her blue eyes shining in the pale glow of her phone. "Lapa do Santo, here we come."

CHAPTER TWENTY

As we started slowly down the steps, our footsteps echoing quietly off the smooth stones, Violet lowered the brightness setting on her phone almost all the way down, which I thought was a pretty smart move, because we didn't know who—or *what*—might be lurking at the bottom of wherever these steps led, and we certainly didn't want them—or *it*—to see us coming. The only problem was that now I could barely see my feet and, only occasionally, the next step down.

When we finally reached the bottom (which felt like an eternity, though in actuality it only took a minute or two), we both froze, and all I could think was, "Whoa."

We were now standing in an enormous, dome-shaped chamber. Pinpricks of sunlight were slanting down through dozens of small openings in the ceiling, throwing long, skinny triangles over sections of the chamber while leaving others in almost total darkness. But there was more than enough light for me to see the theme of the place . . . and the theme was *monkeys*. They were everywhere, twining up the soaring stone pillars, carved into the rock walls, shaped into stony statues and clay figurines that stood in the niches and alcoves. All the little hairy little monkey faces appeared to sneer or scowl, fangs sticking out of their wide, angry mouths, their eyes slitted menacingly like, *Whatcha doing down here, muchachos?* Apparently the interior decorator had a thing for primates.

"So . . . this place isn't the least bit creepy," I whispered, and my voice seemed to echo forever between the pillars.

In the center of the vast space was a huge stone altar— an elaborately carved sort of tablelike thingy that looked like it had been chiseled out of a single enormous hunk of gray-black rock. Great pointed horns curved up and over each of the four corners; along the sides, teeth . . . *actual* teeth (probably from a puma or a jaguar judging by the length of the fangs) jutted out like razor wire, just looking for a bit of skin to snag or tear.

"Okay, now *that's* terrifying," Violet said.

Our sneakers crunched over the rocky floor (at least I *hoped* they were rocks) as we made our way toward it.

"This must be the altar of sacrifice," I whispered, my eyes tracing the intricate zigzag designs along the edges of the stone top.

Turning her phone back on, Violet crouched to examine the dusty floor around the altar, then started around to the other side like she was following a set of tracks. But before I could ask if she actually *was*, I felt something at my back—*a presence*. And a familiar one too. A cold chill ran through my entire body as I turned, slowly. Looming over me, almost completely hidden in darkness, was some kind of ginormous structure. It was pyramid shaped, wide as a house, and looked like some huge ladder with a primitive form of scaffolding supporting it—a jumble of joints and braces and cross sections.

As I stared up at it, my head began to swim, and for a moment I thought I could hear voices, a whole mess of them chatting noisily somewhere close by. They seemed to be coming from everywhere, all directions at once.

"V, do you hear—" I started to say, but before I could finish, somewhere behind me, she shrieked.

CHAPTER TWENTY-ONE

y heart jumped into my throat, and I spun around, my feet nearly sliding out from underneath me on the sandy ground. "What's wrong?" I shouted.

Scrambling around the altar, I skidded to a stop right where she stood staring down at a familiar black-and-gold scarf that lay crumpled—almost hidden—behind a clay pot with, you guessed it, the profile of a snarling, hairy-faced monkey. "That's Joanna's scarf!" I shouted as it hit me. The one she'd used to set that big oak tree on fire before the gang of minairons could squash us with it. And the realization made me so incredibly, unbelievably, *impossibly* happy, I almost broke into the "Macarena" dance right in the middle of this big ol' creepy place.

Violet, meanwhile, was nodding her head up and down like a sugar addict who's just been asked if they'd like another scoop of double chocolate chip ice cream.

"So the minairon was right!" I said.

"Uh-huh."

"But . . . I don't get it," I said as my eyes flicked over the altar, which looked relatively clean and, *thank God*, definitely not recently used. "Why would they bring her to a place like this, a place of sacrifice, if they weren't planning on, well, *sacrificing* her . . . ?"

V considered that for a sec. "That's a really good question. . . ." She bent down to pick up the scarf—and that's when the most incredible thing happened: The moment her fingertips came in contact with the edge of the silky, shimmering fabric, the scarf seemed to come to life, first slipping out from between her thumb and index finger, then floating up into the air like a feather caught in a strong breeze. We both watched in stunned silence as the scarf began to twist and wring itself before suddenly igniting in a blaze of unnatural greenish fire, bathing the entire room in dazzling light. In that instant—just those few seconds as the threads burned and began to sizzle away—the scarf seemed to form the image of land . . . of a hunk of land floating in the middle of the sea . . . an *island* . . . and birds. Seagulls! Then, with the *whoosh* of an extinguishing fire, it burned up into ashy nothingness. *Whoa, did that really just happen?*

For what felt like a very long time Violet and I just

stood there, speechless. And when one of us finally *did* speak, it was Violet: "It's a clue!" she shouted, whirling to face me. "Joanna must've left it behind for us! Like a *bread crumb!*"

And almost before she was finished talking, I already knew what it meant: "*Chiloé.*"

"What?"

"That's it. . . . That's what Joanna was trying to tell us."

Violet looked confused. "What's a *Chiloé?*"

"It's not a *what.* It's a *where.* A tiny island off the coast of Chile. Its name means 'the place of seagulls.'" And it just so happened to be one of the most mythologically *rich* places in the entire world. My abuela had lived there for a couple of years, and from everything she had told me about it, she'd loved it.

A small smile had begun to pull on the corners of Violet's lips, but before she could say anything, a powerful gust of wind swept through the chamber. A split second later, I heard this great swooshing roar and looked up in time to see a vapory whirlwind explode out of an opening in the ceiling. It touched down less than fifteen yards away, swirling dirt and bits of broken pottery before snatching up one of the taller monkey statues and flinging it against a pillar to our right. The ceramic orangutan burst on impact, shattering into a thousand dusty fragments, which clinked softly—almost musically—to the ground.

Then, just as suddenly as it had started up, the whirlwind evaporated, and everything was eerily quiet again . . . eerily *still.*

"The heck was *that?*" I breathed.

"Up there!" Violet shouted, pointing at the ceiling. Squinting, I tried to figure out what she was showing me while she said, "Whoever built this place designed it with a pretty ingenious ventilation system. See those bigger openings in the ceiling? Not the ones letting light in—the others?"

I did. They were large and square shaped, cut sideways into the high arched ceiling. "You're saying that's a *ventilation system?*"

"Obviously old-school. But I'm pretty sure, yeah." She got that much out and not another word before a second whirlwind exploded out of one of the ceiling vents, this one slamming down so close it nearly sucked us off our feet. Rocks and razor-edged hunks of ceramic whizzed past our heads, and as we hunkered down beside the altar, shielding our faces, I shouted, "REALLY STARTING TO HATE THAT VENTILATION SYSTEM!"

Aboveground, maybe eighty or ninety feet straight up, I could hear the wind howling and shrieking through the trees. Madre, it was loud! Sounded pretty close to hurricane-strength winds to me—and I should know, having grown up in Miami. *That's probably what's causing the whirlwinds*, I thought.

"I think it's time we make like space shuttles!" Violet shouted, and we took off for the stairs, both of us running flat out as more and more whirlwinds began snaking down out of the vents. They gusted and roared, flinging up walls of dirt that stung our skin and got in our eyes, blinding us.

Halfway to the stairs, I heard a huge swooshing, swirling sound and snapped my head up just as the mother of all whirlwinds descended from above. It crashed down directly in our path with all the force of an *atomic bomb*.

Violet just barely managed to avoid it, springing to her left. I, on the other hand, hadn't done seven straight years of cheerleading and gymnastics. . . .

CHAPTER TWENTY-TWO

What happened next was simple physics. I was slurped straight up into the air, screaming, flailing my arms wildly, which, just for the record, didn't a) help me fly or b) make me look any cooler as I spun and flipped and basically somersaulted my *brains* out. The world became a whirling, howling funnel of wind and dirt and flying monkey statues. I shrieked as a powerful gust swung me outward, boomeranging me around in a wide, looping circle while somewhere way down below me, I could hear Violet shouting, "CHAAARRRLIEEE!"

In the span of just three, maybe four heartbeats, the whirlwind had lifted me so high off the ground that I was now looking down on pretty much the entire altar room. Distantly, I wondered how many people had survived being sucked up into a whirlwind. I wondered if breaking every bone in your body at the same time hurt as badly as

I imagined it would. I wondered which would feel better: landing flat on my back or taking a bounce on my belly, then started to wonder why I was thinking about it in the first place, when I heard Violet shout, "YINGS!"

Yings? What in the world was she talking about? It made absolutely no sense—like, *cero*—but Violet kept at it, shouting the word over and over at the top of her lungs while madly flapping her arms at her sides like an insane ch—

Finally, it hit me: Not *yings*, but *wings!*

Yes! Of course! All I had to do was sprout a pair and—

Then, just like that, the whirlwind—well, quit.

There were no more gusting winds. There wasn't even a slight breeze.

The air had become so still that for a moment I thought I could hear the tiny, crunching sound of roots as they expanded into the ceiling above me.

An instant later, gravity decided to pitch in and make my life just a *wee bit* more difficult. I started to fall. *Fast.* Out of the corner of my eye, I caught a glimpse of the giant ladder-like thingy; it was super close, less than three feet away, and I reached for it like my life depended on it—which it obviously did—twisting, stretching, straining—but I couldn't get my body around in time. My fingertips grazed one of the upper bars, missing by only inches, and then time seemed to pause just like it did for Wile E. Coyote every time he found himself running off a cliff. Pausing just long enough for me to understand it was now all over. (Cue exaggerated cartoon gulp.)

A spilt second before I crashed back down to earth—a crash that would have no doubt *ended* me—I felt a sudden, vicious yank on my lower back and my momentum abruptly changed directions: I'd gotten caught on the ladder somehow and was no longer falling but swinging . . . once . . . twice . . . three complete revolutions, like a gymnast on a set of parallel bars, before finally slamming to the ground. The breath exploded out of me in a painful gasp—"*Uh!*"—as I landed hard on my side. Although nowhere *near* as hard as I could have.

"CHARLIE!" Violet shouted as she rushed over to me. "CHARLIE, ARE YOU OKAY? CAN YOU MOVE?" I wasn't so sure, so I tried nodding and watched as relief flooded into her eyes. "*Oh, thank God . . . ,*" she breathed, wrapping her arms around me. If I hadn't just plummeted seven stories through the air, I might've blushed.

"I . . . but—*how?*" I saw a slithery, squirmy, wriggly movement to my left, had time to think, *¡SERPIENTE!* and then realized it *wasn't* a snake at all. . . . It was *me!*

I'd manifested a tail!

CHAPTER TWENTY-THREE

Violet spotted it a second later. At first she had no clue what she was looking at, but then she shrieked, clapped both hands over her mouth, and started to laugh uncontrollably. "That's *craaazzzyyy*! Did you . . . do that on *purpose?*"

"Yeah, totally," I lied. "All I was thinking was wings or tail. Those were my top two." The truth, of course, would've sounded a lot less cool. I mean, what was I supposed to say? No, my body just knows how badly I suck at morphing and in the interest of self-preservation decided to save my heinie—*literally*.

My guess was that I must've manifested it a few moments before or right as I was falling past the giant ladder thingy, and as I'd reached out with my hands and legs, which hadn't quite been long enough to grab hold of the ladder, I must've also (*unknowingly*) reached out with my tail, which, fortunately for the rest of me, *had* been.

Feeling dazed—and more than a little amazed—I stared up at my newest and most flexible appendage, watching it swing back and forth like the pendulum of a grandfather clock. Covered in coarse black fur, the thing was close to five feet long and thick as a garden hose, with a fluff of pinkish hair at the tip where it sort of curled back on itself like a question mark.

"Kinda cute, actually," V said, giving it a light poke.

"Hey, grow your own," I said with a smirk, and saw her grin before her eyes drifted up, moving past me—and she gasped.

"What's wrong?" I said.

She was shaking her head now, her eyes jacked wide in fear. "It's another one of those . . . those *things.*"

"What *things?*" Propping myself up on my elbow, I glanced back and thought, *¡Madre mía!* What I had assumed was some sort of giant escape-ladder thing was actually another one of those bone castles—another *castell!*

CHAPTER TWENTY-FOUR

This one was even taller than the first, easily over forty feet high, and constructed of nothing but bones. No carcasses—just pure white bones. And not cow bones, either, but the bones of smaller animals— goats, maybe. I saw thighbones, backbones, neck bones, and everything in between, each one fitted carefully together with the ones around it. Most had been picked clean, but ribbons of flesh and hair still clung to a few. It was without a doubt the most gruesome thing I'd ever seen ... *ever*. Even worse than the one in Portugal somehow.

But the part that had me really freaking out was that this was now the second castell we'd seen. The second in as many days! Why did these things keep popping up? I mean, I knew they had something to do with dark magic, but it couldn't just be a coincidence that Joanna had been kidnapped the same day she'd taken us to see the first of these abominations; and now she'd left us a clue right near another. What was the connection?

The castell's shadow hung over me like a poisonous, dark cloud. Suddenly I felt an overwhelming urge to get away from this thing—to get out of here.

"Let's go," I told Violet. "Vamos."

It felt like we walked through the dense Brazilian jungle east of Lapa do Santo for days, though it was probably only an hour or two before we saw the first rooftop of a small town. A rusty sign nailed to a scraggly old tree growing wild along the roadside read PEDRA PEQUENA—0.8 KM.

The town itself was old but well maintained, with several multilevel buildings and nicely paved streets. The buildings had red Portuguese-style roofs, adobe brick, and glazed tile decorating the doorways and balconies. To our left was a row of stalls with vendors selling a colorful array of fresh fruits. On the front of one was a large plastic sign that said TREM/TREN/TRAIN and had a little arrow pointing up the street to our left. Below the words was a picture of a futuristically styled train station and baggage loading area. Looked pretty cool, actually. But as it turned out, the station was anything *but*. When a business's name seemed to translate into "the pearl of luxury travel and leisure," you'd expect to find a *teensy* bit more than a dusty open-air platform with a single dusty old wooden bench and a tiny (and, yes, also dusty) ticket office at the far end. But that's all there was to the place. Inside the office an older dude in a rickety rocking chair was staring blankly at the crossword section of a newspaper. His eyelids were drooping at half-mast, and the ground-down stub of a pencil dangling precariously from his left ear didn't make it seem like he had any plans to complete the puzzle. There was a map with routes and ticket prices taped up on the inside of the plexiglass window. Violet studied it for a second, then banged on the glass, startling the ticket officer out of a deep, slumbering sleep.

"Two tickets, please," she said, "Five o'clock to Santiago, Chile." According to the map, it was the closest stop they had to Chiloé; we were going to have to hop in a taxi or on a bus and take that down to Puerto Montt, where we could then ferry over to Chiloé.

The ticket dude nodded like he'd understood. He drowsily tapped a few keys on some ancient-looking keyboard, and the printer on the desk in front of him spat out two large red-and-white tickets. "Trinta e nove reais para o par," he said, pointing at the little silver tray that scooped under the window.

I felt around for my tail and realized it was gone. Too bad. Maybe I could've shown it to the guy, pretended it was a magic trick, and got us a couple of free tickets.

Violet slung her backpack around so she could get into

it. "At the current exchange rate that should be approximately ten dollars and fifty cents," she said, and when I just stared at her, she gave a small shrug. "What? My parents' shop has a currency-exchange machine. . . . I play with it sometimes." She rummaged through her bag, paused, rummaged some more, dug a little deeper, then paused again. Her blue eyes, suddenly huge and full of worry, rose to meet mine.

"It's just *junk*," she said finally.

"Well, I mean, it's *paper*, right? Paper money. But it's not *junk*. It's backed by the government or whatever. . . ."

"No, I'm talking about *my backpack*—it's *literally* full of junk!" A mini avalanche of dirt and rocks came tumbling out as she emptied her bag onto the ground. "My clothes, my passport, the golden egg, our money—*it's all gone!*"

"*WHAT?*"

"Check your bag!"

Whipping it around, I unzipped the big pocket—and nearly passed out. *Rice.* My backpack was loaded with probably close to ten pounds of uncooked white rice! "What the—"

"It's all gone!" Violet shouted again, panic making her voice thin. "*Everything!*"

"But . . . *how?* I mean, *HOW?*"

She paused for a moment, thinking, before her gaze suddenly lasered in on mine. "In the cave! Remember how

I thought you were messing around with my bag? And—and *you* thought I was messing around with *yours?*"

"Yeah, and then you tried to play it off—"

"I DIDN'T TRY TO PLAY *ANYTHING* OFF!" she exploded. Her fingers tightened on my arms hard enough to make me flinch. "Don't you get it...? WE WERE *ROBBED!*"

"But—by *who?* We were the only ones in there!" I shouted.

"I know. But there's no other explanation. There's no way some *whirlwind* could have emptied our bags, filled them with dirt and *rice*, of all things, then zipped them back up! And where did all that rice *even come from?*" I opened my mouth to argue (I mean, us getting robbed in a cave when we'd clearly been the only ones in there just wasn't possible), but she did have a point. "Charlie, explain it to him," Violet said, jerking a thumb toward the ticket booth and the dude inside it. "Tell him we were robbed. Tell him we *need* those tickets!"

"Right. Um, señor, necesitamos esos boletos. Alguien robó nuestro dinero."

The guy gave me a sort of squinty-eyed look of confusion. "O qué?"

"Necesitamos los tickets! No tenemos dinero. No money."

"Señor, ¡por favor!" Violet said pleadingly. "We *need* to get to Chile!"

The guy stared at us for a long moment. "Onde estão o seus pais?"

V looked at me. "What'd he say?"

"I think he's asking about our parents."

"*Chile*," she said, turning back to the window. "Our parents are in Chile!"

But Mr. Ticket Dude wasn't listening. Instead he'd already picked up his phone and was dialing a number. "Eu estou chamando a polícia. . . ."

Violet's eyes bugged. "Did he just say 'police'?"

"No, no polícia!" I shouted at him. "Tickets, por favor. Los tickets!"

Only it was too little, too late—he had already gotten through to dispatch and was speaking rapid-fire Portuguese into the receiver. Yep, definitely not good.

"We gotta go," V said. "We don't have passports. The police will take us straight to the American embassy, and they'll put us on the first plane back home!"

So we did the only thing there *was* to do. We ran. Pebbles crunched under our sneakers as we hopped off the platform and raced along the humps of gravelly ground that flanked the train tracks.

I heard the ticket dude shouting something in Portuguese—probably something like, *They're runners!* And then we were gone, disappearing into the forest of tall, spindly shrubs that grew wild along the south side of the tracks.

"Get down!" Violet hissed, pulling me into a crouch next to her.

I was panting but managed: "So what are we gonna do, huh? We're stranded!"

"We're *getting* on that train, Charlie."

"But . . . we don't have *tickets!*"

"So?" Violet's lips broke into one of her trademark dazzling grins, and suddenly I had a really bad feeling in the pit of my stomach.

CHAPTER TWENTY-FIVE

An instant later a high-pitched whistling sound split the air, and less than ten feet away the tracks began to hum.

"You're planning on *sneaking* onto that train, aren't you?" I said accusingly. And when she only grinned at me: "V, we can't do this! We're not little kids anymore. We could get in really big trouble! Plus, like just yesterday my mom was telling me that I was growing up now, that I needed to start thinking and acting more responsibly. And I'm pretty sure this is *exactly* the kinda stuff she was warning me about!"

"Well, try not to grow up too fast, Charlie."

"Why not?"

"Because you'll miss all the fun parts." Still grinning at me, she said, "Now get ready to start running."

"What? *Why?*"

"See that pole with the little metal flags hanging from it?"

I did—there was a green flag and a red flag. "Uh-huh. So?"

"Well, if someone had bought a ticket at this station, the ticket guy would've hit a button, and the red flag would be sticking out to let the engineer know he needs to stop here. But since no one's bought one, the engineer's going to see green and roll right past. The train's only going to slow down a little."

There were so many things I wanted to say, but the first words out of my mouth were: "How do you know so much about trains, huh?"

Violet ignored me, so my next ones were: "V, I am NOT gonna go chasing after a speeding locomotive, do you hear me?"

She glanced back to me, said, "Would you do it for a Scooby snack?" Her grin was getting even bigger now, laughing at me behind those dazzling baby blues.

I narrowed my eyes at her. "I *hope* that wasn't you taking some sly dig at the fact that I recently grew a tail. . . ."

"Wouldn't dream of it," she said, clearly making fun of me, and before either of us could say anything else (and believe me, I had a couple more things to say to her), there was another screeching whistle as the train began to slow, just like Violet had said it would. I felt one of her hands close around mine in that cheerleader death grip of hers, and she pulled me forward to the edge of the tracks just as the engine went blurring by, inches from our faces. White-hot steam billowed up from the undercarriage. It washed over us in a greasy wave, and the sound of metal wheels grinding on metal tracks was enough to make my teeth chatter.

"GET READY!" Violet yelled, but the hiss and chug, hiss and chug, of the train was so loud I had to read the words off her lips. An instant later she took off, and I chased after her, staying right on her heels. To our left, the train thundered violently along the tracks. Passenger cars flashed by, glinting in the sun. Suddenly Violet's idea seemed even worse than it had ten seconds ago, and ten seconds ago it hadn't been looking so hot either.

"HOW ARE WE SUPPOSED TO GET ON?" I shouted as the last passenger car pulled almost even with us. Then I got my answer: Violet screamed and flung herself at the speeding train. I watched—sort of stunned, sort of not—as all ten of her strong and always nicely manicured fingers wrapped around the top bar of the grab rail, and she pulled herself up onto the platform with ease. Geez. Talk about upper-body strength. Maybe I should've gotten into gymnastics. Or cheerleading. Or anything else.

"C'MON!" she shouted. Her eyes were huge with adrenaline as she stuck out a hand toward me. "TAKE IT!"

I'll admit I didn't like my chances. The train was still gaining speed, and I was losing mine. Running on these little slopes of crumbly rock was even tougher than *geometry.* "Trying!" My chest was already burning, my sides aching, and my footing was all over the place. But I pushed all of that aside—all of that plus the panicky, choking fear of totally embarrassing myself in front of arguably the coolest girl on the planet—and made my move. I put on a burst of speed, reaching out with my hands—

And stumbled, one of my shoelaces catching on the tracks. By the time I found my balance again and looked up, I saw that I'd fallen almost ten feet behind in the span of a second.

Violet shouted, "CHARLIE? WHAT ARE YOU DOING?"

C'mon, dude! Gritting my teeth, I ran as fast as my feet could carry me, got as close to the train as my legs could get me, and then made the only move there was to make—I dove for the platform just as the train started to pull away for good.

I'd closed my eyes as I jumped (dust and tiny chips of rocks were blowing everywhere) and felt my hands smack against the grab rail.

My fingers barely had time to close around the smooth brass bar before a bump in the track nearly jarred them loose, and I found myself hanging off the back of the platform, my sneakers bouncing and scraping along the tracks as the train rumbled along, picking up crazy speed. Okay, definitely not my brightest idea.

My panicked eyes found Violet's just as another jolt shook the train.

This time my grip opened up. My fingers started to slip off the bar—

And in the instant before they did, Violet's hands closed around mine, and she quickly hauled me onto the back of the train with a loud grunt.

We both went tumbling to our hands and knees.

I smiled sideways at her. She smiled sideways back at me.

"So, that was fun . . . ," I said, and we both burst out laughing.

CHAPTER TWENTY-SIX

The interior of the train had definitely seen better days. The carpeted floors were dusty and faded, the wallpaper lining the halls (some ancient-looking floral print with white and purple flowers) was stained in places, torn in others, and the flimsy cabin doors rattled and banged with every hump, bump, and lump in the tracks. On the bright side, at least the thing still went *choo-choo!* every now and then.

Tiptoeing our way up the narrow hall, we stopped at the first cabin to our right, pressed our ears lightly against the laminated slab of the door, and listened for voices. When neither of us heard any, I slid the door open, revealing a small room with simple padded benches on either side, and we slipped inside.

The upholstery was a hideous faded yellow—more mustardy than lemon—and the overhead compartments were completely stuffed with mismatching suitcases; they must've been using this particular cabin as a storage room. Perfecto!

I eased the door shut behind us and twisted the little knob labeled ABERTO/FECHADO just in case. As we sat down, I gave Violet a *Let's keep our fingers crossed* look, and she whispered, "It's gonna be fine. Relax."

Relax. Right. I mean, we were only stowaways on some old run-down train traveling through the middle of *nowhere* with no money, no passports, and no idea how we were going to get across the fourth largest continent on the planet. What was there to worry about? "And what are we going to do if some ticket-checker guy comes in here asking to see our tickets, huh?"

"Easy. We just start making out."

I have no idea what kind of face I made when I heard that, but it must've been pretty funny, because Violet exploded into laughter.

"*What?*" I nearly shouted.

"*Shhhhhhhhh!*" she snapped, still giggling as she slapped me on the arm. "Someone's going to hear you!"

"Forget that. What did you just say?"

"That someone's going to *hear you.*"

"No, *before* that."

"What? About us making out?"

"Yeah, *that*. I mean, what—what kind of plan is that, anyway . . . ?" Was it terrible? Was it *ingenious*? I couldn't decide.

"Haven't you seen any of those social experiment videos on the Internet?"

"What *social experiment videos*?"

"The ones they do to see how people react in certain situations. I think they even have a TV show like that."

"Yeah, not following . . ."

"My point is that there's been hundreds of those types of experiments conducted to prove a simple point: People don't like to interrupt people they see kissing. It makes them feel uncomfortable. Like they're interrupting something private. They usually just want to get away as quickly as possible."

"Are you *nuts*? You really think some ticket guy is going to come in here, see us playing *kissy face*, then just turn around and leave without asking to see *our tickets*?"

"Pretty much."

"That—*no*! I mean, that's not gonna work. That couldn't *possibly* work!" *And why is my voice suddenly all high and thin and squeaky? She's the one talking craziness!*

"Trust me, Charlie—it'll work."

I narrowed my eyes at her. "You know, it sort of sounds like you've done this before. . . ."

She smirked back. "Charlie, just chill. Everything's going to be—"

A loud *bang, bang, bang* at the door had me nearly jumping out of my skin.

My eyes flew to Violet. To her lips. And her eyes flew to mine. To MY lips!

Is this seriously about to happen?

Right here?

Right now?

In some random train in the middle of SOUTH AMERICA?

CHAPTER TWENTY-SEVEN

K iss me!" Violet whisper-shouted, and another rush of panic—this one even stronger than the first—surged through me.

Suddenly I didn't know what I was freaking out about more: the fact that somebody was at the door, or the idea of kissing Violet Rey!

"This is *not* the way I've always imagined this going down!" I objected.

Violet's eyebrows shot up. *"Huh?"*

"That's not to say I've *imagined* this before . . . because that—that would be totally *weird!*" My face was burning so hot I didn't even know what I was saying anymore. I was just babbling. Fortunately, Violet shut me up.

"Charlie, just do it!" And she leaned toward me, puckering those glossy pink lips and closing those big blue eyes just as the door slid open.

Not a ticket-checker dude, I saw, which was a huge relief to say the least. And not some security guard type either.

No, it was a tiny old man, thin-framed and hunchbacked, holding a man-purse so big it could've easily doubled as a sleeping bag. He wore a colorful striped shoulder wrap over a dress shirt the color of ripe bananas and a yellow turban, which didn't quite match the shade of his shirt. His neck and wrists were adorned with a whole mess of colorful beaded jewelry, and he had pale, liver-spotted skin that sagged in places, making it look almost like he was wearing a flesh mask. The dude was old. Like had-his-family-portrait-drawn-by-Francisco-Goya old. But probably not quite old enough not to notice us.

Which meant we were in *trouble*.

"Ay . . ." He glanced back at the cabin number on the door. "Fui al baño y ahora estoy todo confundido."

"Charlie?" Violet said out of the corner of her smiling mouth. "Google Translate please. . . ."

"He said he went to the bathroom and now he's all confused," I translated.

"Why don't you explain to him about the mix-up?" Violet said, not so subtly urging me on.

"Well, I would consider it a very fortunate *mix-up*," the man replied, surprising us both. "I could use some company."

"You speak English?" I asked, and he smiled softly.

"It would seem so, yes."

"Yeah, we don't know what happened," I said, trying to think quickly. "They must've double-booked this cabin. We just got on."

Violet elbowed me in the ribs, and it wasn't until the guy said, "The train stopped?" that I understood why.

"Yes, briefly," Violet said quickly.

"*Very* briefly," I put in. "Blink and you would've missed it. *I* almost missed it." Which was actually true.

V elbowed me again, forcing an overly enthusiastic smile to her lips.

The ancient-looking man set his huge bag on the bench across from us, then slowly settled himself beside it. His eyes were so blue that at first I thought he was wearing some kind of special-effects contacts, but he wasn't. He just had really, really blue eyes. "It's been a long trip for me. . . ." He sighed.

"Really? Where are you coming from?" V asked.

"I've spent the last few days exploring Brazil. I've always wanted to travel through South America, and by the time you get to be my age, you have to start doing it or you might not ever get the chance."

"So where are you from?" I asked. His accent was sort of interesting, and I figured the more we were asking questions about him, the less he'd be asking questions about us.

"I'm from Venezuela."

Violet made a face.

"What's wrong?" he asked.

"Nothing, I just thought you'd say something like Suriname."

He arched an inquisitive brow. "¿De verdad? Why?"

"Because of your shoulder wrap. I think it's called a *kamisa*, right? My parents own an antique shop, and there's this guy that's always bringing in old toys and stuff. He's from Suriname and always wears one."

A look of surprise flashed across the old man's face. "Very, *very* sharp eyes you have, mi niña. Yes, in fact, I bought this in a vintage clothing store in Caracas. It may very well be from Suriname." He smiled again, his face crumpling into a maze of wrinkles. "By the way, my name is Henry. Henry Ovaprim." And when neither of us said anything: "And yours?"

"Oh, I'm Ramona," Violet said quickly. "Ramona John."

I tried to come up with a cool alias too, panicked, and said, "And I'm Ra-*món . . . Ramón John.*" Violet rib-smashed me again, and I squeaked, "We're brother and sister. . . ."

Which had Mr. Ovaprim blinking in surprise. "You two are siblings? You don't look very much alike."

He's onto us! I thought. Panicking, I cracked my book bag open an inch, then pitched it sideways, spilling a stream of rice onto the floor.

"Oh, how clumsy of me!" I shouted, winking over at Violet, who glared back.

Next thing I knew Mr. Ovaprim was bent over, picking up the arroz with surprisingly nimble fingers. "You—you don't have to do that . . . ," I stammered. "I'll clean it up."

"Why *in the world* are you still carrying all that *rice* around?" Violet growled into my ear.

"*What?* What's the problem?"

"Well, for one, it's *beyond* embarrassing!"

"How is having a book bag full of rice *embarrassing?*" I shot back. "Arroz is, like, one of the most *versatile grains on the planet.* You can boil it. It goes great with beans or meat. And it's not like we have a ton of money at the moment, so I figured keeping a couple extra pounds of *emergency food* on hand just might not be the worst idea, know what I mean?"

"¡Ya!" Mr. Ovaprim held up the last grain of rice, trapped between his thumb and index finger. Then he dropped it into the neat little mound he'd gathered in his other hand and dumped it back into my bag. "Ahí está. Now hold on to that bag *tight*. We wouldn't want another spill." Slowly his gaze focused on my chest, and I watched his leathery face crease into a confused frown. "Pardon me for asking," he whispered, "but are you wearing a dog collar as a necklace . . . ?"

Great. The guy noticed everything! "Oh, uh, yeah . . . actually I am. It's—it's a memento. You know, something to remember my pooch by while traveling. . . . Just love that furry little bundle of joy!" Awful, I know. But the truth was probably even more embarrassing.

Mr. Ovaprim's frown deepened a bit. "How . . . sweet." Then, after a few awkwardly silent moments, he said, "Ay, perdónenme, I have to excuse myself again. Drank a little too much sangria in the dinner coach. When you get to be my age . . . well, you'll find out eventually. Permiso." And he slipped out into the hall with his man-purse clutched tightly against one hip.

"He's nice," Violet said, watching him go.

"And a human vacuum cleaner apparently. Did you see how quickly he picked up all that rice?"

"Yeah, that was impressive."

"By the way, how much longer do you think before we get to Chile? I might wanna check out that dinner coach myself. . . ."

"But *why*? You have a backpack full of such a *versatile* grain. Just snack on that."

"Ha. Ha. You're *sooooo* fun—" Through the window, I thought I saw a flash of blue light in the trees. Looked like a headlight. But way out here?

"What was that?" Violet said, narrowing her eyes as she turned to stare out the window. Which meant that she'd seen it too.

I shook my head. "No idea."

And just then a shrill croaking sound echoed through the woods that ran along the tracks. Our window was slightly open (or maybe just didn't close all the way) so I heard it pretty clearly; it sounded something like *tué tué tué!* "Okay, and what was *that*?" Violet said.

We both just sat there a moment, listening.

Maybe it was just the train. Squeaky brakes?

The thought had no more than crossed my mind when something slammed into the window less than six inches from our faces.

Whatever it was had struck with nearly enough force to shatter the glass; I heard a sharp *crack* as Violet and I jumped back in surprise; but at first my startled brain was all like, *Gah, what I am even looking at?* On the other side of the glass was arguably the most hideous creature I had ever laid eyes upon. Scratch that—it *was* the most hideous creature I'd ever laid my eyes on. Not exactly bird. In all honesty, it looked more like a face—a *human* face! Except this face had grayish skin, ears that had stretched into long, batlike wings, and a pair of swollen, bulging, bloodshot, purple eyes that were all pupils. Large, taloned feet, which seemed to have grown out from under the thing's pointy chin, scrabbled madly at the window, leaving thin scars in the glass. Its mouth twisted into a snarl. The thing reared back, let out an earsplitting cry (*tué tué tué!*), and struck the window again, hard, with the center of its broad, bony forehead. Spiderweb cracks raced across the glass, branching out in every direction. Violet screamed. Jumping up, she snatched a piece of luggage from the overhead bin and held it up like she was planning to use it as a shield. And she might've had to too, if the tracks hadn't run so close to the woods that a wall of branches raked the side of our car like those foam rollers in car washes, wiping the vicious little sucker away.

V turned to me, her face white with shock. "WHAT WAS THAT THING?" she yelled.

I started to shake my head—and then stopped. I knew exactly what it was. I'd known it since I was *five*. "It's a chonchón," I breathed. "A harbinger of evil."

CHAPTER TWENTY-EIGHT

A harbinger of *what?*" Violet was staring back at me with eyes so wide I thought they might roll out of her head.

"Of evil!" I repeated. "They're the decapitated heads of old sorcerers. They grow feet like birds. Their ears turn into wings."

"The decapitated heads of old SORCERERS?"

"It's not as bad as it sounds. They use a cream on their necks. Detach them from their bodies themselves."

"Self-decapitation. Right. So it's even *worse* than it sounds."

"Some cultures believe that they come to warn you when something terrible is about to happen."

V looked a bit unsure. "You mean, more terrible than *it?*"

Off in the distance, a howl rang out through the night—a wild, bloodcurdling sound that made my skin freeze and the hairs on the back of my neck stand on end.

Violet's eyes, huge and full of fear, stared out at the dark woods racing past. "And what the heck was *that?*"

"The something terrible." Through the cracked, drool-stained window I thought I could make out the vague outlines of shapes—*HUGE* shapes—moving in the darkness. They were too big to be forest animals, but also too defined—and too *there*—to be my imagination. *Do they even have grizzly bears in Brazil . . . ?*

"Charlie, are you seeing this?"

Violet got that much out—and not another word—before the train car suddenly rocked and shuddered as if struck by a giant boulder.

We were thrown sideways into the gap between the seats. At the same time, our cabin door flew open, and literally every single piece of luggage in the overhead bins slid out of their cubbyholes, crashing down on us in an avalanche of leather handles and plastic wheels. Something hard—probably the corner of one of those suitcases with the metal-plated edges—smacked me on the back of the head hard enough for me to see stars.

Next to me, Violet was swiping hair out of her eyes with a dazed look on her face and someone's laminated luggage tag (MARIA RUIZ) stuck to her cheek. Even though we were both a bit out of it at the moment (and at least one of us was hurting), we both thought of the exact same thing at the *exact* same time: "MR. OVAPRIM!"

I scrambled to my feet and was about to run out into the hall (first I had to scale the mini mountain of suitcases that had settled between us and the door) when—

THWUMP!

—something landed on the roof so heavily that it caved in several inches under the impact.

Before I even knew what was happening, there was a shriek of metal as ginormous razor-sharp claws ripped into the ceiling of our cabin, peeling back a triangle-shaped section as easily as if it were a tin of sardines.

An instant later an enormous black snout poked through the gap. It sucked in a huge breath, held it for a split second, then let it out in a mucusy explosion.

What the—

The creature's drool-slicked upper lip pulled back like a rumpled curtain, showing off a mouthful of curved dagger-like teeth.

Violet, thinking fast, grabbed our backpacks and yelled, "Run!" and we both went stumbling into the hall, which now looked like the creepiest level in some horror-themed RPG. Overhead, the strip lights flickered and buzzed. Strange sounds—deep metallic groans that were almost human—were coming up through the floorboards beneath our feet. Ahead of us, more pieces of luggage had spilled out from the other cabins and were now scattered everywhere, some forming freaky shapes that half resembled unconscious bodies. I didn't see any sign of Mr. Ovaprim.

"Charlie, c'mon!" V grabbed my hand and yanked me forward. As we flew up the hall, I turned to look out one of the windows—and felt my insides shrivel like pork rinds. Only, at first I didn't even know what I was looking at. *At first* I thought they were *dogs*—some kind of feral, bear-size dogs with giant heads and rippling silvery coats. But then one threw back its head, letting out a wild, terrible howl—

And just like that I knew.

These were no dogs. . . . These were lobisomem.

These were *werewolves*!

In most cases, having *one* werewolf anywhere in your vicinity (within, say, fifty square blocks) would be bad enough. Especially when you consider that most of them—if not *all*—are strictly meat-eaters, which puts human beings smack-dab in the middle of their favorite foods menu. But I wasn't looking at just one werewolf. I wasn't even looking at two or three or four. I was looking at an entire pack of them, a *hunting party*, maybe as many as twenty or thirty, racing alongside the train, their hungry black eyes glittering in the night, ears pinned flat against the huge domes of their heads. Boy, and I'd *already* thought I knew what it felt like to be at the top of the endangered species list. Just as we reached the door at the end of the car, I became aware of a low, steady growl at our backs. *Don't look!* I told myself, but of course I couldn't help myself. . . . I turned, *slowly*, and saw the creature emerge from our cabin on its hind legs, stalking more than walking, moving more like a person than any canis lupis I'd ever seen. And interestingly enough, it sort of *dressed* like a person too. It wore a long brown cape, cinched at the waist by a thick rope, with a hood that fell over its face. Rosary beads were wound tightly around its muscular forearms. A golden cross dangled from its fur-covered neck. Its hungry, red-rimmed eyes narrowed on me. Then, in one lightning-fast move, it arched backward, letting out a spine-chilling howl.

From right outside the train's window—from *everywhere*, it sounded like, all around us—came the *even more* spine-chilling sound of answering howls.

It's me, I realized with a fresh jolt of terror. *These things are after ME!*

The lobisomem's dark eyes once again locked with mine. I had time to think, *¡AY, DIOS MÍO!* and then the thing exploded into motion, bounding up the corridor after us, its long, curved claws tearing up fluffy chunks of moldy beige carpet.

"CHARLIE, WHAT ARE YOU DOING?" Violet screamed.

I didn't respond. Didn't have time to. Just followed her through the door and out onto the narrow platform that jutted out the back of the car.

The moment I was through, Violet shut the door. But no sooner had she run the steel safety bar than the werewolf slammed into the door from the *inside*, making the entire lower half pop outward.

"WHAT ARE THOSE THINGS?" Violet screamed.

"Werewolves!" I screamed back. "And I think they're after me!"

"Oh, you *think* so, huh? What gave it away?"

"It looked right at me!"

"I know! I was being sarcastic!"

A simple metal coupler held together by two huge screws connected the train cars. Underneath it, dark steel tracks and even darker earth flashed by in a dizzying blur.

"Next car, Charlie!" Violet shouted. "Go!"

As I took my first unsteady step out onto the coupler, a high-pitched whistle split the air, and the wind gusted around me, swirling my hair and blowing it into my eyes—like I needed any help messing this one up, right? I felt myself start to tip sideways . . . felt myself begin to fall . . . and dove for the next car just before my foot slipped off the greasy metal surface. I made it—barely—and Violet was right behind me, landing next to me in a crouch just as the werewolf rammed the door again. This time the safety bar popped off like the top on an exploding pressure cooker. It whistled past my face close enough for me to hear it over the screech of the wind before clanking away into darkness. Another inch to the left, and El Justo Juez wouldn't have been the only headless member of La Liga.

"Quick!" Violet threw open the door, and we hurried into the next car. I could hear shouts of terror coming from behind the row of closed doors to our right as we flew down the corridor and thought about how useful jaguar legs would be in our current . . . *situation? Predicament?* (I wasn't sure what you called it when a pack of man-eating werewolves were trying to make you their next Happy— er, *un*happy—Meal). So I concentrated, focusing my mind, and a moment later felt the tiniest tingle down my spine. It was working! Or so I thought—

"Charlie, what the *heck?*" Violet shrieked, gaping at me, and I had to flinch, she was yelling so loud. Then I turned, catching my reflection in the window, and let out a shriek of my own. No jaguar legs. Instead I'd manifested the strangest-looking pair of ears I'd ever seen: long and pointy and tipped with strands of wispy black hair. ¡Santo cielos! They were the ears of a *lynx!*

"*So freakin' embarrassing . . .*," I started to grumble, and that was when a dozen or so claws knifed through the ceiling like daggers. They speared so far down that I had to duck to avoid an impromptu haircut. The thick metal ceiling whined and squealed as it was peeled viciously back. Two of the overhead lights exploded in a shower of sparks. Moonlight flooded into the car like a spotlight.

"Hurry!" I shouted as we reached the next connector door. "¡Dale!" Violet didn't hesitate; she quickly threw it open, and we scrambled out onto the dark platform. Above us, I could see hulking shapes dancing in the moon's pale glow: the lobisomem tearing their way into the train.

I peered around the next car, trying to see what was going on up ahead. And what I saw was *even more* werewolves, dozens of them slipping out of the pitch-dark woods and pouncing on the engine car like it was some wounded animal.

There was a deafening screech of metal. Orange-red sparks suddenly flew up between the tracks and wheels in a wide, dazzling spray: The conductor had slammed on the brakes. But it wasn't going to be enough to stop the train. We'd picked up too much speed.

"We're going to have to jump!" Violet shouted.

Beneath the platform, the ground was still whipping by, a green-black blur in the night.

"I'm not liking it, V.... What's plan B?"

"We get eaten alive by a pack of ravenous carnivore *freaks.*"

That didn't sound too good, either. "On second thought, plan A isn't looking that bad.... On three!"

"*Three!*" Violet shouted—typical Violet—and she grabbed my hand and leapt off the platform, pulling us both into empty space.

CHAPTER TWENTY-NINE

There was a long, terrible moment of falling, of the wind whipping in our ears, of leaves and branches raking at our arms, legs, and faces.

And then we hit the ground. Hard. My knees buckled, and I felt my leg muscles go. Worse, the ground was sloped—*badly* sloped. Rolling and bouncing and banging my head on pretty much everything within head-banging range, I tumbled over and over again, spinning through the air, until—

Crunch!

I landed about thirty or so yards down below, on a bed of dried leaves. For what felt like a long time I just lay there, staring up at a bright full moon through the black lace of leaves. I felt like I'd been beaten like a piñata, pummeled by a dozen or so mean little sugar addicts desperate for their candy fix. Suddenly I felt very sorry for Mr. Puerquito—

the pink baby piglet piñata my mom had bought for my birthday party when I was six.

Wincing, propping myself up on my elbow, I mumbled, "Qué clase de día, caballero," sounding an awful lot like my abuelita complaining about a rough day, and looked around. We were in deep forest now, out in the middle of . . . the middle of *nowhere.*

"V, you still alive?" I said, pushing to my feet, wiping leaves off my face. When she didn't immediately answer, I checked around me and realized she wasn't there—she wasn't *anywhere*! A surge of panic raced through me as I shouted, "VIOLET! *V?*" Had she been knocked unconscious? Broken something? Been eaten by a lobisomem? The possibilities were endless, and not one of them reassuring. "VIOLET! YO, VIOLET!"

Still no answer. But then—

"Over here!" she called back.

I was so relieved to hear her voice that it took me several seconds to realize just how far away it sounded. We must've tumbled down two completely different paths.

"Charlie, you okay?"

"More or less." Rubbing an ache in my side, I turned toward the sound of her voice, only I couldn't see much of anything; it was all shadows and hanging black vines.

"Remind me never to get on a train with you again," she

said. I could hear the smile in her voice, which meant she was totally fine, and that made me smile too.

"Yeah, well, just remember whose idea it was to *jump*." And for the record, it was *hers*.

I began to pick my way through the trees, careful not to trip over any of the rocks or roots . . . and exactly five steps later, I went completely, absolutely, perfectly *still*.

I thought I'd known fear back on the train, but it was nothing—*nothing*—compared to the sheer mind-numbing terror I felt right at this moment—right as I realized I was now standing face-to-face with another lobisomem.

CHAPTER THIRTY

The thing looked like death itself—and probably smelled *twice* as bad.

Its sleek gray mouth was pulled back in a snarl, exposing row upon row of vicious-looking teeth in serious need of toothpaste, flossing, and as many electric-powered toothbrushes as this thing could get its hairy, over-size paws on. Its eyes, beady and doll-like, glared out at me from deep inside its enormous dome-shaped skull, and from even deeper inside this thing, way down in the black pit of its mouth, came a terrible sound—a low, rattlesnake-like hiss that made my skin prickle and the blood freeze in my veins.

I'd barely gotten a chance to utter a scream that sounded suspiciously like a squeak before the lobisomem shoved me to the ground with its massive front paws and pinned me there, its dark brown cape hanging in my face, its enormous weight pressing down on my chest like an anvil. Then it threw back its head and let out a howl so loud that I literally felt it move through the ground beneath me like an earthquake. *It's calling for its buddies!* was the first thought that popped into my head, and it wasn't a comforting one. Wild with panic, I tried twisting out from underneath it again, and just as I did, a wall of darkness swooped down out of nowhere. It slammed into the lobisomem with a loud *smack!* that sent it tumbling, end over end, into the woods. With no idea what was going on—no idea about anything at the moment, really—I whipped my head around in both shock and panic (and some gratefulness, too, obviously . . . but mostly shock and panic) and felt my eyes bug out.

Looming over me was an ogre. And not just any ogre— an Okpe: a race of baddie *warrior* ogres native to Argentina. The thing stood at least fifteen feet tall and just as wide around, with feet so monstrously ginormous that, initially, I'd mistaken them for boulders.

From my abuela's stories, I knew the Okpe were legendary for being completely invulnerable to human weapons. And now I understood why. Almost every square inch of it was encased in thick rocky armor—from the top of its head to the muddy soles of its giant ogre feet. Pretty much the only part of its freakish anatomy that *wasn't* armored was the ogre's face: a fleshy, flabby, pinkish sort of thing that looked almost half formed, with drooping jowls and a smashed-in lump of a nose. No joke, dude looked like un lechón asado—a roasted *pig*—and an ugly one at that!

As I scrambled to my feet and started to back away— and back away slowly . . . very, *very* slowly—the ogre raised a massive rocky fist in my direction and grunted something that sounded a whole lot like "Jorge." Or maybe "torre."

In that instant Violet came up next to me and whisper-shouted, "Hurry, I think I heard another werewolf!" then must've seen the Okpe, because her face paled like a boiled egg.

"I SAID RUN!" the ogre roared, and his voice rumbled through the forest, making the trees around us shudder. "¡CORRE!"

We didn't need to be told twice.

We took off into the dark woods, running side by side, neither of us even daring to glance back. There was so much panic, so much pure, unfiltered adrenaline burning through my veins right then that my arms swung in blurs and my feet flew over the ground like the wind. But nothing—and I mean *nothing*—was cycling faster than my brain. See, none of this made even *a lick* of sense. Okpes weren't *good* ogres— if there even was such a thing as *good ogres*. No, in fact, they were *terrible* creatures, creatures known for kidnapping little kids and slurping the marrow from their bones just for the fun of it! They were feared all over Argentina, from

Buenos Aires to Ushuaia. Most flea markets in the region even sold charms and bracelets that would supposedly keep them away. So with all that said, what the heck had just gone down? I mean, why had that thing *saved* me? Why hadn't it tried to *kill* us?

Does it really matter, dude? answered a tiny, panicked voice somewhere in the back of my brain. *You're alive! Be thankful!*

Only I got the feeling that it *did* matter. That it mattered *a lot.*

As we reached the place where the slope began to level off, I heard a strange sound coming from above us and craned my neck around to look. And what I saw stopped me dead in my tracks: Hordes of Okpes were streaming toward the top of the slope, flowing toward the train tracks like a rocky tidal wave, their massive shapes seeming to form out of the night itself. They swung clubs and spears and huge rocky battle-axes as they charged out of the tree line on the backs of gigantic, tusked hogs, slamming into the werewolves and scattering them like bowling pins.

Howls pierced the night. The ogres had surprised the lobisomem. But it wasn't enough. The werewolves were already regrouping, already tackling ogres off their hogs by the dozens. The hungry, primal sound of their howls caused gooseflesh to break out over every square inch of my body, and I was still standing there, watching the battle with my eyes bugging and my jaw felt like it had come completely unhinged, when a strong hand gripped my shoulder.

I whirled with a shriek, expecting to see another snarling lobisomem—or maybe another Okpe (and, odds were, one nowhere near as friendly as the last)—

But what I saw was a girl.

CHAPTER THIRTY-ONE

She was young, somewhere in her late teens, maybe, with long reddish hair that was tangled in places, sort of like dreadlocks, and slicked back from the kind of face you really only see in telenovelas—all high cheekbones and sharp angles. She wore a simple white tank top and jean shorts cut off at the tops of her thighs, the strands of blue-white denim dangling like cobwebs. Her eyes were the deepest, darkest shade of brown I'd ever seen, the sort of perfectly earthy color you only find in the bark of the most ancient trees. Her skin was a few shades lighter, and her feet were bare. Lines of dark mud had caked between her toes and up her heels, but she didn't seem to mind. Like, at all.

"Vengan conmigo si valoran sus vidas," the barefooted girl said.

"Charlie, talk to me . . . ," I heard Violet shout from a

few yards away. She'd picked up a fat branch and had it cocked back like a baseball bat. "Is she on our side, or am I gonna have to channel my inner José Canseco?"

"Want me to ask her?"

"Well, what'd she *say* . . . ?"

"Come with me if you value your lives," I translated. Then, glancing around, I realized we were standing on the edge of a dark road that curved around the hill we'd just come tumbling down. Parked at the side of the road beside a sign reading ¡PELIGRO! CAÍDA DE ROCAS—DANGER! FALLING ROCKS (which *should* have read: DANGER! WATCH OUT FOR BATTLING SOMBRAS) was an old pickup truck. It looked like something from the fifties with flared fenders and rust spots dotting the sides of the hood and the driver-side door.

Another howl tore through the night. This one close— nowhere near the main battle.

The mystery girl climbed into the driver's seat of the truck saying, "You either come willingly or I *make* you. The choice I leave to you." Didn't actually sound like much of a choice, but I didn't think the lobisomem would make us a better offer.

Violet shoved me toward the passenger-side door, and we piled into the truck just as another hair-raising howl sliced through the woods. Before I even got a chance to close the door, the girl slammed her foot on the gas, and the old, but apparently still pretty powerful, Ford pickup leapt forward. Moonlight glinted off the polished chrome edge of the rearview mirror as she gunned it around the narrow bend, tires screeching. On either side of us, the stretches of thick forest looked like walls of blackness. I couldn't see anything—*nada*—and that wasn't exactly a comforting feeling. I mean, where the heck had all those lobisomem *even come from?* And how many more were there?

"Los lobos have your scent," the girl said grimly. "They will hunt you as long as they have breath in their nostrils. Or as long as you have breath in yours." Her odd brown eyes slid to me, and she smacked the steering wheel loudly with both hands. "You're both reckless! You have *no idea* what you have gotten yourselves in the middle of!"

"What are you talking about?" Violet said.

"Do you know how much attention you've attracted by using an Espejo? You were spotted by black crows *seconds* after arriving in Brazil. . . . I'm surprised you're both not in the belly of some werewolf right now!"

My eyes were still glued to the truck's rear window, watching out for wolves. "Why are they after us?"

"Not *us*," she whispered. "Just *you*."

And even though I'd figured as much, her words still sent a chill through me. "Me? But why *me?*"

"That is an *excellent* question. How *does* one go about

attracting the attention of such cursed creatures...? Please, tell me. I'm curious as well."

"*Cursed creatures?*" Violet repeated, probably not liking the sound of that, either.

"I thought they were lobisomem," I said.

"They *are* lobisomem." Mystery girl cut me a sharp sideways look and whipped us around another bend. "But how many *werewolves* do you see hooded and caped, their paws wrapped with rosary beads?" When we didn't answer, she said, "Those that hunt you were once men. Priests of the Most High. But an unspeakable fate befell them; their parish was burned to the ground by banditos, their parishioners murdered in cold blood. The priests, in a blind rage to avenge the fallen, struck a deal with a dark sorcerer, a brujo of old, who took the opportunity to exploit their grief. They are now known as Los Embrujados, neither man nor beast, cursed to roam this world in shadows, exiled from the lobisomem clans, for they are not natural born, but also exiled from the tribes of men, for they are no longer human. In truth, they haven't been seen for over six *hundred* years."

Six hundred years . . . ? Why would things that hadn't been seen for more than *half a millennium* be after *me?*

Violet spoke up before I could.

"So who are you?" she asked the barefooted girl.

"Doesn't matter," the girl answered coldly.

"Okay. So why are you helping us?"

"Because I don't want Morphling blood spilled in South America. You two want to kill yourselves, do it someplace else."

Violet's eyes, full of shock, found mine. "How did you know he was a Morphling?"

A small smile touched the girl's lips. "When a boy slays a witch as old and feared as La Cuca, word tends to get around." Her eyes flicked to me in the rearview mirror. "Felicidades, by the way. Joanna must be *very* proud."

"You know Joanna?" I asked, surprised.

"The Witch Queen of Toledo is the only Spaniard I have ever trusted. I would give my life for her, as she would for me . . . as she would for *any* sombra." She paused for a moment as if trying to compose herself. "It has been her tireless work building alliances and bringing together the scattered clans that has saved this world. Both from ourselves and from those beyond."

"Are you with La Liga?" I asked.

The girl shook her head, eyes locked on the rearview. "It is not that simple. But I do not oppose them, if that's what you're wondering."

"Where are you taking us?" Violet asked.

She hesitated for a moment before saying, "Away from here."

"Could you be *a bit* more specific?"

"Far away. Is that specific enough?"

There was a moment of silence, in which the only sound was the low, steady growl coming from the old truck's engine. At least I hoped that's where it was coming from.

"We need to get to Chile," Violet said finally.

"Not tonight, you don't. The wolves will be watching the borders. Tonight you stay in Argentina."

CHAPTER THIRTY-TWO

We drove for probably two hours straight, following barely there paths without signposts or markings through the thick woods. Tall trees crammed around us. The night air was sharp but fresh, pouring in through the half-open windows and carrying with it the sweet scent of blooming flowers. I didn't realize the truck had a radio until about an hour or so in, and before that it was pretty much crickets; Violet said maybe five words the entire time and never took her eyes off the girl, who said even less and never took her eyes off the road. (She did, however, finally give up her name, which was Adriana—Adriana Tovar.) The old-school AM/FM radio–cassette player combo couldn't pick up any of the local stations (if there even *were* any local stations), but I found a tape of a band called Memphis La Blusera in the glove box and put that on. Every time the song "La

Flor Más Bella"—which translates into "the most beautiful flower"—played, Adriana seemed to let off the gas a bit. Other than that the speedometer didn't drop below eighty once.

About an hour or so later I noticed that Adriana had begun to stare out the driver-side window like she was looking for an address or a street sign.

"Are we . . . lost?" I asked, hoping very much that we weren't.

"I will find my way." Moonlight shone in her eyes as she scanned the dark woods. "I'm just not used to seeing the trees like this."

"You mean—*at night?*"

"I mean in so much *dolor. . . .*"

Pain? "How do you . . . know they're in *pain?*"

Her voice was low and grim. "There's a darkness spreading through the earth. Perhaps you cannot feel it, but I can. It is seeping out of the soil like poison, killing everything it touches."

Violet frowned slightly. "What do you think it is?"

"No lo sé. No one does." Adriana gave a small, almost helpless shrug. "Some say it's the season, but I do not believe that. I never heard the trees cry as they do now."

"What's so special about this season, anyway?"

"It's the time of year when our two worlds are closest.

The Land of the Living and that of the dead. It is a time of strange occurrences, without a doubt, but it doesn't explain the death in the air." She paused for a second, as if unsure she should continue. "Of course, some believe the rumors. . . ."

"What rumors?" Violet asked, shaking her head. But she'd barely asked the question when Adriana suddenly swerved the truck around the impossibly thick trunk of a eucalyptus tree.

The Ford's ancient suspension squeaked and whined with every bump, divot, and break in the ground but surprisingly kept chugging along until we came to a hard stop at a stand of pines.

Adriana cut the engine and said, "Do not leave this truck." Then, hopping out, she began to examine the ground like she was searching for footprints; she ran over to a pair of trees, appeared to have a conversation with them, then came back saying, "We're here."

"And where exactly *is* here . . . ?" Violet asked her as she climbed out.

"Argentina," replied Adriana.

V gave her a funny look. "What? No. That's impossible. There's *no way* we would have gotten from central Brazil to Argentina in, what? *Three hours?*"

"Not impossible at all when you know the forests, and even less so when you're traveling through sombra wood."

Confused, I blinked. "Sombra wood?" I'd never heard of that.

"The secret places of sombras. Deep, deep wood—enchanted and magical. Distances and time are not the same in these places. And *this* place, in particular, is special even among sombra wood. This is Regancho de Gordura, perhaps the most famous feasting place in the entire world. In the spring, when the old trees give their fruit and nuts grow on the branches, sombras come from everywhere to gorge themselves on the bounty and wonderful abundance of nature. It is quite the gathering. But anyway—we are in Argentina, and you *are* safe."

"We don't have time for safe," I said impatiently, knowing every second we wasted was another second Joanna's life was in danger. "We need to keep moving. We need to get to Chiloé."

Violet shot me a look, and I realized I'd probably said too much. After all, we barely even knew this girl.

"Is that where you're going?" When neither one of us answered, Adriana nodded like that was all she needed to hear—or, *not* hear. "Then I will take you there myself. You have my word. But first, you are going to help *me* help *you*."

I had no idea what Adriana meant by that, but before I got a chance to ask, she went around to the back of the truck, dug around through a couple of cardboard boxes, and came back carrying three grocery bags full of all sorts of Argentinian treats. There were a few I recognized, like alfajores, which are these awesome cakelike cookies glued together with globs of supersweet dulche de leche, and Bananita Dolca, banana-shaped candy bars with banana-flavored filling and a chocolate coating. But there were also a whole bunch I didn't know, like Mantecol, Bon o Bon, and these delicious square-shaped candies called Vauquita. Adriana told me that I could have as many as I'd like (the more the better), and even though I knew my mom *definitely* wouldn't approve, I was so hungry, I dug right in. Sitting under the stars, chowing down on all these tasty sweets, reminded me so much of my childhood: my abuela and me sneaking outside before dinner to snack on churros and guava and cream-cheese-filled pastelitos while my mom (who didn't approve of those, either) was busy grading her students' tests and waiting for the arroz con pollo to finish cooking.

My abuela had this *huge* sweet tooth—which was probably where I'd gotten *mine*—and we'd had so much fun doing stuff like that. Thinking back to it now made me sort of sad because she was gone, and I knew that we'd never get to do stuff like that again. But it also made me happy because it brought back memories of her, and those were some of my favorite memories growing up.

When Violet and I had stuffed our faces pretty good, Adriana said it was time for us to get some rest—that we'd need it because we had a lot of miles to cover tomorrow.

She told Violet to sleep in the truck, then rolled out a sleeping bag for me in the back. I'd obviously gotten the raw end of that deal (the sleeping bag was about as thick as a *bedsheet*, and the truck bed was just as hard and rusty as it looked), but I didn't mind; I was so stuffed I would've happily napped on a *rock*.

"Sleep with your head here by the tailgate," Adriana instructed me as I climbed onto the back. When I gave her a funny look, she said, "What? I'm superstitious, okay?"

As a cool wind blew through the woods, I watched her lean back against the driver-side door, breathing it in deeply. And as the pine-scented air washed over her, she closed her eyes for a moment and sang a few lines from what sounded like a child's lullaby. It was in Spanish, but I didn't recognize it.

"You have a beautiful voice," Violet said from inside the truck. And that was putting it mildly—I could easily see her onstage at some huge concert, singing side by side with someone like Camila Cabello or Selena Gomez.

A soft smile touched the corners of Adriana's lips, and she looked like she was remembering some sweet memory. "I used to sing every day . . . during happier times." There was a dusty three-string guitarra sticking out of a box by my feet. Adriana saw me staring at it and asked, "Sabes cómo tocar?"

"Yeah, I can play a little. . . ."

She picked it up and held it out to me. "I'll sing if you play."

I glanced over at Violet, who was peeking out the back window now, smiling at me, then took the guitar. The first thing I did was sweep my fingers across the strings to make sure it was in tune, and it didn't sound too bad, actually. Someone must've tuned it pretty recently. A moment later Adriana began to sing. It was a low, haunting melody, and I played slowly, trying to keep rhythm. It wasn't easy playing without a pick, but it wasn't like I had to play fast, either. And I was mostly playing background, anyway, because Adriana's voice really was something—high and pure and tragic somehow, which made it difficult to focus on what she was saying. But it sounded like she was singing about a girl, some poor soul whose village had been raided, who'd been captured and beaten, then burned at the stake but hadn't died—a girl who'd come back as a *tree*. . . .

"That was amazing," Violet said when she was finished. "You have an incredible voice. . . ."

Adriana smiled. It was both happy and sad. "Gracias."

"Who's the girl in the song?" I asked her, but she shook her head like she didn't know.

"No one remembers her name anymore," she said in a hushed voice. Her eyes went to the woods. "But both of you should rest now. I'll be close by." And with that, she slipped into the dark trees.

CHAPTER THIRTY-THREE

A few moments later Violet asked, "Comfy?"

"I actually sort of am," I admitted with a laugh. "Never slept in a sleeping bag before. They're not bad...."

V laughed. "And I've never slept in the front seat of a classic Ford pickup. Not too bad either."

Around us, the woods were silent except for the occasional hoot of an owl. "What are you thinking about?" Violet asked after a minute or two.

"Everything," I said. And that was the honest truth. Between Joanna's kidnapping, those terrifying lobisomem priests, and meeting Adriana, it felt like my brain was being pulled in about a *bazillion* different directions.

"So what do you think we'll find when we get there?" Violet asked me.

"Where? To Chiloé?" I shrugged. "Hopefully Joanna.

And *hopefully* she's okay." When she didn't say anything, I asked, "You have a good feeling about all this?"

"Yeah . . . I mean, I guess. Don't you?"

"I . . . I don't know."

"What do you mean *you don't know?*"

"V, think about it. It's just like you said back at the cave. Let's say we get there and find Joanna, right? You know who we're *also* going to find? Whoever *kidnapped* her . . ."

"Yeah . . . so?"

"Well, can you *imagine* how *powerful* whoever kidnapped her must be? I mean, they kidnapped *the Witch Queen of Toledo*, for crying out loud. How are we supposed to beat it or them or *whoever?*"

"Charlie, when we find Joanna—which we *will*—we'll figure that part out. It's going to be okay. . . ."

"That's easy to say."

"I'm not just *saying* that, Charlie—I *mean* it. We'll figure it out. *Together.* Because that's what friends are for. You've got my back, and I've got yours."

"Violet, you're not listening; I cannot control my manifestations, like, *at all*. In fact, I'm pretty sure I *suck* at morphing. . . . It's like I'm defective or something."

"You'll get the hang of it. Just give it some more time."

"Except time is the *one thing* we absolutely *don't* have."

"Charlie, *chill*. You're fine. . . . You're getting better."

"But I'm *not*," I said with a groan. "And that's not even my point. . . ."

"Then what *is* your point?"

"My point is that I'm *useless* right now. I can't do *anything*. The only reason I'm even still *alive* is because my body just . . . just *manifests* stuff on its own! And I hate to point out the obvious, but if my body *hadn't*, I'd be *dead* right now. You do realize that, right?"

"But you're *not* dead. You're *alive*. We both are. So what are you getting so worked up about?"

I sighed. She just didn't get it, or maybe—and a lot more likely—she just didn't *want* to get it. "This is too much for me, V . . . finding Joanna, trying to stop La Mano Peluda from doing *whatever* it is they're planning on doing . . . It's too much responsibility. I'm not ready for this. I'm not *good enough* for this. . . ."

"Charlie, responsibilities don't fall on us because we're good enough; they fall on us because there's no one else for them to fall *on*." She looked at me, her eyes bright in the moonlight. "We're *it*. It's you and me, and that's *it*, babe. Welcome to real life."

Yeah, well, real life sucks, I thought.

Hold up—did she just call me *babe?*

CHAPTER THIRTY-FOUR

I was pretty sure the two of us just lay there in silence for a long time, but the cool night breeze blowing through the woods and my full stomach were making me so sleepy, I honestly didn't remember when I drifted off.

Sometime later I woke with this terrible pain in my chest. It felt like all twenty pounds of junk food I'd eaten had turned to stone, settled halfway down my throat, and were now pressing against my lungs with the weight of a cruise ship. My first thought was that it was indigestion. Or maybe part of some freaky dream. But then my eyes fluttered open, and all my sleepiness was swept away in a wave of absolute *terror*. Not indigestion—it was some sort of hideous monster—a hag!

She was sitting on me, sort of squatting on my chest with her long bony feet planted firmly on either side of my head. Her face, a terrifying mask of greenish, wart-covered skin, hung just over mine but a few inches past so that I almost had to tilt my head back to look into her eyes. In a sliver of silvery moonlight slanting down through the trees, I could see a snarling mouth full of awful rotting teeth and the horrifying bloodred pupils of her beady black eyes as she stared wildly—*hungrily*—into mine.

I was so terrified that if I'd had any strength left in me—any strength *at all*—it probably would've melted away like butter on a hot pan.

I tried to scream but couldn't; it felt like there was no air left in my lungs. Worse, when I tried to reach up to push her away, I realized I couldn't move my arms, realized I couldn't move any part of me; it was as if she'd paralyzed me!

Panic and adrenaline burned in my veins like acid, but it wasn't nearly enough to break the paralysis. Just a few feet away, I could hear Violet breathing heavily in the cabin of the truck, fast asleep, and thought, *V, wake up! WAKE UP, WAKE UP, WAKE UP!* But she wouldn't wake. In fact, she wasn't *going to* wake. Not in time to help me, anyway.

Black started closing in around the edges of my vision. The pressure in my lungs, chest, and head was almost too much. I needed to breathe. I *NEEDED* oxygen!

Just when I was sure I would pass out, I heard the sound of crunching leaves . . . of footsteps, light and quick, coming this way—

Abruptly the footsteps stopped. There was a squeal of hinges, and suddenly the truck's tailgate slammed shut behind me. It banged loudly off the hag's head, flinging her back against the rear window of the truck. She hit it with a sickening *thwap*, then slumped onto the truck bed, unconscious.

Panicking, finally able to breathe but almost in too much shock to care, I looked frantically around and saw Adriana standing over me, her dark brown eyes glittering in the moonlight. "¿Estás bien?" she asked. "You okay?"

When I gave a shaky thumbs-up, she hauled the hag out of the truck by the shirtsleeves of the long, raggedy light-blue pajamas she was wearing and dropped her on the ground, where she muscled her over onto her back and tore open the neck of the hag's pj's.

"What's going on?" I heard Violet shout as she scrambled out of the passenger door, obviously startled out of her mind.

"Everything's been taken care of," Adriana replied breezily, as if taking out evil hags was her part-time job. I watched her reach both hands around the hag's neck to unclasp some kind of necklace. It almost looked like two ancient skeleton fingers!

"And who the heck is *THAT*?" Violet shrieked, staring down at the woman's deformed, crusty feet.

A split second later, it hit me: She was La Pisadeira! She who steps! How many stories had my abuela told me over the years about the vicious old hag who sneaks into the bedroom windows of kids with full stomachs and sits on their chests, trying to suffocate them? Probably too many, which was why I *never* went to bed right after dinner. But that wasn't all I realized. . . . "You used me as *bait!*" I shouted at Adriana. "That's why you fed me all that junk food!"

"Oye, ¡cálmate!" she snapped back, aiming a warning finger at me. Her fingernails, I noticed, were completely caked with dirt. "I told you—you are going to help *me* help *you*. And *you* agreed. So what's the problem?"

Is she kidding? "The problem is that I almost got *suffocated to death* five seconds ago!"

Ignoring me, she said, "Put this on," and tossed the hag's necklace in my direction.

I accidentally caught it, then nearly threw it down just as fast. "What? Ew! No. It looks like—*fingers!*"

Adriana's eyes narrowed on me. "You lose that and the next head I slam into the tailgate will be *yours*, ¿me entiendes?" I could tell from her tone that she wasn't kidding. Not even a little. "Besides," she added with almost a smirk, "you're already wearing a dog collar as an accessory, so it's not like it's going to hurt your style game. . . ."

Ha-ha, I thought, holding the necklace out at arm's length. "But—what the *heck* is it . . . ?"

"¡Ya! No more questions!" she shouted. "Just put it on

and be *quiet*! There are far more dangerous things out here than this hag."

Without giving me a chance to at least wipe it down with my T-shirt, Violet snatched the necklace, slung it around my neck, and quickly fastened the clasp in back. I shivered, imagining the hag's cooties spreading over me like an army of invisible creepy-crawlies. First Al's dog collar and now *this*. . . . "How many ridiculous necklaces are you planning on putting on me?" I asked Violet.

She grinned, showing me her pearly whites. "As many as it takes."

Sighing, I stared down at the pair of crooked, twisted, gnarled—what were they, fingers? Sticks?—*things* and couldn't help wonder what was so special about them. I mean, why had Adriana thought they were so great that she'd decided to use me as bait to get them? And why did she want *me* to hold on to them? This whole thing was sick. . . . And not in the "sick" meaning "cool," either. "Sick" in the nastiest, grossest possible way.

La Pisadeira, meanwhile, was still out cold. Funny, for someone who preyed on her victims while they slept, she certainly seemed to enjoy a nice nap.

Staring down at her, I asked, "What are you going to do with her?"

"I think I'm going to let her sleep it off," Adriana said. "She's had a rough night."

CHAPTER THIRTY-FIVE

It was past midnight by the time we hit the road again, this time driving west through the deep forests of Argentina. We drove nonstop for hours, still traveling through sombra wood and rolling along until the tall trees gave way to vast, low-lying expanses of sandy nothingness, framed by the rough peaks of faraway mountains. Soon we found ourselves climbing the ice-slicked roads that wound their way up those mountains, lurching around impossibly tight turns and blind corners where one wrong move would've sent us tumbling out of this life.

As early morning turned to late afternoon, the landscape once again changed; we were now moving through Chile's Los Lagos Region, and with its sparkling blue lakes, snow-white mountains, and rolling green hills dotted with fat sheep, it was easily one of the most beautiful places I'd ever seen. *Anywhere.* And it felt almost criminal not to stop and snap a picture or something. But as we traveled farther into Chile, cruising along the blacktop, I began to notice something strange: Everywhere I looked I could see animals fleeing out of the woods. All kinds of animals too—rabbits and foxes, chinchillas, Chilean long-tailed horses, guanacos, and even sleek, loner predators like pumas. At first I thought I was the luckiest kid on the planet; I was getting all these close-up looks at some of the coolest animals in the whole world. But I'd watched enough Nat Geo to know stuff like this wasn't supposed to happen. It wasn't natural.

"This can't be normal," I said, staring out the window. "What's going on?"

Adriana's eyes slid to mine. Her fingers were tight around the steering wheel as she said, "The forests are dying. . . . The animals can sense it. I told you this already."

"You also mentioned something about rumors before," Violet said. "Which ones were you talking about?"

Adriana was silent for so long I thought she hadn't heard her. Finally she said, "Rumors of graves rumbling . . . of things long since dead crawling back up from the deep places of the earth."

Violet and I exchanged tense looks, neither one of us too thrilled to hear that.

"Some believe it is happening again," Adriana said darkly.

Violet's eyes still hadn't left mine, but she spoke to

Adriana, saying, "Why do you say 'happening again'? Has it happened before?"

There was another silence. Then Adriana said, "Sí . . ." and took a deep breath, turning briefly to stare out the window at the scenery whipping by before continuing. "Long ago, the dead and those who refused to remain dead began to rise. Some say it started in Mexico. Others say Portugal. Either way, the world was thrown into panic, into chaos. Everyone was convinced it was the end of days."

"So what happened?"

She gave a small shrug, leaning back in her seat. The bright sunshine slanting in through the gap between the visor and the ceiling turned her hair the color of hay. "The dead eventually vanished. Crawled back into their graves. Who knows? No one likes to talk about those days."

"But why do people believe it's happening again?" I asked.

"Because some claim to have seen corpses walking the earth like before. They also claim to have seen those horrible castells popping up again." My reaction must've given me away, because Adriana said, "You've seen one . . . ?"

I nodded, swallowed hard. "One or two."

"Then the rumors are true. . . ." She turned back to the road with a troubled look in her eyes.

"But what do the bone castles have to do with the dead rising?" Violet asked her.

Adriana's expression grew dark, and she was quiet for several moments before she finally answered: "There was a saying in more ancient times, one as true today as it was then: When castells rise, the dead rise with them."

CHAPTER THIRTY-SIX

It was dark again by the time we finally reached the coast, and the moon was a huge yellow orb in the sky. Adriana pulled the pickup into a tiny gravel lot across from where more than two dozen old fishing boats were moored to rain-beaten docks that jutted out into the water. A few yards up the coast, foamy waves lapped onto a thin strip of sandy beach dotted with seagulls and large gray rocks.

When Adriana cut the engine, the three of us got out and started toward the edge of the docks, where a group of fishermen had gathered to watch the incoming storm. There were about eight or nine of them, all rough-and-tumble-looking dudes in long black slickers, staring expressionlessly at the horizon, watching storm clouds mass and swirl in the distant sky. And they all smelled sort of . . . well, fishy.

Adriana, however, didn't seem to mind. She pushed

her way into the group and asked them if they could take us across to Chiloé; the fishermen looked at her like she'd just asked them to wear their boots as hats and dance "La Bamba."

"¿No ves la tormenta?" one said.

"¿Estás loca?" asked another.

"Mateo say he saw El Nguruvilu swimming out there," said a third, and then all of them made the sign of the cross and shivered.

One of the fisherman dudes glanced back at her. A soggy, unlit cigarette dangled from his lower lip. It barely even twitched as he said, "Storms move fast over open water. No one's risking their boat tonight, amigos. Perdona."

"It's fine," Violet said, gripping my arm. "I have a plan."

Didn't she always?

She nodded past me, up the coast. I turned and saw there was a tall chain-link fence blocking off a narrow path that led out to a strip of beach. In front of it, lounged out on what looked like one of those foldable beach chairs, was some sort of rent-a-guard. He wore a backward ball cap and a dark blue uniform, which weirdly enough included a shiny black radio belt but no radio.

On the gate above the guard's head was a sign that read NO ENTRADA PARA LA PLAYA. ¡PELIGROSO! (No beach entrance. Dangerous!)

"What's your plan?" I asked. "We *swim* across?"

Violet rolled her eyes. "Keep looking. . . ."

And that's when I saw it: At the far end of the beach, where the land narrowed to about a pinkie's worth of a peninsula, was a lone, sad-looking pylon. And tied to it was an even sadder-looking boat—no, two boats: one old propeller boat and one dinghy; actually, calling it a dinghy might've been too much of a compliment—it didn't look like much more than a floating plastic shell.

"Perfecto," Adriana said, sounding very much like she was digging Violet's piratey impulse. "We take the boats. Cross over ourselves."

I glanced between them. "You guys don't have any concept of personal property, do you?"

Adriana ignored me. "I'll distract the guard. You two untie the boats. ¡Y muevesen!"

CHAPTER THIRTY-SEVEN

It didn't take long for Adriana to distract everyone's favorite radio-less security pro. She pretended to drop something in the high grass, then started talking to him about plants or flowers or something else that was growing wild in the bushes that bordered the edge of the parking lot, and before we knew it, he had followed her out to the roadside and was pointing across the street, laughing and talking about God knows what. I guess some things are just that easy. And speaking of easy, the fence blocking off the beach wasn't padlocked or even chained; all we had to do was lift the little fork latch, and we were in. The narrow footpath that led to the beach was choked with thorny weeds and tangles of underbrush, which snaked up the chain link, forming these high, bristly walls that shielded us from view.

The first thing I noticed when we reached the shore was the cold—the air blowing in off the ocean was easily ten or fifteen degrees colder than the air by the docks. I was already shivering, and now we had to go *into* that water. Great.

I slipped off my shoes and socks and slowly, very slowly, waded on in. Yep, this wasn't Miami Beach. . . . "If I get hypothermia, I'm telling my mom it was all you."

"No deal," Violet said, grinning. When we made it out to the boats, I saw that they had been tied together by a couple of frayed-looking ropes. We obviously didn't have any use for the dinghy, so we tried to undo the knots, but no matter how hard we picked at them, they just wouldn't come loose. The ropes had hardened with age and swelled with salt water, which meant that we'd probably need a pickax—and not just our fingertips—to get through them.

Fortunately, the length of rope securing the boats to the pylon hadn't actually been tied to it, more like slung *around* it, so that was no sweat.

I steadied the real boat while Violet climbed on board, and then I pushed us off and hopped in. Even here in the shallows, the current was freakishly strong, and I could already feel it dragging us out into open water.

"You know how to work one of these?" I asked Violet as she studied the controls and the engine.

"It's your basic outboard motor. Sit," she said, and the second my butt hit the bench, she gave the starter cord a savage yank. There was a loud pop and a coughing rattle as the old rusty engine slowly sputtered to life.

The boat lurched forward, and suddenly the beach looked far away.

"Where is she?" Violet said, looking around for Adriana. "I don't see her."

"Me either. She can't still be talking to that guy, can she?" Violet shrugged. "I don't know. Maybe she likes him."

"*Likes* him? Dude looks like he counts his toes for *fun*."

"Hey, some people put love ahead of little things like that."

"Do they also put love ahead of saving the world from an impending demon invasion?"

"Some people put love ahead of *everything*, Charlie." She worked the throttle, fighting the pull of the current, and crept us a little way back toward the beach. I scanned the coast (it took me about two seconds) but didn't see Adriana anywhere. I was about to ask Violet if she thought Adriana was planning to settle down with the guy, maybe start a family before rejoining us, when something terrible happened: The boat's engine began to sputter and spit. Bubbles fizzed up around the propeller, and the little boat started to shudder like a wounded bird.

"What's happening?" I said. And I'd barely uttered the words before the engine suddenly shut off. Just like that.

"That didn't sound good." Violet stood up and yanked

on the starter cord again, but nothing happened. She tried again, and this time the little engine that *couldn't* coughed, once . . . twice . . . the propeller whirling into high gear for a moment before the entire engine—protective steel cage and all—came free, dropping into the water with a quiet *splooosh*.

Violet stared down at the back of the boat where there was nothing now except for a square cutout in the shape of a boat engine. "You're kidding me. . . ."

Before I could say anything, the current suddenly picked up and began to pull us rapidly away from the shore. And without an engine to fight it, we were basically sitting ducks. My eyes desperately swept up and down the little beach.

Nothing. No Adriana. What was she do—

"There she is!" Violet shouted, pointing. I looked around, spotted her just as I managed to slip my freezing feet back into my sneakers.

Adriana had made her way around the foresty area by the fence and was now standing on a rickety bridge on the far side of the beach. Her arms were waving frantically over her head, and she was yelling something—probably something like *Come get me!* Or maybe even *Get the heck out of the water! Jaws is coming!*

But there was nothing we could do. We didn't have an engine anymore.

"The boat's broken! The engine fell off!" Violet cried. "We can't do anything!" Then she started waving her arms around in what I could only assume was some kind of nautical distress sign. Above us, the clouds churned and billowed as the storm grew closer, intensified. The temperature began to plummet. An icy wind picked up, lifting salty spray into our faces, stinging our eyes. Our now engineless boat rose and fell, rose and fell. Lightning forked across the sky—an electric scar in the clouds. I could feel the infinite power of the sea rolling underneath us, doing whatever it wanted with our two sorry excuses for boats. We might as well have been riding a little kid's floatie. Or nothing at all. I doubted it would've made any difference.

Violet must've seen the panic in my eyes, because she said, "It's cool. We're gonna be fine. As long as the waves don't get too rough, we should reach land well before the worst of the storm gets to us. And I'm pretty sure we're heading straight for Chiloé, so we're looking really good, actually." She sat back down, began putting her shoes and socks back on. "Just stay positive. That's the most important thing."

Suddenly the currents changed direction—*we* changed direction.

The waves lifted the boat, turned it slightly sideways,

and set us on a course that was almost perfectly parallel to the docks and the strip of beach.

"And what if we start drifting left?" I asked.

"Well, then we'd be heading out to sea. But don't worry about that. It's the worst-case scenario."

"Actually, it's our *current* scenario."

CHAPTER THIRTY-EIGHT

Violet's head snapped up. I saw her expression go from confused to concerned to mildly panicked before finally settling on outright terrified. "Okay, that's not good."

The storm continued to strengthen. Waves slammed into us, jerking the boat back and forth, and next thing I knew, we were picking up some major speed, and the shoreline and dock were nothing more than a fading smudge on the horizon; I could barely even see Adriana anymore. "How far are we from Chiloé?" I shouted at V.

"Fifteen miles, give or take." Translation: We weren't going to make it.

Just a soccer field or so ahead of us, huge waves were popping up all over the place, giant walls of water taller than most of the buildings in downtown Miami. Our junky little boat wasn't built to handle this. And neither were we.

Dude, freaking do something! I yelled at myself. But what could I do? My manifestations weren't exactly reliable. What if I *did* manifest something, and it was something completely useless like elephant ears, and in the process, I sank this worthless piece of ocean litter?

Bro, you don't do something, you're sunk anyway! I thought. But there wasn't anything I could do! The only way out of this seemed to be *up*, and I couldn't *fly*—

Hold up. Actually, I *could* fly. . . .

Sucking in a deep breath, I tried to calm my racing mind. I pictured birds. Pictured wings. I held the images in my mind just like Joanna had taught me. I saw the wings flapping, the feathers catching wind. I tried to feel myself soaring on them. Tipping them this way and that, rising higher and higher. *I'm a bird*, I told myself. *If you're a bird, I'm a bird.*

No, wait. That was from some romance movie. Not helping. . . .

"Charlie?" Violet called as another wave crashed against the side of the boat, almost upending us and sloshing even more freezing-cold water onto our laps.

I shivered. "Yeah?"

"Are you still wearing your lucky Power Rangers underwear?"

"Yeah. Why?"

"Because I really think it's morphin' time. . . ."

"Working on it!" I closed my eyes, trying to ignore the roaring of the sea, the pounding waves, the way the little boat rocked nauseatingly back and forth. In my mind there were only the wings. I saw them stretching out of my back, long and strong, like they had that afternoon when I'd fought against La Cuca. I tried to imagine them growing out of me. Tried to feel them as *part* of me. *One* with me. But for all my trying, I didn't feel any change. Nada.

In fact, I didn't feel a single thing except for my racing heart and the hollow pit of fear growing deep down in my belly.

"Charlie, we almost ready?" Violet shouted. I could hear the fear in her voice. The panic. It wasn't something I was used to. And it made me even more scared.

"It's not working," I admitted miserably. "Nothing's happening!"

Violet didn't look particularly pleased to hear that. She went quiet for a long moment, thinking. Finally she said, "Okay, plan B." Then she leaned out over the rear of the boat, grabbed the length of rope attached to the dinghy, and began to reel it in.

All I could do was watch, confused out of my mind. "What are you doing?"

"Buying you some time. Now help me flip the dinghy."

Her eyes drifted past me, over my shoulder. "And *quick!*"

I followed her gaze and instantly felt my stomach drop into my toes.

A foaming, bubbling wall of water was coming straight at us—a roaring mountain of liquid trouble! It rose straight up, steep as any cliff, fizzing and roiling and surging as it pulled us into itself with the force of about a *trillion* or so vacuum cleaners.

"I think we're going to need a bigger boat," I heard myself say.

"Charlie, help me!" Violet shouted.

"*Go! Go!*" Even though I had no idea what she was up to, I knew that *a* plan was better than *no* plan—plus the dinghy was made entirely of fiberglass and didn't weigh much at all, so getting it out of the water wasn't going to be a problem.

We lifted it as high as we could, and Violet guided it so that it dropped over us. The flimsy shell of a thing crashed down with a hollow bang, and once she had it settled into place, I realized its dimensions were nearly identical to the wooden boat; both ends came together at virtually the same place, and our boat was just *a hair* or two slimmer than the dinghy. Immediately Violet began to rope the two together with the couple of feet of bungee cord that had been wrapped around the straps of her backpack, snaking it under and around the center benches of both boats, through the foot bracings at the corners, and then tying it off.

"So what's the plan?" I shouted, helping her tug on the knot she'd made.

"In 1620, Cornelis Drebbel created the world's first functioning submarine. It was regarded as one of the greatest feats of nautical engineering at the time. In 1897, John Philip Holland perfected it. Obviously, ours will be closer to Cornelis's version, but as long as it behaves more or less the same, we just might breathe fresh oxygen again."

"All very interesting stuff. But I ask you again, what EXACTLY is the plan?"

"I'm making a submarine, Charlie. A *submarine.*"

CHAPTER THIRTY-NINE

Huh. Pretty awesome plan. Except, of course, for the fact that she was making a sub out of a junky, engineless boat and an even junkier dinghy. Through one of the holes in the bottom of said dinghy (which was now the roof of our homemade submarine—yay, us!), I could see the enormous mountain of seawater bearing down on us, blocking out the dock, the shore, the beach, and any hope of living to see five seconds from now. I'd never seen anything so terrifyingly beautiful in my entire life.

"IT'S STILL GETTING BIGGER!" I yelled back at Violet, who was busy making little adjustments to the bungee cord, tightening it here and there.

"That's not helpful!" she yelled back.

"NO, IT'S NOT! IT'S LIKE FIFTY STORIES HIGH NOW!"

"I meant *YOU! YOU'RE* not being helpful."

"For the record, I don't think this is a very good idea!"

"ALSO NOT HELPFUL!"

The bubbling, roaring mountain continued to rise and rise, and suddenly it felt like the bottom fell out of the ocean—

We dropped thirty or so feet in the span of a heartbeat, bouncing off something hard, the bone-jarring impact punching the air out of my lungs a split second before a hundred thousand gallons of angry seawater came crashing down on us.

We tumbled end over end, water blasting into the boat from every angle, the bungee cord stretching and straining almost to the point of snapping.

I heard a sharp plastic crack below me and the groan of straining wood above, but our little *fake*-marine somehow held together.

Then something slammed into us—or we slammed into *it*—and Violet and I were flung backward. My elbow smashed into her forehead. Her knee slammed into my stomach, driving my organs back into my spine.

We were both screaming our heads off—I knew for sure I was—but any sound was drowned out by the deafening roar of the water rushing around us.

Suddenly the USS *Dinghy* shot straight up like a

rocket and bobbed for a moment, and then the bungee cord snapped, and the two boats came apart.

We found ourselves lying on our backs in the dinghy, coughing up water and staring up at a dark, starless sky.

The only thing I could think to say was "Where's the moon?"

Violet said, "I don't think that's the sky, Charlie. . . ."

A moment later, the "sky" began to bubble and foam, and I realized, Holy Chalupa, she was right! That wasn't the sky at all but another wave—this one probably fifty times larger than the last one!

We barely had time to grab on to each other and scream "AAAAHHHHHHHHH!" before the wave swept over us, instantly swamping the dinghy and plunging us straight down into the murky depths.

CHAPTER FORTY

I'd never known what *truly* freezing water felt like until right then and there. The shock of it instantly paralyzed me on contact; it stole everything—the feeling from my limbs, the breath from my lungs, every thought from my brain. Seawater swirled around us, blinding me with bubbles. Violet and I were ripped out of each other's arms. I went tumbling and twirling and twisting until I was so sick and disoriented that I didn't even know which way was up.

My brain spun. My lungs throbbed. I opened my mouth to scream, but instead of sound going out, a rush of salty water came surging *in*, and I started to choke. Panicking, I kicked and flailed my arms, trying to fight my way to the surface even though I still had no idea which way the surface actually *was*.

As if that wasn't bad enough, a whirlpool—yeah, a legit

spinning *vortex* of seawater—suddenly formed at my feet and began dragging me even deeper into blackness. The pressure of the ocean was incredible. It pressed against me on all sides, squeezing like a giant, liquidy boa constrictor, twisting all my bones out of whack. My ribs ached. Pain lit up the area between my shoulder blades and spine, and when I reached back to touch it, I thought, *Dios Mio!* Because the skin there felt like it had started to peel—and badly! My panic ratcheted up another notch. I could feel my chest burning, my lungs screaming, *begging* for oxygen. I tried to stop myself, tried to fight against the irresistible urge to breathe. But I couldn't. It was nature.

My mouth flew open as my lungs drew in a hungry, desperate breath—

But somehow I didn't suck down another lungful of freezing seawater. Instead I breathed air . . . *fresh*, pure air. Actual *oxygen!* I couldn't believe it.

I sucked in another breath. And another. And immediately the burning in my chest began to fade. My racing thoughts slowed, and my head began to clear.

And with that came a pretty simple but important realization: My nose wasn't just happily stumbling upon little magical pockets of breathable oxygen floating around in the ocean. No, I must've manifested fishy parts—I must've manifested *gills!*

It was the only explanation to why I could now breathe down here surrounded by about *a gazillion* tons of churning water.

And that wasn't all. Glancing down at my hands, I noticed that my fingers were now webbed and scaly, glistening greenish gray in the dim shafts of moonlight that reached this far down. And the same thing was going on with my feet, which, by the way, also looked to be about seven or *eight* sizes bigger.

No joke, they looked like Nike had designed a hybrid between dolphin flippers and clown shoes—minus the cool little swoosh, of course.

I tested them out and felt myself zip through the water quick as an eel!

Oh, man, that's all KINDS *of awesome!* But then another thought hit me, one that was nowhere near as "awesome": Violet was *also* down here somewhere. And, unlike me, she probably *hadn't* manifested gills. Which meant that if I didn't find her—and find her right freakin' *now*—she was going to drown!

I began to turn in fast little circles, desperately scanning the ocean around me. And even though some kind of thin membrane had slid over my eyes, some sort of mucusy barrier that made it übereasy to see underwater (and a whole lot more comfortable, because it kept the salt from stinging my eyes), I didn't see her anywhere.

No, no, no, no! V, WHERE THE HECK ARE YOU?

Catching movement out of the corner of my eye, I whirled: Small dark shapes were falling through the water all around me, leaving trails of tiny bubbles as they sank.

Frogs. Dozens and dozens of *frogs*. Hundreds, maybe.

They must've been raining down from the sky like in Portugal. . . .

Dude, forget the frogs—FIND VIOLET!

Whirling around again, I looked up, down—

And what I saw totally froze me in place. (As if the freezing-cold water wasn't enough.)

Way down below me, rising out of the murky darkness, was another one of those bone castles—a *castell*! But oh, man, this one was huge—at least three times the size of the one in Lapa do Santo, and the bones had been completely picked clean of flesh, gleaming so white—even way down here—that they left dazzle spots in my vision.

This was the second one we'd seen in South America, I realized with a shiver of fear. Third overall. But what was a castell doing all the way down *here*? At the *bottom* of the ocean? And why did we keep running into these things everywhere we went?

Voices echoed around me, a ghostly babble in the rush

and swirl of water. But I didn't see anyone else nearby. So where were the voices coming from . . . ?

The ocean gurgled. A wave swept past. I blinked, turning—and finally *did* see someone: She was flailing around in the water not ten yards away.

Violet!

I sliced toward her, wrapping my arms around her waist, then kicked up with every ounce of strength in me. We broke the surface a moment later, Violet gasping, choking on seawater. Her hair was plastered to her face and her eyes were squeezed tightly shut, but she was managing to suck air in through her mouth, and that was good.

Way off in the distance loomed a black mass, some huge shapeless hump against the starry sky.

Land. *Chiloé!*

"V, wrap your arms around my neck!" I shouted. The ocean roared and the waves lifted us high into the air as I began to swim us desperately toward shore, throwing one arm out in front of the other and kicking my legs until my body burned and my muscles felt on the verge of failing. The moment we reached the shore it was like someone hit the off button in my brain, and I collapsed, blacking out before my head even hit the ground.

CHAPTER FORTY-ONE

When I came to, I was lying on my back on the rocky shore, the seawater washing up to the top of my legs, then retreating slowly back with the constant motion of the waves. Violet, who was sitting next to me on the sand, had her legs curled up to her chest, arms locked around her knees, and was shivering a little in the gusts of cold night air sweeping in off the ocean.

"Have a nice nap?" she asked, peering down at me through tangles of wet hair, a small smile tugging at the corners of her lips. Behind her, a little farther up the beach, our book bags had washed up on shore and, a little past them—*thankfully*—so had my sneakers. They must've slipped off when I'd morphed those awesome flipper feet. Propping myself up on my side, I felt around for the gills, realized they were gone. So was the webbing between my fingers and toes.

"How long have I been out?" I said, still tasting the saltwater coating my tongue.

Violet glanced down at her watch. Waterproof. Of course. "Maybe seven minutes."

Well, that isn't too bad. . . .

Several yards behind us a wall of rocky cliffs jutted out of the sand, their faces carved with caves and overgrown with loops of thick, hanging vines. It looked as if a thousand hungry mouths gaped along the beachhead, just waiting for someone foolish enough to wander ashore so they could feed.

I glanced up at Violet, who was still peering down at me, and just started laughing—couldn't help myself. . . .

"What's wrong?" she asked, shaking her head. "What's so funny?"

"You are," I admitted, and she made a face.

"*Me?* What *about* me?"

"That whole *submarine* idea . . ."

A smile stretched slowly across her face even though she was trying to fight it a little; then she burst out laughing, smoothing her salty, plastered hair out of her eyes. "Guess it was kind of ridiculous . . ."

"And kinda *awesome* . . ."

I was still looking up at her, still staring at that dazzling smile and feeling so lucky that she was alive to give it—and that *I* was alive to *see* her give it—when she said, "Charlie, why are you looking at me like that?"

I shrugged, feeling my fingers sink into the soft sand. "My abuela would've liked you, that's all. . . . She would've liked you *a lot.*"

V looked sort of surprised. "You think so?"

"Oh, yeah. I mean, how could she not? You're smart. You're tough. You're *ridiculously* brave. You're just like she was. . . ."

Even though we were just talking, my heart had begun to pound again—and almost as hard as it had when we'd been swimming for our lives. It was weird.

"You're not so bad yourself," Violet said, giving me a playful punch on the arm. Our eyes held for a moment, then, getting sort of embarrassed or whatever, I turned to face the ocean as another breeze blew in, salty and fresh. A few seconds passed.

Then I suddenly remembered something.

"Oh, and I saw another castell!" I shouted.

"*Where?*"

"Down in the ocean. *Deep* down."

"*Really?*"

"Yeah, which is sort of freaking me out, because, like, what is a castell even *doing* down there?"

The smile had faded from V's face, and she was nodding now, like it was beginning to freak her out too. "Yeah, that is pretty strange. . . ." Leaning back on her hands, she turned to stare at the wall of caves ringing the beach, as if in deep thought. Finally she said, "Well, we made it. We're here. . . . So now what?"

I was sort of wondering about that too, but anyone who knew anything about Chilean mythology would know that there was really only one place we needed to visit on the island. "We have to find the Warlock's Cave," I said.

"The what?"

"It's like this super well known meeting place for brujos and brujas on the island. If any sombras came through here, they would've heard about it."

"And how are we supposed to find this *Warlock's Cave?*" V asked.

And thinking back to the legends, I said, "We just follow the moonlight. Follow it straight into the heart of the jungle."

The Chilean jungle was eerily quiet. No birds chirped. I didn't hear any insects buzzing either. All around us, impossibly tall trees loomed up like giant silent sentinels, their trunks shaggy with moss, their branches heavy with blooming buds. The air was thick. We stuck to the overgrown path as best we could, pushing aside thorny tangles of brambles, following a trail of moonlight, our feet sinking into the squishy ground. Once I stepped on what looked like a smooth gray rock, and the rock sprouted claws and took a couple of fast snaps at my sneaker before scuttling off into a web of mangrove roots. Not exactly a friendly welcome. "Watch your step," I told Violet. "Might cost you a toe."

Maybe half a mile later, the path narrowed to about the width of a ruler, and the trail of moonlight we'd been following vanished behind a wall of wild palms. The trees grew so tightly together here that I couldn't see even a sliver of sky. This part of the jungle felt different somehow— more ancient, *enchanted*—and something told me we'd just entered sombra wood.

"There's gotta be a way through it," Violet said. She pushed aside some of the branches and stuck her head into the gap, looking around. After a few seconds she started gesturing at me wildly and whispered, "Charlie, check this out!"

Making sure to avoid any more of those rock-crab thingies (I'd always liked my toes—especially my big toes), I hopped up beside her and peered through the branches. At the edge of a shallow valley maybe twenty feet below us was a giant rock formation. It looked like a stone hut, but it was probably about ten times bigger than any hut I'd ever seen. A winding ribbon of silver water curved around it, disappearing into thick jungle. At first I didn't see an entrance, but as my eyes tracked along the base of the rock, I noticed what appeared to be a small indent half hidden behind a knot of leafy bushes where the rock, the river, and the jungle all met.

"That's gotta be it!" I whispered excitedly. "The Warlock's Cave!"

At that point, I expected Violet to say something—you know, show some enthusiasm—but it was someone else who spoke up.

CHAPTER FORTY-TWO

Qué está pasando, muchachos? ¿Están perdidos?"

Violet and I whirled toward the voice as a small boy stepped out from behind the trunk of one of the trees. He wore a tattered cloth tunic that looked two sizes too big for his scrawny body, and his face was streaked with mud. His fingernails were long and dirty, and his dark, uncombed hair stuck up in clumpy masses around his pointy head. The kid looked in serious need of parents. Or at least a nice bubble bath.

An evil little half grin split his lips as he looked up at us, angling his head lazily to one side. "You lost?" he asked again.

Even though I thought it was a teensy bit weird for some eight-year-old to be wandering around the jungles of Chiloé all by his lonesome (not that we weren't doing sort of the same thing), I didn't go that route. Instead I said, "¡Hola, amigo! We, uh . . . We're looking for the Warlock's Cave."

He raised an eyebrow at me. "What cave, gamberros?"

"La—La Cueva de los Brujos."

"Why a couple punks like you two wanna find a place like that?"

Did he just call us *punks?* "Come again, little man?"

"Um, sorry," Violet jumped in. "What's your name?"

He shot her a distrustful look. "Me llamo Mario. Mario Ramirez."

"Nice to meet you, Mario. I'm Violet, and this here is Charlie. See, thing is, we're looking for someone. A friend. We think she might've come through the island. That's why we are trying to find the cave."

"What your friend look like?"

"She's tall. Has green eyes. Wears this big golden crown. Have you seen anyone that looks like that?"

"She got glowing eyes?"

"¡Sí, sí!" I shouted as a wave of happiness and relief swept through me. So they *had* brought Joanna here. "That's her! That's our friend!"

Mario was nodding. "She a witch, right?"

"Yes, she's a witch!" Violet said. "So you've seen her?"

"Sí, la vi. . . . She came through with, like, *a group.* All wearing black hoods. She a good friend of yours, amigos?"

"Yeah, she's a really good friend . . . ," I said. "Muy buena amiga."

"You hear that, hermanos? Looks like there's more of them. . . ."

Five more kids stepped out from behind the trees. They looked about Mario's age, but their smiles were bigger, meaner. The taller one winked at Violet and said, "Qué chula."

"More friends of the witch . . . ," Mario began.

"Yep, that's us," I said happily.

And then nearly choked when he finished with ". . . who killed our *brujo!*"

Mario eyes bugged. "Killed your *who?*"

He snarled at me through clenched teeth. "*So* happy we found you, amigo. . . ."

"Whoa, whoa, whoa. Queen Joanna wouldn't kill *anyone,*" Violet said. "She's not like that, all right? She's one of the good guys."

"Tell that to our brujo. Oh, wait—you *can't.* Because she kill 'im! *¡Lo mató!*"

I held up my hands, patting the air in an *everyone-please-just-chill* type move. "Listen to me. Joanna's not the one who killed your brujo, okay? It must've been one of the sombras with her. They kidnapped her! They're the *bad guys.* Joanna's their *prisoner!*"

"Your story is changing fast, muchacho," growled one of the other kids.

"Didn't look like they had no prisoners to me," murmured another.

"We're not lying!" I said. "We're not bad people. I mean, look at her face. . . . Does that look like the face of a villain? Look at those dimples. . . ." Violet smiled to make them even more *dimply*, and I said, "See what I mean?"

"Yeah, and look at his face," Violet said, pointing at me. "Look at those honest eyes! You'll never see eyes like that on someone who'd lie to you."

"These are good, *friendly* faces!" I shouted—not even really sure *why* I was shouting. "*Good people* faces! We're not the bad guys! *You have to believe us!*"

"Oye, Mario, I can't take listening to this no more," said one of the other kids, frowning like he'd just downed a gallon of spoiled milk. "It's hurting *my ears*, man! Can we just roast these bobos already?"

I noticed, for the first time, that all six of them had strange marks tattooed on the backs of their chubby little hands—no, burned there, it looked like. . . . The marks appeared to be an eye with swirly looking lines spinning out from the pupils. Brujo marks, I remembered. I'd seen these before. My abuela had taught me how to draw some.

Just then, three more kids emerged from the bushes to our right.

One of them stuck her tongue out at us. She wore a

T-shirt that read: UN PELIGRO DE INCENDIO, which translates to "A fire hazard." The other had the face of angel. He looked like the sweetest thing in the whole wide world . . . that is, until his lips twitched back, revealing a mouth crammed with pointy, rotten teeth.

Piranha teeth! I screamed on the inside. And that was exactly what they looked like!

Suddenly I had a really bad feeling in the pit of my stomach.

With an evil smirk, Mario crouched down, touching the tips of his dirt-smudged fingers to the ground. Now, to be perfectly honest, I wasn't sure what I expected to happen next, but it certainly wasn't what actually *did* happen: In the next instant, the grass caught fire—just like that! There was this loud, hissing WHOOOSH, and before I knew it, sizzling lines were racing past us, raising fiery curtains on either side.

On instinct, I threw up my hands, shielding my face from the intense heat as the word "anchimayen" echoed through my head like I'd screamed it. And maybe I had.

Thing was, I knew all about these things! I'd heard *soooo* many stories from my abuelita, and to say they were well-known (and well *feared*) in Chiloé would be like saying a humpback whale is big. Anchimayen were basically like the sidekicks of sorcerers (or kalkus, as they were called on the island). And depending on which sorcerer they'd sworn their allegiance to, the anchimayen were either extremely kind and peace-loving or mind-bogglingly wicked, starting jungle fires and burning down any village that wouldn't pay tribute to their kalku. There was even one tale where a group of anchimayen had superheated the core of one of the largest volcanoes on Chiloé, causing a massive eruption and nearly wiping out the entire island. Not exactly the sort of peeps you wanted to mess with. And even though I was hoping *this* particular gang of anchimayens happened to fall under the friendly, peace-loving category, something told me that was probably not the case.

"Those aren't normal kids, are they?" Violet said.

I shook my head. "Nope."

"So what should we do?"

"What we always do . . . RUN!"

CHAPTER FORTY-THREE

oing our best Speedy Gonzales impersonations, we turned and bolted into the trees. (¡Ándale, ándale! ¡Arriba, arriba!)

Only we didn't even make it ten steps before I heard a sizzling roar, and a huge, flaming fireball screamed past us, lighting up the forest in a terrifying orange glow. Or maybe it was just me that was terrified. Either way, I was so mesmerized by the impromptu fireworks display that my foot caught on the edge of a root and I went down hard, sprawling.

"C'mon!" Violet shouted, pulling me to my feet. We ran. Behind us, the fire kids were hot on our trail—literally— flinging volleys of mini fireballs that incinerated everything in their path. One crashed into a tree in front of us, and the whole thing instantly went up in flames. Another bounced past us like a soccer ball, leaving a trail of fiery arches across the jungle floor that sort of reminded me of the big golden ones from Mickey D's. Only, these arches would probably register just a tad bit higher on the old Kelvin scale.

It suddenly occurred to me that running through a forest with a gang of pyromaniacs after you probably wasn't a great idea. You didn't need to be a park ranger to know that mixing fire and wood was a giant no-no. Unfortunately, we didn't have a ton of options.

As we slammed through a curtain of vines (me resisting the temptation to turn and, in my best Smoky the Bear voice, shout, 'Only YOU can prevent forest fires!'), something dropped out of the branches overhead. It fell right into my hands, and I nearly shrieked. It was a cockatoo! One that looked like it had been charbroiled, deep-fried, then flambéed before being tossed into the world's hottest pizza oven. Its bulging beady eyes gaped blankly up at me. Its charred, black feathers singed my fingers, sending up wisps of grayish smoke. For some reason I screamed, "HOLY FAJITAS!" then tossed the baked bird back over my head and started running even harder.

Somewhere behind us, one of the pyro-punks shouted, "¡CANDELA!" and I turned my head around in time to see the biggest fireball yet—it honestly looked like a meteor burning up as it entered earth's atmosphere—come roaring past us.

It was one of the anchimayen! I realized with shock. So the legends were true—not only could they *shoot* fireballs, but they could apparently turn *into them*!

I watched the anchimayen sizzle through everything in its path, leaving a smoking, burning outline in the trunks of several trees. Show-off.

The good news was he'd missed. The bad? Another anchimayen had appeared directly in front of us, less than five feet away. This one was creeping stealthily through the woods on her tippy-toes, like we were playing a game of Hide-N-Seek instead of Find-N-*Roast*, and there was an evil, smoldering grin on her face, which, ironically enough, sent a cold shudder down my spine.

We'd barely had time to start running in the other direction when she yelled, "¡CANDELA!" (which, by the way, was quickly becoming one of my most hated words in the Spanish language) and came crackling toward us with completely unfair speed. She was too close. We couldn't dodge her. In fact, she would've incinerated us in a blink if a thick branch with clusters of bright red flowers hadn't come sweeping down from over our heads that very instant, slamming into her like a giant baseball bat and sending the little punk reeling.

Violet and I stopped to look at each other. *Did that really just happen?*

Then we both shrugged and kept running.

We dashed through the trees as quickly as our legs could carry us, but less than ten seconds later had to slam on the brakes as we came to the edge of a rocky cliff. A dead end. ¡Magnífico!

Below us, maybe seventy or eighty feet straight down, spread a wide oval-shaped lake, its surface rippling and shimmering in the moonlight.

"We're trapped!" I shouted, looking desperately around.

"Not exactly." Violet peered down over the edge of the cliff. "The average dive of an Acapulco cliff diver is about ninety feet. Which is probably only fifteen or so feet less than what we're looking at here." When I only stared, she said, "What? I wrote a piece on cliff diving for the cliff diving festival in Key Biscayne. You didn't read it?"

"No," I said, and was surprised my nose didn't grow out an inch or two, Pinocchio-style. Truth was, I read all of the articles she wrote for our school's newspaper—even the ones that railed against trans fats and sugary desserts, which just so happen to be two of my favorite things in the whole wide world. "But those are *professional* divers!"

"Well, most of them are."

"Yeah, the ones that are still ALIVE!" Behind us, I could hear the sizzling snap of the leaves and branches catching fire: the anchimayen closing in on us.

El que no arriesga, no gana, I thought. It was one of my

abuela's favorite sayings. It basically meant "If you don't take risks, you can't win." And in our case you could've tweaked it to, "If you don't take a risk, you probably won't *live*."

Still . . . "There wouldn't happen to be a Door Number Two, would there?" I asked V.

"Door Number Two: We get flamed by a bunch of fire-slinging, superfreaks."

"Now that I think about it, cliff diving does have a certain appeal. . . . Any tips?"

"Yeah, don't die." Right then, just as her fingers closed around mine, the gang of preteen pyros appeared at the edge of the trees.

"Wait!" I shouted, getting an idea—a crazy one, but one that just might work.

The shimmering orange glow of their fiery little hands lit up the jungle, as did the equally but much more *eerie* glow radiating out of their cunning, vicious little faces.

Mario winked at me, his crew yelled, "¡CANDELA!" and tongues of orange flame exploded out around them as they flew toward us. I waited until they were screaming through the air again, waited until they were too far along to slow down or even think about changing direction— and then I made my move.

"Now!" I shouted, and Violet and I leapt off the edge of the cliff, feetfirst.

CHAPTER FORTY-FOUR

There was a wild, terrifying moment of fear, of falling, of the wind rushing up from below us, swirling through our hair—of me screaming, "COOOOOWAABUNGAAAAA!"—and then we hit the water. Hard. Bubbles fizzed around us. We plunged straight down, our feet actually touching the rocky bottom of the lake. Still holding on to each other's hands, V and I kicked up and broke the surface of the water, both of us panting hard. Violet's wavy blond hair was plastered to her face, and she was smiling so big you'd think we were a pair of adrenaline junkies on some wild South American vacation, not a couple of kids running for our lives.

The lake was cold—I'm talking Okeechobee in winter cold—but that was a total relief after all that heat and running for our lives. The best part, though, was what I saw when I blinked the silty water out of my eyes and looked around: Bobbing up and down in the water like hairy-headed buoys, coughing up puffs of white-hot steam and wiping their eyes, were all nine of the fire kids.

Gotcha! I thought as Violet grabbed the nearest one and dunked his head back underwater. Then she punched another square on the nose with legit kung-fu quickness. I'd always thought Violet would be good at karate (I mean, what *wasn't* she good at?) and I was right. The anchimayen's head snapped back like a Pez dispenser, and he went under with a loud *blurrrp!*

I turned to Mario, who was floating in the water to my left. "Not so much fun when it's a fair fight, huh?"

I put my fists up, Popeye-style, preparing to sock him one. But the little punk surprised me by smiling back. "Who said it was a fair fight?"

Suddenly his eyes began to glow. Ribbons of steam rose off his shoulders in waves. Then the pyro-punk went all supernova, exploding into a blazing ball of red-gold fire. I thought things were looking pretty bad at this point, but it wasn't until the rest of his buddies (including the one V had punched) all did their very own interpretations of the human torch that I realized just how bad things actually were.

I felt the water around me change temperature. It went

from very, very cold to very, very *hot*. Then the water level began to drop—and fast, as if some thirsty giant was sucking up the lake water through an enormous invisible straw.

Within seconds—not minutes, *seconds*—we were standing in the middle of a huge muddy pit. All around us, confused fish flailed and flapped their gills. I could see an array of colorful seashells poking out of the mud between my feet. A tiny crustacean scuttled over one of Violet's shoes, but she was in too much shock to notice.

For a long moment my still-stunned brain refused to process what had just happened. Those punks had somehow managed to evaporate an entire lake in a matter of seconds. A *lake*. In *seconds*. It was *insane!*

"Okay, now *that* was awesome!" I had to admit.

Mario smiled at me. His eyes were black fire, flecked by specks of bright yellow, and their stare was more than a little freaky. "Gracias, amigo."

"Charlie, I think it's time to do that thing we do again," Violet said, giving me a nudge.

"Yep!" And we scrambled out of the pit formerly known as a lake, dashing into the trees that ringed it. Our hope was simple: Lose them in the trees or maybe find a place to hide. Unfortunately, exactly five seconds later, we found ourselves trapped.

We'd run into some sort of giant birdcage!

Violet gripped one of the huge ivory bars and shook it with all her strength. "*THE HECK?*" she screamed, her eyes desperately searching for a way out.

Something heavy and squishy plopped onto my shoe. A moment later, something even heavier and *squishier* plopped onto my head. I flinched, heard a deep, throaty "riiiibbbbiittt," and then Violet was shouting, "Charlie, it's raining frogs again!"

"I noticed!" I started to shout back, but stopped as voices echoed painfully through my brain—a chorus of frantic, raspy, whispering voices. And the creepiest part? They were *familiar* voices . . . the same ones I'd heard back in Lapa do Santo. The same ones I'd heard underwater when our junky shell of a boat capsized off the coast of Chile.

Grimacing, I clapped my hands over my ears. "What is *that?*"

Violet frowned, glancing back at me. "Huh?"

"*The voices* . . . Can't you *hear* them?"

"Charlie, I don't hear any voices . . . ," she said, sounding grim.

I looked up, looked around—and felt my heart stop. The giant birdcagelike thing we'd run into wasn't a birdcage at all—not even close.

It was another *castell*.

CHAPTER FORTY-FIVE

The voices had to be coming from the castell. It seemed like every time we got close to one, I started hearing them. But *why?* And more importantly, why was *I* the only one who seemed to be able to hear them . . . ?

The fact that we'd now run into our *third* castell in South America—and the biggest one yet—wasn't at all lost on me; but we had even *bigger* problems.

The anchimayen had caught up to us. They gathered at the entrance, spreading out to block our escape. Mario picked up a hunk of bark, set it on fire with just his touch, and then flung it our way. The flaming projectile hissed past my face, missing by only inches. A warning shot, obviously.

"Dude, chill!" I yelled, holding up my hands. "You're going to burn someone's butt off!"

He grinned mischievously. "That's the idea, hermano."

"Just stop it, okay? Stop!" Violet shouted, breathing hard now. "Listen to me: We don't mean you any harm. We're not looking for any trouble. But there's something you should all know. He's the Morphling, okay? This guy. Right here. And if you all don't stop messing around and shooting fireballs at us, you're going to get him angry, and he's going to morph and put a serious beating on you kids!" She clapped her hands together a few times to drive home the point. The sound was surprisingly loud in the silence. And not one of the anchimayen moved or even seemed to breathe for several seconds as their dark little eyes looked me up and down, probably trying to decide whether to believe her or not. Then they all burst into laughter. Every. Single. One.

"The Morphling!" Mario cried, bent over, both hands wrapped around his belly. "That's too good!"

"Hey, what's so funny?" I shouted. "It's true!"

"It's not funny, amigo," said another one. "It's freaking *HILARIOUS!*"

I glared at Violet.

She shrugged. "What?"

"You're embarrassing me. . . ."

"*How?*"

"They're all laughing at me now!" Irritated, I glared

around at them. "*What?* You guys never heard of the Morphling . . . ?"

"Oh, sí, sí," Mario said, fighting to catch his breath. "We heard of 'im. It's just that . . . *YOU?*" His laughter pealed out again, a high, crackling sound that made him sound all of five years old. He reached up to wipe a tear from the corner of his eye, but it evaporated off his skin before he could get to it. "Oye, I gotta ask—where you from, amigo . . . ?"

I crossed my arms over my chest and said, "Miami. Why?"

"Nah, I was just wondering why you owner let you go so far from home without your LEASH!" he shouted, and the rest of the anchimayen basically erupted. They were all laughing so hard now that dark smoke was pouring out of their ears in thick billowing columns.

Then Mario squatted down and started snapping his fingers and whistling like he was trying to call a dog over. "Come here, boy!" he shouted at me. "You wanna play fetch? You wanna? C'mon, less play!" He was making this big dumb show of it, too, tossing stick after flaming stick at my feet and whistling and clapping his hands, but I just didn't get it.

"What kind *stupid* burn is that?" I snapped. Then, glancing down, I saw Alvin's dog collar hanging from my neck and felt my ears go red. "Oh."

Meanwhile, the rest of Mario's gang were still laughing up a storm—or rather, a dense smoky cloud that hung over the treetops like a roiling blanket.

"Ay, amigo, you so funny. . . ." Mario sighed, trying to catch his breath. "It's going to be a shame to roast you, ¿sabes? But, oye, if you really the Morphling—and not just someone's runaway *perrito*—then this should be no problem for you. . . ." He held out one hand, palm-up, and big surprise, from between his mud-caked fingers rose a long, flickering tongue of reddish-orange flame. As I watched, the flame grew hotter and redder and denser until it had swelled into a single burning sphere that reminded me of a flaming comet. On a danger scale from one to ten, the thing looked like a solid *fifteen*.

"Hey, hey, hey! Hold on there!" I shouted. "I'm having problems with my—*my manifestation*, okay? So put that out right now!"

"Santi," Mario said to the anchimayen standing beside him, "how you like your empanadas?"

"Extra crispy," answered the grinning, reddish-haired girl with the FIRE HAZARD T-shirt, and raised one flaming fist.

I barely had a chance to shove Violet out of the way before twin pillars of hellfire came spiraling toward me.

CHAPTER FORTY-SIX

T he sound was huge. Deafening. On instinct I threw my arms up, squinting my eyes and praying it would all be over quickly. I wondered how badly being instantly fried to a crisp would hurt and suddenly felt very sorry for every chicken the Kentucky Fried colonel had ever gotten his hands on. The flames washed over me in a wave of incredible heat. Sweat instantly broke out all over my body. My entire world became a fiery orange blur. At any moment I expected to see the skin on my arms start to peel back as it melted off my bones.

But then something weird happened: Mario stopped shooting at me. Just like that. They lowered their hands and just sort of stood there, staring at me with looks of total confusion on their chubby little faces. Almost like they'd spent the last hour listening to me trying to escape the space-time continuum.

"Charlie!" Violet rushed over, but at first she was too scared to touch me—probably scared she'd hurt me. Or that I was in pain. But I wasn't. "Charlie, your skin!" she cried.

I had a moment of terrible panic and shouted, "Is it *HORRIBLE?*"

And when she sort of shrugged like she wasn't sure, I risked a peek and saw my skin was as black as coals, yet *shiny* somehow . . . not fried to a crisp, but smooth and supple, moist even. I ran a fingertip along my forearm. . . . It was soft as velvet.

"Looks like . . . *stingray skin,*" Violet breathed, and she was absolutely right! I'd seen enough of them in the Florida Keys to know that stingray skin was exactly what it looked like. And there was one awesome fact I'd learned from my dad about stingrays, which I'd never forgotten, would probably *never* forget: Stingray skin is *completely* fireproof!

A moment later the youngest of the anchimayen waddled up beside Violet. His cheeks were soot stained, his eyes all round and big. He cautiously reached one tiny, dirt-smudged hand out, touched my arm—and gasped. "How—how you do dat . . . ?"

"Tienes que ser El Cambiador, ¿no?" breathed the one called Santi.

"¡Tienes que ser!" shouted another.

"Bro, so you really the Morphling . . . ?" Mario asked, shaking his head.

I straightened, stood up nice and tall, and said, "*That's what we were trying to tell you! Maybe you guys should try listening more and ROASTING less!*"

Beside me, Violet was grinning from ear to ear. "You tell 'em, Charlie!"

CHAPTER FORTY-SEVEN

O nce the anchimayen finally accepted the fact that I was a Morphling, they were actually supercool (no pun intended). They offered to throw a great feast in our honor and said they'd gladly charbroil our choice of forest creature—flamingos were their specialty. We turned them down; you'd be surprised how cruel it sounds to charbroil an animal when you've recently been on the receiving end of a scorching fireball. Plus, neither of us was all that hungry. (Probably another side effect of almost being roasted alive.) But we did have some questions for them, the biggest of which being *Why was there a* castell *in the middle of their island?* Unfortunately, the anchimayen didn't have an answer to that, and they seemed as terrified of the castell as we were. Mario believed that it had been built by the same people who had murdered their brujo, because one of them had seen "the hooded ones" come in this direction when they'd left the island. The anchimayen just wanted to get away from the thing as quickly as possible.

So we walked with them for a while and talked, and Violet and I explained how we believed that the same beings—or being—that had kidnapped Queen Joanna were probably the ones who had killed their warlock. Mario informed us that La Junta had recently been called, a summoning of warlocks from all over the world. He said they had been discussing something of great importance and that he believed that was why their warlock had been killed—something to do with a vote they were about to have, some big decision. He also said they would do whatever they could to help us find our queen and avenge their fallen brujo.

Then he and the rest of his gang began to whisper quietly among themselves, and Mario turned to us and said that there was something he wanted to show us. They led us through the Chilean jungle with only the moon's pale glow lighting our way, and we eventually wound up back at the spot where we'd all first met: the Warlock's Cave.

The entrance to the cave—just like in the legends— was guarded by a ravine with a fast-flowing river. Mario squatted by a large hole on our side of the ravine and began making all sorts of strange sounds—deep grunts and groans, guttural barks.

Which was freaky to say the least. But even *freakier* was when his grunts and groans were answered by deeper, more guttural ones from somewhere inside the dark hole.

A heartbeat later several squat, hunched figures appeared at the entrance to the hole. They just sort of sat there, half hidden in shadow, like they were scared to leave the familiar comfort of the darkness. Then all six suddenly scuttled out, revealing themselves in the moonlight—and my heart gave a painful jolt.

Invunches!

"What the heck are those *things?*" Violet breathed, retreating a step.

"Invunches," I whispered back. "They're deformed servants of the sorcerers. They guard the entrance to the Warlock's Cave."

"Really? *Those* things?"

"Yeah, the brujos do all these different rites and rituals on them to change their nature, make them super loyal. But they're not *things*—they're actually human." Though you definitely couldn't tell by looking at them. All their limbs were bent at weird angles, and they walked on their hands (well, their *knuckles*), using only one leg, because the other had been twisted around behind their backs so that the heel of their foot appeared attached to the base of their misshapen heads. Their bodies, compact and muscular and covered in coarse hair, were more apelike than anything. They wore simple leather tunics and nothing else.

"They are the only ones who can take us into the cave," Mario explained. "They can run through the magia. Pick one," he said. "Climb on."

Violet did, so I did too, forcing myself to wrap my arms around its wide, hairy, sweaty shoulders and wrap my legs around its even wider, hairier, and sweatier waist. The moment I was "on board," the invunche let out a deep, apelike grunt, popped up on its knuckles, and jumped back into the dark hole.

CHAPTER FORTY-EIGHT

The hole—or, as I quickly discovered, the tunnel—was as dark as blindness. My eyes couldn't make out a single thing. Not the walls, not the ceiling, not the floors—*nada*. The invunche, on the other hand, didn't seem to be having any problems with the total and complete lack of visibility, because he had already begun to pick up speed, scuttling awkwardly (yet amazingly quickly) through a series of twists and turns that left me a little bit dizzy and a *whole lot* lost. I held on tight, feeling the incredible power of the man-beast beneath me as its bulky back muscles bunched and released, as its thick shoulders rolled and its single powerful walking leg kicked, thrusting us forward in a sort of long, loping run that had cold, stale air swirling through my hair and whistling noisily in my ears.

Finally, we escaped the heavy darkness of the tunnels, spilling out into a large stone room lit by skinny, candles as tall as people. Dominating the chamber was a great stone table in the shape of a crescent moon. No chairs stood around it. Just marks on the stony ground: shapes and lines, unfamiliar letters, symbols. One matched the marks on the backs of the anchimayen's hands.

Upon the table sat a single leather-bound book, which was thicker than any dictionary I'd ever seen: the infamous sorcerer's book of spells, I realized. Had to be.

Beside it was a large crystal bowl filled with water. Legend had it that it had been filled with the tears of the first warlocks of Chiloé. With a soft whimpering sound, the invunche lowered himself onto his butt, and I hopped off, turning back toward the tunnel just as Violet's invunche came scuttling out of the darkness. Violet, of course, was practically beaming, her hair a wild, free mess around her face. The girl lived for stuff like this.

"They should sooo have a ride like this in Orlando," she said, hopping down next to me.

There was a soft cooing sound above us. We looked around. Shallow recesses had been carved high along the walls of the cave, and perched among these were dozens and dozens of those hideous sorcerer-head birds. Most were asleep, but a couple watched us from the corners of their strange red-ringed eyes. "Ugh, those things again," Violet groaned.

"The ancient ones keep watch over this place," Mario said as his invunche emerged from the tunnel. He hopped off, grinning at us, his pupils like dark tongues of fire. "They guard El Libro de los Hechizos and the Seeing Bowl."

I noticed the ceilings were hung with paintings—hundreds of them, all shapes and sizes. Some were layered two, three, or even four deep. Many of the frames were cracked, a few had finger-size holes in the canvas, but the colors were so bright and vivid that even in the dim candle-light I had to wonder if they'd all been freshly painted. Mario saw me staring up at them and said, "Those you must never touch. That's why we hang them so high. They not oil and canvas.... Those are *memories*."

I shook my head, confused. "You mean, like, *real* memories?"

"Oh, sí ... If a brujo or bruja wants to forget something, they make one of those—a *lienzo*, they called. This way, their minds can be free, but they are kept here in case they ever need to remember it again." He motioned for us to follow. "Vamos."

As the gang of anchimayen led us toward a passage-way in the back, Santi saying something to Violet about this place being almost as old as the island itself, two chon-chones, one black haired, the other blondish, flew down from their perches to land in the center of the stone table.

The dark-haired one (who I was pretty sure was the one that had crashed into our window back on the train—it was hard to forget a nose *that* busted up and crooked-looking) glanced up at me and said, "Pequeño, óyeme . . . *listen* here."

"Sí, listen to him," cooed the other. A long tongue, forked and purplish, flicked briefly out from between its beaky lips. "Listen closely. . . ."

Then the familiar one said, "There is a *traitor* in La Liga—a *traitor* among your *friends*. . . ."

Which stopped me dead in my tracks. "What'd you say?"

"One from within has turned against the rest. . . . They have begun to pull away from the others. It was inevitable."

"How . . . do you know that?" I asked with a shaky voice.

"Because the Seeing Bowl allows one to *see*. . . ."

Frowning, an uneasy feeling rising in my chest, I stared down at the fine crystal, my eyes almost drawn to it, pulled like magnets. "To see—*what*?"

"*Secrets* . . . ," answered the other chonchón. It skittered to the edge of the table on its stick-thin legs, angling its large, misshapen head to look straight up at me. "Can you hear them, pequeño . . . ?" it asked in a screechy whisper. "Can you hear the voices?"

I nodded slowly, sort of freaking out that this head on legs knew that. "Yeah . . . Can you?"

"No," said the one from the train, "but we can *feel* them. The earth is littered with their bones. We walk upon the graveyard of the ages, largest in all the world."

The other chonchón said, "You have many questions, pequeño. . . . The bowl is an infinite reservoir of knowledge. Perhaps it holds the answers *you* seek."

"Peek inside," whispered the familiar one. "Behold its secrets. . . ."

The water in the bowl began to swirl hypnotically as I bent over to peer in. At first I didn't see anything, but as I leaned closer, I *did* see something. . . . Glittery, glistening, silvery lights were dancing across the surface of the water. I thought it might be moonlight, but that was impossible; there were no cracks or openings in the ceiling of the cave. But even more interesting, as I watched, still trying to figure out what those lights were (or at least where they were *coming* from), they began to form images . . . A large, hairy hand. And it was holding some kind of knife: A wicked-looking thing with a gleaming silver edge. I watched it raise the dagger high, and next thing I knew a man was tumbling, face-first, off a great gilded throne embroidered with what looked like a Spanish coat of arms. The crown, which had sat atop his head, glittered faintly as it fell, striking the ground with a resounding *clang*, and the man, obviously wounded—or *worse*—fell beside it, lying motionless on the red-and-gold mosaic floor. His attacker, however, remained in shadow. Only their hand was visible.

Then the water in the Seeing Bowl began to churn, and a new scene appeared: I saw the same hand being buried in a half-familiar field. I blinked, and now the scene changed again—I saw a row of coffins. Four of them. They'd been chained and nailed shut, hidden deep in the belly of some ship. The bowl water had begun to swirl even faster, and the next moment, there was an earsplitting CRACK! as the ship carrying the four coffins was torn apart by a wild and angry sea.

I saw a hooded figure wearing a large emerald necklace with some sort of crest on it—a shield, twin lions, and a huge black eagle—levitating the coffins and escaping with them through an expanding crack in the hull just as the sea swallowed the ship.

For several seconds, the glittery, silvery lights disappeared and the water inside the bowl turned a deep, oily black. It reminded me of tar—or motor oil. When it clarified again, I saw the hooded figure kneeling in the middle of a vast and rocky chamber—a cave, it looked like. The coffins had been laid out in a circle on the sandy ground, and as I watched, wisps of pale green light flowed from the figure's heavily ringed fingers into each one of the coffins. Then, with nothing more than a lazy sweep of its hand, the figure sent the coffins flying off in different directions; I watched, from almost a bird's-eye view now, as the coffins scattered all across South America, crashing down in thick jungle, inside caves—one in the middle of the ocean.

Suddenly, the scene swirled away and the silvery lights formed a new one: A blazing downtown skyline, its jumble of high-rises and office buildings smoking with countless fires that burned on almost every floor.

"That's downtown Miami," I breathed, recognizing the Panorama Tower and the Southeast Financial Center. The next several images formed in the bowl almost too quickly to process: I saw La Liga's headquarters, the Provencia in North Miami Beach, completely razed; I saw lines of terrified-looking kids, their faces pale and soot stained, their hands bound with ropes, being marched through the streets like prison chain gangs; I saw entire neighborhoods leveled; I saw two bodies lying unconscious in a front yard—*my parents!* Someone screamed—it was probably me—and I staggered back from the bowl, breathing so hard my lungs hurt.

"How . . . ? *What the heck did I just see?*" I whispered, shaking, feeling sweat break out over my face, my arms.

"You saw the world as it was and as it will be . . . ," answered the dark-haired chonchón. "But you did not see all. Merely the shadow of a hand . . ."

"Soon this world will be plunged into utter darkness from which it might never recover," said the other. "All living things shall groan under the yoke of slavery. That is, of course, if your mission ends in failure."

My mission? "You mean if we can't save Joanna?"

Neither sorcerer head answered for so long, I thought they weren't going to.

"You know your path," the familiar one said finally. "It has led you this far, has it not?" The chonchón paused for a moment, its bulging bloodshot eyes staring straight up at mine. "The time of your testing has already begun. Like a sacrifice is blind to its end, so you shall be: an offering, tried by the elements—wind, water, earth, and *fire*. But in the end, it will not be you who will tip the balance of this war, rather he whose end was told of old, yes, even from the beginning."

The time of my testing? Tried by the elements? What was this thing *talking* about? "I . . . I don't understand."

"This we cannot interpret for you, even though we greatly wish to. The bowl speaks of its own will. The waters give only what is yours to know—and what has been given to you is this: Return to Brazil. Lay your trap on the highest hill. There the thief lingers, reveling in his take."

"What *thief*?" I said.

"You know which one," cooed the chonchón. "He will

be the one to lead you. And lead you he will, as a lamb to the slaughter."

In another room came a shrill, high-pitched scream. My blood froze.

Violet!

CHAPTER FORTY-NINE

A shot of adrenaline spiked through me as I ran out of the main chamber and into a small room cut into the cave's walls. Violet was standing in the middle—totally unharmed, I saw with a huge rush of relief—staring at something on the ground. I didn't get a chance to see what it was before she screamed, "It's Joanna's crown!"

And now that I *did* get a chance to check it out, I saw she was right!

V stepped toward it, careful not to disturb the scene. "It's another bread crumb!" she said. "Another clue!" Crouching, she studied the dirt mounds someone had built near the back wall—there were five or six of them. Smooth-sided and sculpted, they reminded me of sandcastles.

As my gaze moved slowly around the room, I said, "Okay . . . so what's the clue?"

"Where exactly was the crown . . . ?" Violet asked Mario.

"On top," he replied, nodding at the baby-faced anchi-mayen. "Goyito found it. Last night."

"Show me." Violet picked up the crown and handed it to Goyito, and the little guy placed it carefully—and very, very *gently*—on the tallest of the mounds.

"Así," he said, and then shyly retreated to Mario's side.

I glanced at Violet. "You getting anything from this?"

But she stayed quiet, her forehead wrinkled in concentration. "When do you think our friend and those other sombras passed through here?" she asked Mario after a few moments.

"No sé. Probably around midnight yesterday. We would've seen them had it been any earlier."

Violet glanced at her watch, then at me. "Almost midnight now," she said.

"Okay . . ." I had no idea how that mattered, like, *at all*. "What are you thinking?"

"Not so much thinking . . . maybe, *praying?*"

We waited. A minute passed, then two. The gang of anchimayen stood in a circle around the room. Not one of them said anything. Santi stared silently at Violet, and Violet stared silently back for a moment before glancing down at her watch again.

I saw her frown. Then she looked up at me and said, "It's midnight."

The disappointment in her voice was clear. But I wasn't sure what exactly there was to be disappointed *about*. "Was something . . . *supposed* to happen?"

V let out a heavy sigh. "I don't know. I thought—*maybe*. But . . ." Now she was shaking her head, looking almost hopelessly around the room. "Yeah, I have no idea what Joanna was trying to tell us. . . ."

"Maybe she just wanted to let us know that she was still alive?" I said.

"I mean, yeah. It's possible. But that's not going to help us *find* her."

Overhead, a thin stream of moonlight had found a crack in the craggy ceiling and was spearing into the room in a bright column. Noticing it, Violet turned. And suddenly she was staring at the crown again. Staring *hard*. Like she'd figured something out.

Before I could ask her if she actually had, though, she bent down, angling the crown so that the moonlight shone directly onto the large emerald on the front of it.

I wasn't sure what she was up to, but *she* obviously was, because that's when something interesting happened. . . . The jewel in the center of Joanna's crown began to glow. It seemed to absorb the moonlight like a rag does water, and suddenly the fist-size emerald began to sparkle. Prisms of dazzling light radiated out, bouncing off the walls and lighting the room in a pale, greenish glow. Steadily the sparkling intensified. The crown itself began to glow. And now a rich golden hue fell over the cluster of mounds. In the glittery yellowish light they looked an awful lot more like golden buildings and towers than simple piles of dirt.

Mario's mouth had dropped open. "*Madre . . .*"

"Looks like—*a city*," Violet said, and it did . . . a big, *golden* city.

"Oh my God," I breathed.

V turned to me. "What?"

"It's the City of Gold. . . ."

"*What?*"

"That's her clue! It's *El Dorado!*"

CHAPTER FIFTY

The fabled city of El Dorado was one of the most famous cities in all of legend and myth, if not *the* most famous. Explorers from as early as the 1500s had risked their lives and reputations in search of its wealth and supposedly boundless treasure. But it also seemed to be impossible to find, because although treasure hunters from all over the world had tried to discover its secret location, none had actually succeeded.

"But does it even really exist?" I asked Mario. "I mean, have you ever heard anything about it?"

The anchimayen's black eyes lit up as he grinned at me. Like, *literally* lit up. They seemed to burn in their sockets like miniature fireballs, casting deep shadows over the rest of his face. "¿Cómo no? It's almost impossible to find, but it's real. Our brujo visited many times. They markets are world famous."

"Mario, could you give us a moment?" Violet said, and when he nodded, she turned to me and whispered, "So that's where they're taking her, then—El Dorado. I mean, if it is, in fact, a real place like he says, then that's gotta be it."

"Seems like it." Honestly I didn't see any other way to interpret her clue.

V frowned. "It's weird, though . . ."

"What is?"

"Well, why are they moving Joanna around so much? Usually when you kidnap someone, you take them to *one* place and just keep them there, tied up or whatever. That way they're out of sight and have less chance of escaping."

"You sound like you have experience. Should I be worried?"

"*Ha-ha.* But seriously. First they took her to a cave— Lapa do Santo; then they brought her here, to this island; and now they're moving her to some ancient and lost city of gold. So the investigative journalist in me has to ask, *Why?* What's the point of all that? And is there some connection between the three locations?"

Interesting questions . . . Why *did* they keep moving her? And what *was* the connection between the locations? But before I could come up with any theories, Violet turned back to Mario and said, "You wouldn't happen to know where we could find El Dorado, would ya?"

"In Colombia. But where exactly? Don't know. . . . We never left this island. But our brujo say it's one of the oldest of all the forgotten cities. He say it was built after the Sun Wars and at the cost of much blood." His voice dropped to a whisper as he said, "But you two should stay *far away* from that place. . . ."

I shook my head. "What? Why?"

"The creatures that live there? They *hate* outsiders, *despise* humans, and don't care *nothin'* for no one 'cept they own kind. But, I can't blame them. . . . They been hunted for their great treasure since the beginning of time. I only ever hear one story 'bout someone who walked into their golden fortress and escape alive." His eyes dimmed, lowering to the brightness of a dying match. "You should stay away . . . and *especially* now."

"Why now?" Violet asked.

"You no heard the rumors spreading through the continents?"

I stared at him with a sinking feeling. "What rumors are you talking about?"

The look of concern in his eyes flickered into surprise. "You no heard? We never left Chiloé, and we heard!"

"You mean the rumors of the dead rising?"

The surprise in his eyes changed back into dread. "You have heard, then."

"Were you guys around when it happened the first time?" V asked.

"No," Mario said, "but our brujo tell us about it sometimes. He say it was darkest time the world has ever known ... *either* world."

"What did he say? What happened exactly?"

"*Terrible things* ..." He was nodding now, but there was a kind of guardedness to it. As if he thought he might have said too much already. "So *many* terrible things ... maybe it is better you don't know."

"Actually, I think it could be very helpful to us," Violet said, sounding quite sincere and not just like someone hoping to hear a scary story.

Mario took a deep breath like he was wondering what to say—or whether to say anything at all. When he finally spoke, his voice was low and tight. "Our brujo tell us that in the thirteenth year of La Catrina, los muertos began to rise. He say that, at the time, no one knew why. The warlocks confused. Scared. They blame it on las brujas. Las brujas blame it on las calacas. Las calacas blame it back on los brujos. Everyone started to believe that death had lost its appetite—they say it was *spitting up* souls. . . . But no one knew that the dead were not rising by they own choice."

Confused, I shook my head. "They *weren't?*"

"No, they were rising b—"

"*Because of el MONSTRUO!*" Goyito yelled, then hid behind one of the other kids.

"El monstruo . . . ?" I turned back to Mario. "What *monster?*"

Surprise widened his eyes. "You two never hear this before?" And when we both shook our heads, he turned and started out of the room, motioning for us to follow.

CHAPTER FIFTY-ONE

We followed Mario through a labyrinth of narrow, echoing, dimly lit passageways until we came to a small square-shaped space flanked by wooden tables. The walls were black quartz, glassy, almost translucent, and had been drilled with a matrix of deep holes from floor to ceiling. The holes had been perfectly measured, perfectly spaced, and formed a flawless dot grid. Within these holes were long, ancient parchments, chipped with age but intact and sturdy looking.

When Mario first unrolled one on the tabletop in front of us, there didn't seem to be anything written in it. But a moment later, he snapped his fingers, producing a lick of flame at the very tip of his thumb, and as he passed it over the parchment, inky splotches began to appear until strange marks filled the page; there were a few Spanish words scribbled in the margins, but nothing I could make any sense of. Mario read silently from the scroll for several moments, then looked up at us again, his eyes like a pair of small round torches in the dimness of the room. The kid was using his eyeballs like a pair of reading lamps. It was crazy cool! "These scrolls were left to us by La Sociedad de las Calacas. They the recordkeepers of the sombra world. But after the Great Shaking, many of their bibliotecas were destroyed. They gave what was left to the warlocks for safekeeping." He passed one hand reverently over the parchment. "The scrolls are written in they ancient language."

Leaning over the scroll, Violet examined it. "What does this one say?"

"It speaks of El Dark Brujo . . . El Hijo de la Tumba."

"Who is that?"

"El monstruo," said the anchimayen, turning his fiery eyes on us. "A sorcerer who can summon *the dead*."

"Like, a necromancer?" I said.

"Sí, *exactly* like a necromancer . . ."

His words sent a rush of fear through me, but I tried not to let it show.

Mario glanced down at the scroll and began to read. "'Soulless, sinister, insidious,' that is what is spoken of him. . . . They say the monster was so wicked, so *powerful*, that when Death herself came for him, he fought her off, wounded her, cleaved off two of her fingers . . ." He held up his hand. "Her *dedos*, man. . . . But did you know that he was once the High Inquisitor of España?"

At this point Violet and I were totally freaking out—at least I was. But the anchimayen kept going.

"He lead the inquisitions when they hunted down all those they believed to be brujas y brujos. They give him this task because of his—how you say?—*unique* gift. . . ."

"Because he could raise the dead," I said, and Mario nodded.

"Correcto. So after they burn someone at the stake, let's say, he could bring them back for even more questioning; and if they still refuse to answer, they could do it all over again. . . ."

"That's . . . *terrifying*," Violet breathed.

The anchimayen's eyes cast bright oval shapes on our faces as he spoke. "But soon he became hungry for even *more* power. . . . He no longer care about helping the crown hunt down brujos y brujas; no, he wanted to learn all they deepest secrets—they darkest spells, they most *powerful* elixirs. He formed his own secret army, un regimiento of undead assassins, sorcerers resurrected by his *own* hand. He even create his own secret prisons where he would bring the witches and warlocks he capture. But when the king and queen find out, they were no happy. They kill him. Burn him at the stake.

But that not the end of him. . . . It was only *the beginning.* He crawl back up from the grave with revenge burning in his *corazón.* His dream? To unite La Península. To bring Spain and Portugal under his rule. He wanna bend the worlds to his will—this one and *the other.*"

I frowned. "But why?"

"Porque la iniquidad absoluta siempre anhelará el poder absoluto."

"What'd he say?" Violet asked me.

"Because absolute wickedness always craves absolute power."

Mario glanced down at the scroll and began to read aloud: "'And it was this dark brujo of unspeakable power, which some claim cannot remain dead, who wielded the armies of the dead like a weapon. Under his control, they swept across the earth like locusts, devouring any who dared stand against him.'"

"So this necromancer basically led an army of—*zombies . . . ?*"

"Zombies, los muertos vivientes . . . Call them lo que quieras. But if you ever face one, you find out fast just how hard it is to kill something that's already dead." He paused for a moment, like he didn't want to continue, and I wasn't sure I *wanted* him to. "But there were more than muertos in his army. There were ogres. Comelenguas from the Black

Mountains. Chupacabra tribes from el norte—thousands of them. They gather sangre—you know, *blood*—for el brujo, oceans of it . . . the blood he need for his rituals. Oh, and don't forget, they masters . . . the asemas, vampires of old."

Just then Goyito, the youngest of the anchimayen, pushed up on his tippy-toes and whispered something in Mario's ear. Mario turned to him and, in a soft, reassuring voice, said, "No, no, no . . . no te preocupes por eso . . . eso no va a pasar, ¿me oíste?"

"What's wrong?" Violet wanted to know.

"The little one is scared of the monster. He saw the castell, and now he worried it's coming back. I already told him to stop listening to what the crazy brujos are saying, but . . . he young."

"What *are* the crazy brujos saying?" Violet asked.

"They saying the monster will soon return. That he resurrecting himself like the last time."

"How do they know?" she wondered out loud.

"Because of the castells. They *always* signal his coming."

I felt my insides tighten even as I asked the question. "What do you mean *always* . . . ?"

"He's been killed *many times*, hermano . . . once in Mexico, once in Spain, and the last time was in Portugal. Each time he return from the dead even more *powerful*, and *each time* the castells announce his return. His followers build them over his grave, you see. And then . . . then he performs his dark *magia*, and he brings himself back."

Which meant is was probably some of his followers that had kidnapped Joanna. But why? What did she have to do with any of this? "So he's coming for sure then, yeah?" I asked.

"No, no, no, no . . . there is no coming back for him," Mario assured me.

"I don't understand. Why not?"

"Because the last time he was killed, it was by a *very* powerful sombra—a bruja. . . . She spread his body into four coffins, cursed the coffins, and then hid them throughout the earth so his followers cannot find."

I stared at him in shock. That was exactly what I'd seen in the bowl! Those had been *the necromancer's* coffins, El Dark Brujo's . . . and the hooded figure must've been the witch Mario was talking about.

"So then why are castells popping up everywhere?" Violet asked.

"I think his followers doing it," Mario said. "They building them again, but this time its un truco—you know, *a trick.* They want everyone to *believe* he's coming back so everyone stay scared—so no one wanna join La Liga. Because now that there's a Morphling in the world again," he said, looking right at me, "now that *you* are here—there's *hope* again, and evil *always* try to crush hope."

CHAPTER FIFTY-TWO

None of us spoke for what felt like a long time.

"What do those castells do, anyway?" I asked finally.

"They the most basic piece of resurrection magic," Mario answered. "They—how you say?—*amplify* El Dark Brujo's magia so he can resurrect himself, raise the dead."

There was another silence. Shorter this time.

"Mario," Violet said, "you mentioned something about an explorer who made it out of El Dorado alive, right?"

The anchimayen nodded. "Sí."

"Do you still remember the story?"

"Some, sí."

"Do you remember how they did it? How they made it out alive?"

He grinned, his teeth bone-white in the spotlights of his eyes. "Ay, sí, was the best part . . ."

"So how'd they do it?" I asked.

"With an alicanto egg."

The word tickled a memory somewhere in the back of my brain. "An ali-*whatto* egg?"

"Alicanto. It is the only thing the inhabitants of the golden city fear more than death itself."

"An *egg*?" I said, shocked. "The inhabitants of El Dorado are terrified of an *egg* . . . ?"

The anchimayen nodded again.

"That's all we need, then," Violet said. She glanced at Mario. "Do you know where we can find one?"

Suddenly he burst out laughing—and I mean really laughing, like V had just told the funniest joke of all time. "You can't just FIND an alicanto egg! ¿Estás loca? They the most precious treasure on *this planet*! Some brujos spend they *lives* searching for one, but only a few ever even seen one. . . . They made of the *purest* gold."

Violet's eyes grew to the size of Frisbees as she turned them on me. I had just opened my mouth to say *What?* when it hit me, too. "Wait," I said, whirling to face Mario. "So you're saying they look like they're made of pure gold?"

He gave a quick little nod. "Sí."

"And are they a little bigger than, say, a chicken egg?"

"Sí."

"And do they sometimes glow a little?"

He chuckled. "Amigo, how you know so much about alicanto eggs?"

"Because we had one!" Violet shouted, smacking her hands on the tabletop.

Mario—along with the rest of the fire kids—burst into laughter again. "You two are muy funny, ¿saben? ¡Son de los más graciosos!"

"No, it's true!" I said. "We found one back in Miami!"

"An alicanto egg in *MIAMI*?" He screamed as his laughter turned hysterical. I could see trails of grayish smoke drifting out of his ears. "You gotta be the funniest Morphling *ever!*"

"He's not joking!" Violet yelled. "We *literally* held it in our *hands!*"

"*C'mon, what you think? I stupid or something?*"

"But it's true!"

The anchimayen went silent for a second. Then he just sighed and threw his hands up like he'd just given up. "Bueno, bueno . . . let's say I believe you. . . . Let's say you actually find an *ALICANTO EGG* in *MIAMI*. . . . One question: ¿Dónde está ahora?"

"We don't know where it is," I admitted. "It was stolen from us."

"*STOLEN FROM YOU?*" Mario screamed. "Do you know how VALUABLE an alicanto egg is? You could buy this *entire island*! No, you could buy *THE AMERICAS!*"

"Yeah, well, we didn't know we were being robbed. There were these whirlwind thingies and stuff was blowing everywhere and . . . *whatever*." I honestly didn't feel like reliving it.

"They stole *everything* from us," Violet told him. "All our money. Our passports. Then they filled *my* backpack with dirt and *his* with rice. I guess so we wouldn't feel the change in weight while they jacked our stuff."

Mario's eyes flicked from me to Violet, startled. "Espérate. So this person who stole from you, who you no see, also filled your bag with *dirt* and *his* bag with *rice*?"

"Yeah, why?"

"And you smelled something, ¿sí? Something *terrible* . . ."

I frowned, remembering. "Yeah . . . yeah, I did smell something terrible. Wait. How the heck did you know that?"

Mario exploded into laughter again. It was starting to get *seriously* annoying.

"What? What's so funny?" Violet said.

"Lemme guess—this happen in Brazil, ¿sí?"

"Yes!" I burst out. "And how the heck did you know THAT?"

"Because it's obvious!"

"'Twas Saci!" said the baby-faced anchimayen. He grinned at me, showing those piranha's teeth again.

"*Who?*" I shouted.

"Saci Pererê!" Mario shouted back. "Have you no heard the legends?"

"Of course I've heard of Saci. . . ." I mean, who hadn't heard of the one-legged, magical-cap-wearing prankster? Stories of his childish antics have been told throughout Brazil for generations. He'd been depicted in TV shows, comic books, songs—in fact, dude was so famous, a soccer team had made him their mascot, and he even had his very own holiday in Brazil! Plus, he was, like, one of my all-time favorite mythological characters. Growing up, I'd practically *beg* my abuela to tell me his tales, because I used to think his pranks were the funniest things in the world. Now? Not so much . . . "But how do you know it was him?" I said.

"'Cause his fingerprints all over it! The whirlwind. The rice. And it happen in *Brazil*, hermano! *Brazil!*" Mario took a breath, smiling a little to himself like he found this whole thing absolutely hilarious. "But I guess you should feel complimented in a way. . . ."

"What? *Why?*" Now, *this* I had to hear.

"Because he make special effort for you. Entiende, most the time he just destroy your crops, spill your milk. You know, kids' pranks. But on *special occasions*, when he take something of great value from someone he *truly* hate, he leave behind a pile of rice. That's where the saying 'Y te dejó un saco de arroz debajo de la cama' come from. He left you a sack of rice under you bed. Like making fun of you. Saci a very naughty boy . . . ," Mario continued. "A very, *very* naughty boy. You know he even pranks las brujas and los brujos? Yeah . . . he take they lienzos—those painting memories I show you? He take some and replace them with *finger paintings*. By li'l kids! He even did that here one or two times." Mario smirked. "He think *everything* one big *joke*—the whole world—and he always trying to prove it."

"He sounds *hilarious*," I grumbled. *And when I get my hands on him*, I thought, *I'll show him just how funny I can be.*

"But why would he target us?" Violet asked.

"It's obvious, no? You carrying an alicanto egg! Now, how he find that out, who knows. But he a special guy." Mario hesitated for a moment, like he was considering something, then leaned toward us with those bright eyes and said, "You two really gonna risk you lives and enter the golden city?"

"We don't have much of a choice," I admitted. "That's where they took our friend."

"Then you must return to Brazil. You must take back your egg from the greatest prankster the world has ever known. And you better find him before someone make him an offer on your egg—which not gonna take long, *believe me.*"

"Great . . . ," Violet muttered under her breath.

I sighed. "It's *fantastic*."

"But I must warn you," Mario said. "He not gonna go quietly, and he not gonna go willingly. He will be the most cunning, mischievous enemy you have or ever gonna face. He will prank you. He gonna frustrate you every chance he get. He gonna be almost *impossible* to track."

"Wonderful," I said. "Any more good news?"

"Sí, one more thing: No one's been able to capture him in *five thousand years*."

CHAPTER FIFTY-THREE

I t was safe to say that the anchimayen didn't like our chances. Still, they wanted to help, so they put together a list of all the stuff they thought we'd need in order to capture Saci. At the top of that list was bungee cord. *Lots* of it. There was also a whole bunch of other stuff, like fruit and candles and milk and those small paper packets of refined sugar—apparently Saci had quite the sweet tooth—and when we explained to them that Saci had taken our money, too, they hooked us up with a sealskin pouch filled with gold coins and said it was the least they could do after trying to broil us. Then Mario showed us a map of the area around Lapa do Santo and pointed out where we could find a market to buy the supplies and the location of a high hill (it was called Cabana Mesa on the map) where we could lay our trap.

We slept in the Warlock's Cave that night (something

I wouldn't recommend if you enjoy pillows or bedsheets or snuggling up under a nice cotton comforter; thing is, anchimayen can't sleep near anything that's flammable), and the next morning, as the sun rose red over the wild Chilean jungle, Mario and his crew led us back toward the coast, where they said they could arrange travel for us. About halfway there we came upon this strange creature creeping along the banks of a fast-slowing stream. The fire kids told us it was called El Nguruvilu, which I already knew thanks to my abuela. I'd never forgotten its frightening tales: the half-fox, half-serpent sombra that liked to lurk near bodies of water in Chile and cause whirlpools and floods to drown those trying to pass over. Santi said that she hadn't seen it in years and *never* this far inland. Mario, for his part, was convinced that the creature was tracking Violet and me, though he couldn't come up with any concrete reasons why it would be. Just to be safe, though, we all hid in a knot of mangrove roots until the thing slithered into the stream, and then we continued toward the coast.

When we finally reached the beach, Goyito, the baby-faced anchimayen, brought the sorcerer's book of spells out of the deerskin pouch he was wearing on his back, waded out a little way into the water, and began to read from its pages, whistling as he did. On his fourth whistle a white, bubbly, frothy scar appeared on the surface of the sea, maybe five hundred yards away. It raced quickly toward shore like a torpedo moving just below the surface of the water; then all at once the ocean seemed to burst apart as an absolutely massive creature emerged from its depths— first a *huge*, elongated horse head with a wild golden mane, then a ginormous glistening body, also horselike, with forelegs that ended on folded fuchsia-colored fins and a powerful whalelike tail.

Violet and I gasped as the thing rose to its full height, easily thirteen feet, and let out a monstrous neigh that sprayed seawater everywhere, instantly drenching the gang of anchimayen—and us—from head to toe.

"El Caballo Marino!" Mario announced proudly, spitting a stream of water out of his mouth. "Dis is how sorcerers leave the island. You two will be traveling in style, mis amigos. . . ."

The seahorse didn't have a saddle or any other safety features that I could pick out, so the fire kids used long strands of brownish seaweed to tie us down. When they were finished, Santi offered us a drink from the husk of a small green coconut. "It's potion mixed with a little mote con huesillo for flavor," she explained. "It will calm your body and mind so you don't get sick from the ride. Los caballos travel very fast, and your bodies not used to this."

Violet and I each took a sip of the warm, sweet, syrupy

liquid—which actually tasted a lot like un cafecito, a strong shot of Cuban coffee my mom and dad always liked to start their day with—then smiled down at the anchimayen as they waved up at us and said they couldn't wait until we met again. They seemed pretty sure we would, too. Then Mario gave the command, slapping the seahorse right on its big ol' butt, and el caballo broke into a furious gallop, crashing into the surf with a rush of wind and sea spray, and I felt my eyelids begin to get very, *very* heavy.

CHAPTER FIFTY-FOUR

Sometime later—I had no idea if it had been five minutes or five hours (I'd blacked out after drinking the anchimayen's potion)—my eyes fluttered open as I felt the seahorse begin to dissolve beneath us, its hard, muscular back turning soft and watery, foaming and frothing as its long neck and head fell away in a shapeless column of seawater. One moment we were seated, and the next we were descending gently toward the ground, riding a small wave of greenish water.

As our feet touched down on the jungle floor, the wave rolled out from between our legs, soaking the carpet of twigs and fallen leaves, and then we were standing in an icy puddle that had once been a majestic seahorse.

Violet turned to me, shrugging off the seaweed seat belt, her eyes all big and blue. "Coolest. Dismount. Ever."

◆ ◆ ◆

The market the anchimayen had told us about wasn't very difficult to find. More like *impossible* to miss. First off, it was next to the main road and pretty much in plain sight. And second, the place was so bustling with activity that you probably could've heard it from the other side of the *continent*. I'd never seen so many people in one place; there was everything from fruit vendors selling camu camu and acai to local artists crafting these awesome paper baskets from the pages of recycled newspapers to musicians playing live samba music on improvised drums made of empty water jugs. My abuela had told me about these kinds of markets—the locals called them ferias. She used to say there was no better way to experience all that Brazil had to offer, and finally I understood why.

But as we walked among the maze of colorful stalls, I noticed V staring hard at some of the signs and posters and making these small, confused, embarrassed faces when any of the vendors or musicians tried to talk to her.

When I caught her frowning at a display that read CANTALUPO, I finally couldn't take it anymore and said, "Hey, you okay?"

She gave a little shrug, shaking her head.

"No, seriously, is something wrong?"

"It's nothing. Forget it."

"No, V, c'mon. What's up?"

She sighed. "I don't know. . . . It's just that I feel sort of . . . *disconnected,* you know?"

"Disconnected from *what?*"

"Well, like—we've been all over South America these last couple of days, right? And the entire time I haven't been able to read a sign or understand a *single word* anyone's been saying. It's *frustrating. . . .*"

"But, V, you don't speak the language. I mean, you're not *from* here. . . ."

"But that's the thing—*I am.* Partly, anyway. My granddad on my dad's side was Spanish. He was born in Spain. Then he moved down here to Brazil when he was, like, eight. He spoke Spanish and Portuguese."

I blinked. "Really?"

"Uh-huh."

"Wow, that's . . . unexpected." And here I thought I was the foremost expert on all things Violet Rey. "But hold up—if you're part Spanish, then how come you don't *speak any* . . . ?"

"My parents always discouraged it. They said that we live in the US and that we should assimilate, whatever that means." She let out another sigh, glancing at a table covered with dozens of colorful handmade ribbons as we passed it. "My dad even made this big stink at school once so I wouldn't have to take Spanish classes like everyone else. He said it was a waste of his tax dollars."

"That's crazy."

"Tell me about it. But you wanna hear the worst part? In the short time I got to know my grandfather—he died a couple of years ago—I barely even got to talk to the man. He didn't speak any English, and I obviously don't speak any Spanish." She wiped at her cheeks. "That sucks, you know?"

Hearing that broke my heart. And not only because I could tell how much she cared about her abuelo from the way she was talking, but also because my grandparents—*especially* my abuela—had been such a huge and wonderful part of my life that I honestly couldn't imagine growing up without them. "I'm sorry," I said.

"Don't be. It's not your fault." Violet looked away, shaking her head, and might've wiped her eyes—I couldn't tell for sure. "But no, I'm fine. *I'm okay.* . . . It's just that being here surrounded by all this beautiful culture, all these beautiful *people*, it kind of reminds me what I missed out on—what I'm *still* missing out on. And it's part of me, you know?"

"Doesn't have to be like that. I mean, it doesn't have to *stay* like that." When she only looked at me, I said, "What I'm saying is, maybe I could, you know, *teach you* some Spanish. . . ."

Violet was smiling now, playing with the ends of her hair. "Oh yeah?"

"Yeah, why not? I'm pretty . . ." "Fluent" was the word I was looking for. But it's kind of a tricky word, and in the time it took me to come up with it, Violet jumped in.

"You are pretty . . . ," she said with a sly grin, and I felt my ears turn flamingo pink.

"No, I mean, pretty good at *it* . . . at *Spanish*. It was actually my first language. I think I'd make a good teacher. . . ."

Violet was still grinning at me as she said, "I think so too."

CHAPTER FIFTY-FIVE

The sun had just dipped below the red rim of the horizon by the time we'd finished buying all our supplies and finally made it over to Cabana Mesa, the place where the anchimayens suggested we lay our trap. The hill was about twenty or thirty feet tall, wide at the top and flat, and probably fifty yards in circumference with clumps of leafy green bushes clustered near the center. There were no trees up here—nowhere else for someone to hide. Which made it just about the perfect spot to spring an ambush. Violet and I got right to work. We put out a picnic with all different types of fruit and a big jug of milk, scattered half a dozen or so of the anchimayen's gold coins around the blanket along with the sugar packets, then lit all the long wax candles we'd bought (they were mango and ocean breeze scented) and spread them out around the hilltop to make sure their flames could be seen from down below. Next, summoning my inner Rambo, I took the bungee cord, tied a wide loop at one end, and set it down right next to the blanket. Then I covered the loop in handfuls of grass and fallen leaves, trying to camouflage it and doing my best to make the whole thing look as natural as possible (although I didn't exactly have a ton of experience setting traps for mythological beings—or any other kinds of beings, for that matter), and tossed the other end into the bushes. And once all of that was done, we waited.

And waited.

And waited.

"It's been almost an hour now," Violet whispered a while later, glancing down at her watch. The two of us were still hiding in the bushes, lying side by side on the soft, grassy ground, both holding on to a section of bungee cord, which we would pull to spring our trap. An occasional breeze blew across the hill, but other than that the night was completely silent. You could've heard a gnat burp. "What if he doesn't show?" V asked.

I shrugged. "Then it's game over."

"How do you say that in Spanish?"

"Fin del juego."

"Sounds even more ominous."

A few minutes later I rolled onto my side and peered through the tangle of leaves, scanning the hillside for movement. There wasn't any. I sighed. "Maybe we should've bought more candles. . . ."

"Or milk," V said. "I'm getting thirsty." And she wasn't the only one.

Licking my chapped lips, I glanced across the hill to my left—

And had to do a double take. A tree, tall and thick limbed with bright red flowers budding on its branches, stood at the edge of the hill. A tree I could've sworn hadn't been there a second ago, because *a second ago I could've sworn* that the hilltop was completely *treeless.*

I nudged Violet. "Was that tree always there?"

She turned, tilting her head to one side. "Hadn't noticed it . . ."

"Looks . . . *familiar*, no?" It looked sort of like the tree we'd seen in Chiloé, the one that had smacked the anchimayen out of the air as she'd come sizzling toward us. Looked *a lot* like it, in fact.

Violet shrugged. "I don't know. Maybe."

A soft wind blew across the hilltop, and we both went quiet.

"V, I've been thinking . . . ," I said after a few seconds. "Don't you find everything that's been going on a little *weird?*"

"What do you mean?"

"Well, for starters—Los Embrujados ... Don't you find it strange that some werewolf priests that no one's heard from for over six hundred years are suddenly after *me*? And don't you think it's a *teensy bit* odd that an ogre from a race of *baddie* ogres known all over Argentina for kidnapping children just randomly decided to *help* a couple of kids? Like, out of the goodness of its black heart? Also, isn't it just *slightly* curious that Adriana—this girl neither one of us has ever met before in our *entire lives*—just happens to show up right in the *nick of time?*"

"Not to mention the fact that we keep running into castells everywhere we go ... ," Violet said.

"Yeah—*exactly*. That, too."

"I'm not gonna say it hadn't crossed my mind, but ... yeah. I guess it all *is* sort of weird...."

"Oh, and that's right," I said, suddenly remembering. "I forgot to tell you—but there's a *traitor* in La Liga!"

Violet's eyebrows shot up in surprise. "*A traitor?* Charlie, how do you know that?"

"One of those warlock heads told me back in Chiloé." Now, there was something you don't say every day.

"A chonchón?"

"Yeah."

"What'd it say?"

"That *one of our own* has turned against the rest. That

they've begun to pull away from the others. Something like that . . ."

Violet was nodding now, her eyes locked on mine. "Makes sense, actually . . ."

"*What?*"

"Think about it, Charlie. Whoever kidnapped Joanna was able to get *inside* the Provencia—all the way into *her study.*"

"Yeah, so?"

"Well, the Provencia is warded, isn't it? There are all sorts of protections and barriers on it to ward off evil. Which means whoever kidnapped her either knew their way around the place, or, and much more likely, is posing as one of the good guys. And the minairon even said that the conversation he overhead started off as *friendly.* That right there makes me think it's someone Joanna knows. A *friend,* even."

"You mean a *traitor,*" I said, and Violet nodded grimly.

"Did the chonchón say anything else? Any hints about who it might be?"

I thought back, shook my head. "Nah, that's it. . . ."

"Well, who's been pulling away from the others, then? Who haven't we seen hanging around the Provencia lately?"

Immediately two names popped into my head—but no, it couldn't be one of them . . . *could it?* I felt stupid and ridiculous and actually sort of *embarrassed* for even *considering* the possibility that either one could be the traitor—I mean, they'd both saved my life. On *multiple* occasions. Why would they have done that even *once* if they were really evil?

Violet must've seen the gears turning in my head, because she said, "Who are you thinking about, Charlie? Who is it?"

"El Justo Juez and El Cadejo. Haven't seen either one of them in *days*. . . ."

CHAPTER FIFTY-SIX

Just as I'd spoken those words, a strong wind blew across the flat hilltop, stirring the bushes and swirling our hair around our faces. I scanned the skies for one of those whirlwind thingies but didn't see any. Not even the wispy beginnings of a funnel cloud. I started to think Saci wasn't going to show. Maybe he'd spotted our trap and given us the slip. Or maybe he'd decided to skip town with our egg. Either way, our grand scheme was going up in flames. And as if that wasn't bad enough, right then I spotted some nosy kid jogging up the far side of the hill, just sort of casually looking around, like, *Oh, hey, I've never seen candles before. Let me go check that out!* He must've noticed them from below and wanted to see what was going on up here.

He's going to ruin everything! I thought, pushing up to my hands and knees, getting ready to leap out of the bushes to scare him off.

But an instant before I could—just a heartbeat, really—I noticed the kid wasn't actually jogging as much as he was *hopping* . . . a sort of one-legged kangaroo-like hop. Then he bounded out of the shadows and into a pale swatch of moonlight, and I saw why: He only had one leg. Just one—and I felt a spike of adrenaline flood my belly.

It was Saci!

CHAPTER FIFTY-SEVEN

t's HIM!" V whispered excitedly. "It's him! It's him! It's him!" She paused, rasped, "*Is it him . . . ?*"

"Oh, it's definitely him!" I said, and there wasn't the slightest doubt in my mind. But the legendary prankster looked *way* younger than I'd imagined, right around our age, give or take a year, which was what had thrown me off. I was expecting, like, at least a teenager or something; I mean, he was, after all, *thousands* of years old. And he was shorter than I'd imagined too—probably a couple of inches shorter than me, but about ten or fifteen pounds heavier. He wore bright red overall-shorts, one strap undone, with a shabby pointed cap, almost the exact color of his overalls, stuffed into the front pocket. His skin was a rich, deep black, like the sky on a moonless night. There were holes in both his hands, each one about the size of a silver dollar and perfectly round. Just like in every tale I'd ever heard about him, he only had one leg, but the leg was freakishly muscular. Sort of like a soccer player's leg, with all the little quad muscles showing above the knee. A pipe made of colorful seashells dangled from his lips, which were currently pulled back in a mischievous grin as his dark eyes flitted over our picnic spread.

My fingers tightened around the bungee cord as I watched the little punk glance suspiciously around the hillside, looking for the picnickers. When he didn't see anyone, his grin widened, and he began to tiptoe around, picking up the gold coins and stuffing them down the front of his baggy overalls while at the same time ripping open the sugar packets and streaming sugar into his wide, smiling mouth. Guess the kid really did have a legendary sweet tooth. He was shaking his head now, giggling as he scooped up the last of the coins.

We got him, I thought. This was *actually* going to work! And it was going to work because the dude simply could not help himself!

Just a little to your left, you sticky-fingered punk . . .

No sooner had the thought crossed my mind than those mischievous brown eyes once again flicked over our picnic spread. I could almost see the gears turning behind his eyes. Naughty ideas were filling his head like helium filling a balloon. He looked around, taking his time, and then waved a hand over the fruit—and instantly it all spoiled! The apples and bananas pulled one of those TV-commercial time-lapse tricks, turning dark purple and moldy right before our eyes. Saci, of course, thought this was the funniest thing in the whole world; he started laughing uncontrollably, all bent over and clutching his little potbelly, but managed to hold himself together long enough to pass a hand over the jug of milk, which instantly began to curdle and clump together like potter's clay.

And then it was too much for him. He fell over on his side, laughing and kicking and rolling around on the ground like he'd just played the greatest practical joke in the history of practical jokes.

Little did he know he was now lying smack in the middle of our trap.

"Get ready," V whispered, doubling her grip on the bungee cord as I did the same.

"Yep."

Had we been overly anxious, we might've sprung our trap a moment too soon. But we both knew we had only one shot at this. So we waited for the punk to get it all out of his system, waited for him to have a grand old time. Then, just as he started to push up, just as he began to rise, we yanked on our end of the bungee cord, and the loop lying hidden in the grass sprang to life with a loud *whoosh*, cinching around his ankle like a belt. The force of our combined yank swept his leg out from underneath him, and he hit the ground with a thud and an even louder yelp of surprise.

For a moment all V and I could do was stare, neither one of us *actually* believing that we'd managed to pull this off. But the fact was we *had*. We'd caught him! ¡Lo agarramos!

CHAPTER FIFTY-EIGHT

Violet and I were out of the bushes in a blur, charging toward Saci as he struggled and flailed and tried to figure out what the heck had just happened to him.

"Charlie, don't let go of the bungee cord!" Violet yelled, and Saci must've heard her, because his eyes snapped in our direction. He saw us, started to panic, and then began to spin in wild circles on his stomach like a break-dancing turtle. As he spun and spun, I noticed that he had cut the name from the back of a soccer jersey—a Neymar jersey— and sewn it onto the back of his overalls. Sort of a cool touch, I had to admit.

Overhead, the clouds churned. The wind picked up. Leaves and grass began to swirl around us, and I realized he was trying to whirlwind his way out of here.

But we were ready for that. Just as the winds began

to lift him off the ground, the bungee cord stretching to its absolute limit but not snapping (which was probably why the anchimayen had recommended it), V dug into her pocket, pulled out a brown-and-copper-beaded rosary that Mario had given us, and flung it right at his face. I knew from legend that throwing a rosary into his whirlwind could help capture him. But what I *didn't* expect was for the long string of shiny beads to fly straight at him through the swirling winds like a heat-seeking missile, wrapping itself around his wrists (even twisting its way through the holes in his hands) like a pair of living, intelligent hand-cuffs. Not a second later Saci dropped out of the sky and hit the ground—hard. Immediately the winds died. The funnel cloud vanished, and Violet and I were on him in a second, dropping our knees across his chest and holding him down with our hands as he glared up at us, struggling against the rosary, with his seashell pipe still somehow dangling from his lower lip.

"Remember us?" Violet asked.

Saci frowned. "You two look muito familiar. Have I pranked you before?"

"Lapa do Santo ring a bell? Didn't think you'd ever see us again, did ya?"

Saci was shaking his head, his eyes huge with shock. "Not really," he said, and it sounded like an honest answer.

"Get him up!" I growled, and while Violet hauled him to a seated position, I quickly yanked the cap out of his pocket and the pipe out of his mouth. Saci probably thought this was all payback. But it wasn't. Not exactly. See, my abuela had told me countless stories of the infamous *Saci Pererê*, and one of my favorites was about this little girl who'd snuck up on him in her kitchen late one afternoon while Saci was sprinkling flies into the large pot of stew her mother had been cooking. The girl snatched Saci's cap, and for the rest of that day Saci had had to obey her, and she made him go around doing good, like untying horses' tails (which he loved tying together) and unspoiling people's crops (which he did whenever he passed a field). Saci eventually got his cap back and went back to his pranks, but my thinking was that maybe that little girl had discovered something in his nature—something we could use to our advantage. Either way, I knew that both his cap and pipe were magical and that he treasured them—*especially* the cap, because it turned the wearer invisible. So I figured (well, *Violet* figured after I'd told her about them while we were shopping in the feria) that, at the very least, they'd make great bargaining chips.

"Hey, gimme dat back!" Saci yelled at me.

"You be quiet!" Violet snapped. "You tried to kill us, you li'l punk!"

"Ei! Hey! Never say dat! Saci never try to kill *no one*,

okay? I jess messin' wit you. Having some fun."

I pointed the pipe between his eyes, said, "Getting sucked up into a whirlwind isn't exactly our idea of *fun*."

His expression turned mischievous. "I know . . . but it's *mine*."

"I hope you know your stupid little prank might have cost a lot of people their lives," Violet said. "We had to travel *all the way* back across South America just to find your prankster butt. Now, you'll note my associate here is holding your beloved red cap and pipe, and if you don't wanna watch your *special* items go *exothermic*, you better give us back what you stole and give it back *right freaking now!*"

"Ei, you better untie these beads, okay? Saci getting angry now. . . ."

"Burn his hat!" Violet shouted, and I brought out the box of matches we'd bought at the feria.

"Ei, ei, ei—wait! Jess *WAIT!*" Saci shrieked in terror. "Saci only making the chitchat, okay . . . ? Why you gotta be so cruel?"

"You've got five seconds. I want to see passports, money, clothes—and most of all, I wanna see that *golden egg*."

His face screwed up in confusion. "Saci don't remember no golden egg. . . ."

"Charlie, how do you say 'ash the cap' in Spanish?"

"Quémalo."

"Then *quémalo!*"

"*Okay, okay!* Saci *may* remember the egg . . . jess hol' on there." A smile dimpled his chubby cheeks. "It's beautiful, no . . . ? Saci never seen nothing like it."

"Two seconds!" V yelled.

"Hol' on! Jess hol' it! You—you want your stuff . . . ? Okay. It's in my safe place, okay? My treasure room."

"Say good-bye to your cap," I said, and struck a match. It crackled to life, an orange halo of flame forming at its tip, and Saci panicked.

"Ei! I telling the truth! All you stuff is there! All safe!" He snapped his eyes to Violet and his voice dropped to a low, silky pitch. "You leave Saci's cap alone, and I even throw in a lovely pair of earrings for the very beautiful senhorita. . . ." He was grinning at her now, trying to look all suave and stuff.

But V saw right through it. "Yeah, no thanks," she said. "Keep your bribes."

Saci looked genuinely hurt. "Ei, you sting Saci's heart with those words. . . . Maybe we start over, okay? Why can't we jess be friends?"

"Because friendship means caring about someone other than yourself," I said. "And from everything I've heard about you, I don't think you're capable."

V glared at Saci. "Also, because I think you're obnoxious,

untrustworthy, and just about the *worst* kind of person."

"You two know me pretty good . . . ," Saci said, and grinned. "So, friends or not?"

"*Not.*" I held the match up to his cap. "Now, where's this 'treasure room' of yours?"

"Peru!" he answered quickly. "IS IN PERU!"

CHAPTER FIFTY-NINE

y eyes bugged. He had to be kidding..."PERU? That's, like, on the other side of the CONTI-NENT!" I shouted.

"And it's a *very* lovely place," Saci said. "Beautiful landscapes. Amazing people."

"But you're from *Brazil*. Why wouldn't you just keep your treasure room *here?*"

"Because that's where *everyone* would *expect* me to keep it. . . ." He looked at me like I was about as intelligent as a domesticated turkey. "Você está louco ou o quê?"

I'd heard enough. "So you want your cap well done or extra crispy?"

"No! PÁRE—I telling you da truth! You stuff is in Peru, okay? Now, you burn my cap, *deal off.* But if you give me chance, I take you to my place, okay?"

"Think we can trust him?" V whispered into my ear.

That was like asking if I thought it would be a good idea to leave our last jar of honey around Winnie the Pooh.

"He's basically the shrewdest, sneakiest, and arguably most *cunning* sombra of all time," I said. "No way we can trust him. But we have his cap; he's gonna play ball."

Violet glanced down at the cap. "Gosh, it really does reek, doesn't it?" she said, pinching her nose.

And she wasn't kidding. The thing smelled like a puke-inducing combination of rotten sardines, horsehair, a laundry basket full of unwashed gym clothes, and oddly enough, *chicken feed*. "The legends say he had a bruja put a spell on it so that everyone smells whatever smells worst to them. It's sort of like his security system. To discourage thieves."

"Pretty slick idea, actually."

"Yeah, he's sneaky smart." Then, turning back to Saci, I said, "Peru is, like, *three thousand miles* away. Do you have any idea how much time you've cost us? It's going to take *days* to get there!" And that was if the lobisomem didn't eat us first. Ya tu sabes. . . .

"Days?" Saci made a confused face. "Why days?"

"All right. On your feet, Neymar," I said, hauling him up. "Which way to the nearest train station? And not the Pearl of Luxury Travel, either. They're not exactly fans of ours."

"Why you wanna go to a train station for, huh?"

"Duh. To get to *Peru*. Were you not listening?"

"No, no, no, no. We don't need no silly train. *Saci* take us to Peru. And in *style!*"

"And how exactly does *Saci* plan to do that?"

"I show you." He held out his rosary-bead-bound hands. "Untie, please."

Violet glanced over at me. I shrugged. "We got his cap."

"You sure that's enough?"

The truth? I wasn't. More like 55 percent, but what I said was, "According to all the legends, it is."

Violet didn't sound very convinced. "If you say so . . ." She began to untie Saci, and when she was finished, he broke out into a little dance—bouncing up and down on his toes, his hips swinging this way and that as he high-stepped, hopped, and bopped all over the place. I thought I recognized the dance too—the samba, maybe? Which made sense, since it was one of Brazil's most popular dances.

"Less do it!" Saci said, offering me a high five. I scowled at him, but it didn't wipe that big mischievous grin off his face. "Ei, start dancing. . . ."

"*What?*"

"You want this to work or not? *Dance!*"

"Is he serious?" Violet said.

"No idea." But since it was impossible to know with this guy, we started dancing just in case. And was this quickly becoming one of the most embarrassing moments of my life? You bet. Let's just say I wasn't exactly J-Lo on the dance floor. More like J-No.

Saci, meanwhile, was laughing his annoying little head off. "You two dance so *bad*! You need lessons! No, forget it—I no think even lessons can help!"

A second before I could say something my mom probably wouldn't have approved of, Saci twirled and shouted "AÇÚCAR!" and suddenly a cold wind picked up around us. It swirled and gusted, flapping our clothes and sending our recently purchased picnic blanket flying off the side of the hill. Lightning crackled across the sky.

Then, with an enormous SAWHOOOOOOSH, all three of us were sucked straight up in the swirling, whirling, roaring heart of a funnel cloud!

For one crazy second, I had an epic bird's-eye view of the entire Cabana Mesa hill and the vast, wild jungle surrounding it. Then it was gone, lost in a blur of whipping, screaming wind as we rose up, up, up into the pitch-dark sky.

CHAPTER SIXTY

eing sucked into a funnel cloud was like being sucked into a giant vacuum cleaner. Or at least what I imagined that would be like. A huge, screaming wind that swept you off your feet and spun you in crazy circles as the world whipped by and even more wind screamed in your ears. Icy winds tore at my clothes. My hair blew around my face, stinging my eyes, my temples. I couldn't see where we were going—the entire world had become this giant, shrieking blur—but I could *feel* us traveling not only up but also *forward* somehow. It was the strangest (and probably most terrifying) feeling I'd ever experienced in my entire life, and I was about 99 percent sure I'd left my stomach somewhere back on Cabana Mesa.

When the world finally stopped spinning, we found ourselves standing in a narrow alley between two tall cement buildings. The ground was gray cobblestone. A pair of large green dumpsters, their lids propped open by piles of overstuffed garbage bags, blocked off the alleyway behind us. From pretty much every direction came the frantic sound of road traffic—honking horns, the high-pitched squeal of slamming breaks, revving engines.

"Where the heck are we?" Violet asked, leaning back against the wall, looking a little green. I wobbled to the mouth of the alley and peeked out. Across a couple of lanes of bumper-to-bumper traffic was a wide slate-paved plaza decorated with colorful flower beds, trees, and a huge concrete-and-bronze statue of some dude riding a horse. Groups of tourists strolled casually about, a few taking selfies by the antique-looking lampposts, others lounging on one of the hundred or so wrought-iron benches. Traffic swirled around the square in a dizzying blur of yellow taxis, red municipal buses, and delivery guys on shiny green mopeds weaving their way between both. Compared to the wild jungles and farmland of east central Brazil, this place looked like downtown Miami on steroids.

"I think we're in Peru," I said, glancing back at Violet. "Lima, maybe." I could feel a stupid smile spreading across my face; we'd actually *whirlwinded* (definitely not a word, but it should be) all the way from Brazil to the opposite coast of *South America*. Just the thought was enough to make my brain spin, not that it wasn't already. . . .

Saci, meanwhile, had strolled up beside me and was pointing across the street with his seashell pipe, which he'd somehow taken back from Violet. I had to resist the urge to smack it out of his hand.

"See that hotel?" he said. "That's where I keep my all my good stuff, entende? It's, like, my home away from home.... You heard this expression?"

He put one chubby little hand on my shoulder, and I shrugged it off. "Yeah, I've heard it."

The hotel across the street—or Saci's "home away from home"—actually looked pretty classy, like the sort of place where dignitaries or even presidents might stay on important visits. It was about half a city block wide and about six stories tall, but it blended nicely with all the other buildings that flanked the square on four sides. A doorman in a sleek black-and-red buttoned-up suit stood by the entrance, greeting guests as they climbed out of limos and expensive-looking sports cars. In all honesty, I was a little surprised Saci had picked such a stylish place to hide his treasures. But it wasn't until I saw the name of the hotel—GRAN HOTEL BOLÍVAR—on the sign above the tall glass doors that I realized the *true* twisted genius of it.

"A hotel?" Violet snatched the pipe out of Saci's hand, sounding more than a little annoyed. "That's, like, the *stupidest place* you could've picked...."

"He didn't pick just any old hotel," I explained. "He picked the most *haunted* hotel on the entire *continent.*"

"*What?*"

"Gran Hotel Bolívar. Anyone who knows haunted hotels knows *that place.*"

"It's true," Saci said with a sort of proud grin.

"In fact, the fifth and sixth floor are so haunted, I heard they don't even let guests up there anymore!"

"Not true!" Saci objected. "Dey let people stay there. Jess no one usually lasts the whole night . . . but dey *allowed.* Don' be scaredy-cats—vamos!"

CHAPTER SIXTY-ONE

The lobby of the Gran Hotel Bolívar had this cool 1910s vibe to it and was a whole heck of a lot nicer than I expected a famously haunted hotel to be, with pink marble columns, polished marble floors, and expensive-looking artwork hanging from the oak-paneled walls. As we passed one of the alcoves where three ladies in fancy flower dresses and pearls were sitting at a table sipping tea, Saci clapped his hands together, and suddenly all three of them spat mouthfuls of tea in each other's faces. At the same moment some young guy in a tux was proposing to his girlfriend on the opposite side of the room; Saci raised his hand, and the bouquet of roses the guy was holding out to the girl along with the ring instantly wilted like month-old lettuce.

Saci giggled under his breath, and V and I both turned to glare at him. "Wha'? It's my nature. . . . Saci cannot help."

Then he snapped his fingers, and a bellboy who was hurrying past us with a handful of luggage slipped on a suddenly slick patch of floor and went down in a tangle of arms and leather suitcases.

"Charlie, how do you say 'You're awful' in Spanish?" V asked me, so I said, "Eres horrible," and she repeated it to Saci with pretty decent pronunciation.

Which had Saci grinning. "Gracias." Then, sticking his tongue out at her: "Saci can speak Spanish, too. . . ."

At the end of the hall we came to a service elevator. A large laminated sign above the doors clearly read FUERA DE SERVICIO/OUT OF SERVICE, but Saci obviously wasn't big on following rules, so—in typical Saci style—he dipped into the front of his overalls, brought out a fat black marker, then turned the sign around and wrote *El ascensor se siente mucho mejor ahora* (which translates to "The elevator's feeling much better now") all while giggling like a five-year-old and punching the up button.

Violet sighed. "If your pranks had a butt, I'd kick it."

A moment later the elevator doors opened with a ding, and the first thing I noticed was that the floor buttons were arranged vertically—and in ascending order—on the elevator's stainless-steel control panel. The second thing was that all of them were available for selection, except of course for the top two—floors five and six—which had squares of cardboard with the international symbol for "no" (a red circle with a diagonal line through it) taped over them.

I said, "Maybe we should take the hint?"

Saci gave me a sideways smirk. "Don' be so chicken, sassy...." Then he peeled off the cardboard square covering the sixth floor, taped it over the button for the first floor, and jabbed number six with his thumb.

Violet looked like she was going to say something but held back. A second later the doors rumbled closed, and a loud, metallic squeal sounded overhead. I pictured busted gears turning—or rather, *trying* to turn but being too twisted or rusted to actually accomplish it.

I was about to ask if this elevator was even safe to use when the whole thing suddenly jerked into motion. "That's reassuring," I mumbled.

"Sassy, I tole already," Saci said, turning to me, "*calm down.*"

"Why do you keep calling me that?" I snapped.

He pointed at Alvin's K-G G-*Shock*, which happened to be hanging out of my shirt again. "That's what you name tag say...."

"It's not a *name tag*," I grumbled. "It's a *dog collar*. And it doesn't belong to me."

"You always wear stuff dat no belong to you?" He gave me a sly sideways grin.

"It's a long story. Plus, it's none of your business."

"You smell funny, too. Like doggie shampoo."

I groaned.

"And I didn't wanna say nuttin'," he went on, "but, *man*, you fashion sense *sooooo* bad. . . . Why you wearing some bony old fingers round you neck, anyway?"

I shook my head. *This guy.* . . .

"What's wrong, Sassy?"

"I told you already—that's NOT my name!"

"You know what dey say: If da collar fits . . ."

"No one says that. That's not a thing."

Facing forward now, Saci began to bounce up and down on his toes like he was warming up for a soccer match. When he caught Violet staring, he was all like, "Wha'?"

"Scared?" she asked.

The corners of his lips curled mischievously. "You have to be *crazy* not to be. . . ."

CHAPTER SIXTY-TWO

The elevator doors opened on a long, freakishly narrow hall lined with ornate wooden doors—about a dozen or so on either side. Cobwebs hung like curtains from the low ceilings. A couple of them even stretched across doorways like dusty, silky barriers. On our left there was a row of ancient-looking sconces set a few feet apart along the wall. Their bleary reddish light cast strange shadows over the ceilings and doors, giving the whole place that spooky, half-lit feel of a haunted house. Even spookier, I could hear strange sounds coming from under those doors and echoing up the hall toward us—heavy footsteps . . . the squeal of floorboards . . . distant moans and groans.

My eyes slid to Saci. "I thought you said there were no people on this floor."

"People?" he whispered. "Nope, no people . . ." The way

he said "people" sent a shiver down my spine. I really, really didn't like this floor.

The elevator gave a sudden jerk, and all three of us screamed. Then the doors began to close, and Saci had to stick his arm out to stop them.

"After you," he said, motioning us out.

Violet narrowed her eyes at him. "Try again."

Saci's lips puckered into a frown. He looked like a little kid who'd just been yelled at for breaking a dish. "Why Saci gotta go first, huh?"

"Because it was *Saci* who decided to prank us. And because it was *Saci* who thought it would be a *brilliant idea* to take our stuff and hide it in *one of the scariest, most haunted places in the southern hemisphere!*"

He gave Violet puppy-dog eyes. "Saci sorry, okay? Forgive, forgive?"

"Just walk." Violet sighed.

As we stepped out of the elevator, I noticed for the first time that there was some sort of greasy fog hanging low and thin over the dusty carpet. It wasn't smoke—at least it didn't *smell* like smoke—but the stuff seemed to be seeping out of everywhere, from the AC ducts, every crack and crevice in the walls, even from under the doors. Almost as freaky was the sharp drop in temperature; the hallway must've been a solid *twenty degrees* colder than the elevator. My breath came out in small white puffs as we followed klepto-Neymar slowly down the hall. I could feel my heart pounding painfully against my ribs. My throat had begun to burn from the cold.

Why the heck did we follow this little twerp up here?

Real smart, Charlie.

As we passed a door—one of the few that stood slightly open—I thought I saw a shadow flicker across it, an almost humanlike shape. It vanished before I could say anything, but I was pretty sure Saci had seen it too, because he started moving faster, hopping rapidly along like a kangaroo late for work.

About halfway up the hall, Saci stopped at a door with a bronze plaque that read 603. "We're here," he whispered.

"Well, let's go," Violet said, and Saci nodded, sucking in a deep breath before wrapping his chubby fingers around the old-fashioned knob.

But he didn't turn it immediately; instead he looked back and whispered seven of the scariest words I'd heard in my entire life:

"Don't believe anything you see in there."

CHAPTER SIXTY-THREE

S uite 603 looked more like the secret hangout of some teenage *bazillionaire* than a hotel room. There were mounds of golden coins scattered everywhere. Gaming consoles—at least two hundred of them, everything from original Ataris to the latest handhelds— were stacked almost to the ceiling on the dining table and the L-shaped countertop of the little kitchenette. Piles of old- and new-school soccer jerseys were draped over the sofas and the row of flat-screen TVs, along with a whole mess of playing gear: shin guards and cleats, yellow-and-green soccer socks, sleeveless undershirts. I noticed that a bunch of the items (especially the jerseys) were signed, and most of the signatures belonged to either Pelé, Kaká, Ronaldinho, or Neymar. "Dude . . . ," I said, picking my way inside in a half daze. I mean, there was more signed gear in here than in the Football Museum in São Paulo! Beyond the living room area, along the back wall of the room, were rows and rows of trophies, almost all of them either silver or gold, including what looked like a genuine Ballon d'Or (which is the equivalent of an MVP trophy), and an *equally* legit-looking FIFA World Cup trophy! I could literally feel my jaw dangling down around my ankles. Who the heck has their very own *World Cup* trophy? Some of the greatest players of *all time* didn't even have one!

"Bro, where did you get all this *stuff* . . . ?" I couldn't help asking.

When Saci didn't say anything, I glanced over my shoulder to look at him—and realized he wasn't there. Neither was Violet.

I had a split second to wonder if they'd gone off into another room when suddenly the world around me changed: I was no longer standing in the middle of Saci's hotel room—no, in fact, I wasn't even in *Peru* anymore! Somehow—*someway*—I'd been transported two thousand plus miles north, back to that little house on Giralda Avenue. To the very kitchen in South Florida where I'd battled La Cuca—the very kitchen where she'd almost *ended* me. To my right was the small breakfast nook. Past it, beyond the counter, stood the sink that overlooked the backyard crowded with palm trees. Dizzy with shock, with panic, I blinked around the room, wondering if a) this was Saci's most elaborate prank yet, or b) I'd accidentally stepped through some invisible rip in the space-time continuum and had actually wound up back in Miami.

"*What's going on . . . ?*" I heard myself breathe.

And the answer that came was: *It's a trap!*

I had no idea where those words had come from. But they *felt* true.

Just then a terrifying—and terrifyingly familiar—cackle echoed around me. Every single hair on my body stood on end as I turned over one shoulder to see a tall cloaked figure in robes as black as the night itself stalk out from the hallway to my left.

The figure stopped less than ten feet away, pushing back its hood to reveal a hard and haughty face with eyes so green they were almost black.

Instantly the blood turned to ice in my veins. My breath escaped me in a half-choked gasp.

No, I thought, dazed. *No, it can't be. . . .*

Yet there she was. La Cuca.

She was *back!*

CHAPTER SIXTY-FOUR

ow? . . . I mean, HOW?" was all I managed. Not
exactly Shakespeare, I know. But I was in so much
shock that the fact my mouth still worked—if only
barely—was a small miracle in its own right.

La Cuca's bloodred lips split into an evil grin as her
eyes locked with mine. "You didn't think you had *actually*
defeated me, did you . . . ? A runt like you?"

Her suddenly furious gaze blazed brighter. In that same
moment some invisible force seized me, pinning my arms to
my sides and making it impossible to move, scream, or even
blink. Immediately my survival instincts began screaming at
me to do something—*anything!*—but before I could figure
out exactly *what,* the witch tightened her hold, tightened it
around my *throat,* and now I couldn't breathe! Another wave
of panic crashed over me as I struggled and squirmed, trying to break free. But it didn't take me long to realize that it

was completely useless. This was just like the last time we'd fought—there was no way to overpower her!

"You're too *weak*, Charlie. . . ." La Cuca laughed, sending a chill, like an icy blade, through my heart. "You can't control your manifestations. You can't help Joanna. You can't save those you love. You can't even save *yourself!*" As she stalked forward, her long, black-nailed fingers slowly curled into fists and the pressure around my throat suddenly clamped down like a vise. Waves of agony crashed over me. Black spots danced in front of my eyes.

I grimaced, crying out in pain, though no sound actually made it out of my mouth. Already I could feel my lungs burning for oxygen, starving for it; could feel myself teetering on the verge of consciousness. Worse, there wasn't a single thing I could do about it. *Nada!*

But even more terrifying was the realization that when la bruja was finished with me, she'd go after Violet next. And then she'd go after my par—

Hold up a sec! I shouted at myself. *This makes, like, ZERO, sense. . . .*

How could La Cuca be here with me when *here* didn't even exist anymore? This house had been *obliterated* during our battle. And how could she be standing right in front of me, looking as whole and evil as the first day we'd met when I'd already defeated her, when I'd already watched her burn up in the mesosphere like a falling comet?

Two really good questions. And the answer, of course, was pretty simple: She couldn't.

Which meant that none of this was actually happening. . . .

"This isn't real," I heard myself say.

And it was right then, right as the truth of those words sank in, that the scene around me once again changed: Suddenly La Cuca vanished, as did the rest of the house on Giralda.

I was back in Saci's hotel room again. And the second *that* sank in, I looked wildly around and spotted Violet first, then Saci. V was off in the far corner, crying and shivering, while on the other side of the room, by the row of flat-screen TVs, Saci was on his hands and knees pleading with a stack of Blu-ray players in Portuguese). Kind of curious what that was about (but also kind of *not*), I rushed over to Violet and hauled her up by her shoulders.

"V, snap out of it!" I shouted. "It's not REAL!"

I'd basically shouted it right in her face, but it didn't seem to have gotten through, because she was fighting me now, struggling and squirming like a rabid raccoon as she yanked madly at my wrists, trying to break my grip. "WHY? BUT WHY?" she kept yelling over and over again.

"Violet!" I yelled into her ear. "WAKE! UP!"

Her eyes seemed to focus for a second. But instead of snapping out of it, she screamed and slapped me. *Hard.* Which wasn't exactly the response I'd been hoping for.

I shook her, shouted, "HEY, NOT NICE!" And, naturally, she slapped me again, this time making cartoon birdies fly lazy circles in front of my eyes. There weren't any mirrors around so I couldn't tell for sure, but I was willing to bet she'd left a Hollywood-Walk-of-Fame-style handprint on my left cheek. Nice.

I rubbed my face, trying to get the sting out, and could hear Saci yelling something about sparing his Ballon d'Or— "Take me!" it sounded like he was saying. "Just don't hurt the trophy!" I had no idea if these hallucinations could leave permanent brain damage, but I *did* know that we didn't need to make Saci any more of a wild card than he already was. I had to do something. And fast.

"Violet, c'mon!" I shouted. "We don't have time for this!" When she ignored me, I looked around, spotted a signed Gatorade bottle (it looked like it had been signed by Dani Alves) inside the mouth of the World Cup trophy.

Thinking fast, I snatched it up, twisted the cap open, and squeezed. An icy blast of blue nitro nailed Violet square between the eyes, and she let out a huge gasp.

Her eyes blinked into focus. Sticky bluish tears streaked down her cheeks.

"That wasn't—"

"*Real?*" I asked. "No. Now help me get Saci and let's make like trees!"

"Huh?"

"Haven't you ever watched *Back to the Future*? I'm saying we gotta leave!"

Violet didn't need convincing. We rushed over to Saci, V taking one arm, me the other; then we began to haul him toward the door. No easy task considering the guy probably weighed as much as a fridge. He wore the weight well, though—I had to give him that.

"WAIT!" Violet shouted suddenly. "OUR STUFF!" She hustled over to the table in the dining room, where, I now saw, our money, passports, and clothes had been stacked into a big messy pile next to an equally messy pile of signed trading cards. "Your book bag!" she shouted. So I tossed it to her, and she quickly dumped the rice and put all our stuff back where it belonged.

Okay, so maybe I should've dumped the rice myself a while ago, but the truth was my mom's Cuban, which meant I'd basically grown up on the stuff, and I hated the idea of wasting any. Especially when it could be used to make a rockin' plate of arroz con frijoles.

While Violet was gathering our stuff, I happened to glance around the room—and spotted our egg! It was on

Saci's couch, trapped between two cushions and glowing faintly. Not wasting any time, I snatched it up and slipped it into the inside pocket of my shorts (making sure Saci didn't see me do it) for *extra* safekeeping.

"Wait! Where's the egg?" Violet shouted.

"Already got it!" I shouted back. Then together we hauled Saci the rest of the way across the room. The instant we dragged him through the door and out into the hall, his eyes snapped open, and he began flailing around.

"QUE, WHAT—WHO?" His gaze rose to meet Violet's. "Did we make it out?"

She nodded. "Barely."

"Oh, and thank you *so much* for storing our stuff in such a *wonderful* place," I said, rolling my eyes. "Had a blast in there."

Saci looked around at us, giving a sleepy-eyed, dazed sort of grin, and said, "Me think dis is da start of a beautiful friendship!"

"Shut up!" Violet and I snapped.

CHAPTER SIXTY-FIVE

By the time we made it down into the hotel lobby and back outside, the sun was setting again (which was one of the side effects of traveling backward through time zones—Lima, Peru, time was exactly two hours behind central Brazil), and the sidewalks were packed with people in suits and other business attire catching rides home or heading out for the evening. Still feeling a little dazed (actually feeling like someone had dropped my brain into a meat grinder, then ran it through a high-speed juicer), I asked, "What the heck happened to us up there, huh?"

"Da spell that protect my room," Saci explained, "it makes you see you worst fear. That way no one wanna stay there, snoop around, entende?"

Yeah, I definitely understood. It was hard not to once you'd experienced it.

Violet, who was looking a bit dazed herself, nudged me on the arm. "Charlie, we need to focus. We have to get to El Dorado already."

And she was right. So we both turned to look at Saci, who stared back at us, shaking his head. "Wha? Wha you lookin' at Saci for? I not some mythological tour guide. . . ."

V's eyes flicked back to me. "So . . . ?"

I shrugged. "So . . . ?"

"Where do you think it is?" she asked me.

"You mean El Dorado? How am I supposed to know?"

"Well, Mario did tell us it was somewhere in Colombia. You don't remember anything from any legends that might give us a little more to work with."

I tried to think back. "I mean, I know most explorers and treasure hunters believed it was inside Lake Guatavita, which I think is somewhere in central Colombia."

Violet beamed at me. "I think you're starting to get the hang of this investigative journalist thing."

"But, V, none of those treasure hunters ever found it. Which means it's probably not there."

"True, but we know it's somewhere in Colombia, so we might as well start there. Plus, it's our only lead." She turned back to Saci. "Okay, here's the deal, Neymar. Whirl-wind us over to Colombia—*Lake Guatavita*. And after you help us find our friend, you're free to go. Deal?"

The sweet-toothed prankster snickered at that. "Ha. Colombia. From here? Você está louca?"

"What's the big deal?" I said. "You got us *here* all the way from *Brazil*."

"Saci not *machine*, manequim! Saci need *rest*. Saci need *food*. Saci need pranks and funnies to get him excited and happy!" He paused, giving us a pouty look as his dark eyes moved past us, up the block. "But maybe Saci know another way...."

"Well?" Violet said.

"Is right on the tippy of my tongue...." He smacked his lips together, grinning at her. "Hmm. Maybe you give Saci some sugar it help jog my memory."

V cut him a sideways look. "*Excuse me?*"

"I talking about those sugar packs you use to lure Saci onto the hill. *Hellooooo?* What you think I mean, huh?"

"Never mind." She took out one of the leftover sugar packs from her bag, tossed it to him, and we both watched as he tore it open and poured a stream of sugar into his mouth.

Okay, now, I had a pretty big sweet tooth myself. I could probably live off tres leches, which is this sugary, milky, custardy dessert. But just eating the stuff right out of packets like that ...? Yeah, that was a whole 'nother level of sugar cravings.

Violet only stared. "You do know that refined sugars

have been linked with a whole mess of health issues, including obesity and diabetes, right?"

Saci nodded, loudly chewing sugar. "I know. But Saci love it! I addicted. You know Saci's dream? Own a *huge* sugarcane farm with all different kinda sugarcane, make lots and lots of sugar, and jess eat it all day long!"

"Cool story," V said. "Now are you gonna tell us the other way to get to Colombia or what?"

"Hmm . . . still right on the tippy of my tongue. Maybe you gimme my pipe back, that *really* help jog my memory?"

"Oh, c'mon, now you're just messing with us!" I shouted.

"No, dis *true*! It could help . . . *maybe.*"

Sighing, Violet reached into her bag, came out with his pipe.

"Obrigada, obrigada, obrigada!" Saci chanted happily as she handed it to him. "You *soooo* much nicer than Sassy"—glaring at *me* now—"I like you much better!"

"For your information," Violet said, "smoking is a disgusting habit. It kills millions of people. *A year.* And it's responsible for tooth decay and a whole bunch of other respiratory issues I don't really feel like getting into."

"Man, you like a walking public service announcement!" Saci shouted, sounding almost impressed. "But no worry . . . Dis pipe ain't for smoking."

Violet didn't look convinced. "What's it for, then?"

"My apartment is where I keep my *good* stuff. My pipe is where I keeps the *rest* of my stuff. Plus, I like to chew on it." He grinned at her and V gave an annoyed sigh.

"You going to get us to Colombia or not?" I said.

"Ei, sim, sim. Come!"

We followed him to the corner of the busy street, where an open-backed shipping truck with crates of raw vegetables and freshly picked flowers sat parked along the curb. The driver—or at least a man I assumed was the driver—was standing in the loading bay of the tall building to our left, talking to some lady in an orange hard hat.

"Climb on back!" Saci whispered. "Go! Go!"

Violet's eyes narrowed. "*What?*"

"Rápido, por favor! No waste time!"

Shaking our heads, we both climbed on, glaring at him.

"I got a bad feeling about this," I admitted.

Violet dug the heels of her hands into her eyes. "And I'm feeling a little light-headed."

"You need food!" Saci said. "Same thing happen to my cat. Hol' on!" He peered cautiously around, like a bandit just before a bank robbery. Then he turned sideways, hiding his pipe (and his hands) from the view and seemed to reach *into* the mouth of said pipe. His arm went in almost to his elbow (at least it appeared to), and he came out with—a *chicken* . . . ?

I had to blink. I almost couldn't believe my eyes. But there it was, some strange orange-and-blue-feathered chicken, clucking and *bawk-bawk*ing and peeking airheadedly at nothing. "Ay, sorry. Wrong thing." He stuffed the chicken back into his pipe and this time came out with a couple of nice-looking yellow bananas. He grinned. "Saci *love* plátanos! Yellow Saci's favorite color, you see. Green, number two." Handing one to each of us, he said, "There you go. Now eat you plátano. Relax. Fique tranquilo. Saci gonna handle everything."

He'd started to turn when Violet grabbed back of his overalls, stopping him. "Hey. You try anything funny, and your cap's toast. *Literally.*"

"C'mon, you know Saci . . . ," he said with a sly grin.

"I do. That's why I'm warning you."

His grin widened. "Eat you plátano. Saci be right back."

Watching him go, I said to Violet, "Wouldn't eat that if I were you. You don't know where his pipe's been."

Two minutes later Saci came back, grinning widely, and climbed onto the truck beside me. "We go to Colombia now," he announced proudly. "Lake Guatavita. Is all taken care of . . ."

Violet shot him the same sort of deeply distrustful

look teachers reserve only for the most devious students. "What? You paid the guy or something?"

"Pay him?" Saci sounded insulted—hurt, even. "No, no, no, no . . . Saci change his papers and add Lake Guatavita as his next stop. Then I sneak and put it in his little GPS machine too!" He burst out laughing. "You two proud of Saci or what?"

Or what, I thought. "That's the guy's livelihood you're messing with," I pointed out.

"Ei—*relax*. He heading north anyway. Now he just going *a little bit* farther north, okay?" Clasping his hands behind his bald, shiny head, he lay back against a stack of crates, stretching his leg out in front of him and wiggling his toes as the truck suddenly lurched into motion. "Saci take care of everything. . . . Dis gonna be one *smooth* ride."

But there was something about the mischievous twinkle in his eyes, about the way his lips curled up at the corners, plus everything I'd ever heard about him from my abuela's stories—not to mention the seemingly never-ending string of pranks he'd pulled over his thousand-year-plus existence— that made me think it was going to be anything *but*.

CHAPTER SIXTY-SIX

A few hours later I jerked awake. It was dark now, and the delivery truck was droning along some winding stretch of blacktop framed by little hills and trees silhouetted against the starry night sky. I didn't remember falling asleep, but with the cool wind blowing in my face and the way the truck rumbled and hopped and hummed underneath us, it was no surprise I had. Something had woken me, though—not quite a sound or a touch, but a *feeling*. . . . Something was up.

Blinking, I looked drowsily around and saw *exactly* what that something was: Saci. The guy might've been fast asleep, snoring up a storm, but he *also* happened to be clutching Queen Joanna's crown tightly against his chest like it was his favorite nighttime snuggle toy. Which meant the sticky-fingered punk had been going through our stuff again!

"Can't *believe* this . . . ," I grumbled, and reached over to snatch it away. But his fingers wouldn't give it up; the dude had a *killer* grip—even in his sleep!

Scooting closer to him, I brought my legs around so I could plant my feet firmly on his shoulders and rip the crown out of his greedy little paws, but I accidentally kicked the pipe out of his mouth in the process. It clattered onto the truck bed, emitting a wisp of gray smoke.

Wait. Was it . . . *lit?* Because forget about a health hazard. Sleeping with a smoldering pipe around all these crates and boxes would've been a full-blown *safety* hazard!

Frowning, I picked it up. A faint reddish glow shone deep down in the bowl. But even weirder, the bowl looked impossibly *deep.* . . . I couldn't see the bottom.

Except it had to have one. Everything did.

Squinting, thinking what an odd pipe this was (which, in all honesty, wasn't that surprising considering its owner), I peered closer, almost touching my eye to the bowl. . . .

And suddenly the world around me began to spin and sway like a top!

The trees, the road—even the boxes and crates on the back of the truck—swirled into a dizzying, dark brownish blur. Somehow only the seashell pipe remained in focus, and I watched it grow larger and larger while at the same time I felt myself tipping forward as a strange sensation began to prickle over my skin: a feeling of tightening, of shrinking—of *falling*. I plummeted through the swirling, spinning world, screaming, my arms and legs flailing, searching for something to grab on to—something to stand on—but not finding anything.

Then the ground rushed up to meet me, and I landed hard enough to feel the jolt of the impact shudder all the way up my spine and to the top of my reeling brain.

Gasping, wobbling, my heart flopping around in my chest like a drowning fish, I blinked my streaming eyes, looking left . . . right.

I was now standing in the middle of a small, cluttered room that smelled oddly of smoke and something else . . . *banana milkshakes*, maybe?

The walls were some kind of corky wood; so were the floors and the soot-stained ceilings, which sloped up to a big, circular opening way high above.

All around me rose huge mountains made up of the most random stuff: marbles, packs of playing cards, candy bars, sunglasses, car keys, bags of cassava chips (Mama Mia brand), books, vinyl records, and, yep, bananas—there must've been *truckloads* here. From neon green to bright sunshine yellow, most still clinging to the wide flopping leaves they'd grown on. Neat foot-high piles of rice littered the floors. Old-school aluminum toys gleamed on the few tables and chairs scattered about. The place looked like some sort of hoarder's paradise.

But what *was* this place? And more importantly, *where* was this place . . . ?

And where was Violet? And Saci? They'd been right next to me just a sec—

Just then the peak of the nearest mountain of junk began to rumble. A stack of Blu-rays cascaded down its side like a mini avalanche. Something soft and plasticky-sounding went *POP!* I froze like I was playing a life-or-death game of Red-Light, Green-Light and felt my heart somersault into my throat as some sort of tiny-headed monster poked its tiny monster head out from between a pair of old tennis shoes.

Wait, not a monster—it was a *chicken.*

And a familiar one too . . . Orange and blue feathers. Brown beak.

I'd seen that chicken before. And recently.

Suddenly it all clicked. The chicken. The random piles of junk. The stink of smoke.

¡DIOS MÍO! I'VE BEEN SUCKED INTO SACI'S PIPE!

"HEEEEELLPPP!" I began to shout wildly, turning my face up toward the big hole in the ceiling, which was very obviously now the opening in the pipe bowl. "VIOLET! I'M IN THE PIPE! V—HEEEEELLLP!"

I shut up for sec, listening for a reply. Some sign that

someone—*anyone*—had heard me. But all I heard were crickets. Like, *literal* crickets. They were hopping around everywhere. High-diving off the mountains of junk. "Why isn't anyone talking back . . .?" I wondered out loud.

Because they can't hear you, answered a tiny voice inside my brain. Which, of course, sent another rush of panic swirling in my chest. *You're probably like AN INCH tall right now, dude!*

I started turning in fast circles. I had to find a way out of here. ASAP! But *how?* Climbing out of the bowl was a total no-go; the opening was *way* out of my reach, and when I say *way out,* I mean like past Pluto, round the bend of the Milky Way, and halfway out across the known universe. Not even the tallest junk mountains rose that high.

But there had to be another way. Another end to this thing, didn't there?

Of course there was—the stem! That was my way out!

Now, was it going to be super gross? Duh. Saci always had that end stuck in his mouth. But crawling through a tunnel of nasty, sticky saliva was definitely better than spending the rest of my life with El Pollo Loco over there.

I'd just started my climb up Mount Everjunk, my feet slipping and sliding on the mess of old toothbrushes, remote controls, and empty leather wallets, when a painting caught my eye. It was half buried in junk, but the half I could see stopped me dead in my tracks: It was a painting of *Queen Joanna*!

She was kneeling, weeping, beside some elaborate wooden coffin, a dark veil pulled low over her pale, tear-streaked face.

The mood of the painting was obviously somber, but the colors were so bright and vivid, they appeared almost *wet*. In fact, the tears running down Joanna's face looked like they were running *down* the painting, down the canvas itself!

It reminded me of the paintings I'd seen in the Warlock's Cave—the lienzos—and I remembered Mario telling me how Saci loved to take these things and replace them with kids' finger paintings to mess with the witches and warlocks.

Without thinking, I reached out to touch one of wet-looking tears on Jo's cheek—

And the moment my fingertips grazed the paint—the very instant my skin made contact with the oil or acrylic or whatever it was—a web of dark tendrils exploded right out of the canvas!

Tentacle-like and slimy, they wrapped themselves around me, the tendrils tugging and pulling on my arms, my back, even as I struggled and screamed, and then they were snaking around my head, over my eyes, and before I could scream again, my entire world went pitch-dark.

CHAPTER SIXTY-SEVEN

When the tendrils vanished, I was standing in a vast, ancient-looking church. Candles in gilded candlesticks glowed on the walls, their flames burning low, casting long, flickering shadows over the endless rows of empty benches.

Up near the front stood a large wooden casket, etched with an intricate coat of arms—castles, roaring lions, golden eagles—surrounded by great wreaths of colorful flowers; it was the same casket I'd seen in the painting . . . and the same person I'd seen kneeling beside it was still here now, still weeping.

"Queen Joanna!" I shouted almost automatically. And even though I couldn't have been standing more than ten yards away, it didn't seem like she'd heard me. She just kept weeping over the casket, her arms stretched over it in a sort of awkward embrace. Still a little dazed, I opened my mouth to shout her name again when I realized it was pointless—she wasn't going to be able to hear me.

And that was because *I* wasn't actually here.

Or at least, *hadn't* been.

This was a scene from Joanna's past—a memory she'd turned into a lienzo!

"You don't touch the paintings," Mario had told us, and now I understood why. Because apparently these paintings touched *back*.

"You have to let them bury the body . . . ," said a tight voice at my back, startling me.

I spun around to see a young woman in a simple black gown standing in the aisle. Her hands were clasped politely in front of her, and she was staring anxiously at the queen. "It's been almost ten days now . . . ," she whispered. "The priests are beginning to complain about the smell." Joanna, meanwhile, hadn't stopped sobbing—hadn't even looked up, in fact. "Mi reina, you must leave this place. . . . You *must* return to your throne or the politicians will run you off it. Some have already begun to incite the people; they've come up with a nickname for you—Juana la Loca."

I stared at her for a moment, confused. Juana la Loca was a famous Spanish queen from the sixteenth century. But the woman currently kneeling and weeping beside the big fancy casket was very *obviously* Queen Joanna.

So why had that lady just called her Juana la Loca . . . ?

"If you keep this up, they'll have you locked up," said the lady. "Or *worse*."

Finally, Joanna looked up. Her face was a trembling mask of tears. "You know I'm not crazy, Yolanda—I'm in *love*."

The girl offered her a sympathetic smile. "Mi reina, what's the difference?"

Suddenly Joanna scrambled to her feet. She fumbled past the casket, nearly tripping in her haste as she came rushing up the aisle, rushing toward me—and then passed right *through* me as if I was nothing more than a vapory mist!

My heart stuttered. My breath caught. Every single muscle in my body went absolutely rigid.

But it wasn't "the ghosting" that had me feeling like I might pass out.

No, it was what I'd seen hanging around Joanna's neck: What appeared to be some sort of royal crest—two lions flanking a shield and a great black eagle, its wings spread in flight, in the background. It was the same necklace I'd seen in the vision in the Seeing Bowl . . . the *exact* same necklace the hooded figure had been wearing.

I thought back to what the anchimayen had said: how a powerful sombra—a *bruja*—had cursed the necromancer's coffins. And all of a sudden, everything fell into place.

It was *her*. . . . Joanna had been the hooded figure! *She* was the witch who had taken the necromancer's coffins off that doomed ship; *she* was the witch who had spelled them—who had hidden them throughout South America!

The realization slammed into me with the force of a freight train, and for a moment it seemed like the entire room had begun to seesaw around me.

"Mi reina, dónde vas?" asked the lady in the gown—Yolanda. And when the queen didn't respond: *"Juana, where are you going?"*

"To resurrect the monster," Joanna answered quickly. "There is *no* other way."

And there it was again—the lady calling her *Juana*, and Joanna responding to it.

With surprising quickness, Yolanda stepped in front of her, blocking the queen's path. "Mi reina, *no!*" she said in a firm voice. "You cannot bring that thing back into this world!"

"But I *have to*, don't you understand? The king was *murdered* by the necromancer's *own hand*! Only *he* can resurrect my Philip now!"

Hold up. So the necromancer had killed King Philip? King Philip *the Handsome*? That was Juana of Castile's husband—Juana la Loca's. But Joanna was talking about him like he'd been *hers*. . . . What the heck was going on here?

"Mi reina, control yourself—" Yolanda began, but Joanna cut her off.

"We spoke. . . . Did I tell you?" Jo's voice was soft now, vulnerable. "I spoke with him. . . ."

"With *whom?*"

"Philip . . . He *wants* to come back—he's *begging* me to bring him back!"

A shocked look crossed Yolanda's face. "Mi reina, this is not right. . . . You're violating the laws of nature. . . . This—*all of it*—it is *wrong*." Her hands gripped Joanna's shoulders. "I know how much you loved your husband, but bringing this monster back—even if it is to resurrect Philip—cannot end well. Consider the *pain* El Brujo could unleash upon this world. Consider the suffering—"

"CONSIDER *MY* SUFFERING!" Joanna roared, her expression turning suddenly vicious. Her eyes began to glow a deep poison green, and for a moment my heart stopped, positive she was about to attack this lady. But she never did. Instead she blinked several times, and after a few seconds all the anger seemed to drain from her face. The two of them hugged it out, and Joanna whispered, "I'm sorry, Yolie. . . . You are right . . . but I . . . It seems I can no longer trust myself."

"Mi reina, you are *Juana de Castilla*. You are *our queen*. You must be strong. For España!"

A chill ran down my back. Whoa. . . . So there it was, out in the open, and Joanna wasn't even denying it.

Which meant that Queen Joanna—*our* Queen Joanna, the leader of the League of Shadows (and the current president of Spain)—was a five-hundred-year-old ex-monarch who had lived and ruled way back before even *toilet paper* had been invented!

And now she began to weep. "But I want him back, Yolanda. . . . I want him back more than anything. . . . It's the *only* thing I WAAAAANT!"

That last word rang in my head like a bell struck by lightning, and I felt myself jerked backward off my feet. The marble floors vanished. The church seemed to stretch out forever. I went tumbling down the aisle—no, down Mount Everjunk—landing, sprawled, on the pipe floor with El Pollo Loco strutting around my head, pecking at the ground.

I barely had time to sit up when the entire pipe—scratch that, my entire *world*—was suddenly flipped on its head. Gravity immediately took hold and the junk mountains turned to junk hailstorms as the pipe was shaken once . . . twice (and *hard*) . . . and on the third time I was spat out in a screaming, swirling, whirling gust of wind. I felt my body unravel like a ball of yarn, felt my arms and legs and head expanding back to their normal size, and I crashed down in the middle of the truck bed, flat on my back, my mind racing, reeling. Shapes crowded around me, the outline of faces.

A moment later they swam into focus.

"CHARLIE, YOU ALL RIGHT?" Violet screamed.

I shook my head to clear it—didn't work. "Yeah, just feel a little *squished*. . . ."

"What HAPPENED to you?"

"Honestly?" I said. "No friggin' idea . . ."

Saci shot a warning finger at me. "Hey, you no EVER go in my pipe ever again, okay? It's *PERSONAL SPACE*, ouviste?" He whipped his head around to Violet. "And *YOU*—where you get dat crown, huh?"

Joanna's—or should I say, *Juana's*—crown winked in the moonlight as Violet held it up for me to see. "He was going through our stuff again . . . ," she said. "Caught him *sleeping* with it!"

"I say, where you get *dat?*" Saci snapped, pointing at the crown.

"None of your business," V snapped back.

"You got *any idea* who dat thing belong to . . . ?"

"Of course I do. We're not thieves, like *somebody* I know, if that's what you're thinking. . . . It belongs to a friend of ours."

"A *friend* of yours?" Saci made a face like *Yeah, right.* "I no think so. . . . *Dat* crown belongs to a *witch queen*, and they not friends of *no one*."

"You're not dumb. Untrustworthy, unscrupulous, and generally *underhanded*, but definitely not dumb."

"How you two know the mad queen of España, huh?"

So apparently Saci knew her secret too.

Violet blinked. "Excuse me?"

"Juana la Loca. Juana of Castile. Look!" He pointed at the base of the crown, where some small markings had been carved into the soft metal—it was the same royal crest from the necklace I'd seen Joanna wearing twice now. "Dat's her crest!" he shouted.

"Wait up," Violet said. "Are you saying that *our* Queen Joanna is Juana la Loca? That famous Spanish queen from the fifteen hundreds?"

"Duh! She the Witch Queen of Toledo! Don't you two know NOTHING?"

Violet looked skeptical. "Charlie? You listening to this?"

"He's telling the truth," I said, but could hardly believe it myself.

V gaped at me. "*What?*"

"In fact, now that I think about it, *Joanna* is actually English for *Juana*. And Juana of Castile was born in Toledo, just like *our* Queen Joanna!"

Violet only stared, her mouth hanging open in shock, the wind tugging at her hair and T-shirt.

"Course she was!" Saci burst out. "Because is the SAME person. Pão, pão, queijo, queijo!"

"But if that's true," Violet said, "why wouldn't she have told us?"

Which was an *excellent* question. Why *hadn't* she told us? Why hadn't she wanted us to know?

Saci huffed. "More like, what *else* hasn't she told you . . . ? But dat's not so surprising to Saci."

"Why not?"

"Because that's one CRAZY WITCH! She the one that carried the dead body of her husband around with her everywhere she went for almost *TWENTY YEARS!*"

"People . . . grieve in different ways," V said lamely. "Though, now that I think about it, she *has been* acting kinda weird recently. . . ."

"Duh! All brujas and brujos get crazy around dis season. Especially *that* bruja. She's already loca!" Saci began chewing nervously on the end his pipe.

"V, I think it's even worse than that." I couldn't believe what I was about to say out loud, but I made myself say it anyway. "V, I think it's *her.*"

"*What's* her? What are you talking about?"

"I think Joanna's the one trying to raise the necromancer. . . ."

Violet's eyes nearly flew out of her head. "*WHAT?*"

I gripped her shoulders to steady her. This was crazy, I knew. But I had strong reasons to believe everything I said and everything I was about to say. "Remember what Mario told us . . . that the castells were signs of the necromancer raising himself? But that this time he thought it was just the necromancer's followers building them to make people think he was coming back, to keep everyone scared? Well, I don't think that's what's going on, and I don't think his followers have anything to do with it. . . ."

Violet was looking at me like I'd lost it. But I didn't let it slow me down.

"V, Joanna's been wanting to raise the necromancer since almost *the moment* King Philip died. . . . There's a painting in Saci's pipe—"

"Dat's not a painting, irmão—"

"I know," I said. "They're memories." Then, to Violet: "Like the paintings in the Warlock's Cave . . . Anyway, there's one in there that belonged to Joanna—when I touched it and I went *into* it, it was like I was there, at Philip's funeral. Joanna was arguing with a friend of hers—her friend *literally* called her Juana of Castile, but that's not where I'm going with this. Where I'm going is that her friend was *begging* her not to resurrect the necromancer. See, Joanna wanted to resurrect him so *he* could resurrect King Philip. From what it sounded like, it seems like the necromancer might've murdered him; *and,* from what it sounded like, only the necromancer could resurrect him."

Violet was shaking her head now, opening her mouth like she had something to say, but I wasn't finished yet—and she *needed* to hear this.

"But, V, that's not all. . . . Get this: Joanna's the *only one* who knows where the necromancer's coffins are hidden; she's the one who hid them!"

"How do you know that?"

"I saw a vision in the Warlock's Cave. In the Seeing Bowl. It didn't mean anything to me until just now—I didn't know it was *her*!"

Violet threw up her hands as the wind swirled around us. "*Whoa, whoa, whoa*—you saw a vision in *the Seeing Bowl* in the Warlock's Cave? When were you planning on telling me this . . . ?"

"I didn't say anything because it didn't make sense to me then. But I *saw* her do it, V. . . . I saw her curse those coffins, and I saw her hide them with my own eyes."

Saci was nodding along, still chewing on his pipe. "Things making *good* sense now to Saci. . . ."

"What are you talking about?" Violet snapped at him. "What's making *good sense?*"

"He right!" Saci burst out. "It's *HER!* Your queen friend behind all this!"

"Hey, *reality check*," V said, "to BOTH of you. Joanna's one of the *good guys.* She's not running around trying to raise the necromancer and building those . . . those *bone castles.*"

"For you informação—it's in her blood!" And when we both only stared, Saci said: "Raising the dead started with *her* family—jess look where dey name come from!"

"Where—*Castile?*" Violet said—and froze with the last word still hanging on her lip.

"Castile, *castell*—don't you get it? The spelling change over time—you know, slowly, slowly—but in old Spanish, they the same word. The dark magia of necromancy runs in they blood. Her family the ones who figure out how to raise the dead!"

"Joanna of *Castile,*" V murmured, as if giving the words a taste test.

"Man, and you know that necromancer everyone's so scared of? He Juana's *half brother!*"

"*What?* No way!" she shot back.

"*Yes* way! It's the worst best-kept secret in the world!"

"Now you're just making stuff up. . . ."

"Yo, I no making *nothing* up! Most of her family are *bad* sombras! Dark brujas and brujos. She's the only one who came out okay, and she's not even *that* good." He let that sink in before adding, "Joanna's loca, yo! Half of her is good. But the other half . . . ? That side is so bad I pray you never see it. There's always a war going on inside her. Good versus evil. And maybe her good side has been winning for a while, but what about tomorrow? Next week? A hundred years from now? Her bad side could take over any second, and trust Saci, she's not going to be so friendly with you *or* La Liga when dat happens. And things gonna get *ugly* when dat happens. Real *ugly.*"

It was still dark, and I was lying wide awake on my back, staring up at the starry night sky, when I heard a small, anxious voice whisper, "Charlie . . . you up?" It was Violet.

"Can't sleep," I whispered back. In fact, with how many freaky and terrifying thoughts were currently racing through my mind, I'd be surprised if I ever slept *again*.

She rolled over to face me, the wind whipping her hair into tangles. "Me either," she said.

There was a moment of silence during which the only sound was the hum and whine of the delivery truck's huge diesel engine. Then Violet asked, "So you really believe everything you said—everything Saci was saying . . . ?"

"I do. V, it just all makes perfect sense to me." I sat up so I could look at her. "And I was just thinking about this—but I got a *bad* feeling that Joanna's the traitor the chonchón told me about. . . . I mean, who else in the League would have reason to wanna team up with La Mano Peluda and try to raise the necromancer? Not El Cadejo. Not El Justo Juez."

"*True*—but . . . I don't know. . . ." Violet sounded conflicted, torn. "I mean, do you honestly *believe* all this?"

"I don't want to, V; trust me, I don't. But just look at the facts. We know the necromancer killed King Philip. We know Joanna was *madly* in love with him and wanted to bring him back from *the second* he died. We *also* know that Joanna is probably the only person on earth who knows where the necromancer's coffins are hidden; *she* hid them, for crying out loud. *And* we have reason to suspect there's a traitor in La Liga. I hate to point fingers or whatever, but if I did, all ten would be pointing straight at *her*."

Violet frowned as the trees whipped and flew by. "But . . . Joanna being evil . . . it feels *wrong*." And she had a point. It did feel wrong. Unless . . .

"But what if she's not?" I said. "Not really. What I mean is, what if Joanna really does have two sides to her like Saci said . . . ? What if it's her evil half going around building castells and trying to resurrect the necromancer while her good half is trying to stop her, leaving us clues and stuff?

She might not even realize *she's* the one doing it!"

Violet sat up. The moonlight filtering through the stack of crates at my back shone in her eyes. "But—but Charlie, it's *Joanna*!"

"I know. It's pretty convincing, though, isn't it?"

Violet was quiet for several seconds as she tried to process everything. Finally, she just shook her head. "Something's off. . . ."

"What do you mean?"

"Okay, for one—that would mean that Joanna staged her own kidnapping."

"Not necessarily. Maybe she really did fight someone in the monastery. Remember all the plant guts we saw? What if Madremonte found out what she was up to and tried to *stop her*? See, that would make sense!"

V considered that, then started shaking her head. "Eh, I guess—but I feel like . . ." Her voice trailed off.

"Like what? What is it?"

"Honestly? I feel like we're being *played*. Like someone, somewhere, somehow is pulling the strings, making us dance." She paused again, her blue eyes fixing on mine, holding there. "But okay, fine. Let's just say you're right. About everything. Where exactly does that leave us?"

She wanted my honest opinion, so I gave it to her. "I'm thinking we're gonna have to save a witch queen from herself."

CHAPTER SIXTY-EIGHT

Sometime early the next morning the delivery truck came to a screeching stop on the side of some tree-lined road in the middle of nowhere. I had no idea if the driver had spotted us in his rearview mirror or if he had just realized that Saci had messed with his delivery/drop-off sheet, but I didn't think we wanted to be around to find out. Fortunately, all three of us were awake, and the second the truck stopped, we hopped out the back and slunk off into the trees, hoping to stay out of sight. I hadn't caught a glimpse of any road signs (not that that probably would have helped much), so I didn't have the slightest idea where we were, but Saci kept telling us to relax—that we were close. We hiked for maybe twenty minutes through dense jungle and soon found ourselves approaching a huge, shimmering lake hidden deep in the woods. The shoreline was all rocky dirt. A rumpled carpet of green hills rose up around us, blocking out the reddish glare of the blazing sun. Less than five feet away, Lake Guatavita—or at least what I *hoped* was Lake Guatavita—rippled in every shade of blue, black, and green, as if some giant invisible hand were trailing its giant invisible fingers across the surface of the water.

"What Saci tell you?" he said, gesturing grandly at the lake with a big smile on his chubby little face. "Saci get you here safe and sound!"

Squinting, Violet pointed up at my forehead. "What does *b-a-r-a-t-a t-o-n-t-a* spell?"

"Sounds like Portuguese. . . ."

"It spell 'silly cockroach.'" Saci grinned at me. "Sorry. Couldn't help myself."

"Did he write on my face?" I asked V, but it was Saci who answered.

"Sim, and with permanent marker, so that gonna be hard to get off. . . . I suggest soap and hot water."

Violet pressed her lips together like she was trying not to laugh.

"Is it big?" I asked.

She nodded, still pressing her lips together. Still trying not to laugh.

"I hate him," I growled.

"Me too," V said, but a snort of laughter slipped out. "Sorry . . ."

As I peeled off my shirt, Saci said, "Ei, you not *really* going in dat lake, are you? You even know how to swim?"

"Course I know how to swim—I'm from *Miami*." I tossed my shirt onto a rock near the lake's edge and waded into the shimmering turquoise water. "Now, let's see if those old legends are true."

"How is it?" Violet asked me.

"Freezing." Holding my breath, I went under. Lake Guatavita, like most lakes, was freshwater, so opening my eyes underwater wasn't a problem; the problem was visibility—the lake was an underwater galaxy of swirling grit and lazily drifting clumps of algae that made it hard for me to even see my toes.

When I came up for air, Saci called, "You find a golden city down there?" then had himself a nice, hearty laugh about it.

I ignored him. "I don't see anything, V. . . ."

"Maybe it's deeper in?" she guessed.

I heard a soft splashing sound behind me and turned. Rippling rings of water were spreading slowly outward from the middle of the lake. There might or might not have been a golden city in here, but there were *definitely* fish.

"Ei! Stop wasting Saci's time!" Saci shouted. "El Dorado is not at the bottom of some lake, idiota!"

"Then where the heck is it?" I started to say. And that

was when something huge and fur-covered (it felt like a hand—an *actual* human hand!) closed around my right ankle—and yanked.

I was instantly pulled off my feet and went under with a garbled cry, choking on a mouthful of silty water as the hand or fish or plant or whatever the heck had grabbed me began to drag me rapidly through the water and toward the middle of the lake. Half-blind with panic—and the tiny chunks of sediment swirling around me, stinging my eyes—I kicked out wildly with my other foot—my *free* foot—trying to fight myself free, and when that didn't work, I stabbed my toes into the sandy ground and pushed up hard enough to just barely get my nose and mouth above the water. I managed, "HE—!" (though I was going for HEEELLLLP!), before I was pulled back under again, this time so hard that my shoulder slammed viciously into the lake floor. I cried out, swallowed another mouthful of the oh-so-delicious algae-flavored water, and started to choke. My fingers raked blindly across the bottom of the lake, trying to find something to hold on to, and when they scraped over a large rock, I gripped it with both hands and swung it down toward my legs.

Choking, being dragged roughly along the sandy bottom, I really didn't like my chances. But I hit the jackpot, the rock smashing solidly against whatever the heck was holding me, crumbling a little from the impact. An instant later a shrill high-pitched shriek echoed through the lake— and suddenly I was free! I kicked up, breaking the surface of the water with a gasp, and began to swim desperately— *blindly*—toward shore.

"Wha' happen?" Saci asked as I staggered out of the lake, panting, coughing up water, and collapsed onto the sand on my back. "Can't swim after all?"

He was standing on the edge of the shore now, facing me, his back to the lake. Meanwhile, I was shaking my head, pointing past him, trying to tell him what had just happened but still choking too badly to actually form any words, mostly just grunts.

"I already *tol' you!*" he shouted, wagging a finger at me, the bright morning sunlight spearing through the hole in the middle of his hand and getting in my eyes. "There's NOTHING down there. NADA—"

As if on cue, a ginormous fur-covered hand attached to what looked like a never-ending cord of fur-covered tail exploded out of the shallows. Great sheets of water went flying in all directions as it snatched Saci up like he was some little kid's plaything and dunked him, headfirst, into the lake.

"*Oh my God!*" I heard Violet shriek.

Without thinking, I scrambled to my feet and started

into the water again, not sure what I was planning but knowing I had to do *something*—when Violet grabbed me around the waist, stopping me.

"Charlie, you can't!" she shouted. "It's *suicide!*"

There was another high-pitched shriek (it sounded like some helpless baby crying out), and the water around where Saci had been dragged under began to hiss and splash. I could see shadows moving just below the surface, a frenzy of dark shapes. A heartbeat later, Saci burst up out of the water. He sucked in a great wheezing breath through his pipe (which was kinda weird) and then began swimming furiously back toward us (which was kind of expected). When he reached the shore, he kept moving, hopping speedily along now, shouting, "VAMOS! VAMOS! INTO LA CAVERNA!"

There was a small cave in the hills that butted up against the lake. We raced inside, and once we were deep enough to hide ourselves in shadow, Saci said, "Don' worry. . . . An ahuizotl will never come this far in. They scared of the dark."

"Good to know," Violet said, panting.

An ahuizotl—*that's* what that thing was! Those awful dog-monkey-hybrid things with hands on their tails that supposedly lurked in rivers and lakes. Except in all the stories my abuela had told me, they were usually spotted in Central America. Apparently these things (like a lot of animals) had some sort of migratory pattern. At least this one did.

I turned to V. "That *thing* is probably protecting El Dorado! What are we gonna do?"

Saci cut me an annoyed sideways look. "You really thick in da head, huh?"

"Makes sense, doesn't it?"

"No, it makes *no* sense! El Dorado *huge*! How can it fit at the bottom of some teeny-tiny *lake*?"

"Then we have to search the jungle around the lake," Violet said. "Find whatever clue Joanna may have left us. Maybe it'll tell us the real location of El Dorado."

"But that'll take ALL DAY!" Saci snapped.

"Then we'll stay here *all day*!" V snapped back.

"FINE. YOU WIN. Happy? You. Win!"

We both turned to look at him.

"But Saci ONLY telling you dis because I not gonna spend the rest of life searching around some *stupid* lake with some *stupider* ahuizotl inside!"

"We're listening," Violet said.

"Everybody who has a brain—obviously not *you two*—but everyone who *does* knows that if you wanna find the golden city you have to ask the cave anões . . . *los enanos*."

I felt my brow furrow. "The *cave dwarfs*?"

"Did Saci stutter?" He made an annoyed face, then

reached down deep into the bowl of his pipe and pulled out that orange-and-blue-feathered chicken of his by its scrawny orange-and-blue-feathered neck. Without even bothering to look down, he raised the chicken's head to his mouth and opened wide like he was getting ready to bite its head off. He might've, too, if El Pollo Loco hadn't let out a terrified *BAAWWKKKK!* startling Saci.

The legendary prankster made an embarrassed face. "Thought dat was a banana . . . ," he said, and then stuffed Mr. Pollo back into his pipe. "Dat's Paco de Barcera, by da way. Coolest chicken in all of Brazil. He got his own website, you know."

I sighed, rolling my eyes. "Yeah, we've met. He's super cool. Now, would you please tell us where exactly we might be able to find one of these *cave dwarfs?*"

"Madre, you people *slow!* It's in the name—*cave. Dwarfs.* You find dem in caves!" He turned, pointing back over his shoulder. "Olhe, look, you just wander on in there a little deeper, and I sure you find one. . . ."

"Perfecto. Lead the way, capitán."

Saci seemed to flinch at that. "Wha'? *No, no, no, no, no!* Saci say, *YOU* go in, not me. I no go any deeper. Not one step!" He sniffed lightly at the air, then grimaced. "I can smell los enanos *already!*"

I noticed one of his eyes was twitching a little, a tiny,

jerky movement. "You're not *scared* of them, *are you?*"

"Ei! Saci not scared of *nobody, nowhere, nohow*, entende? I jess don't wanna go, because I jess don't *wanna!*" Crossing his arms over his chest like an angry two-year-old, he grumbled, "Saci could be in São Paulo right now . . . by *the beach!* Drinking coconut smoothies. Watching soccer on my *flat-screens!*" Then he looked up, looked straight at me, and shouted, "Ei, I bring you here. Now you gotta let me go. So gimme my cap, please and thank you, and I be on my way!"

"That wasn't the deal," Violet said. "The deal was *you* get us to El Dorado and help us find our friend, *and then* we let you go. And we *still* need to get to El Dorado, and we *still* need to find Joanna."

"Hey, you two deaf? I not going one step deeper into dis cave! And you wanna know WHY? Because there's only *two things* Saci hate in dis world. And the first is people who stereotype other people."

"Right . . . and what's number two?"

"Number two is *CAVE ENANOS! THEY ALL EVIL! YOU NOT LISTENING TO SACI OR WHAT?*"

"But why do you hate them so much?" Violet wanted to know.

"Because those anões are the nastiest, greediest, ugliest, *SMELLIEST—*"

A figure melted out of the shadows behind us—a little guy in a yellow miner's hat with forearms like pythons.

"—most *wonderful* creatures in the *whole wide world!*" Saci grinned brightly at him. "How you doing, hermano? So glad to see you!"

CHAPTER SIXTY-NINE

The mini miner stepped forward, and I saw he was wearing beat-up dungarees and studded black boots that were big enough to double as clown shoes. His long dark beard, which hung below his knees, glittered with flecks of gold dust, and his bright little eyes glowed like polished onyx. In my shock, it took me several seconds to realize that he was a muki, a race of awesome cave-dwelling dwarfs with the ability to transform rock into precious metals. But that's exactly what he was!

Which, by the way, was insanely cool (at least to me) because I'd grown up hearing all about these little dudes. Now, this wasn't the first time I'd run into a muki in real life; V and I had spied a whole bunch of them working in some kind of coffin manufacturing plant beneath La Rosa Cemetery back in Miami. But I'd never gotten this up close and personal with one, and I was actually feeling the same kind of tingly, nervous-excited rush I'd felt when my dad had first taken me to check out the hippopotamus exhibit at Zoo Miami. I had to fight the urge to reach out and pet the dude!

"Tell him we're looking for El Dorado," Violet whispered to Saci.

"You tell 'im!" he snapped. "They speak Spanish. I *Portuguese!*"

"I'll tell him," I said, turning to the muki. "¡Hola, amigo! Estamos buscando the City of Gold." I was trying to sound really friendly, but also trying to keep my cool; I didn't want him to think I was some kind of silly fanboy (which I sort of was).

A sprinkle of pulverized gold drifted down from the muki's thick beard as he shook his head. "¿Qué buscan?"

"The City of Gold? El Dorado? ¿Sabes dónde está?"

"Ah, *El Dorado* . . . sí, sí. ¿Cómo no?" His tone was flat, his voice as rough as the rock he mined and as hard as the tools he used to mine it. He took another step toward us, the massive silver head of his ax hanging by his ankles. "But first I have a question for *you*, amigo. . . . Why have you come to this place? Do you intend to take the rest of our land? Or just to spill the rest of our *blood?*"

I blinked. "What? *No.* We—we're just looking for a friend. . . . We think she might've passed through El Dorado, that's all."

"We mean you no harm," Violet assured him. "We just want to find our friend, like he said."

Even with V working on him too, the muki didn't seem to be warming up to us. If anything, he looked like he was getting angrier. His eyes narrowed in a not-so-friendly way. "That's what your kind told us the first time. Before the dawn of the Sun Wars. But look around you. . . . My hermanos and I have been driven underground. You stole our cities from us. You stole our wealth. You even stole the sunlight from our eyes and its warmth from our skin. You forced us to make our homes in the *deepest darkness.*"

"I tol' you this was bad idea . . . ," Saci rasped into my ear. "*I tol' you, tol' you, tol' you!*"

Violet shushed him, banging him on the side with her elbow, as the muki said, "Tell me, enemigos, do you intend to finish what your ancestors started?"

I heard myself swallow. Enemigos. He'd just called us *enemies.* I guess it was safe to say that this conversation wasn't exactly heading in a *pleasant* direction. . . .

So, instead of words, I tried offering the little guy a nice bright smile, the extra-toothy, extra-dimply one I reserved for my teachers when I needed a couple of extra days to turn in a homework assignment. Unlike my teachers, however, the muki was totally unfazed.

"Look, if you could just point us in the direction of El

Dorado," Violet said, "we'll get out of your hair—oh, or *beard*, in your case. . . . We just want to find our friend."

"No, you just want to find *gold* . . . ," said a new voice. "That's what your kind craves most." The fingers of panic began to close around my neck as three more mukis emerged from the darkness. These, too, wore miner's outfits and hard hats and carried a mix of shovels and pickaxes. And they didn't seem friendly. Like, *at all*. Convincing one skeptical cave dwarf to help us was going to be hard enough. But *four* . . . ? Yeah, didn't think that was gonna happen.

Worse, we were now outnumbered. They might've all been a couple inches shorter than us, but they *were* carrying weapons and also happened to be incredibly thick, built like miniature fullbacks, which made me not like our chances so much.

The oldest (which was the one who had spoken) held an old-fashioned oil lamp over his head, casting eerie shadows across the cave walls and over the folds of his craggy face. He said, "You crave it more than life itself. . . ."

"Hey, that's not true!" I objected, and then fumbled back a step, bumping into Violet as two of the mukis raised their heavy tools like they were getting ready to start swinging.

Not good! I thought, and felt V's fingers wrap tightly around my arm, which probably meant that she agreed.

But right at that moment—*thankfully!*—I remembered one *very* important fact about mukis: these itty-bitty rock-smashers loved to make pacts! My abuela had told me countless stories of them striking deals with miners and making those miners insanely rich. Most of the stories centered around the miner not holding up his end of the bargain (which most of the time was as simple as never telling anyone they'd met a muki), and the mukis making him pay, sometimes causing cave-ins, injuring the miner, or causing a tunnel collapse to shut off access to the mine.

But the point was, making deals with people seemed to be something they did for fun—like, it was ingrained in their DNA or something—which gave me a bright idea.

"I wanna make a pact!" I shouted, and it was as if I'd spoken magical words.

Instantly all four of them froze. They blinked their big shiny eyes at me, once, twice, then slowly began lowering their tools.

¡Muchas gracias, abuelita!

"What *pact* would you like to make with us?" asked the one with the studded boots, leaning lightly on his pickax as he scrunched his thick black eyebrows together. His voice was still as deep and rough as before, but there was something else in it now—intrigue, maybe?

"Simple," I said. "You guys show us the way to El Dorado and we'll make sure no one ever hears about this little meeting. Plus, as a bonus, we'll throw in bagged lunches for everyone!" Now, that probably sounded ridiculous (no—I *know* that sounded ridiculous because Violet was giving me a look that was all like, *Charlie, are you still on planet earth?*). But if I knew anything about mukis it was that a) they valued their privacy above just about everything, and b) they had a thing for bagged lunches—they'd steal them from miners on the regular.

The mukis considered my offer, gathering into a tight circle and whispering quietly among themselves while Violet and Saci watched them with funny looks on their faces.

Finally a lady muki looked up at me and said, "What *kind* of bagged lunches . . . ?"

I glanced at Violet, hoping she had a bit more catering experience than me. "How about some bologna sandwiches, apples, and a few cartons of milk?" she said.

Which sounded pretty good to me. Grinning stupidly—but nodding agreeingly—I turned back to the mukis. "Think that just about covers all the food groups! Whaddya say?"

The mini ax-swingers went back to whispering; I could hear tell they were speaking Spanish but couldn't quite make out what they were saying. A few seconds later the same muki turned to me again and said, "Will you throw in some buñuelos as well?"

Violet and I looked at each other, sort of shrugging our shoulders and nodding our heads. I mean, it sounded fairly reasonable to me. After all, who doesn't like buñuelos?

"Sure, why not?" I said, grinning brightly.

The muki holding the oil lamp grinned back at me. And just as brightly. "Then I think it's settled," he said. But right as he began to extend a tiny meaty hand in my direction (mukis always shake hands to finalize a pact), the muki standing beside him, the one in the studded boots, took a good long look at Saci, and I watched in what felt like total slow-mo as his huge steel shovel slipped out from between his fingers. It clattered nosily to the ground, the sound like thunder in the quiet of the cave. "Ay, madre mía," the muki murmured, touching one suddenly trembling hand to his beard, "do my eyes deceive me, or is that truly *Saci Pererê?*"

Saci laughed. Too hard. Too loud. "No, no, no, no, no . . . You are mistaken, hermano. I not Saci. I someone else. Someone you *never ever ever* meet before, okay?"

The muki holding the lamp shone it at the nearest wall, throwing a square of bleary light over what looked like a WANTED poster. And whose face was grinning back at us from the WANTED poster? Saci's. Who else? According to the poster, Saci was numbers one, two, three, five, and seven on their most-wanted list. Oh, man, what could he have possibly done to these guys? Replaced all their gold nuggets with Chicken McNuggets?

"Dat's definitely not me . . . ," Saci said, shaking his head. "Maybe some long-lost relative. Very handsome guy, though. Beautiful eyes. Silky skin."

"That is the rascal who took our Joya del Sol and replaced it with a giant hot-air balloon!" shouted one of the mukis.

Saci let out a snort of laughter, then tried to cover it up with a cough.

"¡Lo mató!" cried another muki, raising her silver ax, but the little miner with the oil lamp snatched it out of her hands.

"¡Espera! We bring him back alive, and our reward will be great. . . . Then our people can throw a feast and boil him in front of our children!"

"Guys, violence is never the answer," I said, trying to pass on an important lesson my mother had taught me. "I usually want to strangle him too—*believe me*. But it's not worth it."

One of the mukis smiled at me. "You speak muy wisely, amigo. . . ."

"Sim, he is very wise!" Saci agreed. Then he leaned over

and whispered, "The egg . . . *Now is the time to use THE EGG!*"

"Amigo," said another one of the little dudes, "take a look at your reflection in my shovel. . . . Tell me what you see."

There was something about the way he'd said "amigo" that I really didn't trust, but not wanting to offend the dude, I leaned down to look at his shovel, and the last thing I saw was my own confused expression, and the last thing I heard was Saci begging me to bring out the egg, and then the backside of the muki's shovel clunked against my forehead—

And everything went dark.

CHAPTER SEVENTY

ometime later I woke to a strange noise. *Tink, tink, tink. Tink, tink, tink.* It sounded like someone was picking at a block of ice with a chisel.

I groaned, opening my eyes, and had to squint against the harsh blast of yellow sunlight blazing down on me. For a moment I just lay there, listening to the soft tinking sounds, wondering where those evil little dudes had decided to dump my unconscious body. But as my vision adjusted, I realized the glowing golden circle above me wasn't the sun at all, but the *ceiling.* Confused, I propped myself up on my forearms. I was lying on a cot, in one corner of some kind of ultra-luxury prison: smooth gold walls, golden cell bars, yards of golden thread sewn into the sheets and pillows underneath me—there was even a tiny golden toilet in the corner. *Where the—*

"Oh, would you give it a rest already?" said a familiar voice. It was Violet.

I turned and saw her sitting cross-legged in the opposite corner of the cell. She had her hair pulled back from her face in a fresh ponytail and didn't really look all that worried, actually—mostly just annoyed.

"You're never going to get through," she said. "You're just gonna get us—" She broke off when she looked over and saw me sitting up. "Charlie!"

She rushed over, crouching beside the cot.

I rubbed the center of my forehead where I could feel a huge, swollen knot. Oh, right. The shovel . . . "Where are we?" I asked her. "And how the heck did we get here?"

"They brought us over on mine carts," Violet explained, "then locked us in this cell. You've been out for, like, ten minutes and change."

I heard that soft *tink-tink-tink* again and looked around for its source: Saci was kneeling in front of the golden cell bars, chipping away at them with a tiny chisel and an even tinier hammer. "What are you doing?" I asked.

He glanced my way briefly, then continued chipping away. "Trabajando."

"And what exactly are you *working on*, if I may ask?"

"What it look like, bobo? I take these from one of the

mukis after they knocked me unconscious. They got me right after you."

V looked confused. "Don't you mean *before* they knocked you unconscious?"

"No, I'm pretty sure it was after. . . . What can I say? It's a gift."

I held up my hands. "So let me get this straight. You stole from the same guys who are currently getting ready to *boil* you for *stealing* from them in the first place?"

"Ei! I no *steal*. . . . Saci ain't no *thief*. I the greatest prankster that *ever* live! But dat's the circle of life, you unnestand . . . ?"

"Actually, Simba, that's *not* the circle of life."

"It's the circle of my life." He grinned at us. "Anyway, I figure, we all gonna die—what's the harm?" And he went back to chipping.

"Charlie, we gotta get out of here," Violet said, looking like she might strangle him if we didn't. "We have to get to El Dorado already; we're running out of time!"

"*Get to El Dorado?*" Saci glanced back at us, his eyebrows raised halfway up his forehead. "Look around you. . . . You *in* El Dorado!"

CHAPTER SEVENTY-ONE

I t took a second for that to sink in. Then Violet and I scrambled to our feet, climbing up onto the tiny golden toilet to peer through the even tinier window above it. And my jaw instantly dropped. All I could manage was "Whoa . . ."

The view was *incredible*. From our little prison cell maybe twenty stories up, I could see a vast, gleaming city spread out below us like a sunrise—the golden city of El Dorado. It was way bigger than I had imagined, probably as big as any major city in the world, with giant golden archways, twisting mazes of bridges and roads, and fields of bright red and blue orchids. To our right, almost at the edge of what I could see, a river of gold—yeah, pure liquid gold—flowed from one end of the city, vanished beneath a stretch of golden hills, then reemerged, bubbling through a massive crystal fountain on the other end. To the left, skyscrapers, towers, and other tall golden buildings stretched hundreds of feet into the air, creating one of the most epic skylines *ever seen*. But at its center stood the most impressive building of all—a slim cathedral-like structure that made the Empire State Building look vertically challenged. Its soaring yellow-gold towers were inlaid with blue and red gemstones, and at the peak of its tallest tower was a bloodred ruby so huge that at first I had a hard time even processing what I was looking at. Roughly the size of a blimp, it radiated a clear, reddish light that seemed to sparkle over the entire city, reflecting off the golden streets, bouncing off golden roofs, and sparking tiny rainbows everywhere. El Dorado made Fort Knox look like some five-year-old's piggy bank.

"See dat big red gem?" Saci asked, squeezing in between Violet and me. "They call dat they Joya del Sol. Is nice, eh?"

"Dude, so you *took* that thing?" I asked, gawking at it.

"Not dat one—da one that was next to it. Its big sister."

It had a *bigger* sister? That I couldn't wrap my head around. Not figuratively, not literally—in no way, shape, or form. "But . . . how did you move something so—so GINORMOUS?"

Saci grinned like he'd been waiting all his life for someone to ask him that. "Simple. I use fifty feet of basajaun hair braided into a single strand, a basket of pine needles, two small fish, and the undying gratitude of an old llama."

"I don't even know what to say to that. . . ."

"I know. The gratitude of a llama is especially hard to earn," Saci said solemnly.

"That's not what I meant."

"I have an idea!" Violet said suddenly. "What if Saci just offered to give them their gem back? I mean, it's probably sacred to them. I'm positive they'd be willing to cut some sort of deal."

"Yes! I like it!" I shouted, but Saci was shaking his head.

"Impossível," he said. "Already traded it."

"To *WHO?*" Violet and I yelled at him.

"This nice old witch with a farm. She gimme oxcart full of sugarcane. The chewable ones!"

Violet said, "You sold a *priceless gem* for some edible *grass?*" She sounded like she'd just been told—well, that he'd traded a priceless gem for some edible grass.

"Ei, no one been selling sugarcane to Saci for *long time* now, okay? And you think you can get better deal? Then take da other one. Is right there!"

Violet glared at him, then hopped off the toilet. "Gimme that chisel. I wanted to wait until Charlie woke up, but there's a shot I can pick that lock."

"Not yet," Saci said. "I wanna get a few more shavings. . . ." He held one up for us to see—it looked like a curly, solid gold pig's tail. "Saci big fan of gold. It's yellow. My favorite color, remember?"

"I don't give a rat's *behind* what your favorite color is," Violet snapped. "Give me the chisel or you're gonna be the first *dead guy* to attend his own boiling!" And she lunged at him. They wrestled over it, pushing and pulling on each other until a squad of mukis appeared at the end of the hall, marching our way. Not regular mukis either—muki *soldiers*. Each one was completely encased in golden armor—old-school comb-topped helmets and breastplates, shirts of chain mail, and shiny five-fingered gauntlets. Golden swords hung from golden scabbards, which dangled only inches from the gold-paved stones that the soldiers' gold-stitched sandals trod upon as they marched up to our golden cell, tried a little golden key.

"No trabaja," one of them said. "No es la llave."

"¡Te van a matar!" his buddy shouted. "¿Dónde la pusiste?"

"¿Qué sé yo?" And they all took off running back down the hall, their swords scraping along the ground, their heavy golden armor clinking and clacking.

"Charlie, what's going on?" Violet wanted to know.

"I think they lost the key to our cell." Just then I became aware of a strange sound: a soft crunching, cracking noise somewhere close by. Like, *very* close by. "What is that?" I said.

V made a face. "Sounds like . . . *crunching potato chips?*" And it sort of did.

Violet was looking around for its source when Saci suddenly shot a finger at me.

"It coming from *him!*" he cried.

Panicking, I looked wildly around. "Me? What? Where?"

His eyes slid down to my shorts. "In you bolsos! You pockets!"

"My *pockets?*" Then I remembered: the alicanto egg! I'd hidden it in the inside pocket of my cargoes to make sure Saci wouldn't try to take it again.

When I dug it out, Saci cried, "Madre! Did you just *lay* that?"

"No, you moron! Do I look like classification *avian* to you?" In all fairness, I had sprouted feathers once (and wings), but he didn't need to know that. . . .

Another *crack, crunch, crunch* and now a long, zigzagging crack ran up the side of the copper-colored shell. All three of us froze. Something was in there . . . something *alive!* Which I guess should've been kind of obvious, it being an egg and all—but still!

The egg quivered between my hands; I heard another *crack!* and then a huge section of shell fell off and a tiny coppery bird—it looked like a newborn chick that had been dipped into a bucket of liquid pennies—pushed itself out through the gap. Twin beady eyes looked up at me. Its tiny coppery beak opened, and it chirped something that sounded suspiciously like "*Mama!*"

"Oh my gosh, Charlie—that's, like, the *cutest* thing EVER!" Violet cooed.

The tiny bird chirped again, "Mama! Mama!" and this time Violet heard what I'd heard.

"Charlie, it thinks you're its *mother!*"

"*What? Why?* Why would it think something like that?"

"I know—it's weird. . . . I mean, for a bird to think that you're its mother, you would have had to have incubated it for an incredibly long period of . . . *hold on.* How long have you had that thing in your shorts?"

Too long, obviously, I thought, but what I said was, "Uh . . . a while?"

A second later the baby bird hopped out of my hand, its itty-bitty little baby wings a blur, and landed on the floor between my sneakers. All three of us watched it waddle over to one corner of the cell and begin pecking at the golden wall. *Tap-tap-tap, tap-tap-tap!* Its tiny beak must've been made of something pretty hard, because next thing I knew there was a chunk about the size of a Ping-Pong ball missing from the wall.

"Charlie, I think it's *eating* the gold . . . ," Violet said, sounding a little bit concerned and a lotta bit amazed—and finally everything clicked together in my brain.

"Of course it is!" I shouted. "It's an *alicanto*!"

V was shaking her head like, *No comprendo.*

I gestured wildly at the bird. "An *alicanto*! My abuela loved these things! Well, she loved telling me stories about them. . . . They're, like, these legendary birds known all over South America! Their feathers light up at night. They've also been known to lead people to vast treasures and stuff like that. Greedy people they lead off cliffs. But, yeah, they're super famous!" I couldn't believe it had taken me until now to remember about them.

Saci was nodding along, like he'd heard the same stories—or, maybe had tried to follow one. "And dey the mukis' natural-born enemy. Those birds feed on precious metals. How you think dey feathers get such beautiful colors?"

A jingling: One of the soldiers had returned to our cell holding three different rings of golden keys. But the second he got one look at the alicanto in the corner, he let out a shriek (something like, "CHICHICHICAAAA!"), dropped the keys, and took off down the hall again.

Saci grinned. "See what Saci mean?"

I felt Violet's fingers tighten on my upper arm. "Charlie, look!"

I turned and almost choked on my own tongue. The

baby alicanto had almost doubled in size; it was now about as big as a full-grown duck, and the chunk it had taken out of the wall had expanded to about the size of a beach ball! Dang, that little thing knew how to chow down!

"It's gonna eat through the wall!" V shouted with a rush of laughter.

The alicanto glanced back at me, chirped. "Mama!"

The hole it had made must've been almost two feet deep; there couldn't have been much wall left. "Sí, sí, eat, my child!" I shouted, pointing back at the wall. "You must be hungry! Eat!"

From behind us came the wild jingling of keys—I turned, saw a different guard fumbling around with the keys the other one had dropped. He was trying to find the right one, but his eyes kept flicking up to the alicanto, and in his terror he was having a tough time sliding the keys into the lock. "¡No te muevas!" he warned us in a voice that was more scared than scary. "D-D-D-Don't move!"

My eyes flew back to the alicanto: The once-tiny baby bird had grown to nearly the size of an ostrich! Even more amazing, it had already managed to eat all the way through the prison wall! The hole was just big enough for us to run through; only problem was, if any of us actually *ran* through it, we'd plummet twenty stories straight down to a resounding KASPLAT!

"Meu Deus, that bird can eat!" Saci cried.

V whirled around. "Can those things fly?"

"Of course they can fly, chica! They *birds*!"

"Not all birds can fly, smart guy. Ever heard of an emu?"

Saci thought for a second. "No."

"Whatever!" Her eyes locked onto mine. "Charlie, I think we've found our way out!"

I was shaking my head, wondering if she'd gone bananas. "What?"

"We have to ride that bird out of here!"

"*What?*"

"It's the only way!"

"*WHAT?*"

"You have a better idea, or are you just going to keep sayng 'what'?"

I was actually going to stick with my "what"—it seemed like the only sensible thing either of us was saying at the moment. But a loud metallic click behind us had me whirling: The guard had finally found the right key. Which meant there wasn't any time for more "whats" or even any better ideas.

"C'mon!" Violet shouted, pulling me toward the alicanto, and all three of us quickly climbed onto its back, Saci yelling, "Fly, you crazy bird, fly!"

But instead of taking off, the bird craned its head around and squawked, "Mama!"

"This isn't going to work!" I yelled as the guards threw open the door. They rushed into the cell, swords drawn— and I panicked. Right before they'd unlocked the door, I had spotted a fist-size hunk of golden brick hanging off the wall by my head; now I yanked it loose, showed it to the alicanto long enough for its eyes to light up a brilliant greenish gold, then tossed it in front of us, out into the open air. The alicanto took the bait. Literally. It sprang forward, snatching the golden nugget out of the air with its shiny beak before we had even started to drop. I had a split second to think how brilliant my move was—and then we *did* start to drop.

CHAPTER SEVENTY-TWO

The good news: My plan had worked—we were out of the prison. The bad news: In all its hungry excitement, the alicanto had forgotten the number one rule of gravity—no flapping, no flying. We plummeted straight down like a bag of rocks. The wind screamed in our ears. The giant canvas ceilings of the market way down below rushed up toward us in a dizzying blur. of red, yellow, and blue stripes. At the very last moment the alicanto threw open its wings, which would've been perfect like five seconds ago. All it did now was slow our fall a little.

We crashed through a canvas top, splitting the fabric with a great tearing sound, and landed smack-dab in the middle of a huge crate of—*SQUISH!*—fruit. Juice sprayed everywhere. A sharp, citrusy scent rushed up my nostrils. Oranges. We'd fallen into a crate of oranges. Around us, several mukis who had been shopping at this fruit stand shrieked. One saw the alicanto and fainted on the spot.

"Vamos! Vamos!" Saci shouted, frantically climbing out of the crate. And then I saw why: A band of muki soldiers was pushing its way through the crowd less than thirty yards away. "TO THE CARTS! RÁPIDO, POR FAVOR!"

There was a row of golden mine carts sitting along the far edge of the market, where the golden brick floors turned to golden tracks that ran out in all directions, winding and crisscrossing into a complex highway system.

We zigzagged our way through the maze of tables and stalls—the alicanto right on our heels, Saci snatching up anything that wasn't tied down—and jumped into the first cart in the row. The moment we'd all piled in, I heard a crackling, electric *zap!* and the cart immediately lurched forward, shooting off the line like we'd hit the turbo boost in Mario Kart. As we zipped along the tracks, going from zero to *at least* sixty in all of a blink, I remembered that gold was an amazing conductor of electricity and couldn't help wonder if that's how they were getting these carts to move.

"ONLY WAY OUTTA DIS PLACE IS THROUGH DA PURPLE CAVES!" Saci yelled.

There was a metallic screech as the cart began to pick up incredible speed. It bounced. It wobbled. It trembled, and Violet shouted, "WHICH WAY IS THAT?"

"Dey comin' up!"

There was a tunnel up ahead, four tracks wide. As we zoomed into it, another mine cart came screaming up behind us, then suddenly hopped the tracks, pulling alongside our cart. The driver, an older-looking muki with a chin-cape of curly white hair that flew out behind him in the wind wagged his fist at us, shouting, "¡Aprendan a manejar, gamberros!" which basically translates to "Learn how to drive, morons!" And then he sped away. Huh. I guess even mukis suffered from road rage . . . well, track rage, anyway.

"How do you switch tracks with this thing?" I asked Violet.

"Probably with that!" She was pointing at a golden lever sticking out of the front of the car. "Looks like it's some kind of primitive steering column."

As I wrapped my fingers around it, I noticed there were strange symbols carved into the top. "What do these things even mean?" I started to say, and then—

Clink, clink, clink!

I whirled, saw a bunch of muki soldiers on our tail—five of them packed into a single mine cart with another bunch crammed into the cart behind them.

Three of the soldiers in the closest cart were holding sleek silver bows. They aimed them at us, making my insides twist into a pretzel, but apparently Saci didn't share the same fear of being mortally *skewered* because he suddenly sprang to his feet, shouting, "Here! Right here!"

Good thing for him Violet was right there and dragged him down before one of them could score a bull's-eye. "HELLLOOOO! They're trying to SHOOT you!"

"I know—and I *want* dem to! Those arrows solid *gold*!"

Clink, clink, clink! The mukis missed again, the arrows bouncing harmlessly off the back of our cart, but they were gaining on us. Which meant they wouldn't be missing for long.

Violet shouted, "CHARLIE, DO SOMETHING!"

She'd barely spoken the words when the mukis unleashed another barrage of arrows, and Saci fell back with a loud yelp. My first thought was, *Oh yeah, sure.* I was convinced he was messing with us—you know, pulling one of his old prankaroos.

But then I saw the gleaming golden arrow sticking out of the middle of his chest and my heart slammed so hard I was positive I'd busted a rib.

"SACI!" I shouted.

Violet's panicked eyes found mine as we both leaned over him.

"I feel so cold, irmão . . . ," he whimpered, gripping my hand in both of his. I could feel his fingers trembling, the strength seeping out of them as his body went into shock.

"Dude, it's okay—you're going to be okay!" I looked at

Violet, feeling dread beginning to crawl up my throat. "I mean, you can fix him, *right?*"

"Charlie, I don't have the tools to perform SURGERY on him!"

"Just do something! He's gonna die!"

She leaned closer, examining the wound.

"WHAT YOU DOING?" Saci yelped. "HURTS SO BAD!"

"I haven't even *touched* you yet! I'm just looking. . . ."

"Is it *muito, muito* bad?" he asked her.

Violet's eyes narrowed. "It's *TERRIBLE!* I'm gonna have to operate after all. And by hand."

"*WHAT?*" I couldn't believe what she'd just said. I mean, first off, it sounded *highly* unsanitary. But before I could say anything else, she yanked out the arrow, and I almost passed out right then and there.

"Yep, just as I suspected—a kill shot." She held up the arrow, and when I finally forced myself to look, I saw that the tip had embedded itself into a nest of curly gold shavings—the stuff Saci had been chiseling off the bars back in the prison! "Something tells me he's gonna make it," Violet said with an annoyed look.

"Oh, shiny!" Saci sat up, snatching the arrow from Violet's hand. "GOOOOOOOOOOALLL!" he began to shout, but just as he did, the alicanto glanced over and gobbled up the golden arrow in a single slurping gulp.

"NOOOOOOOOOOOO!" Saci cried as the alicanto let out a satisfied burp.

"Charlie, get us out of here!" Violet screamed while more arrows swooshed by overhead.

I spun around and grabbed the steering column, but wasn't sure what to do with it.

"Just do something!" she yelled at me.

Fine. I slammed the lever forward and then had to clench my teeth as an earsplitting shriek of metal rose up from the tracks, and we began to slow. The cart shuddered. My teeth clattered. The alicanto let out another loud burp.

"Do something else!" Violet said, so I did, yanking back on the lever. But this time there was no slowing down. In fact, it felt like I'd hit the warp-speed button on the *Starship Enterprise!* The mine cart shot forward like a rocket, the sudden acceleration snapping our heads back and slamming us against each other as we zoomed down the tunnel in a frenzy of speed and sound.

"Maybe dis a little *too* fast!" Saci yelled.

Ahead the tunnel opened up, creating a fork in the road—or rather, in the *mine.*

"Go right!" Saci yelled. "That's the caves!"

"*Hold on!*" I shouted, and started to pull the lever to the right, but Violet stopped me.

"I think the controls are inverted!" she said.

I shook my head. The tunnel was coming at us fast. We didn't have time for thinking. "Meaning?"

"Meaning forward is stop and back is go, right? So then left is probably *right*. And right is *left*."

"So then left is right, right?"

"Right."

"Wait!" Saci said. "So, *his* right or *your* right?"

"Enough!" Violet wrenched the lever left, and the mine cart swerved sharply into the middle lane, cutting in front of the other cart of muki soldiers just as they came zooming up on us. The tiny bearded driver tried to slam on his brakes, but it was too late. The front of their cart played bumper tag with the back of ours, then tilted sideways. A mesmerizing shower of golden sparks leapt into the air as their mine cart tumbled once, twice, then went flying off the tracks.

"AGAIN!" Saci cried, playing bongo drums on my back with his fists. "SWITCH AGAIN!"

Violet gave the lever another yank, and we sliced right, our wheels squealing against the inside rail as we shot into the narrow opening.

We blasted down the tunnel. Rocky walls zoomed past. The wind howled around us. Then our cart bucked and nearly jumped off the tracks as the second cart of soldiers rammed us viciously from behind. The wheels on our cart whined and shuddered. The angry pint-size driver pulled his cart closer and closer until he was tailgating us. And just as he did, one of the mukis tried to board us, swinging his sword inches from my face.

He'd almost crawled halfway into our cart when the alicanto finally decided it'd had enough. Our big, *beautiful* bird snatched the muki's sword, swallowing it down in a single gulp, then batted him away with its wings, sending the muki tumbling backward into his cart. Then it stretched out its long, feathered neck and bit a chunk out of the front of their cart, chomping through the tough gold ore like it was sponge cake. The muki driver let out a terrified shriek, twisting the steering column, and the mine cart wobbled suddenly and then came off the tracks. It crashed into the rocky wall and was out of sight a split second later.

"GOOD PÁSSARO!" Saci cried, stroking the alicanto's broad, coppery head. "WHAT A BIG *WONDERFUL* BIRD!"

But no sooner had he said that than the big wonderful bird turned into the big *gluttonous* bird and craned its neck around to bite a massive chunk out of the back of *our* mine cart. And then another. And another.

The cart began to shake. Now I could see our back wheels grinding along the tracks, sending up spurts of fiery yellow sparks.

Oh, man, oh man, oh man! Las cosas están malas! BIEN malas!

"He's eating us out of house and home!" Saci cried, wrapping his arms around me.

"Doesn't matter," Violet shouted. "Looks like it's time to move, anyway!" She pointed up ahead, where the tracks dead-ended at an untidy heap of rotten planks, and not for the first time that day, I heard myself swallow.

CHAPTER SEVENTY-THREE

A large rectangular sign had been chained over the pile. It read VÍA CERRADA.

"JUMP!" Violet shouted, and no one hesitated—not even the alicanto.

We hit the ground hard, tumbling for several feet, and when the world finally stopped spinning, I looked up just in time to see our cart smash into the pile of planks. Splinters and chunks of stone flew in every direction.

The thud of the crash echoed through the tunnel, rattling off the walls and making bits of rock rain down from the impossibly high ceilings.

Gingerly I pushed up to my knees and ran a quick diagnostic. Alvin's smelly dog collar? Check. Freaky finger-necklace? Check. Skeletal system still in one piece? Más o menos . . . "Everyone still breathing?" I asked.

"Think so." Violet sat up, wiping sweat off her face.

"You two *dangerous* to be around, you know?" Saci was already up, looking around at the ginormous cavern. Stalactites hung down from the roof like fangs while stalagmites shot up from the ground like spikes. He turned to glare at the alicanto. "And I not even going to talk about dat *crazy* bird. . . ."

"There!" Violet said, pointing. Through the blackness, maybe ten yards ahead of us, I could just barely make out a bridge—some kind of long plank-and-rope setup that must've stretched a hundred yards or so over a pitch-black chasm. It should've been impossible to see with how dark it was in here, but something nearby had started to glow. And when I looked around to find out *what* (I was hoping one of us hadn't unknowingly caught on fire or something), I saw it was the alicanto! A bright radiant light was spreading like luminescent ink through the veins of its feathers, shining out in every shade of copper, gold, and brown imaginable. The bridge, which, like everything else in this place, appeared to be made of pure gold, shone dully in its fierce glow.

"What a *beautiful* pasarro. . . ." Saci's voice had dropped to an awed whisper as he stared up at the glowing bird with wide, googly eyes. "What you think it's made from?" he asked, reaching out slowly to touch it.

Violet smacked him on the back of his head. "It's made

out of *bird*, you idiot. Now keep your hands to yourself!"

"C'mon," I started to say. *Let's get out of here* was how I meant to finish. But before I could, the jangle of swords and armor echoed from the tunnel behind us.

Saci's head snapped around. "*Mukis.*"

"¡Corran!" I shouted. Then, thinking it might be a good time for another quick lesson—seeing as we were probably about to *die* anyway—I turned to V and said, "That means 'run'!" And we all took off for the bridge as an entire battalion of gold-plated soldiers came rumbling out of the same tunnel we'd just come tumbling out of ourselves. There had to be close to three hundred of them, all fit, bearded, angry little dudes waving swords and flaming torches over their heads. Their golden breastplates gleamed like jewels in the torchlight.

"I'm curious," Violet shouted as we ran for dear life, "what makes those alicanto eggs so valuable?"

"The bird, duh!" Saci shouted back.

"But all it does is *eat* gold!"

"Ah, but you should see what it *poops!*" he said, grinning at us.

We'd just made it halfway across the bridge when another couple of mukis—huge ones, both a little taller than us, with broad barrel chests and arms so muscular their biceps looked like they had biceps!—appeared at the other end of the bridge.

"We're trapped!" Saci yelled. And for once, he wasn't lying.

I was pretty sure things were about as bad as they could get. Then I glanced back again and realized that a few of the soldiers were using their torches to light the ropes at their end of the bridge on fire.

When I saw *that*, that's when I *knew* things were about as bad as they could get.

CHAPTER SEVENTY-FOUR

"GRAB ON TO THE BRIDGE!" I shouted, dropping flat on my belly, wrapping my arms and legs around the planks. Not exactly MacGyver-level, I know, but it was the only thing I could think of to do. Maybe the only thing there *was* to do.

Within seconds the superheated ropes began to bubble and melt. Golden droplets ran down the sides of the bridge posts like raindrops, and suddenly the ropes came loose, and we fell into the chasm, all four of us screaming our heads off. (Well, except of course for the alicanto, who was, in fact, *squawking* its head off.) We swung through the chilly darkness and slammed into the cliff face on the other side. The impact nearly shook me off, but I managed to hold on—*barely*. Hunks of broken board tumbled past on my left while on my right the two super-size mukis, who had both lost their grip on the bridge, plunged, shrieking, into the abyss.

I caught the glint of their golden breastplates as they dropped away, and then they were gone, swallowed up in darkness.

Somewhere above me, I could hear Violet screaming as she clung to a plank. Below me, similar panicky shouts were coming from Saci and the alicanto as they did the same. I had just opened my mouth to yell *We gotta climb!* when the mukis did something that, basically, said it for me: They started shooting arrows at us.

The sleek golden projectiles whistled through the air, screaming down around us and embedding themselves into the cliff face.

The four of us began to climb like our lives depended on it, but not two seconds later one of the two ropes still holding the bridge up suddenly snapped, and we sagged another twenty or so feet down into the chasm—dangling by a thread now. *Literally.*

"THIS THING'S ABOUT TO GO!" I shouted.

Violet looked around desperately. "Grab the arrows!" she yelled down at us.

There was no time to argue. I dove for the pair half buried in the rock to my left just as the bridge suddenly collapsed on my right.

As my hands closed around the shafts and my full weight bore down, their sturdy metallic bodies groaned and bent, but they didn't snap or come free. Thank you, muki craftsmanship! Even better, the arrows were jutting out all over the cliff face, which meant we'd have plenty of handholds all the way up. Still, the climb up was probably the most exhausting thing I'd ever done, and by the time I reached the top and pulled myself over the edge—with a little help from Violet, who had beaten me by a few seconds—I was as done as a turkey on Thanksgiving.

I rolled over next to her and stared blankly up at the dark, crusty ceiling of the cave, wheezing, every single fiber of my being crying out in absolute pain. But, hey, at least I was still alive enough to hurt, right?

Saci pulled himself over the edge a moment later, a half dozen or so golden boards stuffed down his jersey clanking back and forth. Surprisingly, the guy looked as fresh as a daisy, not even breathing hard. Guess he was used to this, though. In his line of "work," someone was probably always after him. "DON'T JESS LIE THERE!" he yelled, hopping past us. "DIS NO PLACE FOR NAPPY TIME! GO, GO! RAPIDO!"

We scrambled after him and soon found ourselves sprinting across some kind of land bridge, running through a glittering purple tunnel about as wide and high as a soccer stadium, with the alicanto leading the way, looking like a golden-brown light bulb scuttling around on a pair of chicken legs.

"We did it!" Saci cried, waving one of his golden planks triumphantly over his head. "We actually gonna get out of dis place alive!"

He held up a hand for a high five, and I laughed, about to give him one, when I heard a sound that sent the needle on my Uh-Oh Meter spinning in crazy circles: a deep, reverberating, earthshaking rumble, seemingly rising up through the ground itself.

Then, from way down below in the pitch-dark blackness came another sound—a great gasping, sucking sound that seemed to snatch every last bit of warmth out of the air—and that was when something dark and gelatinous and absolutely *massive* surged out of the chasm! It slammed into the underside of the bridge with a deafening *crack*, crashing straight through the thick, calcified rock maybe ten yards ahead of us and gobbling up a huge section of it in its enormous, toothless maw.

My heart stopped as I watched the thing stretch to its full height above us—and when I say full height I mean *incredible* height, *impossible* height, eye-bulging, mind-bogglingly *ridiculous* height. It looked like a cross between an earthworm and a *skyscraper*. The word "Minhocão" flashed through my mind, but in that moment, in my terror, only some distant part of my brain registered that that was *exactly* what this thing was—a Minhocão: a species of gigantic (and supposedly) amphibian earthworms native to South America. According to some old legend, one of these things had swallowed an *entire* city—the lost Incan city of Paititi!

Before any of us could react, before any one of us could even scream, another earthworm exploded out of the pitch-dark chasm. Its massive mouth opened wide, opened directly below us, giving us an up-close-and-personal look down the rough, dark tunnel of a throat as it smashed through the bridge beneath our feet, gulping down everything in its path—including *us*.

CHAPTER SEVENTY-FIVE

Getting swallowed alive by a Minhocão was one of those "once-in-a-lifetime experiences." There really aren't any words to describe the utter skin-crawling horror of being gobbled up by a segmented worm the size of a cruise ship. But if you've ever ridden a water slide where the water and slide are both made out of the driest, dustiest, grainiest earth on the planet, then you'd have a pretty good idea what it was like. We tumbled down a sandy, pitch-black tunnel, sand stinging our eyes and faces, and landed in a great fluffy pile of—you guessed it—more sand. In the bright glow of the alicanto's feathers, I got a good look at the thing's guts and it honestly reminded me of the inside of a giant sandcastle. Sandy floors, sandy walls, sloping sandy ceilings. I half expected to see a couple of little kids with plastic beach buckets running around building little castles of their own. Anyway, the bad news was that we now found ourselves sitting squarely in the digestive track of some ginormous, earth-gobbling invertebrate. The good news? We hadn't quite been digested yet. . . .

"Dat wasn't too bad," Saci said as the creature's insides started to rumble. A gush of sand cascaded down from overhead, pouring over him like a waterfall. Saci didn't even try to avoid it. Just let it flow over him. Then he shook himself off. "At least we survived the worst part," he said, sounding rather happy about it.

And, naturally, we started to sink. Which meant that we hadn't, in fact, survived the worst part.

"You *had* to say that, didn't you?" I grumbled, and the alicanto squawked like it agreed with me. Meanwhile, I could feel my feet being sucked down. Worse, the more I struggled, the faster I sank. Saci tried to hop out, almost made it, then started to sink faster than anyone.

"Intestinal quicksand!" Violet screamed, yanking uselessly on her legs. She was sinking slower than I was but not by much.

I tilted my head. "Is that even a thing?"

V shrugged. "At the moment, it seems like the logical answer would be *yes*, don't you think?"

I wouldn't know—the logical part of my brain had already shut down, thanks to my rising panic, and the frantic side of my brain was racing in a totally different direction, trying to come up with a plan to get us out of here. Problem was, how did you fight your way out of a hungry pit of quicksand inside an even hungrier monster *also* made out of sand when everything in that monster was made out of the same stupid, silty sand and there wasn't anything you could grab on to or sling a rope around to pull yourself out with? I began to sink faster, the sand climbing past my knees, then my hips, and up to my belly button. I couldn't believe we were going to die like this—suffocated to death in a quicksand pit in the stomach of a spineless, brainless, oversize lumbricina! It was so sad. And gross. And on so many different levels. . . .

Behind me, Saci was flapping his arms like a wounded pigeon and yelling, "I feel like I sinking in a quicksand pit of despair!"

"Uh, what's he doing?" I asked Violet.

"I think he's trying to make a metaphor."

"But you can't make a metaphor by *literally* describing what's happening to you. . . ."

"You explain it to him," V said.

Saci suddenly gripped my shoulders, his eyes huge, fingers digging painfully into my skin. "Bro, we sinking like *skunks!*" he cried. "And we gonna die like dem, too!"

"Except skunks wouldn't die like this," I said without thinking. "They're burrowers. They'd just burrow their way—"

That was as far as I got before I knew what I had to do. Closing my eyes, I concentrated, letting everything else fade to a blur. I could hear Violet shouting my name, could hear Saci yelling at the bird, telling it to fly him out of here, could feel myself sinking deeper into the sand, the pressure pushing against my chest and back, squeezing the air from my lungs. But I blocked it all out. I pictured claws, long and pointed, pictured them as my own hands, imagined them extending from my fingertips, searched for the animal trapped inside me, groping for it like a light switch in a dark room. The sand rose up around the base of my throat, and the image of the skunk, the image of those curved, razor claws began to flicker, being choked out of my mind by a rising wave of panic.

I can't breathe, I realized. And just when I opened my mouth to scream—it happened.

CHAPTER SEVENTY-SIX

That familiar icy tingle down my spine. The animal inside me was waking up—*had* woken up. "Both of you, grab on to the bird," I said, my eyes still closed, feeling my hands shrinking, my fingers widening to accommodate claws. "Do it now!"

I heard Violet say, "Charlie, *what?*"

"Just grab on to the alicanto and hold your breath. I'm gonna dig us out!" I began to struggle to make myself singk faster. And as the sand rose up and over my head, swallowing me completely, I felt for the nearest wall, sank my claws into it, and began to dig.

At first it was slow and tough, my back and arms burning with the effort; apparently the oldest layers of dirt in this thing's body, the layers closest to his gut, had hardened over the decades or centuries—or maybe even *millennia*. But the deeper I dug, the softer the dirt became, and soon tunneling was as easy as walking or swimming or even breathing.

Around me the Minhocão began to shudder and shake like a building on the verge of collapse, and then I was through; I moved out of the way to let the fast-flowing river of sand escape until I felt the alicanto (along with Violet and Saci) come sliding past me, and then I grabbed on myself. The alicanto, realizing it was now free, began to flap its giant feathery wings. It caught a gust of air sweeping from below, and we suddenly shot upward, surging toward the pinprick of light way up in the distance.

Violet and Saci were too terrified to do much more than scream, but I couldn't help looking down to make sure the Minhocão wasn't coming after us again. It wasn't. But what I saw down there, what I saw rising out of the blackness, scared me more than any earthworm—

Another castell!

CHAPTER SEVENTY-SEVEN

This one was made out of huge gray bones, the bones of something ancient and prehistoric. It rose out of the dark pit like a skyscraper of death, glistening palely in the shine of the alicanto's feathers. I frowned, a panicky feeling rising up in my stomach as I realized two things. First, one of the necromancer's coffins had been buried down there. Second, Joanna had beaten us here by *a while*. How else would she have had time to build something so absolutely *enormous*?

And how had she managed to even build that thing way down in that pit . . . ?

I stared at it—too long. Voices began to echo through my mind, whispers and groans, shrieks and moans. The world around me started to tilt. I felt myself falling. Instinctively my hands shot out, trying to grab on to something—*anything*—but my fingers closed on nothing but empty air.

I had time to think, *Ayúdame—help!* (but not quite enough to shout it). Then I felt a hand clamp down on my shoulder. It yanked, and suddenly the world was right again.

"Don' let go!" Saci shouted. And he didn't need to tell me twice.

I wrapped both arms around his waist and held on tight as the alicanto gave a shrieking, high-pitched cry and arrowed us out of the Purple Caves.

As we burst into a world of blazing yellow sunshine, I heard Saci yell, "Sim, sim!" Then: "Ay, no! *No, no, no!*"

And we hit the ground with a bone-shattering jolt; the alicanto sprawled out, squawking; and Violet, Saci, and I went flying.

I went end over end once . . . twice . . . then crashed into a clump of thorny bushes. It wasn't a soft landing, but the bushes probably saved me from a few broken ribs.

Wincing, I crawled out, yanking at a handful of tiny barbs as I pushed unsteadily to my feet.

To my left, Saci was lying on his back on the grass, sort of half smiling, looking like he was seeing stars, watching them do the samba or something. His overalls were all rumpled and dirt streaked, but apart from that he seemed okay. He tried to sit up, couldn't quite manage, muttered something that sounded suspiciously like, "Sufferin' succotash," and then sprawled back out.

Violet and I looked at each other. "Did he just say what I thought he said?" I whispered.

"Sounded like it."

"Do they even *have* Looney Toons in Brazil . . . ?"

V shrugged. "I'd hope so."

I thought about that for a sec. "Yeah, me too . . . For the children's sake, you know?"

Violet, grinning at me now, said, "Yeah, Charlie, for the children's sake."

A moment later, Saci staggered awkwardly up and looked over at us. "You know, a witch once tol' me, 'Saci, you a true son of Brazil. Brazil love you! She herself gon' keep you alive till the end of time. She never gon' let you die.' And dis witch the no-nonsense type. She no lie. So you two unnerstand the risk I taking for you, eh?"

Yep, he'd definitely hit his head. Probably pretty hard, too. "You wouldn't happen to know how to treat a concussion, would ya?" I said, turning to look at Violet, who was now staring back at the cave with a troubled look on her face. I frowned. "Hey, what's wrong?"

"We're going to have to go back down there," she said. "That's what."

"Back down where? Back into El Dorado? Why? I mean, *why*?"

"Because we didn't find Joanna *or* her clue. And that's where she would've hidden it."

"You CRAZY?" Saci screamed. "We can't go back in there! We never make it out alive! Not two times!"

"He's right, V. There's no way . . ."

"Now, dat's the truth! Listen to Charlie, okay? Yes, he got terrible taste in necklaces, but in this case he know wass up."

"Wait, wait. Just—*chill* for a second!" Violet said, raising her hands. "It doesn't make sense. . . ." She started pacing purposefully around, which I knew meant she was onto something. "Joanna's brilliant, right? And she's cunning. I mean, she's led us this far, hasn't she?"

"What's you point?"

"My point is that she wouldn't have hidden the clue somewhere we couldn't find it. She would've put it someplace obvious."

"But El Dorado is *huge*," I said. "It would take forever and a day to search it." That is, in the highly unlikely event we didn't get *boiled* first.

"Exactly. So she must've hidden it somewhere she'd know we'd absolutely have to pass through."

"Okay, that makes sense. But, like, *where?*"

"There's only one place. The exit."

"The Purple Caves?"

"Maybe. But I don't even think there, because Joanna is smart enough to know that there'd be a pretty good chance the mukis would be all over us at that point."

"So where, then?"

Her blue eyes flitted around our surroundings. "How about right here . . . ?"

"*Here?*" Saci sounded more than a little confused as he looked slowly around. "Like in da trees . . . ?"

"Well, anywhere. See, she'd know that if we made it out, we'd have to pass right through here. It's the only way out of the city, isn't it?"

"And she'd also know that the mukis would never leave their mines to chase us," I said as it hit me.

"Which would make this the *perfect place* to hide a clue!"

Saci, who was trying to keep up, turned to me with something like awe in his eyes. "Dang, she pretty smart, huh?"

I smirked. "That's Violet."

"Start looking!" V shouted. "The clue's gotta be around here somewhere."

So that's exactly what we did; we searched high and low, in the tangle of thorny bushes near the mouth of the cave, behind all the tall trees, under every rock and log, even up in some of the lower branches. But twenty minutes later we hadn't found a thing. Nothing that looked like a clue, anyway.

"Not seeing anything, V." I rolled a rock over with the bottom of my shoe and remembered I'd already checked under this one. "There's nothing out here. . . ."

"Nutting!" Saci shouted. "We wastin' our time. We could be halfway to Brazil by now!"

"Just keep looking . . . ," Violet said. "It's *gotta* be here."

Right as she said that, one member of our search party decided they'd had enough; there was a loud squawk, and suddenly the alicanto exploded into flight, rising up over the tops of the tall trees and disappearing into the fierce jungle sky.

Watching it go, I felt the strangest tug on my heart. Sort of like when I watched Alvin accidentally flush his pet goldfish down the toilet in second grade.

"Charlie, you all right?" Violet asked, putting a hand on my shoulder.

"Yeah, it's just—the bird and I really bonded, you know?"

"Are you . . . *crying?*" she whispered.

I shook my head, blinking my suddenly misty eyes. "It's just the rain."

"It's not raining," she said.

"Probably that, um, empty-nest syndrome thing, then."

"Yeah, I'm pretty sure that's not it either."

A moment later there was a loud shout behind us, and

I turned to see Saci come scrambling out of the cave, swatting at something around his head.

Violet frowned, and I shouted, "What's going on?"

"Stupee bug flying in my face!" he shouted back, still swatting at something. "Stupee *butterfly*! Is all over me!"

Violet sighed. "Oh, just ignore it."

"I trying!" Saci said. Then he screamed and fell sideways into a bush.

"Are you *serious?*" I couldn't believe this guy was getting beaten up by a friggin' *butterfly*. Shaking my head, I went over to see if he was all right and found him lying on his back with a bright yellow mariposa poised on the very tippy-tip of his nose. Dude had literally been taken down by something that weighed less than *a penny.*

"Nobody move!" Saci whispered through gritted teeth. "I gonna get dis sucker myself. . . ."

Violet was standing over him too, and now, as Saci slowly raised one hand, preparing to squash the butterfly against his face, she yelled, "Wait! That's not a butterfly!"

Saci shot her an annoyed look. "Ei, menina, *please* . . . Saci *know* a butterfly when he see one, okay?"

"No, she's right!" I shouted, realizing it. "It's *Joanna's brooch!*" The one she'd used to mesmerize that big crowd of people and the police officers the day she'd taken us to see that first castell!

Then, with a blur of golden wings, the butterfly brooch lifted off Saci's nose and began flying slow, floaty circles around our heads.

As we watched, it flew ahead of us, toward a path in the trees, and when we didn't immediately follow, it floated back over to us and tried again.

"It looks like it's trying to lead us somewhere . . . ," I whispered.

"That's because it is!" Violet shouted excitedly. "It's Joanna's clue!"

CHAPTER SEVENTY-EIGHT

We followed Jo's butterfly pin north through thick jungle and along winding silver streams, occasionally crossing over barely there paths that zigzagged around clusters of grassy foothills and log bridges. The terrain was tough, the ground littered with knots and bumps and twisted roots, and studded with these huge mossy rocks that looked like they'd make good footing but were actually as slippery as banana peels. We all found that out the hard way. Still, no one—ahem, *Saci*—complained. We were all too jacked up about having found Joanna's clue. That, and having made it out of El Dorado alive. The only bad part, I guess, was that none of us had any idea where the heck we were or where the heck we were going. The Purple Caves could have let out anywhere in South America, anywhere in *the world*, for that matter, and it wasn't like we had a GPS or anything to tell us where we were. Twice, Saci mentioned that the jungle smelled like Costa Rica to him but that he couldn't be positive because he'd banged his nose pretty hard back when we'd crash-landed outside the cave and still wasn't sure it was working right. Wherever we were, my only hope was that Joanna was close by, because we were running out of time.

As the sun began to set, we found ourselves following the golden butterfly down a side of the mountain where the land flattened out and formed almost a plain cut into the steep slope. We were now in sombra wood. At least I was pretty sure we were. I could feel the magic in the air like a cool breeze, like electricity. I watched the butterfly flit in lazy, erratic circles near a stand of trees. Then I watched it pick up speed and fly straight into—*a rock . . . ?*

What the—

Wondering if all this hiking was making me see things, I raced over, Violet right behind me. "How did it do that?" she asked, panting.

"No idea." I pressed the palms of my hands against the big white boulder, which was a little taller than us, about the size of a minivan, feeling for any cracks or openings, but there were none. Something squawked above us.

We both looked up. A fat black crow with big black eyes was perched on the boulder. It peered down at us, squawked, "*Password! What's the password?*"

"Did dat thing talk?" Saci asked as he hopped up behind us.

"*Yes, dummy!*" the crow answered.

Saci glared up at it. "Wha' you jess call me?"

"Password!" I shouted. "It's asking for a *password!*"

Violet looked at me, and we both look at Saci, who shrugged.

"Wha'? I don't know no password for *no rock.*"

V's eyes flicked back to mine. "Charlie?"

"A password . . . ?" How should I know? I mean, who had ever heard of a password to get into a *rock?* But the longer I thought about it, the more I felt like there was something familiar about it all . . . the huge white rock, the black-as-night crow perched atop, asking for a password. Legends began to bubble in my mind, stories of a terrible witch, one who could turn people into animals and entire cities into stone—a witch of the wild . . . a terrifying sombra people had come to fear for hundreds of years. "*Zarate,*" I breathed, and the crow's black eyes sharpened on me.

It angled its sleek, dark head, as if eagerly anticipating my next words. And suddenly I remembered the password: "For the love of the peacock, open the stone!" I shouted, and then knocked three times, just like the legend said to.

On the third knock, the crow leapt off the rock with a

loud squawk and disappeared into the trees in a flurry of black feathers.

"You scare it off!" Saci cried. "*Now* what . . .?"

But no sooner had he spoken those words than a gust of laughter swept through the trees. We all froze. Heart leaping into my throat, I scanned the woods around the rock, but didn't see anyone hiding in there. Nada. Then, a second later, the laughter came again, and this time a great voice—seeming to come from everywhere and nowhere all at once—suddenly spoke up.

It said only five words, but they were five of the most terrifying I'd ever heard:

"BRING LOS NIÑOS TO ME!"

CHAPTER SEVENTY-NINE

At that moment, the ground under our feet began to tremble (which was more than a little freaky, considering earthquakes weren't exactly *rare* in Costa Rica), and I saw a circle of pure white light glowing in the center of the large rock.

At first I thought it had to be one of the last dying rays of sunlight piercing the tree cover and shining right onto the rock's face like a mini spotlight. But the light kept strengthening, expanding outward in overlapping rings of brightness that never wavered or dimmed, until the entire rock shone like a blazing sun.

Shielding my eyes, squinting against the intense glare, I caught glimpses of what looked like dark shapes in the rock . . . dark shapes moving *inside* the rock . . . moving *through* it, through the light. And they were coming toward us, growing bigger and more defined as they did, their inky black shadows seeming to stretch out behind them forever.

"WHAT THE HECK ARE THOSE THINGS?" I shouted.

But before Violet or Saci could answer (not that either one probably had any *clue*), the figures emerged from the light, melting right out of the rock *itself*!

There were maybe ten of them, all oddly shaped, a couple hunched over or seeming to walk on all fours. And now, as they came toward us, walking across solid grassy ground and moving far enough away from the rock that the dazzling light no longer hid their forms, I saw what they actually were—and what they *actually* were was a gang of wild animals. There was a brown pelican, five white-faced monkeys (capuchins, it looked like), a pair of coatimundis (supercute members of the raccoon family), three collared peccaries (basically hairy pigs), an iguana, and a giant green macaw. But even weirder than what they were was what they were wearing: The monkeys had on pleated white pants and red belts; one of the coatimundis was sporting a pair of tiny diamond earrings on its fuzzy half-moon-shaped ears; the macaw wore a necklace of white pearls; and sitting slightly sideways on the pelican's feathered head was a fancy straw hat adorned with a bright red flower and ribbon. No joke, it looked like they were on their way to a quinceañera—at Zoo Miami. The sight was so bizarre, so out-of-this-world ridiculous that I could hardly process it. In fact, I hadn't even finished gaping at their clothes when I realized the animals were *also* carrying weapons—machetes, shovels, and a whole bunch of sharpened twigs and sticks—well, at least the ones with opposable thumbs were. Before I knew it, they'd surrounded us and began herding us toward the glowing rock at twig-point. Like *we* were the wild animals!

One of the capuchins jabbed Saci on the butt with his sharp little stick, shouting, "Marcha!" and Saci immediately whipped his head around to glare at him.

"Hold up—you can *talk*, too . . . ?" I shouted at the monkey. But these were Zarate's woods, after all, which meant that these animals weren't necessarily animals—or at least they hadn't always been. . . .

"Ei, who care if dey can talk?" Saci growled. "Hol' on to you shirts—I gonna whirlwind these furry little freaks to Rio!"

But Violet grabbed his arm, shouting, "Wait!" Which had Saci and me frowning. I'd thought his idea of sending these militarized mammals on a wild ride sounded pretty good actually. "Joanna's butterfly pin went *into* the rock they came *out of*," she explained. "We have to let them take us. Might be the only way in."

And, as usual, she was right.

CHAPTER EIGHTY

As we started into the rock, the intense white light washed over us like a wave, turning everything bright, snowy—and even though I was trying to keep my eyes open, I could already feel them squinting shut. We might as well have been walking into the sun.

Slowly—thankfully—the light began to dim. The back of my eyelids turned from white to red to a darkish golden color, the color of honey in a honeycomb. The heat blazing off the rock was replaced by coolness . . . a gentle breeze. And a scent—faint but sweet: bananas and coffee. I opened my eyes. We weren't in Costa Rica, anymore. Well, at least not in the same *place* in Costa Rica: The grass was still high and wild, but we weren't up on a mountainside anymore. No, we were standing in the middle of a huge, wide-open garden dotted with flower plantings and ringed by dozens of species of fruit trees, their branches heavy with mangoes and papayas, guavas and bananas.

A stone building sat in the middle, right where the flowers and trees grew thickest. It looked like a regular old thatched-roof hut. What I mean is that there wasn't anything particularly strange about it, except for the fact that it seemed to be sitting under its very own dark cloud even though the trees were too far back to cast their shade and there were no rain clouds overhead. In fact, there wasn't a single cloud anywhere in the bright blue canopy of sky. I noticed that the front had no knob, which I found a *tad bit* weird but didn't actually turn out to be a problem, because no one bothered knocking, and the door apparently didn't need any help opening; it just swung slowly inward without anyone having pushed it from our side or pulled it from the other, groaning miserably on oversize steel hinges. *Gulp.*

"After you, chicos, chica . . . ," said one of the capuchins, motioning us inside. The monkey clearly had, like, *zero* intention of joining us inside—neither did any of his buddies.

Saci looked at me, I looked at Violet, and she stared back at me with a look that said, *What choice do we have?*

Not so surprisingly, the place didn't get any less creepy on the inside. Actually, the creepiness factor probably *quadrupled.* The main living area was crammed with all sorts of strange objects: There were fur rugs so thick your feet could get lost in them, and a stack of miniature cauldrons in one corner that gurgled with a tarlike liquid and overflowed into one another. Fancy lamps with what looked like glass eyeballs for bulbs sat on end tables with genuine-looking bones for legs, alongside rows of clear glass jars containing a whole mess of powders and liquids. There were cages, too. A bunch of 'em. They dangled from the ceiling on strings and metal wires. In one a poison dart frog stared out at me with curious bulging eyes; in another was a family of golden silk orb weaver spiders—freaky hand-size arachnids known to catch birds! And as if that weren't freaky enough, a moment later a low silky growl reached my ears. I froze, following the sound with my eyes to the shadows between two tall wooden bookcases—

And felt my heart stop as the bright yellow eyes of a jaguar rose to meet mine. The huge jungle cat tilted its head curiously to one side as it flashed its deadly fangs, and I'm pretty sure I would've let out the world's shriekiest shriek if some part of me hadn't noticed that it, like every other animal in here, was trapped behind wooden bars.

Worse, as my eyes cautiously scanned our surroundings, I saw that the jaguar probably wasn't the most dangerous thing in here. A woman stood at the back wall, hunched over a sink. She was short and fat, bundled up in layers of dark robes, which pooled around her feet. A bright red shawl was knotted around her shoulders, and her eyes, black as liquid tar, stared out at me through the tangles of dark hair hanging over her pale, wrinkly face. I couldn't tell for sure, but it looked like she was peeling fruit with her left hand, effortlessly working the razor-sharp nail of her thumb under the skin of an apple, maybe, and raising a tight curl of peel. Her other hand hung loosely at her side. In it was a short chain made of glittering silver links. Attached to the other end of it was a studded collar, which had been clamped tightly around the slim neck of a beautiful blue-and-black peacock.

"Oh my God," I blurted out, "you still have that peacock?"

Zarate's dark eyes slid to mine. "I've been very much looking forward to meeting you," she said in a scratchy, whispery voice that made all the hairs on the back of my neck stand on end. "I've heard so much about you, many different tales from many different sombras. . . . But to answer your question: Why wouldn't I still have my peacock? He is *my* peacock, and he will always be *my* peacock."

"Um, Charlie, what's going on . . . ?" Violet wanted to know.

"That peacock's *a dude!*" I whispered. "Or *was.* She turned him into that because he didn't love her back."

"Wait. She turned a human being into a *bird* because he didn't love her? That's . . . *creepy.*"

The witch had been stooped over the sink. Now she turned fully to face us, the peacock turning with her, spreading its huge tail feathers like a fan. The feathers had begun to glitter in stunning iridescent shades of blue, brown, green, and yellow. The large eyespots seemed to blink up at us like a hundred winking eyes.

"*Creepy?*" la bruja repeated in her raspy, gravelly, grating voice. I had to fight the urge to clap my hands over my ears, but I could feel my lips pulling back into a grimace. "I think not. . . . I met Governor Pérez at a ball, at the great gathering at the city gates. He was as charming as a mortal man can be, as beautiful as any purple orchid. And like a fool, I fell in love with him . . . sí, como una *loca*. But he *despised* me . . . despised me for my appearance, for the toll the years and suffering had taken on this body. . . . A shallow, *shallow* man he was, so I swore my *revenge*."

Saci giggled. "You turn him into a bird. . . . Now, *that's* a good prank! Saci approves!"

"It wasn't *a prank*, idiota. I *loved* him, ¿no entiendes? And he was *repulsed* by me! How would any of *you* have felt . . . ?" The witch raised a wrinkled, pockmarked hand in our direction, and without thinking I quickly stepped in front of Violet. I'd done it to protect her, I guess, but apparently Zarate had just been pointing.

Now the spooky old bruja grinned, deepening the map

of wrinkles across her face as understanding seemed to illuminate her cold black eyes.

"Qué lechero . . . ," she cooed, wrapping the silvery chain tighter around her hand. "What a *special bond* you two must share. . . . A *very* special bond, indeed." Beside her, the peacock stretched its wings to their full length and began to flutter about, tugging nervously against the chain. "Is your friendship *truly* so precious? Am I to understand that you would gladly sacrifice yourself for this niña . . . ?"

I didn't respond to that—didn't know she'd expected me to—and for a moment there was complete and total silence. Then, suddenly, la bruja's eyes blazed out like red-tinted spotlights and, well, things started to get scary. She roared, "I ASKED YOU A QUESTION, MOCOSO! WOULD YOU SACRIFICE YOURSELF FOR HER? ¡CONTÉSTAME!"

All at once the witch went into this insane growth spurt. Her body stretched like taffy, growing wider, taller, towering above us now, the shadows darkening around her, creeping slowly up the walls and out from under tables and furniture like something alive and slithery.

Behind us, the shutters on the only window began to slam open and shut. Lamps flickered. A few buzzed and went out. Closer, the animals trapped in the hanging cages had begun to go wild, howling and jumping and chittering and making the cages swing back and forth on the ceiling like pendulums. Zarate's peacock also seemed to have lost it: the thing was screeching at the top of its lungs now, loud enough to make me worry my eardrums might burst, while at the same time flapping its wings and dancing wildly about the little kitchen, hopping from one leg to the other, as if the old wooden floorboards had suddenly turned into burning coals.

Not liking where this was going—okay, more like *terrified* where this was going—I forced myself to speak. I shouted, "Yes, okay? I would. Happy?"

"¡MENTIRAS!" la bruja snapped back. I could feel anger boiling off her like waves of heat. It pulsed through the floorboards, making them tremble beneath us. "ALL LIES! WHAT DO *YOU* KNOW ABOUT SACRIFICE? ABOUT *TRUE* FRIENDSHIP? WHAT DO *YOU* KNOW ABOUT THE MISERY BETWEEN LOVE AND HATE WHERE ALL BECOMES BLURRED AND THERE IS NO ONE YOU HATE MORE THAN THE ONE YOU ONCE LOVED?"

"Dis not good . . . ," Saci said, backing slowly toward the door. "Dis *muito* not good, bro!"

"YOU KNOW NOTHING OF IT!" Zarate's voice boomed through the small room like an explosion, rattling the tables and shelves, sending jars and plates crashing to the floor. "HOW DARE ANY OF YOU JUDGE MY ACTIONS? HOW DARE *ANY ONE OF YOU* JUDGE ME?" The tips of her fingers shone with a fierce reddish light so dark it was almost black. Her pupils had expanded to fill her eyes almost completely. It was freaky to say the least. "I SHOULD CURSE YOU! I SHOULD TURN *YOUR* PRECIOSA INTO A *PEACOCK!*"

La bruja's craggy hand stretched toward us. Violet gasped. She staggered on her feet, and I looked downt to see that her legs were changing, thinning, the skin thickening, becoming those of a bird—a *peacock!*

CHAPTER EIGHTY-ONE

WHAT ARE YOU DOING?" I yelled as bright green feathers began to pop out all over Violet's arms. Her lips were changing too—hardening, turning beaklike. Her eyes bulged; her skin rippled and discolored beneath the sprouting feathers. "OYE, ¿ESTÁ LOCA? STOP! STOP IT!"

I screamed at the witch, but she totally ignored me, cackling at the top of her lungs. I didn't know what else to do, so I just kept screaming at her, screaming with everything in me: "PARA! FOR *THE LOVE OF THE PEACOCK,* PLEASE JUST STOP!"

And somehow—I honestly had no idea how—it worked. I watched Zarate blink her eyes slowly, as if coming out of a deep trance. Then, even more slowly, the anger began to drain from her eyes, her face—the room seemed to brighten, and I saw, with a huge rush of relief, that Violet's legs were turning back to normal again, the skin smoothing and losing that bumpy texture as the feathers dropped away to seesaw lazily to the ground around her sneakers.

"Perdóname . . . ," Zarate breathed, stumbling back a step, her dark eyes wild, unfocused. She had shrunk back down to what I guessed was her usual size and her fingertips were no longer blazing. Thank God for that. "It's the season. . . . It makes me un poquito—*uneven*."

I didn't think the word "uneven" was—no pun intended—even in the ballpark (more like *psycho*), but I wasn't about to say a peep.

The fingers of la bruja's left hand loosened. The silver chain she was holding slipped from her grasp, and her peacock immediately scampered out of the house through the back door. Zarate's wavering gaze sharpened on me like a laser. "No eres como los otros. . . ."

"I'm not like the others?" I asked, shaking my head.

"The other Morphlings." She hesitated, her eyes once again narrowing in that dangerous sort of way. "You can hear the voices, can't you . . . ?"

"The voices?" My heart was still pounding so hard and so fast I could barely make sense of her question. "What voices?"

"The ones no one else can. The whispers, the groans."

Yeah, that made my arms tingle with goose bumps. How did she know that? "Yeah . . . who are they?"

"Those who have passed yet are to come. Who else?"

I was still shaking my head, the goose bumps now working their way up my neck, over my scalp. "But—how come I can hear them?"

"Because of El Ojo. The Eye. It watches you day and night. It has already bound the sacrifice to its offerer. I can see it on you. . . . You now hear without limitation. Your ears now perceive both the living *and* the dead."

"I—I don't get it. . . . What *eye*? What *sacrifice*?"

"The more I say, the less you'll understand. But now, for the reason you have come . . ." Moving quickly, she picked up a small wooden bowl filled with the leaves of marigold flowers. She ran some tap water into the bowl. Then she brought out a stone pestle from a drawer below the sink and began to grind the flowers into a thick yellowish paste sort of the way I'd seen my mom do when she makes mofongo, that tasty dish of smashed fried bananas. But la bruja didn't stop there. Next she plucked a strand of thick, sticky web from the cage of those bird-eating spiders, thumbed a finger's worth of slime from the back of a poison dart frog, flicked all of that nastiness into the wooden bowl, and a second later I saw her eyes roll to white as she began to mutter something under her breath. Her muttering quickly turned to chanting, and maybe it was my imagination but I thought I could see some sort of vapory mistiness escaping the witch's mouth and flowing into the bowl, mixing with the marigold paste. Then she dipped her thumb and index finger into the yellowish goo and touched them to my forehead. Finally, her eyes rose to meet mine.

"It is the final step of preparation," she whispered. "La Marca will give you a second chance. But only *one*."

I felt my lips pull down into a frown. "I—*what?*"

Zarate didn't answer; instead she just smiled at me. It was a sort of apologetic smile—one that said, *Cheer up; things will get better . . . maybe.*

She didn't seem like she was going to say anything else, so I said, "I didn't come here for any *mark*. I came to find Joanna."

"Yo lo sé. You followed her butterfly." With the tips of her fingers, la bruja peeled back the collar of her robes, and I saw Joanna's butterfly resting quietly on her shoulder. Its wings were still, and it now appeared more pin than butterfly. "She wanted you to find me."

"Why would she want us to find you?"

Zarate frowned. "I've already told you why. Were you not listening?"

This bruja clearly put the *k* in kooky. Maybe *both ks*. But Joanna *had obviously* wanted us to find her. So maybe she could help. "Look, we're running out of time. Where do you think Joanna could have hidden her next clue?"

"There are no more clues," she replied quickly. "I am the final bread crumb in the path that has been prepared for you."

"So you know where she is?"

"No. But I know where she will *be*. Mexico. San Miguel de Allende. In El Jardín. The heart of old San Miguel. You must be there by midnight. *Tonight*."

This was big. No, this was huge. But . . . "Midnight tonight? *Why?*"

"Because events that cannot be reversed have been set into motion." Zarate cast a quick look around, frowning. "Y algo más . . . something else I needed to tell you . . . ¿Qué fue, Dios mío?"

In the distance, a single piercing howl split the air.

Every cell in my body seemed to turn to ice, and Zarate's eyes, now wide with panic, flew to the window.

"Los Embrujados," she breathed.

"*Ay, no* . . ." Saci whirled, staring out the same window. "Not lobisomem!"

"Tómalo. Take this!" The witch shoved a basket of grapefruit into his arms.

"What dis? Saci no want no stinkin' *fruit!*"

"Do not lose those! Carry them with you until the very end!" La bruja's dark eyes found Saci's. "Can I trust you to do that, *traitor?*"

"*Wha' you call me?*" Saci said, but Zarate had already turned, motioning us toward the back of the house.

"Out through the kitchen!" she cried. Saci and Violet took off for the back door, but the witch grabbed me before I could. "There is one more thing you must know. . . . This path you walk, the path of the sacrifice—*you* must walk it, ¿me entiendes? It must be your feet! And remember: Castells are the pathway to the High Altar." Before I could ask what any of that meant, she said, "You are the fifth and the final, the last of five. You must do what your predecessors couldn't—you must do what no one else can. You've already come *so far*, mi niño, tried by the elements—earth, wind, water, fire—and proven true. . . . But you *must* finish this."

Finish it? I didn't even know what *it* was. "And what if I can't?"

"Then this world will fall to the hand of darkness."

Saci and Violet were standing on Zarate's back porch, staring up at a couple of camels chained to a post.

"Take them!" the witch cried as we spilled out the back door to join them. She smacked her hands together, and the chains began to unwind themselves, clinking and clanking as they loosened. "And treat them harshly! These rascals deserve it."

Another howl—and bloodcurdlingly close.

"Out of the way, lady!" Saci screamed. "We not riding any of your nasty people-animals. And dey ain't no slow-poke camels in da world that gonna outrun lobisomem!" Then, winking back at me, "But Saci can." He raised a hand, cried, "AÇÚCAR!" and suddenly a swirling, screaming whirlwind snaked down out of thin air, gusting around us and slurping us up into the clear blue sky.

From way down below, I heard Zarate shout, "*¡Hasta la muerte, hasta que veas la Catrina y la Calavera te retenga en sus brazos!*" (which basically translates into "Until death, until you see La Catrina and she takes you in her arms!"), then: "*¡Pura vida!*" (which translates into "Pure life!"), and then we were gone.

CHAPTER EIGHTY-TWO

When we touched down again, we were standing in the middle of some dusty little town . . . what looked like a *ghost town.*

"This isn't San Miguel de Allende," I couldn't help pointing out.

Saci frowned, embarrassed. "Not as far as I hoped . . . Saci a bit tired."

Worse, as the world steadied around us, I saw that the town wasn't exactly uninhabited . . . and *even worse,* I saw that what I'd first thought might be an injured, limping, overly dressed couple ambling slowly, arm in arm, across the desolate intersection was actually a couple of zombies—yes, *zombies.* And what I'd mistaken for some kind of calaca-inspired decoration was really a severed zombie head trying to roll itself across the strip of grass that ran along the sidewalk just off the road.

"The heck's going on . . . ?" I started to say, but as I took a closer look around, I realized, with a spike of panic, that the town was actually *crawling* with these things! And I meant that both figuratively *and* literally. They limped and lumbered and dragged themselves through the streets and alleyways, dozens upon dozens of walking, disheveled, undead corpses in various stages of oh-so-yucky decay: men with greenish skin and moth-eaten tuxedos, women with curls of fingernails that hung below their knees and patches of stringy white hair down to their ankles.

Some wore shoes, but most didn't. Some had eyeballs swimming around in the sockets of their sagging, melted faces—but a *lot* didn't. And their smell? Well, let's just say it registered off the charts on my 'Bout-to-Barf Meter.

I remembered what Adriana told us about the days when the dead walked the earth. I remembered what Mario had said about how the necromancer's zombie army had nearly overrun the entire *world*. And, no big surprise, I shivered. Shivered even in the dry heat of this dusty little town.

"It's happening again," Saci breathed, hardly daring to look around. "Dey already rising. . . ."

That there was zero question about. The only question was, *why?* Was this some side effect of Joanna preparing to raise the necromancer? Had something gone wrong? Or—

and no doubt the *scariest* possibility—had Joanna gone full-blown evil and decided to raise her *own* army?

"V, I see dead people . . . ," I whispered. Couldn't help it.

"Jess keep walking," Saci said, focusing his eyes straight ahead. "And whatever you do, *don't* look dem in dey face!"

Violet cringed. "I don't think that one even *has* a face."

We walked on through the town, pretending not to hear any of the gruesome moans or groans coming from inside the buildings or notice any of the decaying, bedraggled bodies lumbering their way through the streets, and we reached the next town over about an hour later—just as the sun had begun to set over the stretch of hills that marked the horizon. The first thing I noticed was the people: Unlike the zombie town we'd just walked through, this place was absolutely *packed*—and, even better, with genuine *living* bodies this time. There must've been thousands, maybe several thousands, crammed along the board sidewalks and wandering almost aimlessly up and down the narrow two-lane road that cut through the center of town. The second thing I noticed was what *wasn't* there: There were no cars anywhere along the road, no taxis waiting at the curb in front of the office buildings, no buses sitting in the pickup zone to our left. I didn't even hear the distant whine of an electric scooter.

"Guys, I don't like this," Violet said, looking around uneasily.

Off to our left, a mother with two young children was holding up a shoddy cardboard sign that read HAVE MONEY—NEED TRANSPORT. Farther up the road a man was waving one that said WILL PAY FOR GAS. I realized a lot of the people sitting or standing along the dusty street were carrying similar signs, and most were in Spanish. I saw children standing next to suitcases with name tags stapled to the sleeves of their T-shirts. Abuelitas were crying. Men and women were poking their heads out of the second- and third-story windows of the short brick-faced buildings that flanked the road, shouting the names of family members or asking for people to help them pack their belongings. I had no idea what was going on here, but something was seriously wrong.

"Hey, what's going on?" Violet said to a dude in an Astros cap as he came toward us.

"¿Qué?"

"What's going on?"

"What does it look like? Everyone's trying to get north."

"Why?" I asked.

"You joking, kid? Central America's being overrun by the dead, and you're asking me why people are trying to *leave?*"

"Wha you mean overrun?" Saci asked the man.

"I mean they're crawling out of their graves, attacking people! It's happening all over South America too, I heard."

He narrowed his eyes at us. "Esperate. Where are you three from? Where are your parents?"

"They're, uh, in Oaxaca, Mexico," I lied. "We're trying to get there."

"You and everybody else, kid."

"Where are the taxis 'n' stuff?" Saci wanted to know.

"*Taxis?* I haven't seen *a car* in over a week. The government is sending buses around, but we're not exactly the biggest town, so we haven't seen one yet; but everybody and their cousin is trying to get a ticket." His eyes moved up the street, past us. "Oye, I gotta go. I got a wife and two small children I have to get out of this place." Then, turning around, he shouted, "¿Oye, Paco, encontraste el carburador? ¡Paco!" And he ran off down the road.

"This is jess *perfect,*" Saci grumbled. "How we supposed to get to Mexico now?"

Out of the corner of my eye I caught a flash of blue light between the buildings to my left, and when I turned to look, thinking it might be the headlight of a motorbike, I saw a familiar wrinkly face beneath a familiar yellow turban heading straight for us.

"Mr. Ovaprim!" I shouted.

"¡Niños! We meet again!" He grinned broadly at us, but the smile didn't quite reach his eyes. "I only wish it were under better circumstances. . . ."

"Me too," Violet said. "But you made it off the train okay, huh?"

"Sí, sí. On my way to the bathroom I slipped and hit my head, but when I woke up, we had arrived in Argentina and everything was fine. They even refunded my ticket money."

The least they could do after a werewolf attack, I thought.

Mr. Ovaprim hesitated for a moment like he was trying to think back. His cheeks and forehead creased like a rubber mask. "By the way, do either of you know what happened after I left the cabin? It felt like the train might have hit something. . . ."

Violet and I looked at each other. "Uh, yeah," V said. "I think it might've. . . ."

"Yeah, there were some animals on the track . . . ," I said, (which wasn't even telling the *half* of it), and Violet had to hide her smile. "But you're okay, right?"

"Sí, sí. I'm fine. I'm just trying to find a ticket to Mexico."

"Seems like everyone's trying to do that," I said.

"It's true. But I've done a bit of traveling over the years and learned a few tricks." He brought out a handful of small red tickets, about a dozen of them. "I was able to get my hands on these. They're raffling off the last twenty seats on a small plane that's leaving not too far from here. They're going to announce the winners in the town hall. I'm making my way there now to ensure that I get a seat. These old knees much prefer to sit. Meet me there in ten minutes, and we'll test our luck!"

"You got it, Mr. Ovaprim!"

"Oh, I almost forgot. I'm looking for my son. He was supposed to meet me here. His name is Ronald. He has black hair, a nose ring, a couple tattoos. If you see him, would you please let me know?"

"Definitely!" I said. "You're a lifesaver, Mr. Ovaprim!"

Now his grin did reach his eyes. "Let's hope so, niños. And nice grapefruit, by the way," he said to Saci. "They look tasty." Then Mr. Ovaprim began to waddle away, moving so slowly and carefully that it made him look like he was wearing a skin suit he was afraid might fall off.

When he disappeared into the press of bodies crowding the sidewalks and streets, Saci turned to me and said, "Maybe we win?"

"Maybe. But we need a backup plan," I said, and Violet, who was usually one step ahead of everyone else, pointed up the narrow street to what was very obviously some kind of bus station; the sign over the front door read AUTOBÚS, and there was even a picture of a speeding red bus below.

"Worth a shot," she said.

The El Camacho bus station was pretty big for a bus station but still overflowing with bodies. The lines *literally* were out the doors. In fact, right where we stood to *open* the door was where we joined the line.

"We gonna be here all night," Saci grumbled.

V glanced at him. "You got something better to do?"

"Saci can think of a few things. . . ."

I saw his dark, mischievous eyes surveying the room and said, "Well, you better *stop* thinking."

He sighed. "Can I at least put this basket down already . . . ? This stupid fruit *heavy*."

"Just don't lose it," Violet said. "You heard the witch."

To our left two men in leather vests and faded jeans were sitting on the inside sill of the front window. They were wearing guns on their hips, even though there was a NO PISTOLAS sign hanging on the window above them, and talking so loudly that they reminded me of two overly caffeinated first graders exchanging wild stories in the school cafeteria. The one wearing a cowboy hat said, "Oye, forget the zombies. Olvidalo! It's *the bloodsucker* that worries me. . . . And like I tol' you—there's only *one* bloodsucker. There's this guy I know. He seen it face-to-face. *Cara-a-cara.* Thinks it's after him. But I think it's after *all of us* . . . this whole freaking town."

Wannabe number two was shaking his head. "Esta loco, compadre. . . ."

"¿Yo? No, *you* just blind! Don't you see what's happening?

The thing's herding us up. Like cattle! Cutting us off from the rest of the world. And then, well, then it's *feeding time.* . . ."

"You listening to that?" Violet whispered.

I nodded.

"Should we . . . ?"

I nodded again. "I think we should."

V turned to Saci and handed him some cash. "Hold our spot in line. But if you make it to the front, buy us three tickets and one for Mr. Ovaprim. And no fooling around, okay?"

Saci gave her a mischievous grin, and since that was probably the best the guy could do, we left it at that and strolled over to the two vaquero wannabes like a couple of hotshot detectives from telenovelas. I decided to let Violet do the talking.

"I'm sorry," she said, "but we overheard your conversation. . . . Did one of you say that you know a guy who's seen *the bloodsucker* face-to-face?"

The guy in the hat crossed his arms over his plaid shirt. "That's right."

"Is he still in town?"

"Sure is."

"I know this is going to sound strange, but could you take us to him? We'd love to ask him a few questions."

"I don't think so, señorita. . . . He's locked himself up pretty tight and isn't much interested in company at the moment."

"We can help him," I said.

The man's eyes narrowed skeptically. "Oh yeah? And how's that?"

"Do your friend a favor," Violet said. "Tell him to talk to us. You just might save his life."

"Well, for starters, the guy ain't my friend. . . . He's a customer. And for seconds, I don't see what I'm getting out of all this."

V brought out a wad of cash. "How about a couple of Benjamin Franklins and an Andrew Jackson?"

I heard him swallow hard. "Always loved those two gringos. . . . Name's José. Follow me, por favor."

CHAPTER EIGHTY-THREE

The building attached to the bus station had three floors connected by a rickety wooden staircase; it creaked and groaned as we followed José to the third door on the top floor, where he raised a silver door knocker, then paused. "This fellow's been through a lot recently," José whispered, "so no sudden movements. No sneezing, coughing. Don't reach into your pockets; don't tie or untie your shoes. Try not to smile. Oh, and do either of you have any open wounds? No? Good. Because he's not too keen on blood at the moment. Also, don't look him in the eye for too long either. In fact, maybe avoid eye contact altogether."

Geez. . . . "Anything else?" I asked.

He thought for a second. "Nothing comes to mind." Then he banged the knocker once, twice, and shouted, "Oye, Ronny, I got some visitors for you. . . ."

"¿Qué? ¡No! ¡No visitas!" came a loud voice from the other side. "Tell 'em I not here!"

"But they say they wanna hear that story you tell! The one ab—"

"WHY YOU TELLING PEOPLE ABOUT THAT, MAN? YOU CRAZY?"

José glanced down at the money V had given him, sighed, then brought out a ring of keys and began to unlock the door. "Oye, my friend, please don't shoot!"

We followed him into the tiny apartment, which reeked of vinegar and something else . . . something *stronger*—fermented garlic, maybe?

None of the lights were on—only a cluster of wax candles burning over the cold fireplace, but even in the semi-dark I could see dozens of silver crucifixes dangling from the ceiling fan on fishing lines and strips of fabric.

"Oye, what's wrong with you, man?" a voice yelled from somewhere in the shadows. "You deaf? I said NO VISI-TAS!"

My eyes flew around the room again, and I *still* almost missed the guy. He was sitting on the love seat next to the sofa, half hidden in the dark and buried almost to his knees in a mountain of uncooked rice, his bare toes poking out the bottom like hairy little foothills. The guy was somewhere in his early forties with dark eyes peeking out from under a mop of darker hair and a silver nose ring glinting dully in his left nostril. Slung around his upper arms were wreaths of black garlic, and in his trembling right hand I saw a sharp wooden stake. Looked like he'd carved it out of a spatula. Yep, the dude was definitely one bean short of a cafecito. Suddenly I wished I'd paid a little more attention to that long list of don't-dos José had given us.

"I—I'm gonna leave you three alone, okay?" José said, already backing out of the room. "Have a nice chat!"

He closed the door behind him, and for several seconds no one spoke. In the silence I could hear a TV in another room, some news anchor talking about how the Spanish president had been missing for days now—how no one had heard from her or had any idea where she'd gone. *We're working on it*, I thought.

"What do you two want?" the man finally asked. He sounded angry, borderline furious, in fact—but also scared; his voice trembled like a plucked string.

"We wanna help," Violet said.

"Okay, so help."

"Look, my friend here is an expert on all things . . . *freaky*, you could say. So if you just gave us the four-one-one on the thing you saw, we might be able to stop it before it hurts anyone else."

Ronny—or whatever his name was—laughed, but it

wasn't a *ha-ha* sort of laugh; there was bitterness in it, and fear . . . much fear. "You have no idea what this creature is, do you, señorita? You think *you two* can stop it?" He leaned forward to whisper, "This thing will suck every last drop of blood out of your bodies before you can even muster up the courage to open your mouths to scream for help."

I heard myself gulp. Yep, that was a visual I didn't need. "So what is it exactly?"

"At first? Una luz—that's all, just a light . . . but then the creature takes its true form, and you see it for what it *truly* is."

He was silent for so long, I found myself stepping forward to ask, "And what is it?" Half of me was dying to hear the answer, the other half, well, not so much.

Then Ronny spoke two words—just two—but they were enough to make my insides twist into the twistiest pretzel you've ever seen "Un vampiro . . ."

"A *what?*" Violet asked.

"A vampire," I translated. "He said it's a vampire. . . ."

CHAPTER EIGHTY-FOUR

The dude's gaze drifted down to my feet and his eyes went glassy for a moment, like he was no longer really looking at me but rather staring back into the past. "I've never seen anything move so fast. Its fangs are daggers; its eyes a hungry fire." He brought a candy bar from his pocket, tried to unwrap it, but his hands were trembling too badly. He sighed and tossed it onto the couch. "Those things are no good for you, anyway...."

"Where did you see it?" Violet asked, her blue eyes locked on his.

"I was working overseas ... herding cows ... before it *slaughtered them.*"

Violet and I exchanged looks of shock. The words "cow" and "slaughtered" rang through my mind like a gong, and suddenly I was picturing that first castell Joanna had taken us to see . . . the one made up of all those sucked-dry cow carcasses.

Every inch of my skin rippled with goose bumps.

"Let me guess," I said. "You're from Portugal?"

And just from the way his eyes flashed with surprise I knew I was exactly right. "I—I'm from España. But I *was* working in Portugal. . . . How did you know?"

"Lucky guess." I turned to Violet. "So Joanna is working with a vamp, then—*a vampire*."

"Sounds like it."

"What are we gonna do?"

"You're asking me? That's *your* specialty."

"*My* specialty? Who do I look like, Buffy? I'm not a *vampire slayer*."

"Well, you better start acting like one."

I opened my mouth to say something, but Ronny spoke first. "It's hunting me . . . ," he murmured as if talking to himself. "Once a vampire knows you've seen it, it will hunt you until you're dead. It's why I haven't stopped running." He laughed humorlessly. "The only reason I'm even still alive is because the monster got tripped up, lost its shoe. That gave me enough time to get to my car and—"

Just then the door to his apartment flew open, and Saci came scrambling in with the basket of grapefruit clutched under one arm. He made a funny face as his eyes flew around the room, but then he spotted us and quickly closed the door behind him, slid the bolt.

"Ei!" he said, panting. "Been looking for you!"

"Who THE HECK are *you*?" Ronny blurted out, leaping from his chair. Grains of rice flew everywhere. A handful pelted the side of my face.

"It's okay," Violet said. "He's with us."

"And that's supposed to do exactly *WHAT* for me?" he shot back. Candlelight glinted off the point of his deadly spatula-stake as he aimed it threateningly (well, as threateningly as you can aim a *spatula*) at Saci, who'd probably broken Jose's entire don't-do list in about three seconds after entering the room.

"Dude, what are you doing here?" I asked Saci.

His breath was wheezing in and out of his lungs like a busted bagpipe, but he managed: "The guy in the cowboy boots . . . wass his name? He tol' me you were here."

"That doesn't answer my question," I said.

Saci grabbed my arm, started pulling me across the room. "I think we should probably go. . . ."

I yanked my arm free. "What? *Why?*"

"Did you get the tickets?" Violet asked him.

"Oh, sim, sim . . . four tickets just like you wanted." He pulled them out of his overalls and handed them to her.

"Wow. I thought they'd all be sold out by now," Violet said. "Did you get change?"

"Sim, sim, sim." Nodding, he handed that over too—all of it, everything Violet had given him. Which started to make me really, *really* nervous.

Violet stared down at the bills. "So the tickets were . . . *free?*"

"You could say that . . . ," Saci mumbled, looking down at his toes.

Pounding footsteps echoed in the hall outside. Lots of people, from the sound of it—heavy boots. Someone shouted, "¿Dónde fue?"

And someone else answered, "He went that way!"

The footsteps grew louder, closer.

"*Or* you could say something else . . . ," Saci said in a low, embarrassed voice.

"In here!" someone shouted, this time just on the other side of the door.

Violet aimed a threatening finger at Saci. "You didn't prank those guys by *taking their bus tickets*, did you?" she whispered harshly.

Saci nodded shyly, and I was surprised that I didn't spontaneously combust on the spot. "Well, give them back!" I roared.

"Saci can't!" he said.

"Why not?"

"I try! But dey don' care! Dey too mad!"

I glared at him, trying not to a) strangle him or b) bite his head off. (The first was going to be harder to resist.) "What exactly did you do to them?"

"Exactly?" he asked meekly.

"Yes, *exactly!*"

He took a breath. "Okay, here go. After I take tickets, I tie dey belts together and dey shoes, write silly things on dey faces, like I did to you. I take dey wallets and switch everyone's licenses. I tape, 'Kick Me' notes to dey backs. I shoot spitballs at meanest-looking guy and blame it on someone else. Oh, and then I sour dey cups of hot cacau."

"You did all that in *ten minutes?*" Violet asked, sounding almost impressed.

But now Saci looked downright *de*pressed. "I know . . . slow day for Saci."

"V, go out there and negotiate some kind of peace treaty!" I shouted.

She glared at me. "What do I look like, a UN ambassador?" And before she could say anything else, a storm of bullets ripped through the door, sending metal and chunks of wood flying.

"Don't look like dey want peace!" Saci shouted. "Jess a piece of *ME!*" Then he grabbed Violet and me by our shirtsleeves and dragged us across the room to the window overlooking the main street. He threw it open, started to climb out. When we didn't immediately follow—I was still staring back at the door, terrified out of my mind—he grabbed us again and pulled us, side by side, through the small rectangular opening. We crawled out onto the little slope of the roof just as the door on the other side of the room was kicked in.

"VAMOS!" Saci screamed at us. "*MOVE!*"

The roof had been weatherproofed with rocky shingles that bit painfully into the palms of my hands and my knees as I scampered across it. When we reached the edge, Saci hopped off, landing in the middle of a dumpster overstuffed with plastic bags. We went next, crashing down on either side of him, and just as we fought our way out of the stinking thing, one of the guys Saci had pranked stuck his head out the third-story window, scanning the street below. I could see the word 'burro' (which is Spanish for donkey) scrawled clearly across his forehead in black marker, and on either side of his mustache Saci had drawn in some oversize curly ends so that the dude looked like a fancy French chef. He spotted us, then drew a pistol and squeezed off a couple of fast shots. One went whizzing by over my head and pinged off a telephone pole. Another shattered the window of the old-fashioned ice-cream parlor down the street.

Everyone on that side of the street—actually, pretty much *anyone* within earshot—started screaming and running for cover.

I wanted to yell, *Aim for the barefoot pickpocket!* But then the maniac was sighting me down his barrel, and I was done trying to talk any sense into him.

"Are you INSANE?" Violet shouted up at him. "You're shooting at *kids!*"

"C'mon!" Saci yelled. He grabbed me by the shirtsleeve again and took off down the middle of the street, weaving recklessly through the crowds as two of the gunman's friends spilled out of the first-floor doors and gave chase.

As we ran, I heard a soft tinkling sound, something like a wind chime, and looked down to see that the dozen or so plump purple grapefruit Saci was carrying in the basket had suddenly turned to gold—*solid gold!*

Saci, who'd also taken note of this *interesting* turn of events, was staring at me with eyes the size of soccer balls. "BRO, YOU SEE DIS?" he cried, giggly with joy. "IT'S A MIRACLE!"

Only it wasn't—not really. It was actually *legend!* In one of Zarate's most famous tales, she'd been tracked down by some poor farmer who had been robbed of all his animals and lost his land. He wanted the witch to give him money so he could feed his starving family. But when he finally found her and told her his story, Zarate gave him a basket of grapefruit and told him to go on his way. The farmer was obviously disappointed but left since he didn't think there was anything he could do to change the witch's mind. Later that day, as he was making his way back home through the woods, he began to dump some of the grapefruit because they were getting so heavy. It wasn't until he was almost home that he realized the grapefruit had all turned to gold. Apparently the kooky bruja was still up to her old tricks.

There was another burst of gunfire behind us. More screams erupted.

What is up *with these dudes?* I thought, fighting the urge to look back. *Okay, fine. So they got punked by an overall-wearing klepto with a seashell pipe. Stuff happens. But that doesn't give them the right to start shooting at people!*

As we reached the near corner, where a set of train tracks ran through town, I finally couldn't fight it anymore, and I glanced back but couldn't pick out any of the trigger-happy psychos in the scramble of bodies. Then another volley of gunfire ripped through the air—at least ten or fifteen guns going off almost in unison.

"WHAT'S WRONG WITH THESE PEOPLE?" Violet shrieked, looking back.

"Dey not shootin' at us!" Saci cried. "They shootin' at *dem!*"

He was staring past me, off to my left, and following his gaze, I saw the first of them—a huge, hulking shadow racing along the rooftops, its fierce, bright eyes like twin laser beams against the darkening desert sky.

And worse? Those eyes were looking right at us. Looking right at *me*.

CHAPTER EIGHTY-FIVE

Watch out!" Violet screamed as another lobi-somem leapt down from somewhere overhead, landing in the road in front of us, cutting us off.

It threw back its head with a howl that turned my blood to ice. Then it snarled at me, fangs bared, and lunged—

Time slowed. A million and one panicky thoughts raced through my mind:

Ay, mi Madre!

I'm so dead.

Dude, do something!

RUUUUUUUUUUNNN!

My body, however, was scared stiff. Frozen like a snow-man in winter.

Before I could react, the werewolf was flying through

the air at me, massive razor-tipped claws rising, preparing to slash—but Saci was faster.

He shot out a hand and shouted, "Açúcar!" and a whirl-wind funneled down out of the cloudless sky, lifting the werewolf off its feet and sending it crashing through the display window of the bakery across the street. The wolf tumbled through about half a dozen full-size baker's racks, sending doughnuts, bagels, baguettes, and a whole mess of other freshly baked goodies flying as shards of glass rained down around it.

My eyes, still jacked wide with fear, flew to Saci. Had he just saved my life? Again? "Dude, thanks!"

He grinned at me, but it was a weak sort of smile. Beads of sweat had popped out on his forehead, and his usually bright eyes were dim and unfocused.

"Not sure I can do that again, irmão," he choked out, which wasn't *exactly* what I wanted to hear, because right then another wailing howl pierced the night, and I looked back to see a literal *army* of lobisomem—hundreds, if not *thousands*, of werewolves—charging toward us, bounding over the sidewalks and streets and trampling anyone in their path as they fanned out across the town like a swarm of locusts. Their yipping and braying echoed around us like ghostly laughter.

More gunfire rang out. I could see the silhouette of

bodies being tossed around in the air like rag dolls. And I didn't need to be a lycanthropologist to know they'd overrun the town in a matter of minutes.

We only had one move.

"V, give me Saci's gorra!" I shouted.

"Huh?"

"His cap! Give it to me!"

She dug into her bag and handed it over, and I had to grimace against its brutal stench. Gosh, it was almost like that thing was smelling *worse*, somehow.

"What are you thinking?" Violet wanted to know.

"They're after me, remember? I'm going to lead them away from you guys and everyone else. Meet me in the restaurant up the street. Paco's!"

Violet shouted, "Charlie, are you sure?" but I was already moving, already darting into the side street to our left—and then I was gone.

CHAPTER EIGHTY-SIX

The howls seemed to chase me, growing louder, closer. Shapes and shadows flitted along the rooftops. They stretched long across the sides of buildings, over the streets and storefronts. The town was officially crawling with lobisomem; I could feel them lurking around every corner, gaining on me block by block, herding me, corralling me, forcing me right to where they wanted me. Or so they thought.

I ran flat out, flying down one side street, then another. The paths between buildings got narrower, the smooth brick walls seeming to hem me in as they twisted and turned like a maze. Shouts of terror came from every direction.

My pounding footsteps bounced off the walls as I raced around another corner, then cut across a side street somewhere on the edge of town.

Soon I lost all sense of direction and found myself running through an abandoned parking lot behind an even more abandoned-looking warehouse topped with a red-and-white striped smokestack.

There was a large grassy field bordered by a fence to my right and a couple of warehouses with an alley running between them to my left. I chose left and had just run past a row of trash cans when I heard a low, vicious growl behind me. I froze. Behind me, a pack of lobisomem was stalking up the side street, the entire pack creeping in the shadows, only those glowing red eyes clearly visible. Gulp. And there were even more peering down hungrily at me from the ledge of every rooftop in sight.

Probably three times as many. Double gulp.

I couldn't wait for them to make their move. So I made mine, slipping behind the trash cans, pulling on Saci's cap, and watching my arms and legs—along with the rest of me—vanish completely out of sight before taking off down the alley.

I made it just as one of the wolves sprang down from overhead in a blind attempt to cut me off. And it would've gotten me too, if there hadn't been a tree in the way, a tree growing right up through the pavement by the mouth of the alley. I hadn't even noticed it until that very moment, and apparently neither had the lobisomem, because it slammed straight into it, the werewolf's arms wrapping around the branches heavy with clusters of beautiful red flowers almost in an embrace.

For a split second, I thought, *Whoa, that tree looks familiar!* And in that *same split second* another thought struck me, one that made me feel a little bit stupid for thinking it: *Isn't that the exact same tree I saw back on Cabana Mesa Hill?*

But it wasn't like I had time to stop and stare—or even to think very much about it—because the rest of the werewolves were already after me, their claws scrabbling over the sidewalks and rooftops as they chased the sound of my pounding feet. I knew that was the only way they could track me now—by the sound of my footsteps (smell was probably out of the question thanks to the stink of Saci's cap)—so I ran into a wide-open area of town where the sound would be harder to make out and started zigzagging my way up the shop-lined street, alternating between tiptoe and heel running to make it even harder to lock in on me. And it worked. By the time I reached the far end, my lungs were burning and my legs felt like pastelitos, like they were filled with cream cheese and guava, but there wasn't a single lobisomem in sight.

Now to get the heck out of this place.

CHAPTER EIGHTY-SEVEN

Paco's restaurant had apparently been evacuated (maybe earlier this week with the wave of zombie fear that had probably swept over the town or maybe more recently with the howl of hungry werewolves echoing through the streets), but I found Violet and Saci hiding out in the kitchen, Saci snacking on a big bag of tortilla chips and queso. I pushed through the swing door, and the moment I took off the cap, Violet shouted, "Charlie!" She rushed over, throwing her arms around me, and all I could do was smile. "Looks like you owe me a World Cup trophy," she said, glancing back at Saci.

He tossed another chip into his mouth. "I know . . . I know. Don' gotta rub it in, okay?"

I was shaking my head. "What are you guys talking about?"

"Saci wanted to bet on whether you'd get eaten or not. I won."

I grinned at her. "Thanks for the vote of confidence," I said. But my grin quickly faded as I became aware of a low clicking sound coming from the dining room. Balancing up on my toes, I peered through the little window—and saw another lobisomem. An enormous gray-black one with its nose low to the ground and those glowing red eyes searching. There was a rainbow of colorful sprinkles stuck to its front paws, two streaks of whitish icing smeared across its furry side (which for some reason made me think of racing stripes), and half a jelly doughnut dangling from its large and rather hairy behind. Realizing this was the werewolf Saci had sent flying through the window of the little pastry shop, I almost burst out laughing. *Almost.* What I actually did, though, was freeze. V and I both did. But *behind* us, Saci *didn't.* Instead, he obeyed his tummy and slipped a hand into the bag of tortilla chips, making a soft crinkling sound.

Violet glared at him, mouthed, *STOP!*

Saci nodded *all right, all right,* then popped a tortilla chip into his mouth.

Crunnnnnchhhh!

The lobisomem's head snapped in our direction.

Violet and I immediately ducked out of sight.

If we'd had a couple of seconds to spare, I think I would've really enjoyed strangling our little tortilla-loving comrade—only we didn't. Already I could hear the were-wolf's claws clinking on the glassy tiles as it made its way toward the kitchen to investigate. We had five seconds, maybe six.

I glanced frantically around, searching for an exit, but I didn't see any; there were no holes in the walls, nothing leading up to any windows we could escape through.

Just rows and rows of stainless-steel cabinets.

So many stupid cabinets and not a single place to hi—

"I have an idea!" I whispered. I whipped around to face the cabinet at my back, the low one on the center island, and began to roll it open, praying that there wouldn't be any loud squeals from the wheels. There weren't, and once I'd gotten it all the way open, I gestured for Violet and Saci to crawl inside, and the three of us quickly piled in.

If only this thing came equipped with a dead bolt and a panic bar, we might still be breathing in two minutes.

Saci nudged me with his elbow. "Where'd the lobo go?"

Ignoring him, I peered through a narrow slit between the doors. The slit gave me a pretty good look at the door to the kitchen and the dining area beyond, but I didn't see any werewolf. I held my breath, listening hard. Nada. No soft padding of paws, no claws clicking on the tiles. *Where the heck did it go . . . ?*

I scooted to my left, my face still pressed against the

gap, trying to get a better angle into the dining room—
 And my world stopped.
 I didn't get a better angle into the dining room.
 What I got was an eyeful of snarling werewolf.

CHAPTER EIGHTY-EIGHT

The word "terrifying" didn't even begin to describe this thing—and that's when it had been a safe distance away (if there even was such a thing as a *safe distance* when dealing with bloodthirsty lobisomem). But up close and personal? Well, there really weren't words. The thing's head must've been the size of a grizzly's, covered with matted fur the color of dirty snow. Its fangs were as long as my forearms and twice as thick. Long ribbons of milky drool dribbled from the corners of its snarling mouth, and its eyes glowed like burning logs. Not one of us dared to move. We didn't even dare breathe. Out of the corner of my eye, I saw the werewolf raise its fang-lined snout and sniffle at the stale kitchen air. Then it lowered its head and began to sniff about, nose pressed to the cabinets, its furry sprinkles-checkered brow wrinkled in a sort of furious concentration. I held my breath. My blood roared in my ears. Beads of sweat broke out all over my arms and chest. *Go nose deaf! Go nose deaf! Please, oh please, oh please, go nose deaf!* That was pretty much the only thing running through my head at that moment. I was trying to think it into happening. But my psychic game obviously wasn't on point because I suddenly saw the thing's eyes light up like it had picked up a scent—and almost certainly mine!

I was pretty sure things were about as bad as they could get. I mean, here we were trapped in a steel box with about a dozen square-shaped openings all around us and less than half an inch of flimsy metal separating us from a ravenous, five-hundred-pound, man-eating werewolf who was currently very intent on having the three of us as an early dinner. But then things got *even worse* when said five-hundred-pound, ravenous man-eater began pawing and scratching at the drawer directly in front of me, rolling it back inch by terrifying inch.

Had I thrown up right then I wouldn't have been too surprised. After all, there's only so much fear the human body can take. But there wasn't any excuse—at least not that I could come up with—for what Saci did next. He didn't scream or whimper or even close his eyes and send up a string of emergency prayers. Quite the opposite. Saci—ever the prankster—decided that now would be a great time to make a funny and began emptying an extra-large bottle of ketchup over the top of my head. Guess he wanted to die the way he lived. The interesting thing,

though, I was having a hard time holding it against him. . . .
He was, after all, about to become something's *snack*. We
all were. But then—and this part nearly blew my mind—
Violet joined in, basically doing the exact same thing! She
had a squeeze bottle of some yellow hot-dog mustard in
her hand and was squirting it over my legs, my shoulders,
and across the front of my T-shirt. Now, *this* I didn't get. I
mean, what were they thinking? That a *food fight* would be
a great way to go? I had just started to wonder if this were
all some twisted joke—if I were actually trapped in some
sort of bizarre nightmare, when I finally understood what
they were doing: They were trying to mask my scent!

Quick! Violet mouthed. *Put the cap on!*

I barely had time to do just that before the lobisomem
(whose giant dome of a head was way too big to fit into the
smallish square-shaped opening) jammed his furry, teeth-
choked muzzle into the cabinet. His huge black knob of a nose
came within an inch of mine—maybe less—then stopped as
the rest of its head butted up against the cabinet. I held my
breath. The wolf did the opposite: It began to suck in deep,
snuffling breaths. I felt all the tiny little hairs on my cheeks and
ears get suddenly pulled forward. Panic surged up in me like a
soda bomb, but I forced myself to sit perfectly, absolutely still.
My eyes were half shut with dread, but they were still open
enough for me to see the wolf's lower jaw unhinge slightly.

A long, purple tongue slid out from between its rows of glistening teeth to sample the orangey (and probably pretty tasty) puddle of ketchup and mustard that had run together in the hollow above my collarbone. Immediately my toes began to curl, my fingers tightened into fists, and it was a small miracle that I didn't gasp or scream or just flat out jump out of my skin! But did the freakish, sauce-loving, tickle-monster stop there? Not even close. It began to lick. And lick. And lick. And for some weird reason the only words running through my panicking, terrified brain were: *How many licks does it take to get to the Tootsie Roll center of a Tootsie Pop?*

But the worst part, I WAS THAT TOOTSIE POP!

The lobisomem's flavor-taster was rough and warm and wet and sent a shiver through me as it dragged back and forth across my face, lapping up the rivers of sauce. Its low snarling turned into a sort of pleased humming, and its wrinkled gray muzzle pulled back in almost a half smile.

The facts were in: Choosy lobisomem choose JIF—er, *ketchstard*! I mean, the thing *loved* it!

Beside me, Saci was shaking with silent laughter. Violet, meanwhile, couldn't have looked more terrified. Her face had gone completely pale, and her eyes were so big I thought they were about to pop.

A moment later the lobisomem began to shake its

head, sending ribbons of drool flying in every direction as it backed its snout out of the cabinet.

And as it turned and started back toward the dining room, I felt a sudden and overwhelming sense of relief sweep through me, and I did a mental fist bump: us—one, werewolves—zero.

My eyes flicked over to Violet and Saci, and I saw that now they *both* had their hands clasped over their mouths, trying to hold back laughter.

I took off the cap to glare at them—and suddenly it was too much.

Saci let out the faintest of giggles. *Heh!*

I felt my heart stop. Violet stiffened.

I started to raise a finger to my lips, but it was too late. Saci let out another, this one longer than the first and much, *much* louder. *Heh-heh!*

My blood froze. My world froze.

In the doorway of the kitchen, *the lobisomem* froze.

Its rear legs tensed. Its ears perked up.

I thought, *No, please. PLEASE!* And quickly slapped Saci's cap back on just as the lobisomem swung its giant head around to look straight at me.

It knew I was here.

Even if it couldn't see—or smell—me.

CHAPTER EIGHTY-NINE

Suddenly the lobisomem lunged. All I saw was a blur of grayish fur, and then the werewolf slammed against the edge of the island, making the entire thing jump as it tried to force its head into the rectangular opening. Its jaws slobbered and snapped. Ribbons of drool flew everywhere. The werewolf whipped its head viciously from side to side, crumpling the stainless-steel cabinets and lifting one corner of the island almost a foot off the floor. Metal groaned. Wooden support beams bent and popped above us. The top of the island bucked inward as I scrambled out through the cabinet on the other end, Violet and Saci already bolting ahead of me.

We made it through the kitchen door before the lobisomem could yank its head out of the cabinet, and Violet held the door closed as Saci and I dragged a table over, creating a makeshift blockade. Now, did I think some ten-pound table was going to slow down a legendary half-ton man-beast? Not even a little. But something was better than nothing, right?

"C'mon!" Violet shouted. We raced out the front of Paco's, the shrill sound of tearing metal and crashing tables chasing us from inside the restaurant as we spilled into the busy street. I didn't even have time to look around, to ask any of the running, screaming people which way the wolves had gone, before a terrible howl ripped through the night. I turned and felt my heart crawl into my throat.

Lobisomem were swarming from every direction, bursting out of second-story windows, streaming out of the alleys and side streets, charging down the main road in a stampede of flying fur, glinting claws, and wickedly sharp teeth. The ground literally rumbled with the pounding of their paws.

"Oh meu Deus," Saci whispered, which sounded a lot like "Dios mío" or "Oh my God" and pretty much summed up my feelings too.

We ran. We ran through the busy streets, dodging bodies, the werewolves right on our tails. Their snarls and howls ricocheted through my brain like Ping-Pong balls, and as their massive shadows began to overtake us, another howl pierced the night, this one horrifyingly close. I whipped my head around just as the lead wolf lunged at me, arms out, claws poised for the kill. I'd like to say I did something cool right then like a backflip or maybe a baseball slide under the wolf's belly, but the truth was I didn't. I just made a stupid, terrified face and raised one arm, preparing for the blow that would most likely end me.

Only it never came. Instead I felt a rush of wind, heard the clatter of hooves, and caught a glimpse of something huge as it blurred between us, a silver-white streak in the night. Somehow the lobisomem got spun around. It did a legit 360 in midair, then hit the ground with a loud *smack!* Before I could even begin to make sense of what had just happened, a wall of reddish-orange fire blazed down from the sky, raising a fiery curtain between us and the wolves. The flames were huge, licking up more than twenty feet into the air and billowing columns of thick black smoke.

Great tongues of fire seemed to lash at the wolves like whips. Most of them shrank back with howls of fear and dismay, but some held their ground even as the flames licked at their paws, leaving dark charred marks on the cement.

A moment later the lobisomem began retreating— dozens of them at a time. Soon only a handful remained, their burning eyes fixed on me through the boiling, roiling flames, but as the fire grew hot enough to shimmer the air and a roar that seemed to shake the earth echoed through the night, even those turned tail and ran. And that's when I saw the source of the fire, the source of the roar. That's when I saw who'd saved us.

CHAPTER NINETY

E l Cadejo! Justo Juez!" I shouted, and could only stare, shaking my head as the divinely ordained protector of mankind, who takes the form of a great white dog, and the headless rider himself, the king of Salvadorian legends, trotted up beside us, Juez's armored horse breathing out sizzling columns of bloodred fire. "WHAT ARE YOU GUYS DOING HERE?"

Helping friends, replied El Cadejo, speaking directly into my mind as he affectionately nuzzled my side with his huge furry head. His glistening white coat was unbelievably soft, almost airy, his deep azure eyes bright as starlight.

"Unless you three don't require help," Juez said, and I thought I could hear a smile in his voice. It was always hard to tell, with him having no head and all. . . .

"Oh, no—we require it!" Saci screeched. "We require it *badly!*"

"But how'd you even know we were here?" Violet asked, looking between them.

"You stand on Salvadorian soil, señorita. Nothing happens on this soil that I am unaware of." The wispy column of smoke that was Justo Juez's head snapped, crackled, and popped as he said, "The real question is, what are *you* doing here?"

"We're trying to get to Joanna," Violet said. "We think she might be up to something bad."

"Like trying-to-raise-an-ancient-evil-necromancer-in-order-to-resurrect-her-dead-husband bad," I pitched in.

Juez said, "¿Sabes dónde está?"

"Yeah. She's in Mexico. In—"

Tell us no more! El Cadejo ordered. *It can only jeopardize things.*

"Jeopardize what things?" I started to say, but Juez cut me off.

"Charlie, Violet—you both must go to Joanna. Save her if you can. But stop her by *any* means necessary."

We will find you when the time is right, said El Cadejo. *But ask no more questions, for our enemy's spies listen even now.* And he must've seen the confusion on my face because he quickly added, *Carlito, we all have our parts to play. But if you've trusted in us before, trust in us now.*

Okay, I thought back. *I trust you.* Beside me, Saci began kicking around a couple of the golden grapefruit Zarate had given us, playing Hacky Sack with them. Trying to ignore him, I said, "A witch told us we had to get to Joanna tonight. Before midnight. But there's no way we can get to Mexico that fast."

Just then a shrill, shrieking cry split the night as a huge shape sliced through the air just inches above our heads. It snatched one of the golden grapefruit Saci was playing with out of the sky and landed a foot or two away.

It was the alicanto—our favorite gold-munching bird was back!

Juez's smoky head flared a fiery orange. Its sizzle rang out in the night. "Divine providence! Your journey is blessed. Go now. ¡Apúrense!"

We all climbed onto the back of the alicanto, which looked like it had put on about two hundred pounds since the last time we'd seen it; the crazy bird had probably stumbled across a gold mine somewhere in Colombia.

Violet sniffed the air, made a disgusted face, then snatched Saci's cap out of my hand and stuffed it into her backpack. "But does the alicanto know where we need to go?" she asked Juez, confused.

"Alicantos are the smartest birds in the sky. Just whisper where you want to go into its ear," Juez said, so Violet did. Then he shouted, "Llévelos, pajarito. ¡Y no se demore!"

Our coppery-feathered friend seemed to nod at that. It craned its neck around, screeched at Saci, then gobbled up the entire basket of golden grapefruit in a single bite.

"NO! BAD BIRD!" Saci shouted back, trying to pry open the alicanto's mouth. "Give dat back! La bruja gave dem to me!" The alicanto shoved him away with its sleek feathery head, then nuzzled my face with its beak and squawked, "*Mama!*"

Juez gave me a funny look—or at least it *seemed* like it might've been a funny look from the way he angled his smoky column of a head.

"Is this something I should know about?" he asked in an embarrassed voice.

CHAPTER NINETY-ONE

oaring through the cool night sky on the back of the alicanto was easily the highlight of my day— okay, probably of my life.

I mean, sure, I'd flown before (during my battle with La Cuca), but that had been all panic and nerves and choking fear. This was something else. . . . *This* was pure, unfiltered *exhilaration!* Way up here, higher than even the loftiest clouds, the air was thin and freezing cold, but I'd never felt more alive. More *free*.

There was no race against the clock, no pressure to find Joanna—no trying to figure out who was doing what and where they were going next. There was only the tingling of my skin, the wind in my hair, and the clever flex and twitch of the alicanto's glowing coppery wings as they tilted this way and that, effortlessly catching the thermals and rocketing us along the blue-black curvature of the earth.

I had no idea how long we flew, but it felt like forever, a lifetime of sailing across a vast, endless sky, none of us bothering to say so much as a single word—not *having* to—until the sun hid itself on the other side of the world and the moon rose to become a pale, shining disk before us.

Deep down inside, I wished the ride would never end, but too soon the alicanto began a steady earthward descent, and the familiar shapes of mountains and valleys, buildings, homes, and the neat little grids of streets broke through the misty cloud cover like old friends eagerly awaiting our return.

We touched down on the crest of a ring of high hills, overlooking a town that seemed to have sprung out of the mountains themselves. With all its old-school buildings and manicured gardens, the place looked like it belonged on a postcard. In fact, my mom *had* a San Miguel de Allende postcard.

"Dis da place?" Saci asked, sliding off the alicanto and trying to pluck one of its brownish-golden feathers as he did. The alicanto snapped at his hand and moved away.

"Hey, leave the bird alone," V said; then she nudged me with her elbow and began rooting around in her backpack. A moment later she came out with Saci's red cap, and I saw Saci's eyes nearly pop out of his head when she handed it to him. "Almost forgot. Probably should've given you this back in El Salvador, but better late than never, right?"

"Wat dis for . . . ?" he asked, confused.

"You're free," Violet said. "Our deal was for you to get us to El Dorado and help us find Joanna, and you pretty much held up your end, so . . ."

I raised one hand in a little wave. "Hasta luego, amigo."

"*Amigo?*" Saci's gaze slowly shifted from Violet to me, and I thought I saw a flicker of something in his eyes. . . . Was it *joy?* "You mean dat?"

"We do." Violet put a hand on his shoulder, smiled. "We couldn't have done it without you."

"No way," I agreed, and couldn't believe I actually *meant* it. Less than seventy-two hours ago I would've given almost *anything* just to get him out of our hair, but now, after we'd been through so much together—after he'd even saved *my life* a couple of times—it was like we were losing a teammate . . . losing a *friend.* "Hey, and just so you know—I grew up listening to your stories. You're, like, one of my all-time favorite myths—er, sombras. I would have asked you for your autograph, but I'm afraid where you might sign it . . . ," I said, sort of joking, sort of not. I watched Saci's face slowly light up, and he suddenly looked all of five years old. There he was, this thousand-plus-year-old legend looking like a kindergartener whose buddy had just told him that he was his best friend in the entire world. He blinked at me, and it now seemed like he was fighting back tears.

"Saci so glad he prank you two . . . ," he said in a shaky whisper. "So glad I punk'd you . . ." He started to back away, hopping sideways now, maybe so we wouldn't see him cry. "Ei, Saci see you two soon, okay?"

"Definitely," Violet said. "Stop by Miami sometime. Like for Christmas or something."

"Sim! I do that!" Saci said, but I thought I detected a note of sadness in his voice. "Saci be there . . ."

"See ya," I said, waving, and he gave me a small, almost regretful wave back. I felt something inside me sink a little.

Next to me, Violet was smiling. Trying to, anyway. Smiling through shiny eyes. "You take care, okay?"

"Okay . . . And you two take care too. Jess be careful and stuff. You never know whas out there."

"We will," I said—

And then he was gone, hopping away down the side of the mountain.

For what felt like a long time, Violet and I both just stood there, staring after him. I tried to swallow the big lump in my throat, but it wouldn't go down. Finally I said, "Is it weird I feel totally sad right now?"

"Little bit. Kid was a menace."

"But he was, like, *our* menace. . . ." And now he was gone.

CHAPTER NINETY-TWO

r so I thought.

Not ten seconds later, while the two of us were still standing there, someone tapped me on the shoulder. I whirled with a scream, ready to judo chop whoever (or whatever) had snuck up on us—and saw that it was Saci, grinning from ear to ear.

"How did you . . . ?" I started to say, pointing, suddenly really, *really* confused.

Violet looked almost as confused. "Forgot something?"

"Saci don't know how to say this . . . ," he began, looking all shy now.

"What happened? I asked. "I was pretty sure you'd be halfway to São Paulo by now. Beaches, coconut smoothies—watching soccer on your flat-screens . . . remember?"

"Dat's the thing about São Paulo this time of year . . .

beaches kinda cold, and there's not too much good soccer on TV, you know?"

I felt this huge, stupid smile spread across my face. "What are you trying to say?"

Saci was smiling too—smiling hard. "Saci trying to say, maybe you two come with me, huh? Let's all go have some coconut smoothies . . . together."

"We'd love to," I said, "but we can't. We have to help Joanna. She's our friend too."

Saci opened his mouth to say something, his face creasing into a frown, then closed it. "No way Saci can change you minds . . . ?"

"We have to help her," Violet explained, and Saci gave a frustrated sigh.

"Okay then," he said. "If it's like dat, den Saci wanna go with you all da way to da end. Maybe lend a helping hand."

"You sure about that?" Violet asked, and I could hear the happiness in her voice. "Wouldn't lending a helping hand sully that reputation of yours?"

"Saci not so worried about his reputation no more." He grinned at me. But it wasn't a Saci smile. It didn't light up those brown eyes. After a moment he said, "So let's go find this friend of yours, den. . . ."

CHAPTER NINETY-THREE

El Jardín was a huge cobblestone plaza lined with bustling cafés, markets, touristy shops, and about a block of outdoor restaurants. Its name means "garden" in Spanish, and it was the most famous plaza in San Miguel de Allende's historic district. On the south side was the world-famous Parroquia de San Miguel Arcángel, an old-fashioned stone church with pink spires that rose up to gleam against the black night sky. Usually the square was packed with tourists sightseeing and people-watching and street vendors offering up homemade recipes from their carts or stands, but not today. Today it was filled with *the dead*. Women in elegant bridal gowns and marigold crowns, their faces painted to look like calaveras. Men wearing vaquero jackets and cowboy boots. Little kids in homemade skeleton costumes and skull masks. I could see a whole bunch of them playing tag under the lollipop-shaped laurel-trees in the middle of the square. One—a little girl in a frilly black gown—was standing on a bench, gazing around and nibbling on a skull-shaped pretzel that was almost as big as her head. There were easily a couple thousand people out here. Maybe more.

"What day is it today?" I asked, frowning.

Violet looked down at her watch. "November first."

And suddenly the realization smacked me like a soccer ball straight to the face!

"I can't believe it . . . ," I said. "How could I be *so* stupid?"

V turned to me. "What's wrong?

"Today is Día de los Muertos—the Day of the Dead! That's why everyone kept mentioning the season!" Thanks to my abuela, I knew that the season when the Day of the Dead was celebrated was known as the Season of the Living; supposedly every day of that month, the boundaries between the Land of the Living and that of the dead grow thinner and thinner until the Day of the Dead, when they are at their absolute thinnest—in other words, the perfect time to resurrect an ancient necromancer. "It's going down *right now*, V. She's going to resurrect him *here*. Tonight!"

I could see the fear in Violet's eyes, but she didn't let it get the best of her. She narrowed her gaze, nodded. "Okay. So how do we find her?"

Great question. My eyes swept over the crowds, over

the painted, smiling faces. The street vendors and kids. Over the mariachis playing music in the soft yellow glow of the antique street lamps. There were so many people here. How *were* we supposed to find her?

"Wait a sec," I said, feeling this strange sense of déjà vu. "I've seen this place before."

"What do you mean? Like, in a book?"

"Maybe." But I didn't think so.

Then Saci said, "Look like we come to the end of da path, irmão. . . . Now wha'?"

Which made me think of something Joanna had said to me—

And suddenly I remembered!

"V, Joanna's crown! Give it to me—*quick!*"

She brought it out of her backpack and handed it over, and when I held it up . . . there it was—the exact cityscape of San Miguel de Allende carved into the band of the crown!

"But—how . . . ?" Violet whispered.

"No idea. But I remember Joanna telling me that when I came to the end of my path and couldn't go any farther, to look to the crown."

"Maybe she in da old church," Saci guessed. "Look pretty much the same as on da crown."

"Maybe . . ." My eyes drifted down the etched cityscape, and I noticed a tall, upside-down triangle, a tower of bones—no, *a castell*! Flipping the crown over, I realized there was a second cityscape etched into the band. But this one was upside down.

"A world . . . *beneath* the world?" Violet whispered.

Saci leaned over my shoulder to peer at the crown. "Beneath *which* world?"

"This one," Violet and I answered in unison.

Glancing up at me, she said, "But how do we get down there?"

"You need a guide," Saci told her. "*Duh.*"

"A guide?"

"A calaca," I explained. Then I had to laugh as Zarate's words now came back to me: *Hasta la muerte, hasta que veas la Catrina y la Calavera te retenga en sus brazos.*

It was almost as if the witch had known. But how?

"What is it?" Violet asked.

"This is *her* city. This is *her* celebration."

"Whose?"

"*La Catrina's.*"

CHAPTER NINETY-FOUR

ait, wait. You saying La Calavera Catrina is *here* . . . ?" Saci said, sounding more than a little spooked. "You sure 'bout dis, bro?"

"Pretty sure." I mean, what better guide into the underworld than the Lady of the Dead herself?

Violet was shaking her head. "But how do we find her?"

"I don't know. She's definitely here, though . . . *somewhere.*" Problem was, the place was packed; everywhere I looked, crowds of people were marching giant papier-mâché skeletons through the streets. I could hear them laughing and telling stories while others sang along to the mariachi music that seemed to be coming from every direction. The square smelled of incense, baking bread, and caramel.

"C'mon," Violet said. We started into the crowd. All around us, colorful streamers blew in the breeze, and lacy paper cutouts of calacas danced between the stone arches and covered walkways that lined the square. We slipped between the streams of bodies, careful not to trample on any of the winding trails of marigold petals that had been laid out pretty much all over the place. They were called caminos de los muertos—or paths of the dead. Family members put them out for their relatives that had passed on. Most led to elaborate altars decorated with bright red cockscombs, wild-flowers, and mounds of fresh fruit. There was also bottled water and cans of soda to refresh wearied spirits.

"You see anything?" I asked V.

She stood on her tippy-toes, trying to see over the crowds. "I don't even know what the woman *looks* like."

"You'll know if you see her," Saci said. "*Trust me.*" He gripped my arm. "Ei, Saci thinking, maybe we come back some other time. . . . Maybe we go now."

"We *can't* go," I said. "We *need* to do this."

He blinked slowly, and his expression turned grim. "If you sure 'bout dis, den maybe Saci know a way down. . . ."

"You do?"

"Long time ago I hear rumor about an entrance near da . . ." He let his words trail off as his eyes drifted past me, over my shoulder.

"Dude, what are you—" I turned.

And suddenly felt my blood freeze when I spotted a lobisomem moving slowly through the crowd behind us.

With its inhuman size and height and the long hooded coat it wore to conceal its hairy arms and legs, it wasn't exactly hard to pick out. The creature was maybe forty yards away, sniffing the air near the entrance to the garden.

The gate *we'd* just walked through.

Violet squeezed my hand. "Charlie . . ." Following her gaze, I saw that the lobisomem wasn't alone—in fact, it had *plenty* of company. Its buddies were spread out everywhere— half a dozen of them prowling the dark hills just beyond the square, a spotter pacing back and forth along the roof of the old pink church, a pair lurking right outside the gate, scanning the crowds with those glowing red eyes. My heart started to beat harder. The blood thrummed and pulsed in my temples. I wasn't sure about a whole lot at the moment (it was hard to be, with the hand of fear that had closed around my neck), but I did know this: The lobisomem had set a trap. They'd set it right here in El Jardín, and we had just walked *straight* into it.

But how did they know we'd come here . . . ?

Of all the places in Mexico. Of all the places in *Latin America*.

How could they have known?

Violet's eyes, full of fear, rose to meet mine. Her voice was barely a whisper as she said, "Charlie, what do we do?"

The question was, *what could we do?* There was a whole lot more of them than there was of us, and they also happened to be a whole lot bigger and a whole heck of a lot faster. We weren't about to just give up, though. Not by a long shot. "We have to find La Catrina," I said. "And quick!"

We started across the square, cutting through streams of happy, laughing partiers. Wax candles burned everywhere, casting a hazy yellow glow over everything and every*one*. With my pulse pounding in my ears and the way my nerves were scrambling my brain, it wasn't long before the painted calaca faces of the festivalgoers started looking real to me. I was now having a hard time differentiating between imagination and reality, fiction and real life. Voices, music, and laughter melted into a single dizzying rush, and my panic kicked up another few notches.

Just as we swerved around a group of rhinestone-studded mariachis singing "Calaverita," Violet said, "Oh no," and something warty and green plopped down between my sneakers. A frog. I squinted up to see about another thousand or so free-falling through the sky toward the square. It was raining frogs again—no, *pouring* frogs. They tumbled through the air like candy out of a busted piñata.

"Dis can't be good," Saci started to say, and then shut right up as another lobisomem emerged from behind the wall of hedges to our left.

This one had its hood pushed back to reveal its sharp, furry features, almost as if he didn't care people might notice him. The only good thing was it hadn't seen us. Yet.

I grabbed Violet and Saci and steered them into a tight circle of people marching up the middle of the square, lifting a ten-foot-tall papier-mâché calaca.

We stepped on a bunch of toes, got a few angry looks. The lady working the skeleton's left leg (they were trying to make the calaca look like it was walking around and waving at people) almost tripped over us.

"¡Ay, Dios mío!" she shouted.

"Perdone," I said. "Mi culpa. Perdone."

"Miren dónde van, gamberros," yelled a voice behind us.

Through the forest of swinging arms and legs, Violet spotted another lobisomem. Ten yards ahead of us, coming this way.

The second she pointed this out, we pushed our way out of the circle and headed in the opposite direction—

Only to walk straight into *another lobisomem.*

Bad news: This one *had* seen us. Worse, it was already raising its fang-lined muzzle, preparing to alert the rest of the pack.

But an instant before it could let out its terrifying howl, a chorus of screams erupted from the far side of the square. Screams of panic. Terror.

I whirled, expecting to see more werewolves, but what I saw was even worse—what I saw was *zombies!*

CHAPTER NINETY-FIVE

What looked like an army of zombies had surrounded the square. Not tens or hundreds or even thousands, but *tens of thousands*—thousands upon thousands upon thousands more. I could see them lined up in legit battle formation just beyond the high iron gates of El Jardín: A horde of pale, stick-thin bodies wielding swords and spears and carrying shields. And, like you might expect with things that had spent the last hundred or so years rotting away in the earth, they were totally *gross*. Their skin had begun to melt off their bones. Their fingers were clawlike and twisted with age. Teeth that had stretched into fangs grew out of their mouths. Just one look at them was enough to send my Panic-O-Meter spiking. Then they began marching upon the square, marching as one, and my Panic-O-Meter basically exploded. Next thing I knew the zombies began to attack the festivalgoers, swatting aside children, swing-ing their weapons at the men and women. I heard shrieks and saw dozens of bodies crumple to the ground. And the zombies would've no doubt hurt many more had the lobi-somem not immediately engaged them. Werewolves and zombies clashed in a blur of teeth and steel. Howls ripped through the square. Terrified wannabe calacas fled in every direction, tripping over one another, knocking over tables and food carts. One dude—a sombrero-wearing mariachi—broke his guitarra over the head of one of the zombies, then took off running. Unfortunately, none of this distracted the lobisomem standing directly in front of us. Its glowing red eyes were still locked on me, and it was now reaching one clawed hand out toward me.

"Charlie, run!" Violet shouted, but before I could, there was a loud *crack!* and I saw the werewolf's eyes roll up to whites an instant before he collapsed, facedown, on the cobblestone street. Standing over the body of the KO'd werewolf was a hooded figure with what looked like a thick tree branch growing out of its right sleeve.

"Now we should *definitely* run!" Saci shouted.

But just then the figure reached up to push back the hood of its dark cloak, revealing a familiar face. "Adriana!" I shouted, shocked. "What are you doing here?"

Her lips curved into a smile as she said, "Let's just say

that looking after you two is a full-time job. But we don't have much time. I'd like to introduce you to my amiga." She glanced to her left, where a lady dressed in a frilly white bridal gown stood facing the opposite direction. "Perhaps you'll recognize her. . . ."

Now the lady in white turned to face us, rising to her full height—and my jaw dropped somewhere near my ankles. Yeah, I recognized her all right. . . .

It was her. The Lady of the Dead.

CHAPTER NINETY-SIX

L a Calavera Catrina was easily over seven feet tall
and telephone-pole slim, and radiated with a powerful otherworldly presence—something you had to
experience to understand. Her face, a bony white
skull the color of freshly fallen snow, was as terrifying as
it was beautiful. Her eyes were dark, bottomless sockets.
Her teeth were perfect and white. Her forehead and the
smooth ridges of her cheekbones were decorated with
intricate designs—geometric patterns and swirls, spider-
webs, and the long stems of roses seemingly carved right
into the bone. They reminded me of fancy henna tattoos.
Only, unlike any henna tattoos that I'd ever seen, these
sparkled in the moonlight, appearing to swirl and dance
as she moved. Her old-fashioned bridal gown clung to her
ultra-slim frame, and she wore this wide-brimmed hat
decorated with bunches of yellow marigold flowers, red

roses, and wide purple feathers—ostrich, maybe. Beneath it, where her ears would've been, were two bright red rose-heads, each almost the size of a softball and glistening as if freshly plucked. I'd never seen anything like her. Nothing so regal and ancient and utterly mesmerizing.

Paralyzed by fear and wonder, I just stood there, staring up at the Lady of the Dead as the dark sockets of her eyes bore deeply into mine. Which, by the way, was more than a tad bit freaky, considering there were no *eyes* in there. Finally she said, "Es mi placer, Charlie."

"You—you know my name . . . ?" The words trembled on my lips, barely audible over the shouts and howls rising above the square.

"She knows more about you than that," Adriana whispered into my ear—and then, "It was my pleasure to watch over you." With that, she stepped back, smiling, and spread her arms wide.

Before I could ask her what was going on, what she was talking about, Adriana began to sing, that soft haunting voice of hers echoing out across the square. And then . . . well, something *strange* happened: Even as she sang, her body began to change. And when I say change, I mean *change*: Her upper half began to swell, her shoulders ballooning outward as she grew several feet taller right before our eyes. The skin on her arms and legs darkened, turning a rich coffee color. Then it began to harden, becoming rough, grainy, marked with honey-brown ringlets and knobby little bumps. Cracks appeared in the cobblestones around her feet as her toes sank into the stones, lifting some several inches and vanishing beneath them. As I watched, gaping, the fingers of her hands stretched out impossibly long, twisting and twining, forming a network of spindly branches. The branches closed into a canopy, and as her voice grew louder, buds suddenly appeared. Then leaves, bright red and glistening, burst to life.

With a soft moan, Adriana threw her head back, and I realized that her face was changing too—her features fading, melting into the coffee-colored bark that now covered her from twigs to roots. And it was only when her face had completely vanished into the bark that her song ended.

Shocked—beyond shocked, really—I stared up at her, beginning to wonder if I should trade my eyes in for a pair that worked a little better. Except that wouldn't have helped any. Because it wouldn't have changed the facts, and the facts were simple: Where Adriana had been standing—and not even *twenty seconds* ago—now stood a tree, huge and timeless. A kapok tree. The national tree of Argentina. Suddenly an old story came back to me, one that had been nipping at the edges of my memory back in the woods when Adriana had sung her song and I'd played the guitarra. It was another legend taught to me by my abuela, the story of a young indigenous girl called Anahí, who lived with her tribe on the shores of the Paraná River. Every evening she would sing to her people about her love of their land and its beauty, and her voice was so lovely that everyone considered it a blessing and always looked forward to her song. But one day a group of conquistadors came to conquer their land and took her entire tribe prisoner. Anahí, who had always spent her days free, roaming the forests and frolicking in the great river, could not take being chained to a post. So one night when her prison guard fell asleep, she saw her chance and tried to escape. The guard, however, happened to wake, and in their struggle Anahí accidentally stabbed him with his own sword. His dying cry startled the rest of the soldiers, who then captured Anahí and sentenced her to death. On the day of her execution, after they'd tied her to a tree and lit a stack of firewood at her feet, the soldiers were astonished to see that the girl did not scream as the flames burned hotter and brighter, but rather *sang*. And the following morning they got an even bigger surprise: They woke to discover a kapok tree blooming in all its glory at the very spot where the girl had died.

Finally—*finally*—everything clicked together for me.

"It's *her*," I whispered to Violet. "The girl from the story she sang to us . . . the one who was burned alive and came back as a *tree.*"

But that wasn't even all of it. No, see, I remembered this tree—this *specific* tree . . . Remembered seeing it back in Brazil when we laid our trap for Saci. Remembered seeing it in Chiloé when one of its great branches had swept down to swat an anchimayen out of the air just before she could incinerate us. I even remembered seeing it back in the town where the lobisomem had attacked, where it had saved me as I'd escaped into the alley wearing Saci's cap.

It was her the entire time. . . .

She'd been tracking us, protecting us without us even knowing.

She'd never left.

La Calavera Catrina had once again turned the empty sockets of her eyes on me. The patterns carved into her cheekbones seemed to swirl and dance. "A kapok tree's roots run deep and strong. They are a perfect access to the realms that lie beneath."

As she spoke, the trunk of the tree pulled apart like a yawning mouth, revealing a sort of entrance . . . a descending, spiraling staircase, but instead of stone or concrete, the steps were the loops and knobs of tree roots. The whole thing was mind-boggling. Like something you'd see in a theme park. Only, it was *real.*

La Catrina ducked into the opening, but before I could follow, Saci grabbed my arm. "Don't go," he said, his dark eyes as intense and serious as I'd ever seen them. It was honestly a little unsettling. "Don't do it."

"Don't be such a scaredy-cat," Violet told him. "C'mon, Charlie."

CHAPTER NINETY-SEVEN

The stairwell—or rather, the *treewell*—was cramped and dark and smelled not so surprisingly of bark. We followed La Calavera deep underground, our footsteps echoing loudly in the gloomy silence. Maybe fifty yards down, the world opened up around us: We were no longer moving through tree roots but some dark underground chamber with stony walls and floors that looked like they'd been paved with ash. I began to hear voices again, the same whispers and groans I'd been hearing around castells. They were louder down here, more desperate sounding.

La Calavera's eyeless gaze narrowed on my face. "Do you hear them? ¿Las voces?"

I nodded, slowly, wondering how she knew. "Who are they?"

"The voices of the forgotten," she said, and nothing

more. Apparently she didn't care to elaborate, and I was too terrified by what it could mean to ask her to.

As we followed the Lady of the Dead through a series of twists and turns, Violet whispered, "This place is completely bonkers. . . . It's *literally* a maze down here."

"La Sociedad designed it like this in the ancient days," La Catrina said. She spoke slowly, as if she had all the time in the world. Which I guess she probably did. "It was the only way to keep dead things from finding their way out."

"Ei, we not going to the Land of the Dead, are we?" Saci asked her. "Because that ain't no place I want to visit anytime soon. . . ."

"We are not going that far down," La Catrina replied in that hollow voice of hers.

"So where we going, then?"

"An in-between place. Somewhere neither here nor there. A place of sacrifice."

"You mean an altar?"

"The *highest*," she said, and Saci's anxious eyes found mine.

"I no like dis, irmão. . . . *You* should definitely turn around."

The Lady of the Dead's hollow laughter echoed softly off the tunnel walls. "Already betraying your deal, Saci Pererê?"

Saci seemed to stiffen. "*Wha*'? I don' know what you talking about, lady, okay?"

After a few more turns, we came to what looked like a dead end—a huge stony wall that stretched from floor to ceiling and across the width of the chamber.

"We are here," La Calavera Catrina announced. "El Muro de Partición . . ." She turned to me. "The altar lies beyond this gate, but I can take you no farther. I cannot enter, for it is forbidden to my kind."

Intricate designs and stunning geometric patterns just like the ones we'd seen underneath La Rosa Cemetery back in Miami had been carved into rough, grayish rock. Right where there should've been some sort of keyhole, there were two sets of five almost finger-size holes, four on top, one on the bottom.

"So how do we get inside?" I asked La Catrina, but the Lady of the Dead shook her head grimly.

"I have lost the ability to open such gates myself."

"What do you mean?"

Her right hand slipped out from the sleeve of her silky skull-embroidered gown, and I saw that two of her fingers were missing—index and middle. "All ten are required to open this gate."

I stared silently at her hand. Her fingers looked *so* familiar. . . . Where had I seen them before?

Suddenly a thought occurred to me, and digging into the front of my shirt, I brought out the necklace Adriana had taken from La Pisadeira back in Argentina.

The dark sockets of La Calavera Catrina's eyes seemed to light up.

"Where did you find those?" she breathed.

"Took them from a *surprisingly* heavy hag."

"Wait," Violet said, "so you're Death. It was *your* fingers the necromancer sliced off."

La Calavera nodded, like that had impressed her. "You children are full of surprises, aren't you?"

"We try to be," I said, grinning.

She held out her hand toward me. "May I have my fingers back now?"

There's something you don't hear every day. "Oh. Yeah . . ."

There was a sick snapping, crackling sound as La Catrina reattached her fingers. Then she slipped all ten into the holes in the wall and turned her wrists like a key.

At that same moment, a huge rumbling shook the chamber. The ground bucked and trembled beneath our feet, and all four of us staggered backward as the entire wall sank slowly and noisily into a wide slot in the ground.

"*Increíble,*" I started to say, but my words fell away as I realized La Calavera had vanished.

"Where'd she go?" Saci wondered out loud.

I blinked around the dim hall. "No idea."

Beyond the wall was another chamber: a narrow peninsula of ground that seemed to run on forever; surrounding it on all sides, though not quite even with it, spread a vast ocean of ashy whiteness—some kind of powder, obviously.

Violet was the first to muster her courage. "Let's go," she whispered, and wandered out into the wide-open chamber, walking along the crooked peninsula of cobblestone.

After a moment, Saci and I followed, our footsteps clattering loudly on the stone, the chorus of whispering voices in my head growing louder and louder with every step.

Their combined voices were almost painful now—a splitting headache that began in the center of my forehead and radiated outward like spreading fingers.

Finally, we reached the end of the peninsula, where the ground fell away into the ocean of powdery white stuff, and Saci said, "Wha's all this?"

Violet had crouched to examine the powder. Now she looked up at me with panic clearly visible in the bottoms of her baby blues.

"What's wrong?" I said. "What is that stuff? *Flour?*"

"Try again," she whispered, so I looked closer—and felt my chest go numb. Dios mío . . .

It wasn't flour—in fact, it wasn't *any kind* of ground powder.

They were bones. An ocean of bones . . .

CHAPTER NINETY-EIGHT

The first thought that went through my head was something like, *What kind of freaked-out, awful place is this?* The second was, *And what the heck are we still doing here?* There were a couple other thoughts in there too—mostly, *Ugh, gross!* and *Run, dude, run!* and *What if I'm allergic to powdered bone?* But that last one didn't seem too likely.

Although most of the bones that spread out around us as far as the eye could see were so ancient or damaged that, up close, they reminded me of baking flour, there were plenty that had more or less kept their original shapes. I could pick out shinbones and spines, fist-size skulls and rib bones that resembled empty birdcages; these jutted out of the surface of this ancient graveyard, creating almost a ripple effect. The bony white ocean seemed to stretch out forever, like an endless desert, and beyond it was only shadow.

"Why are there so many bones here?" Violet asked.

"This is the burial yard," I said in a low voice. "This must be where the priests would discard the bones of the sacrificial victims. The altar must be out there somewhere . . . hidden in the cleft of a rock." Or at least that was what some of the legends claimed.

"So we just have to walk over the bones, then?"

"I wouldn't chance it," Saci said, but Violet stuck her foot out over the edge anyway, testing to see if the bones would support her weight. Which they didn't. Even the ones that looked somewhat intact crumbled under the slightest pressure.

She backed away from the edge, saying, "They're too old, too fragile. The whole thing is unstable. We'll fall right through."

That, and who knew how deep this thing went? Which, by the way, was definitely *not* a question I wanted to learn the answer to. "There's gotta be another way," I started to say, but a sudden sharp pain in the middle of my forehead cut me off.

It was the voices—they were chanting now, shouting in unison, and for the first time I thought I could actually understand what they were saying. And it sounded like: *STEP OUT! STEP OUT! STEP OUT!*

Just like that I knew what I had to do. "That's it . . . ," I breathed.

Violet turned to look at me. "What is?"

"We have to use a castell. They're the pathway to the High Altar. It's just like what the witch Zarate told me!" But that wasn't *all* she'd told me. She'd also happened to mention that it had to be *my feet* that walked the path. Mine. It all made sense now. At least I hoped it did. Or else, in a few seconds, I would find out that I'd been *dead wrong*. And in the very literal sense of the phrase.

Violet was shaking her head. "Charlie, I don't see any castells. . . ."

"Not yet you don't," I said, and with my heart now beating in my chest like un tambor, I did either the stupidest or bravest thing I'd done in a while: I closed my eyes, sucked in a deep, steadying breath, then stepped slowly—yes, *very* slowly indeed—out onto the ocean of bones, hoping it wouldn't be the last step I ever took.

For a split second I saw a terrible vision of me floundering around in there. Arms flailing, head turned up to take one last gasping breath before I disappeared below the surface. Basically drowning in the stuff. But that wasn't what happened. Not even close.

Instead, a heartbeat later, as my foot crunched down on bone, it somehow found *solid* bone—and even more surprising, the bones held! I let out a shaky breath, smiling back at Violet—and that was when something really strange happened: The ocean of bones began to vibrate as if the world's largest amp, buried deep beneath them, had suddenly been turned on. A fine layer of bone dust rose high into the air, a shimmering white cloud in the semi-dark. Then the bones that were still intact began to interlock with each other, clicking together like puzzle pieces and forming a solid bony base beneath my foot, and directly above and in front of it. I risked another step. More bones joined the party. They flew out of the dusty ocean as if drawn by giant invisible magnets, combining with the base and rising up, up, up until they formed a towering castell that stretched toward the ceiling of the chamber, becoming lost in shadow. It happened so fast that for a second I had to wonder if it had really happened at all.

"Okay, now dat was freaky," Saci said.

CHAPTER NINETY-NINE

Standing there, staring up at this winding, seemingly never-ending stairway of bones, I had to keep pinching myself because part of my brain kept trying to deny the existence of what I was very *clearly* seeing. Sure, it hadn't been here a few seconds ago, but now it was. Incredibly.

The castell itself kind of reminded me of an ancient Egyptian pyramid, partly because it looked about as wide around and partly because it had that whole stepladder effect going on. There might've been as many as eight or nine hundred steps going almost straight up, though there was no way to know for sure because I couldn't see the top of this thing.

Violet nudged me on the arm, whispered, "C'mon . . . ," and the three of us started up the wide, makeshift staircase with the old bones that made up said staircase creaking and crunching under our sneakered feet. On the outside I was trying to play it all cool, strutting up the steps like, *Climbing a set of giant bony stairs? Please, I go grave-robbing every Tuesday. . . .* But on the inside I was screaming, *Please don't break, please don't break, PLEASE DON'T BREAK!*

When we finally reached the top, the voices in my head (which had quieted a bit since I'd stepped out onto the bones) went *completely* silent, and we found ourselves standing in some huge, dimly lit, underground cavern. Except the word "huge" didn't quite cut it, because this place was mind-bogglingly *massive*, about the size of a soccer stadium, with skull-paved floors and walls like jigsaw puzzles of longer, paler bones. The walls went twisting up to impossible heights, easily over nine hundred feet tall, and I could see niches and windows (and even things that looked sort of like balconies) overlooking the main space. There were halls on the other side of those walls, I realized. I could see some through the niches. And through several of the windows I could just make out the faint greenish glow of torchlight . . . no, *bruja* light.

"Da High Altar . . . ," Saci murmured, looking nervously around.

Although most of the chamber sat in semi-darkness, there was enough light for me to see that he was exactly right: Rising out of a platform directly in front of us was a great stone altar. It looked just like the one we'd seen back in Lapa do Santo, only this one was at least twice as big and even more terrifying, because the rows of teeth that jutted out along its edge were bigger than any teeth I'd ever seen, each one probably as long as my arm. The room pulsed with magia—hummed with it. I could feel it creeping out of the floors between the cobbled bones like mist, urging me forward with invisible fingers, pushing me deeper, toward the altar.

As we approached the center of the room, movement to my left caught my eye. A figure stepped out of the shadows, her eyes like glowing emeralds.

"*Joanna!*" I shouted. Instantly, joy flooded my body, and I felt numb all over. I almost couldn't believe it . . . *seriously*. After all we'd gone through, after all the fighting and close calls and clues, here she was. *Finally*. And she seemed to be in her right mind. "Oh my gosh . . . You have *nooooo* idea how glad we are to see you!" Understatement of my *life*.

"Charlie, stay back," she warned.

"It's okay. We know everything!"

"We're here to help you," Violet explained.

"You don't have to do this," I started to say—and then realized Joanna's hands were bound, tied tightly with ropes the color of fresh vines. "Jo—what's going on . . . ?"

Two pinpricks of harsh blue light shone out of the

darkness behind her. They glowed steadily, growing larger
and brighter until another figure emerged from the shadows: a man, old and hunchbacked, carrying a large bag—
no, a man-purse.

"*Mr. Ovaprim?*" Violet breathed, shocked. "What are
you doing here?"

But the old man didn't answer; instead he hooked his
fingers into the sides of his mouth and, in one grotesque,
stomach-churning move, began to peel his face back like he
was tearing open the neck of a T-shirt. His skin stretched
and squeaked as he forced it up and over his head and
then down his neck—it tore a little when he shrugged
his shoulders through the narrow opening, and then it
slipped smoothly down his body to pool at his feet like
a heavy coat. Without his skin, Mr. Ovaprim didn't look
old anymore—he didn't even look *human*! His head was
shaped like a deer's, but without ears or antlers, narrowing
to a wide, lipless mouth choked with fangs. His body was
a mass of ropy, sinewy muscle, which flexed and rippled
with his every movement; his real skin must've been semi-
translucent, somehow giving off a poisonous bluish glow,
and there wasn't an ounce of fat anywhere on his entire
body. As we watched, he stepped easily out of the mass of
skin, gathered it up in his clawed hands, then stuffed it into
his giant purse.

For almost a full minute I couldn't breathe. I was so stunned by everything. I felt paralyzed. In fact, I had to work my jaw for probably *half* that minute before my mouth could finally form words. And even then they pretty much only stated the obvious. "You—you're a *vampire*. . . ."

ut he wasn't just your garden-variety bloodsucker, either. His skin suit and the harsh blue light radiating from his entire body practically *shouted* his vampire type, and that, my friends, was an *asema*. A race of ancient Surinamese bloodsuckers, the oldest and most vicious of *all* vampires.

I closed my eyes, feeling suddenly dizzy. And *epically* stupid. Man, how could I have not seen this coming . . . ? All the signs had been right there. Staring me straight in *my face*. His ridiculously huge man-purse. His sagging, flabby skin that always made it look like he was wearing a flesh mask or skin suit. That eerie blue light we kept seeing whenever he was around. The way he'd compulsively picked up the rice I'd accidentally-on-purpose spilled on the train—which, by the way, was an obsessive behavior asemas were well known for.

Pssh. And I hadn't even gotten to the cherry on top of it all. . . .

"The clog," I said, meeting the vampire's poisonous blue gaze. "That was *yours*. . . . You lost it chasing after Ronny, the cow herder whose cows you *vamp'd* in Portugal."

The asema gave me a slow smug nod, but I didn't need it to know I was right. See, history might not have been my best subject (it was actually way down at the bottom of my best subjects list, along with math and home ec), but I'd paid enough attention in Mr. Henry's third period to know that Suriname was once a Dutch colony. Had been from back in the mid-1600s to pretty recently. So it was really no surprise that an ancient Surinamese blood-sucker would probably have a soft spot for classic Dutch footwear.

I squeezed my hands into fists.

There had been clues of an asema everywhere. Right from the jump!

If only I'd tried using just a bit of my gray matter. . . .

"V, you were right," I said. "That thing's from Suriname. Just like you thought on the train!"

"Suriname?" Violet made a confused face. Then something seemed to click behind her eyes, and she must've realized the Suriname-Dutch connection because she said, "*No . . .*"

The vampire's fangs gleamed wickedly in the torchlight as it smiled at us. A vicious sort of smile. If looks could kill, we'd already have our headstones carved. . . .

"He's the one who's been working with Joanna," I said, my voice hardly more than a whisper. "Slaughtering all those animals and building those . . . those awful *castells*."

"Not *quite*," the asema replied rather casually, and now he didn't sound at all like the old Mr. Ovaprim. The vampire's voice was . . . *weird*. Impossibly deep yet velvety smooth, tinged with an odd Spanish accent. "While it is true that I *have been* the one constructing the castells, I have not, as you put it, been working with your beloved and *pathetic* queen. ¿No hay comunión entre la luz y la oscuridad o no has oído esto?"

No fellowship between light and darkness? What did he mean? That Joanna was all good? That she hadn't played a part in any of this? "I . . . I don't understand."

The asema's face twisted in a mocking grin. "Are you really so dense, pequeñito? You were *fooled*. ¡Engañado! All this time you believed you were following your queen's clues you have been, in actuality, following *mine*. I was the one who left the alicanto egg in the Provencia for you to discover; I planted your queen's scarf in Lapa do Santo; I left her crown in the Warlock's Cave in Chiloé; and it was I who spelled her butterfly so that it would lead you to la bruja Zarate—the final step of your preparation."

"Preparation for *what?*" I asked without thinking.

"*For sacrifice,*" answered another voice—and now the witch Zarate herself stepped out from behind the vampire, her beautiful black-and-blue peacock waddling neatly at her side.

"You—you're on their side . . . ?" I asked dazedly, but la bruja stayed silent.

"You have been unwittingly walking the path of the sacrifice," said the asema, letting out a hollow, haunting laugh. "Every place I led you, every place you saw a castell, was one of the secret locations where your beloved queen buried one of the four cursed coffins. You see, it was your queen who captured the necromancer nearly eight hundred years ago to the day, and it was *your queen* who thought it would be wise—in an effort to avoid him resurrecting himself a third time—to chop up his corpse, divide it among four coffins, and then scatter said coffins all over the world so as to never again be found. And to seal his fate forever— or so she thought—she bound each coffin with ancient ele- mental magia—four coffins, four bonds: wind, water, fire, and earth—ensuring that the necromancer would not be able to resurrect himself until those bonds had been bro- ken *and* the *breaker* of those bonds offered as a sacrifice." If possible, the asema's grin widened even more; it reminded me of a shark. "Perhaps your queen thought it would be appropriate to make the bonds elemental, seeing as it was a Morphling—a girl a little older than you—who helped her capture the necromancer all those years ago and since only a Morphling would be capable of breaking all four. A Morphling. Just. Like. *You*."

Which explained why they needed me. Probably even why they had sent La Cuca to try to take me out and steal my powers—so they could break the bonds themselves. Things just kept getting better and better, didn't they? Whatever. This wasn't going to go down like that blood-sucking leech had planned. Not if I had anything to say about it. "Well, it sounds to me like you wasted a whole buncha time," I said. "'Cause I'm definitely not gonna let you offer me as a sacrifice, and I'm not gonna break any of those bonds for you either."

"But don't you understand, pequeñito? You already *have.* . . . Think back to Lapa do Santo, where you were tried by wind; to Chile, where you were tried by water; to Chiloé, by *fire*; and finally, to El Dorado, where you were tried by earth. At each castell, each secret burial site, you were tried and tested by an element, and by surviving it, you proved yourself a worthy sacrifice and broke the elemental bond placed on the coffin by your queen. Now all that is left is to sacrifice you upon that altar and El Hijo de la Tumba will rise once again." While the vamp was still yapping away, three more figures melted out of the shadows: two of the anchimayen kids, Mario and Santi, along with El Nguruvilu, that fox-serpent creature we'd seen back in Chiloé. Perched on Santi's shoulder was the dark-haired chonchón I'd talked to in the Sorcerer's Cave. It winked at me with a bulging bloodshot eye.

"Hold up," Violet said, sounding shocked, angry. "*You* guys were in on this too?"

Mario grinned. His bright eyes smoldered like lit fuses. "Perdona, chula, but we bad to the *bone!*" Then he and Santi burst out laughing, bumping fists, and glanced back over their shoulders. "Oh, and we brought some friends . . . ," Mario said.

Call it intuition, but the way the little punk said "friends" set off all sorts of alarm bells in my head. The floor began to rumble. Tiny fragments of loose bone leapt up around our sneakers, and from the wall of shadows behind the vampire emerged a horde of Okpe ogres—easily two or three thousand strong. Most rode those huge, husked hogs; some, armored llamas; but they all carried clubs and battle-axes and spiked iron maces. Something that wasn't particularly comforting especially when you considered that we were already massively outnumbered. Being *outweaponed* as well only made the remote possibility of us surviving to see the next two minutes even more remote. Like, virtually nonexistent. A moment later what looked like a human hand skittered up beside the asema. At first I thought it was a spider, a great big black one, but no . . . it was a hand—an actual human hand! Hairy and calloused and severed at the wrist.

"Alas, but I am merely a tool," said the vampire, grinning down at it. "Behold the *architect* of your demise!"

I recognized that hand. Vaguely. But from *where* . . . ?

My pulse began to thud painfully in my ears. Then, like a bolt of lightning, my mind flashed on the visions I'd seen in Chiloé, in the Seeing Bowl: That was the hand I'd seen in the throne room—the hand that had killed the dude with the crown!

The asema must've read my face because it said, "¿Lo reconoce? How long has La Mano Peluda haunted your dreams?"

I blinked. *La Mano Peluda?* Why would he call that thing La Mano Peluda . . . ?

Suddenly there was an itch at the back of my mind; a memory had been tickled . . . an old and almost forgotten legend, the story of a man who had been buried in a haunted cemetery, the story of a man whose hand had crawled out of the grave.

Had come back for revenge.

"No . . . ," I breathed. It couldn't be—*could it?*

The asema was nodding now, urging me to put the pieces together, to get there already. And a split second later I did: La Mano Peluda wasn't just the name of an organization; it wasn't just the name given to a cabal of evil sombras who wanted to expand their dominion from the Land of the Dead into this world; it had been a *person* once—or part of one, anyway—and that person had inspired a legend, maybe the most terrifying one in the *entire* Spanish-speaking world.

The legend of La Mano Peluda. *That* thing's legend.

My heart was now pounding like a hammer. My palms dampened with sweat, and as I wiped them over the pockets of my shorts, my eyes still glued to *easily* the most frightening and feared hand in *all* of human history, Joanna's words echoed through my mind: *The king was murdered by the necromancer's own hand! Only he can resurrect my Philip now!*

I thought back to the lienzo where I'd heard her say that, to the casket she'd been weeping over. The casket of King Philip. Then I thought back to the king I'd seen in the vision in the Seeing Bowl, the one who had been murdered by La Mano Peluda.

Both were kings.

Both were *Spanish* kings.

And they'd *both* been murdered. Coincidence? I didn't so. And that's when it all finally clicked together for me— *todo.* They weren't two different kings—they were one and the same!

Which could mean only one thing. . . .

CHAPTER ONE HUNDRED ONE

The asema began to clap its slender clawed hands together in mock applause, grinning wickedly. "¡Qué inteligente! I'm impressed!"

"Wait," Violet said. "So *that* *thing's* La Mano Peluda? *And* it's the necromancer's hand . . . ?" When I nodded, she frowned and said, "But if that's true, how was it resurrected? Even if all the bonds really have been broken, the sacrifice—that'd be *you*—still hasn't been offered."

The answer hit me even before she'd finished her question, my mind flashing on another vision I'd seen in the bowl: the hairy, severed hand being buried in a field I half recognized.

The field in Portugal! I nearly shouted as it hit me.

The one where we'd seen the first castell. The hand had been buried there . . . buried right under that awful castle of bones.

"Because Joanna hadn't known about it," I said out loud, feeling every inch of my skin prickle. "No one did. He must have buried his own hand before he got captured. It didn't get put in any coffins. It didn't get bound."

"Muy bien," the asema purred, those razor fangs stretching out of its smiling, lipless mouth. "When El Brujo felt your queen closing in, he hid his hand in a field to make sure there was a piece of him in this world that he could bring back at *precisely* the right time to orchestrate his grand plan. And that time is *now*."

"But why now?" Violet asked. "Why did he wait so long?"

"Because not until recently did we learn the whereabouts of all four coffins. Not until recently has La Liga experienced a bit of—¿cómo se dice?—*trouble* keeping their secrets *secret*." Its poisonous blue eyes narrowed on me. "Ah, but our scheming did not end there. . . . No, you see, in order for our plan to be completely *foolproof*, we required someone to watch over you, someone who could make sure you made it to this place alive and unharmed and well prepared for sacrifice. We required someone with a reputation, someone who could—eventually and *believably*—worm their way into your hearts." The asema's eyes flicked to Saci. "Ay, Saci Pererê—there you are! Ven aquí, ven aquí, don't be shy now. . . . Claim your reward."

I turned to Saci. "Dude, what's he talking about?"

But Saci didn't respond. Wouldn't even look at me. Instead he hopped slowly over to the grinning, gloating asema, who handed him an old scroll tied with a red ribbon.

"The deed to the finest sugarcane farm in el mundo entero," said the vampire. "Six thousand six hundred acres already planted with every species of sugarcane know to mankind and dozens found only in the deepest of sombra wood."

I could feel my jaw hanging, my eyes bulging as I stared at Saci, shocked beyond words. Beyond *thoughts*. I mean, was this *actully* happening right now?

"You've been playing us this whole time, haven't you?" Violet said to Saci. "You *wanted* us to capture you. That's why you pranked us in the first place, why you took our egg." Her voice trembled with anger, with disbelief, as she said, "You tricked us."

Saci, meanwhile, hadn't even looked up. He hadn't made a single sound or spoken a single word, but he didn't have to. His silence said more than words ever could.

The asema, now laughing its fangs off, turned its fierce gaze on me. "La niña is quite right . . . this has all been an elaborate show. And I do hope you have enjoyed it. Because it is now time for the final act—time for you to *die*."

CHAPTER ONE HUNDRED TWO

Espere un momentito," Joanna said, her voice ringing loud and clear through the dark castle. "Before you spill el niño's blood and raise your master, I have something I'd like to share. While it is true that La Liga has, in more recent times, been experiencing a problem with traitors, we do still have quite a number of allies, which means that we see much and hear *even more*. And while you were busy scheming, so were *we*. You could say that we knew vaguely of your intentions . . . that we had an idea as to what was in your mind. *Or* you could say that we knew *exactly* what you and your cohorts were planning . . . that *every single move* you made, from capturing me in my study to leading Charlie through South and Central America, breaking the elemental bonds, were moves we *allowed* you to make, moves we *wanted* you to make, and that, very much like *you*, we have been simply biding our time, awaiting this grand reveal." The asema's eyes, now widening with shock, focused on Joanna as she said, "You should also know that, again, like you, we haven't schemed *alone*."

No sooner had she spoken those words than a deafening neigh split the air, followed by the thunderous clatter of hooves. I whirled as a rider charged up the bony staircase behind us: a headless figure clad in black-as-night armor— El Justo Juez. Columns of thick, dark smoke trailed back from his horse's fiery nostrils as he galloped past me, pulling up next to Joanna and turning to face the asema and the Okpe hordes.

Oh, heck yeah! *Now* we were talking. . . .

But the best part? He wasn't alone.

A split second later El Cadejo came bounding up the castell along with Juan the basajaun and at least five hundred basajauns in full battle armor; they looked like an army of blond-furred yetis with silver breastplates, enormous broadswords, and tiny (at least in basajaun terms) wooden daggers strapped to their impossibly long, impossibly muscular legs. Juan, I knew, was one of the smartest and fiercest warriors that had ever *lived*. He'd fought alongside La Liga for decades, and Joanna trusted him so much she'd basically made him her personal bodyguard (even when she was on her "official" duties as president of Spain). He'd also nearly single-handedly fought off an entire clan of weather fairies back in Compostela de Santiago, and if that didn't prove just how tough the dude was, then *nothing* would.

"V, we're about to *own* Mr. Mosquito and his piggies!" I shouted.

And I believed it, too. At least until I glanced over my shoulder and saw the largest pack of lobisomem I'd *ever seen* come streaming up the same bony staircase in a blur of fur and teeth.

Worse, they were being led by none other than those terrifying lobisomem priests—*Los Embrujados*!

CHAPTER ONE HUNDRED THREE

Panic rose in my throat so thick I could almost *taste* it. And for the record, it tasted *terrible*. Whirling back around, I opened my mouth, preparing to shout a warning to Juan and the others, when I got the shock of a lifetime: The werewolves didn't attack the basajauns—no, they fell into rank *beside* them. Like they were on the same team. Like we *all* were.

Yep, something totally loco *is going on here. . . .*

"You've put on quite the show, vampiro," Joanna said with a wry smile, "but it seems the show was even more *elaborate* than you knew."

"Whoa, whoa, whoa," I shouted, raising my hands. "Everyone just hold your horses. . . . How can *the lobisomem* be on *our side*? They were trying to EAT ME!"

Joanna smiled sheepishly. "I'm sorry for any scare they might have caused you, Charlie—I will explain later. But for now, rest assured that they won't bite—at least not you."

Just then the witch Zarate cleared her throat and marched over to "our side," bringing her peacock along with her. As she turned now to face the asema and the rest of them, she gave me a small nod and smiled. I smiled back, thinking it wouldn't be too bad to have the kooky bruja with the awful temper on our team.

"Oh, and of course we've had our own spies as well," the queen said to the vampire.

For a second I was tempted to shout, "BOOM! Mic drop!" but I decided to hold off on any celebrations. For the moment, anyway.

The asema grinned, but his face was as hard as stone. His eyes had begun to pulse, alternating in color from that hazy, poisonous blue to a deep dark red. "I see you have managed to open El Muro de Partición, which means you found La Catrina's fingers. A pity, really, because we took such great care to avoid this very inconvenience. There is only one other entrance into the castle, the one Saci was *supposed* to lead the boy through and which we had heavily guarded." The asema looked even more furious than he had moments ago, yet his grin widened. "Congratulations on figuring out a way to get your army in here. You have always been a worthy adversary, Juana. *Quite* worthy. Unfortunately, all your grand scheming has been for *naught*...."

Suddenly a series of torches flamed up in the recesses of the castle. Harsh green light flooded the room, chasing away the shadows and revealing what appeared to be an innumerable swarm of muertos vivientes—zombies. They crowded the stadium-size space from end to end and as far back as the torchlight reached. Growling and hissing, their scraggly, emaciated bodies lumbered and lurched as they marched forward, their pupil-less glassy eyes reflecting the soullessness within.

"Dead things are notoriously difficult to kill," said the asema haughtily, "but I'm sure I will enjoy seeing all of you try. Let us not stand on ceremony—shall we?"

Joanna whirled to Violet and me and said, "Find La Mano Peluda. It controls los muertos vivientes. If you destroy the puppeteer, his puppets will cease to be."

I looked around for the hand and saw it was gone; so were the anchimayen and El Nguruvilu. I guess everyone was happy to let the zombies do their dirty work.

"It fled up into the catacombs," the queen said, "but it cannot go far from its army."

Violet tapped Juan on his side. "Can I borrow that?" she asked, pointing at the small wooden dagger strapped to his leg.

He handed it over, and the moment it changed hands, I saw just how "small" it was—the thing was probably as long as my leg. Looked wicked sharp, too.

"Go now!" Joanna shouted. "¡Y apuracen!"

CHAPTER ONE HUNDRED FOUR

There was a shadowy opening in the wall to our right, and we took off into it, following a twisting maze of halls that gradually spiraled upward, slowing only to peek into the rooms we passed to make sure the hand wasn't hiding inside. As we raced along, I could hear the sounds of battle reverberating through the castle—shrieks and howls, the high, clear ringing of steel. They rattled through the bones that made up the castle floors, making it shudder beneath our pounding feet. Three floors up, the walls that blocked the view of the altar room below had sort of crumbled away, and as we ran I looked down to see a terrifying sight—well, it wasn't exactly *terrifying* at first. *At first* it looked like La Liga was kicking butt. Directly below me, I could see El Cadejo tearing through the ranks of zombies in a flash of teeth and bursts of dazzling white light that rippled off its coat, exploding through the ranks of the undead like shock waves and sending dozens tumbling into the shadows; to my left, the basajaun and lob-isomem clans had formed battle lines and were advancing on the Okpes, smashing through their heavy rock armor with claws and swords and tackling the ogres off their hogs. On the far side of the altar, galloping through the center of the zombie horde, El Justo Juez swung a sword the size of an SUV and his massive, armored horse shot hellfire out of its nostrils, while Joanna, Zarate and, of course, Zarate's *peacock* unleashed great blasts of blinding light that cut through the marching muertos like molten laser beams, searing flesh and sending up thick columns of oily gray smoke. But the problem was—the *terrifying* part was—as I watched, I realized that each time they downed a zombie—it didn't matter if they'd blasted it or stabbed the thing—it wasn't long (maybe eight or nine seconds) before the zombie would just get back up again, pick up its arm or leg or head off the ground, reattach it, and then go right back to fighting. And this happened every time. Every *single* time. Those things simply refused to die! Well, die *again* . . .

"We have to hurry!" I shouted to Violet. And we'd made it probably another five or six floors up when we came around a bend and had to skid to a stop—

Standing in the middle of the corridor, towering almost as high as the bony ceiling itself, was an Okpe ogre—and not just any Okpe: It was the same ogre that had "saved" me from the lobisomem back in Argentina. His rocky armor shone faintly in the greenish torchlight. His fleshy piglike face crumpled into a snarl as he reached up to grab the large metal box on his humped back. The box—which was a sort of cage Okpes transported kidnapped children in—was attached to a heavy metal chain wrapped around one of the ogre's wart-marked forearms.

"You again," I breathed.

The ogre's misshapen piggish mouth pulled open in what I guess was supposed to be a smirk but was much too hideous to actually be considered one.

"V, stand back," I shouted, squatting into my fiercest-looking ninja pose. "I got this. . . ." Then I gave the waistband of my Power Ranger's undies a lucky rub, shouted, "IT'S MOR-PHIN' TIME!" (which just so happened to be one of my favorite superhero catchphrases), and began concentrating like I'd never concentrated before in my life. I imagined horns and claws and fangs. Even that freakish crustacean-like hand thingy I'd manifested thanks to La Cuca feeding me poisoned lobster bisque. Basically anything I could use to teach this overgrown boulder a lesson. I was hoping to morph at least a couple of them. Hey, the ogre was *ginormous*, after all. Not to mention *rock-plated*. But for all my concentrating, for all my imagining and visualizing and *praying* (yeah, I was silently doing plenty of that, too), what I actually ended up manifesting was a big steaming platter of nada! I didn't feel the slightest change. . . .

The Okpe, of course, being the big jerk that he was, let out this huge earth-rumbling chuckle. You would've thought me failing to manifest anything was the funniest thing he'd seen in his *entire life.*

"*NOT* MORPHIN' TIME!" he roared mockingly. "BUAHAHAHAHAAHAHAAA!"

And that ticked me off. "Hey, you watch your mouth, piglet! I'm a one-man *ZOO* over here! I'm just having a little trouble unleashing my—my *inner animal* at the moment...."

Grinning now, the Okpe unwound a long length of chain, letting the steel box hang by his knees for a moment before beginning to swing it in a tight circle at his side. The box whistled through the air as the ogre, still eyeing me, whispered, "*Corran*"—i.e. run. Only without actually giving us *a chance* to, he swung the chain so that the box came arching down in a screaming blur. Violet and I dove out of the way as it slammed into the ground between us. Chunks of bone flew everywhere; the hall shook.

As I rolled to one knee, I saw Violet raise the dagger, and the ogre's murky green eyes instantly flicked in her direction. There was a loud jangling sound as he gave the chain a vicious yank, and the box went tumbling along the ground.

When it rolled past her, I thought he'd missed—or messed up.

But then the ogre yanked on the chain again, and this

time it swept up and out like a jump rope, catching Violet across the back of the knees and sweeping her legs out from under her. She landed hard on her back, the dagger clattering to the floor.

"VIOLET!" I shouted, starting toward her, but at that same moment, the Okpe whirled, giving the chain another powerful yank, and the box came arching back around. It screamed past me, the chain looping around my shoulders once, twice, three times and pinning my arms painfully against my sides before the Okpe caught the box with his other hand.

He pulled. The chains tightened around me. The breath exploded out of my lungs in a gasping cry.

I flailed and kicked and struggled, but the chains only got tighter, squeezing me, crushing me. I could feel my bones beginning to bend in the wrong direction, could feel my spine creaking and cracking under the incredible pressure.

I heard Violet shout, "CHARLIE!"

But what could she do? This thing was *literally* invulnerable. Even if she still had the sword—even if she had a *rocket launcher*—there wasn't any way she could hurt this monster. No way she could penetrate his rocky armor.

Okpes didn't have any weak spots—

Except . . . they *did*.

And remembering the legends, remembering *exactly* where that weak spot was, I opened my mouth to shout,

"V, go for its heel!" but all that came out was a strangled wheezy squeak. In my panic, my eyes frantically scanned the ground for a weapon. And I spotted one! Violet's dagger! It was right there, not five inches away, resting on a hump of bone between the ogre's massive armored feet.

Just one little problem: My arms were currently being *crushed* into my sides, so reaching out for it was going to be more or less *impossible*.

Just then a movement caught my eye. Something was flicking near my left leg. A ... tail?

No, *my* tail!

Desperate, pain lighting up my entire body like a Christmas tree, I reached out with it, clumsily at first, until I'd wrapped the fluffy end tightly around the sword's hilt. Then I spun it around and drove it, pointy end first, into the soft pinkish flesh at the back of the Okpe's foot.

As it turned out, I learned two very interesting things: a) the stories about Okpe's having weak heels were much more fact than fiction, and b) basajauns might've been the most talented woodsmiths on the planet, because I hadn't exactly gotten a lot of power behind my poke, but the razor-tipped hunk of wood still sank in like a fork into freshly baked flan. And as pretty much everyone knows, when someone drives something sharp and pointy into your foot, you usually scream. Okpe were no exception to this rule. The rock-encased piggy let out a squeal that could've probably been heard all the way to downtown *Fort Lauderdale*. He stumbled backward, releasing the box or cage or whatever, and the chains immediately fell away.

Gasping for air, I dropped to a knee, watching as the giant ogre began hopping around on one foot, clutching the other between his two rock-plated hands and shouting, "¡Mi talón! ¡Mi talón!"

"What'd you do to it?" Violet shouted as she ran up beside me.

"Nothing it enjoyed," I said, grinning.

"Did you stab its *foot?*"

"Basically. The heel's their weak spot. Just gave it a little poke."

"Nice!"

"Yeah, I think he got the *point*. . . ."

V had to laugh at that (though she tried not to). Then she asked, "But will it, like, put him out of commission?"

I thought back to the stories and shook my head. In the ones I remembered, the tribespeople always defeated the monster by pushing it off a cliff; that was usually what it took to crack an Okpe's armor. And now, as the ogre skipped and hopped dangerously close to the edge of the hallway, I saw my chance.

Dragging in one last gulp of air, I charged the Okpe,

dropping my shoulder at the last moment, and slammed into the side of his leg like an angry billy goat.

I hit with a loud *smack!*

My head banged against his hip, and I just sort of bounced right off him, feeling like I'd run into a, well, a massive ogre leg encased in rocky armor. . . .

But it was enough. If just barely.

The Okpe tipped, tilted, tottered—and then, like Humpty Dumpty before him, had a great fall. He tumbled backward into empty space, huge arms and legs flailing, but finding nothing to grab on to.

Watching him fall, I had a sudden urge to shout, "Hasta la vista, *bebe!*" So I did. I mean, the thing *had* just tried to squash us.

But as I turned back to Violet with this big stupid grin spreading across my face, I felt the weirdest thing: Something had tightened across the front of my legs.

Something hard and cold and metallic-feeling.

I frowned, realizing what it was even before its loud jangling clatter reached my ears.

Jump! was the first thought that screamed through my mind. And I didn't get a chance for a second before the chain swept through, spilling over the edge along with the box and taking *me* with it.

CHAPTER ONE HUNDRED FIVE

plummeted, tumbling through the cold, stale air, turning over once, twice, the wind whooshing and roaring in my ears as the ground rushed up to kiss me goodbye. There was no time to scream, only to think, so as what I fully expected to be my final act on this side of things, I thought, *Wings!* I didn't really expect anything to happen—it just seemed like a much nicer thought than picturing myself going *splat* surrounded by a swarm of dead things.

I felt a tingle down my spine. A rush of heat. And then something was pushing its way up through the skin and muscle of my back! I had another split second to think, *No way!* And next thing I knew wings were exploding out the back of my T-shirt with a great flappy, tearing sound! Now, I didn't have a *ton* of flight hours logged with these bad boys. But I remembered enough from my little aerial scrum with La Cuca to instinctively stretch them out as wide as they would go—you know, to avoid making my very own Charlie Crater in the middle of the bony floor. Fortunately for me—and also for the zombie or two that I would've pancaked—it worked! Immediately the air caught me, and I soared up, up, up above the main altar, where the battle was still raging. Below, I could see what looked like a rolling carpet of scraggly, lumbering, desiccated bodies pressing mindlessly forward while a blur of claws and teeth and bursts of bright light tried to drive them back. Which, from the looks of it, seemed like a fairly impossible task.

There were just too many. Plus, those things couldn't even *die*!

We needed to hurry.

Violet had just leaned out to peer down over the edge as I flew up toward it, and we almost knocked heads.

"Oh my gosh!" she breathed as we caught each other in big bear hugs, her eyes huge and wild. "I thought you were . . ."

I smiled. "Not yet. But c'mon—we have to find La Mano!"

We made it maybe halfway around the next bend when another familiar creature suddenly appeared in our path—the fox-serpent, El Nguruvilu! Standing on its rear legs with that strange tooth-lined tail curled up underneath itself like a coil, it looked like the result of some secret government experiment gone horribly wrong.

Its dark foxy eyes were fixed on mine. The witch light glistened off the matrix of reptilian scales that ran along its long, slender body.

"Ah, if it isssn't the captainsss of the two *leassst* impressive boatsss I've ever had the pleasssure of capsssizing!" it hissed, grinning evilly.

"Charlie, what's it talking about?" V asked me.

"It tried to drown us in Chile . . . ," I said as it hit me. "It caused the waves and the whirlpools! That's what that thing does!"

El Nguruvilu nodded proudly. "Esss verdad . . . and sssoon I'll make you wisssh that I'd *sssucceeded!*"

The fox-serpent's sleek serpentine tail had begun to swell up like a balloon. Now its jaw came unhinged, and my heart stopped as a torrent of water spewed out from its mouth, slamming into us and knocking us onto our butts. The current was so strong, it carried us, kicking and screaming, down the center of the hallway and back around the bend. Before the wave of water had even fully died away, I saw El Nguruvilu come slithering rapidly into view, its scaly, slender tail already swelling up again.

"Violet, watch out!" I shouted, scrambling awkwardly up, my feet slipping and sliding on the smooth and now *soaked* bones.

But it was too late. The creature opened its foxy

fang-lined mouth again, and another powerful blast of water gushed toward us.

It raced along the ground, bubbling and foaming, and swept Violet and me right off our feet, sending us crashing against the wall with enough force to snap my head back. My right shoulder hit hard. One of my wings got twisted underneath me; pain shot down my side. I cried out, sucked in a mouthful of silty water, and started to choke.

As the force of the water ran out underneath us, Violet, who was lying a couple of feet away, rolled over, wiping hair out of her face, and shouted, "Charlie, how do you beat that thing?"

I was still coughing up water but managed, "Huh?"

"I'm talking about like *in the legends!*"

Great question. "I—I think you have to capture it! Hold its mouth shut like those alligator wrestlers in the Everglades do in the shows!"

"Seems like that might be difficult."

"*Seems* like it?" *Impossible* was probably closer to the truth. How were we even supposed to get within five yards of the thing without being Super Soaker'd, much less hold its mouth shut?

V pushed unsteadily to her feet. "We're gonna have to find a way to get close to it." And she was right; problem was, the floor was so slick now that we might as well have been standing on a Slip 'N Slide covered in *banana peels.*

I could've probably slid for half a mile on th—

"I have an idea!" I shouted.

"I'm all ears," V said, but before she could say anything else, I took off down the hall, using my wings like two extra limbs to keep from falling over. With perfect timing this might actually work; but we didn't have time for *perfect timing,* which meant I was just going to have to "wing" it. (Pun intended.)

Nearing the bend in the hall, I leapt forward, feetfirst, throwing myself into a baseball slide just as El Nguruvilu slithered around the corner.

Its black eyes flashed as it caught movement in its peripheral vision, but it was too late. I popped to my feet, flicking my wings out like an overturned beetle, and wrapped my arms around the creature's head, clamping its mouth shut.

It wriggled and writhed and hissed, but its slender snakelike body wasn't all that strong, so it wasn't going to be able to shake me off. Behind us, its strange tooth-lined tail had swelled up to about the size of a beach ball and was quivering angrily now.

"V, I got it!" I shouted.

A second later she came sliding around the bend, hands out at her sides like she was just learning to ice-skate. When her eyes found mine, she grinned. When she saw me in full gator wrestling pose, her face broke into a huge smile. But then her gaze drifted past me, up the hall, and her smile instantly evaporated. "CHARLIE, LOOK OUT!" she screamed.

I snapped my head around and thought, *Uh-oh*. Mario and Santi were standing less than twenty yards away, eyeing me with mischievous little grins on their mischievous little faces. Their eyes burned brighter than any torch, and I could see the trail of charred, smoky footprints their tiny fiery feet had left as they'd come running around the corner.

"¡Agárralo!" Mario shouted, and they both burst into fireballs. I blinked, and they were already sizzling through the air toward us, huge tongues of orange-yellow flames licking at the walls, the ceiling. I swallowed—hard—and because I didn't have a whole lot of options, I did the first thing that popped into my brain: I whipped El Nguruvilu's head around to face them and stomped on its swollen tail at the exact moment I let go of its mouth. A jet of super-pressurized water gushed out, crashing into the anchimayen. The water hissed and boiled, dousing them in an instant and sending up puffs of white-hot steam. The pair of anchimayen went flying backward, knocking their heads against the wall, then slumping to the floor, side by side, unconscious.

"BULL'S-EYE!" Violet shouted, pumping her fist in the air.

Grinning, feeling pretty good about it myself, I said, "Thought they looked a little hot under the collar. . . ." Which, in my mind, was probably the best burn I'd dealt out all day.

But apparently El Nguruvilu disagreed, because it craned its long, slim neck around to hiss: "That hasss to be the lamessst one-liner I've EVER heard!"

And since I couldn't think of anything better to do (I didn't have any other "lame" burns in my back pocket), I just slammed its head against the wall, felt it go limp, and called it a day.

"How's that for a one-liner?" I said.

CHAPTER ONE HUNDRED SIX

I was about to ask Violet if she had her phone handy so I could take a selfie with El Nguruvilu (you know, the way fishermen do when they catch a huge marlin or whatever)—when another thought filled my mind— no, not a thought exactly . . . but a message: *Charlie, hurry! ¡Apúrate!*

It had come from El Cadejo. I knew it like I knew the sound of my own voice.

I hear you, I thought back (though I had no idea if he could hear *me* through thoughts) and said, "V, c'mon! We gotta find the hand already!"

As we flew up the spiraling hallways of bone, rising higher and higher into the dark castle, Violet said, "So we took care of water and fire—Saci, that dirty little traitor, is obviously wind—who's left?"

"Earth, right? Those giant Minhocão things?"

"You don't think there's one of those in here, do you?"

"I sincerely hope not."

We rounded another bend and came to a skidding stop as a figure appeared before us, tall and curvy, with a mass of writhing purple vines for hair.

"Madremonte!" I shouted. "*Thank God!* You have to help us find La Mano Peluda. . . . It's around here *somewhere*."

She stretched her buff, green-skinned arms out at her sides, and beneath us the jigsaw puzzle of bones that made up the floor began to buckle and crack as skinny twiglike branches pushed their way up through it. The branches grew branches themselves, thickening as they did, budding thorns as well as leaves. They twisted and twined, rising up on either side of her like a hedge.

One of the thorns pricked the back of my hand, and I flinched as blood ran warm down my index finger. "Madremonte, what are you *doing?*" I shouted. "We have get *through*—we have to stop La Mano!"

The mass of vines that grew out of her head began to change color, turning from a pale green to a dark reddish orange. Her voice was oddly cold as she said, "Perdóname, but I'm afraid this I cannot let you do . . ."

"*What?* Why not?" Violet snapped.

"Because she's the traitor," I said as it dawned on me. I watched a slow smile begin to tug at the corners of

Madremonte's lips as her glowing yellow eyes narrowed on mine. "You're the one who told the vampire where the coffins were hidden. . . . It was *you* who kidnapped Joanna." Which explained all the splattered plant guts we'd seen in the queen's study. And *also* explained how an evil sombra had gotten past all the wards and spells that protected La Provencia.

And that explained all the slimy green plant guts we'd seen splattered over the furniture and floor in Joanna's study.

"Eventuality is like a tsunami," Madremonte replied calmly. "Either you embrace it or are *crushed* by it. The time of La Liga has passed. I have chosen to accept that. Will you?"

"So you're the reason the forests are dying," Violet said beside me. "Because you're changing. . . . You're turning *evil*." Whipping around, she gripped my arm tightly. "Charlie, you can do this!" she rasped. "I know you can!"

"Wait, wait, wait. Do what, V? What are you talking about?" Because she couldn't *possibly* be implying what it sounded like she was.

"Charlie, I believe in you! You got this!"

"Have you gone cuckoo for Cocoa Puffs? Listen to what you're saying!"

"No, you listen to *me*! You can take her, Charlie. You *can*! You can *beat* Madremonte!" Violet paused for a moment, frowning. "Okay, now that the words *actually* came out of my mouth, I'm not feeling so good about this anymore...."

"*Thank you!* Now what are we gonna do?"

She glanced briefly toward Madremonte. "I'll tell you *exactly* what we're going to do. You're going to give your lucky pair of underwear another rub, morph something SPECTACULAR, and just take her *out!*" She paused again, making a sad face. "Yeah, I gotta stop saying that out loud.... It's just making things worse."

"You think I got any chance?" I whispered.

"Not really. But I'll be trying to come up with a plan before she kills you."

Now, *there* was an idea! "I like it!"

"Go buy us some time."

"It's what I do best! " Giving my wings a quick flap, I turned back to Madremonte and smiled, hoping maybe she'd take it easy on me. Surprisingly, she smiled back, a sort of regretful smile, and raised one hand in my direction. She said, "Hasta luego, Charlie...."

In the next instant something whistled out of the thorny hedge to her left. It streaked through the air, a greenish-brownish blur and, before I could react, pierced my chest like an arrow.

At first I didn't feel anything. Not fear. Not pain. I just stared numbly at the skinny, ruler-length thorn sticking

out of the front of my T-shirt. It looked so odd there—
so out of place—and it felt wrong too. Like when you get
sand stuck between your fingers or toes.

In what felt like slow motion, my eyes rose to meet
Violet's, and suddenly all the energy drained from my body
and I collapsed at her feet.

I hadn't even closed my eyes before the world went
completely black.

CHAPTER ONE HUNDRED SEVEN

When I opened my eyes again, I was sitting in a familiar room, on a familiar red-and-yellow carpet, staring at a familiar television set with a familiar show playing on it: *SpongeBob SquarePants*. A familiar episode, too—when SpongeBob meets Jack M. Crazyfish and tries to save a lady who got tied to the railroad tracks. All around me, scattered over the Spanish-tile floors, were hand-drawn sketches of sombras: basajauns, chupacabras, acalicas. Some had been colored messily with crayons; others had been scribbled over with markers and had pencil holes punched through their faces. I realized I was sitting cross-legged on the floor, wearing my absolute favorite pair of pj's, my Power Rangers pj's—the ones I hadn't been able to fit into since I was *eight*.

"*What's going on . . . ?*" I said out loud, feeling my skin prickle.

How the heck had I gotten here? And where *was* here...?

No sooner had the last question crossed my mind than I knew the answer: I was in my room, my *old* room, back in my *old* house—the one La Cuca had burned down—and somehow...*someway*...it looked just like it had when I was *eight years old*.

"¿Mi hijito?" whispered a warm and familiar voice at my back.

I turned—and my entire world froze.

Sitting behind me, on the edge of my bed with the *Dragon Ball Z* bedcovers and matching sheets, was the person who'd been there for every birthday, every Christmas, every time I'd scraped my knee or needed a hug. The one person I missed most in this world.

"*¿Abuelita?*" I heard myself whisper.

Tears welled in my grandmother's eyes, spilling down her brown and wrinkled cheeks as she grabbed me up in her arms. "Mi niño precioso..."

That voice, so kind, so full of *love* and everything I remembered most about my childhood, seemed to fill this huge hole in the middle of my heart that had been there since the day my mom had told me she'd died.

"Ay, so long I've waited for this...," she murmured as she stroked my hair, her touch as familiar as her voice, imprinted in my soul.

I started talking without even realizing it. "But, Abuelita . . . how are you . . . ? Am I—*dead?*"

"No, no, no, no, no . . ." She pulled back, shaking her head, those large brown eyes as beautiful I remembered them, as loving. "¡No digas eso *ni jugando*! I just wanted to talk to you. . . . Watching over you all these years, watching you grow into this *incredibly* brave and beautiful boy, I—I'm just *so proud* of you, mi hijo. . . ." Another rush of tears spilled down her cheeks, falling to the carpet below us, splashing my feet.

I was in so much shock I could hardly think. "You . . . watch over me?"

My abuela gave me a smile that was so warm and full of love that I felt my heart melt in my chest. "I've been watching over you since the moment la enfermera brought you out of the nursery wrapped in that little blue towel with the initials of the hospital on it," she said. "And I remember turning to your father—even *before* the nurse had told anyone whose you were—and saying, 'Look! That's him! ¡Ese es Charlie!' And the *first time* I ever held you in my arms, I made you a promise—whispered it into your little ear even though you were too young to remember or understand. The promise was that I would always—siempre—look after you, para el resto de tu vida, and no power in this world or the other will stop me from *keeping* that promise. After all, an abuela's job is never *really* done. . . ."

For a moment her eyes drifted up to gaze at something behind me, but when I turned to look, there was nothing there—just my bedroom wall.

A shudder shook the room. Windows rattled. Behind me, the TV blinked off.

My abuela gripped my shoulder, still smiling. "Mi corazón, it is time to go. . . ."

"What? *Why?* I just got here. . . ." I felt a single cold tear roll slowly down my face to drop into her palm. "And . . . I miss you *so much.*"

"And I've missed you." Her hand came up to wipe my cheek. Her voice was thick as she said, "One day we will be together again. But right now there is something you must finish—something only *you* can finish."

I knew what she meant. Only, I wasn't so sure that I *actually* could. "But I *can't*. . . . I can't stop La Mano. There's nothing I can manifest to beat Madremonte. I—I'm not *strong enough.*"

My abuela leaned in close to whisper, "Charlie, your strength doesn't come from your manifestations. . . . Your strength comes from *your heart*—your loving, selfless, *incredible* heart." Her eyes smiled into mine, and she said, "You might be able to manifest animal traits, mi hijo, but you're more *human* than all of us." As she spoke, the edges of my abuela's face began to glow, her outline blazing out, blurring into pure white light. Before I could ask what was going on, she said, "¿Y Carlito?"

"Yeah?"

"Evil has always drawn its power from fear, from anger. So don't hold on to any and it won't have any power over you."

CHAPTER ONE HUNDRED EIGHT

CHAAARRRLIEEEE!"

My name echoed through my head like thunder, and my eyes burst open and I sat up, gasping, a circle of white-hot pain burning—*blazing*—in the center of my forehead. My eyes flew to the thorn that had pierced my heart, and I saw that it had begun to sizzle and burn as if someone was blasting it with a blowtorch.

At the same moment I noticed a fine yellow dust drifting down from between my eyes; it fell in tiny flakes and smelled faintly of wet hay.

¡Santo cielos! It was the stuff Zarate had dotted onto my forehead! And just like that la bruja's words came back to me: *La Marca will give you a second chance. But only one.*

I felt a tingling sensation in my chest and looked down again to see that the thorn had completely burned away, leaving nothing behind but a crumble of brownish ash that had gathered in the center of my lap. The hole in my shirt was still there, but the hole in *my chest* was not—and there wasn't even a scar.

Madremonte gave me a puzzled look. "Tricky bruja," she said. "Pero no es un problema—we'll simply try that again."

She let out a loud roar, and the walls of hedges began to tremble as if there were some wild animal trapped inside trying to break free. A hail of thorns shot out, arching through the air as they flew toward us.

There were too many. Way too many. There was no way to dodge.

The thorns came screaming at us like a prickly wall of death—

And less than three inches from our faces they seemed to hit an invisible barrier, which flickered with bursts of greenish light as the thorns embedded themselves into it. For a crazy second I went all Urkel, thinking, *Did I do that?* Then the barrier must have dissipated because the thorns clattered harmlessly to the bony floor.

Without thinking, I picked one up and saw that its razor tip had been seared flat, like someone had taken a butcher's knife and hacked off the end.

They were basically harmless now. Harmless twists of dried-up leaves. Violet's eyes, wide with shock but relieved—really, *really* relieved—found mine.

"*Tsk, tsk, tsk* . . . ," said a low, smooth voice at our backs.

I spun, saw the Witch Queen of Toledo standing there, her green eyes like fire, her long jeweled arms hanging loosely at her sides.

Relief crashed over me like a tidal wave—we weren't going to die after all!

Joanna was shaking her head disapprovingly at Madremonte, her expression one of barely contained fury. "Not playing nice with los niños . . . I'm disappointed."

Then, in a blur of motion, she charged forward as Madremonte unleashed another volley of thorns, raising some sort of greenish-bluish shield that expanded over her like a liquid bubble, repelling the thorns, and tackled Mother Mountain (or should I say, the Mother of All Traitors) around the waist, both of the them vanishing out of sight with a crack of thunder the instant their bodies touched.

I stared at the spot where they'd just been standing, dazed. "Where'd they go?"

"Charlie, the hand!" Violet shouted, hauling me to my feet.

"Go . . . go!"

We raced past Madremonte's thorny hedge but didn't make it more than four, maybe five steps before a roaring, shrieking column of wind snaked down from out of nowhere, lifting us off our feet and sending us flying. Violet was thrown one way, almost ten yards up the hall, crashing down so hard she didn't even scream, and I was flung the other, the entire left side of my body going numb as I slammed against the wall, hitting the floor a moment later like a sack of bricks.

My head spun. The ground seemed to seesaw around me. Rolling onto my side, I grimaced at the pain in my ribs, my neck, my spine—and turned my bleary, tear-filled eyes up the hall to see the hand—La Mano Peluda itself—dancing along the edge of a cutout in the far wall, which overlooked the main altar. There it was . . . prancing around on its fingertips, like some hairy, deformed, five-legged spider, flicking and kicking its fingers as it played puppeteer over the zombie horde below.

"You're mine," I growled, but as I clawed at the gaps and cracks in the floor, trying to pull myself toward Violet, toward the hand, someone suddenly appeared in front of me, seeming to materialize out of thin air. And there *he* was—the legendary overall-wearing traitor himself—Saci Pererê, removing his stinking red cap and glancing around at us with that seashell pipe hanging off his lip.

CHAPTER ONE HUNDRED NINE

I felt my hands ball into fists. "Saci, you backstabbing *punk!*"

"Traitor!" I heard Violet shout.

Saci turned those big brown eyes on me. "Dis no personal . . . ," he said. "Saci hope you two understand."

"HOW COULD YOU DO THIS?" I screamed up at him. "WE *TRUSTED* YOU!"

"Saci got problem, okay? You know dis. *La Mano* know dis . . . and dey use it to make Saci do thing Saci no wanna do."

"Like betraying your *friends?!*"

"Addiction's a cruel master, irmão. . . . It take you farther than you wanna go and make you hurt people you don' never wanna hurt." His expression turned hard, like stone. "But Saci don't have no friends. . . . Saci don't *need* no friends."

"You're wrong," I said. "You *had* friends. You had *us.*

But"—I flinched against a stab of pain in my ribs—"I guess you're right, too, because we're not your friends anymore."

A flash of hurt flickered across his face. "You think dis new for Saci?" he snapped, his voice bitter, his hands clenched fists at his sides. "Saci been alone his whole life! Saci don't have no parents. Saci don't have *no* family. SACI DON'T EVEN KNOW WHERE SACI COME FROM!" His dark eyes seemed to swim in their sockets. "And nobody ever like Saci when Saci was little. . . . Ain't nobody wanna be Saci's friend, because Saci *different*. . . . Saci only got one leg. He hop, not walk. . . . Saci got holes in his hands, can't scoop water from the river to drink like everybody else. Nobody like Saci, nobody *need* Saci, so Saci don't like or need *nobody*. . . . Like I say, Saci born alone, Saci gonna die alone—and that's *that*."

"You talk like you're so tough," I said, "but all that stuff about not needing people—you're *lying*. You want people to remember you, to talk about you. That's why you behave the way you do; that's why you play all those pranks! You're crying out for attention, dude! You want people *to know* you exist, so that maybe one day—*just maybe*—you'll find that one person who'll give you the only thing you ever really wanted, the *one thing* you could never prank your way into getting . . . *friendship*."

Saci blinked, and a single tear streaked down his chubby cheek. "You don' know Saci. . . . You don' know what it's like being *different*."

"Except I know *exactly* what it's like! I've had horns growing out of *my head*, lobster claws for hands—I *currently* have wings stretching out of *my back*. I'm, like, the biggest freak in the whole world! And I was terrified—*sooo terrified*—that someone would find out just how different I really was. . . . But you wanna know what I learned? I learned that what makes you special aren't the things that make you *like* everyone else; it's *every single little thing* that makes you *unlike* them."

Saci was shaking his head now, tears free-falling down his face.

"¿Qué esperas?" roared a voice behind us. "Kill him already!"

I snapped my head around, grimacing against the pain in my neck. The asema was standing in the middle of the hallway, just beyond the thorny hedge. Its face was twisted in an angry snarl, revealing a bloodred mouth choked with jagged fangs. Its eyes burned with hate.

Saci looked from me to the vampire, then back again. He wiped tears from his face, stretched one hand out toward me, palm out. I couldn't believe it. He was seriously getting ready to whirlwind me into the afterlife. Getting ready to, quite literally, blow me away. Even after everything we'd been through—after everything I'd said!

"FINISH HIM!" cried the asema. "¡TERMÍNALO!"

Saci's lips had begun to tremble. He flexed his fingers. His expression changed, becoming fierce, his dark eyes narrowing . . . but then his face changed again, softening; all the anger, all the venom vanishing from his eyes in an instant. He lowered his hand. His lips stopped trembling.

The asema started to come forward. "What are you doing? KILL HIM!"

But Saci said, "No."

Which stopped the vampire in its track. Its furious, hate-filled eyes bore into Saci. "¿Qué?" it hissed through its fangs. "Shall I take back the deed to the sugarcane farm? SHALL I TAKE BACK OUR *ENTIRE AGREEMENT?*"

"Go ahead." For several seconds that was Saci's only answer. Then his head turned, his dark eyes found mine, and he said, "Because friendship mean caring more about others than you do 'bout youself." He paused, glancing briefly toward Violet, before turning his gaze back to the vampire and adding, "And Saci don't want no sugar farm anymore, anyway. Eating too much sweets been linked wit obesity and diabetes. A friend I once had taught me dat. So you can take it back. Take it *all* back."

And as you can imagine, that wasn't exactly what the asema wanted to hear. The vampire let out a shriek high-pitched enough to shatter glass. My entire being seemed to flinch against that awful sound—and next thing, the asema transformed into a ball of light, a vapory, bluish orb that streaked up the hall toward us. It reappeared behind Saci, close enough to stare directly down at his shiny bald head; Saci had a moment to smile at me, just a second or two for his lips to begin to curl mischievously up at the corners. Then one of the vampire's clawlike hands snapped out, and I saw Saci's eyes widen in shock—in pain.

"NOOOOOOOO!" I roared, and in what felt like slow motion, began pushing up with my legs even as Saci's gave out underneath him.

The asema, holding him up now, smiling wickedly, bent its head down to snarl into his ear, *"How does it feel to be stabbed in the back . . . ?"*

But an instant later its eyes too widened in a look of shock and pain.

"You tell *me,"* growled another voice—*Violet's.* She'd snuck up behind the vampire, Juan's wooden dagger in her hand, and now she gave it a vicious twist.

The asema's face instantly drained of color. Its mouth

opened in a soundless scream of horror, and before I could flinch, it exploded into a swirling cloud of bluish, chalky ash.

Without the vampire holding him up, Saci collapsed to the ground like a sack of rice.

"SACI!" I screamed, and Violet and I knelt down beside him; I lifted his head off the floor, resting it on my lap. Those big brown eyes rolled up to look at me.

"Forgive me. . . . Forgive Saci," he said, reaching out for me with trembling hands.

"There's nothing to forgive . . . ," I told him as he gripped my hand between both of his. His fingers were cold—freezing cold. "Just hold on! Hold on, okay? Zarate can help. She can make you all better." Her yellowish marigold goo had helped me, hadn't it? I turned, shouting, "ZARATE! CAN YOU HEAR ME? ZARATE, WE NEED YOU!"

But the sounds of battle were still reverberating through the castle, and I knew there was no way the witch could hear me.

"ZARATE!" I turned to call for her again, to stand up—but Saci grabbed me.

"Don' go. . . . It's too late; no one can help Saci now. . . ."

"Don't say that," Violet breathed. "Just hold on. I'll get her!"

"No." Saci's trembling fingers closed around V's wrist. "Stay with Saci. . . . Just stay."

Violet was nodding now, tears filling her eyes, streaming down her face like rain on a windowpane. "Okay. I'll stay. . . . We'll *both* stay."

My voice was thick, shaky, as I said, "You're gonna be all right, you hear me? You're going to be back in Brazil and pranking people in no time. Just relax." I tightened my grip on his hands.

Saci flinched. "I guess it's too late to make whirlwind and go bye-bye, huh?"

Violet and I both had to laugh at that. Laugh through the tears.

"We're ready to go if you are . . . ," I said.

Saci smiled up at me, wincing with the effort even that tiny movement had cost him. "Dis not such a bad way to go, you know," he said, his voice little more than a hoarse whisper. "Surrounded by meus amigos . . . by my *first friends* . . ." Dipping one trembling hand into the front of his overalls, he brought out a fat magic marker. After uncapping it with his teeth, he held it up, motioning for me to come closer. "For old time sake?" I grinned, leaning down so he could write on my face. When he finished, he motioned to Violet, and she also bent down so he could write on her. This time when he was done he looked up at us, smiling, and whispered, "Pranked you both once las time. . . ."

On the last word, Saci's breath wheezed out of his lungs in a low sigh, his eyes closed, and his grip on my hands went limp, his fingers falling open, lifeless.

"No . . . no, no, no, no." I grabbed his shoulders, shook him. "C'mon, don't give up, dude. . . . SACI, LISTEN TO ME—DON'T GIVE UP! DO YOU HEAR ME? WAKE. *UP!*"

Violet touched her hands to mine. "Charlie . . . he's gone. . . ."

But I shook my head, not about to accept that. No, we had Zarate. We had *Joanna.* . . . One of them could bring him back—*couldn't they . . . ?*

Even as tears blurred the world around me, in my mind it was like I was watching clips from old home movies. I was seeing my abuela in her favorite rocking chair, telling me Saci's stories in the little living room of my old house. I saw myself lying out on my bed, no more than five years old, drawing pictures of Saci on the inside cover of my math book: Saci tying someone's shoelaces together, Saci sprinkling flies in a bowl of soup. I saw my mom and dad running around my backyard on a sunny afternoon, chasing me, while I dodged between lawn chairs and potted plants, wearing Saci's trademark red cap and overalls, pretending to *be* him.

He'd been one of my all-time favorite sombras for as far back as I could remember.

His stories had made me laugh. And smile. And dream.

He'd been a hero to me. The Prankster King of the World!

Back then I would've given anything to hang out with him. To go pranking with him.

And now I was watching him *die*.

Right here. In my arms.

It was too much. It was all just too much.

Violet met my eyes and, as if reading my thoughts, reached out to wipe a tear from my cheek.

"It's okay," she whispered. "He's free now. . . . He's free."

With my heart pounding in my throat, I said, "What did he write on my face . . . ?"

I heard V swallow as she said, "*Best.*" She paused to wipe her eyes. "And what about on mine?"

"*Friends,*" I answered, reading it right off her cheek—and the moment the words left my lips, it was as if everything inside me—every last ounce of strength—instantly crumbled.

I started bawling. Crying harder than I almost ever had. I probably sounded like a newborn *baby*—maybe even looked like one too. But I didn't care. Not even a little.

I'd just lost a friend. And right now that was *all* I cared about.

Choking on tears, I started to hang my head—

And caught movement out of the corner of my eyes. I turned, saw La Mano Peluda still dancing along the windowsill, strutting proudly around on its thumb and forefinger

And as my gaze narrowed on it, all my sadness, all my grief instantly turned to anger, a hot, boiling rage that burned in my veins like acid. I stared at it a moment longer, and my rage turned to fury, and suddenly the world seemed to fade away.

There was only me and *it*.

I didn't think, just grabbed the dagger poking out of the asema's ashes and took off toward the hand.

Less than five yards away, I beat my wings and lunged, hurtling through the air as I raised the sword over my head, preparing to bring it down like a stake.

I hated that hand like I'd never hated anything before in my *entire* life.

That was the hand behind my abuela's murder.

That was the puppeteer that had been pulling the strings when Violet had almost been poisoned, when my parents had been turned into dolls and nearly died.

That was the evil behind so many bad things that had

happened to the people I loved most, and now I just wanted to make it pay. No, I *would* make it pay.

As my sneakers touched back down, I brought the sword around in a sharp downward arc, intending to impale La Mano to the windowsill.

The tip of the dagger was less than four inches from the hand when it suddenly whirled around, fingers raised like a scorpion's tail, and the dagger froze in midair—

Froze completely.

Gritting my teeth, I began pulling down on the dagger with all of my strength, with every last ounce of my bodyweight. Only nothing happened.

It wouldn't budge. Not even an inch.

The hand had taken hold of it somehow. And even if I hadn't been feeling it, I could now see it: Dark, smoke-like tendrils were seeping out from beneath La Mano's fingernails, curling around the blade of the dagger even as I tried to force it down. Twisting and tightening, they climbed up the steel like some vapory, otherworldly ivy, overpowering me as it did. And the fact that I could now feel myself losing this struggle made me mad, made me even more *furious*.

Problem was, the angrier I got and the more I let myself hate La Mano, the stronger it seemed to get, and the stronger it got, the more furious and scared I became, and soon it was overpowering me with ease, turning the dagger back in my direction, aiming it straight for my heart, and there wasn't a *single* thing I could do about it.

I'm so gonna die. . . .

The smokelike tendrils darkened, thickened as the tip of the dagger grazed my chest, drawing blood. My arms were getting weaker. La Mano Peluda was getting stronger. My muscles were on fire, about to go. Translation: La Mano had won.

And just an instant before my grip opened up, an instant before La Mano could drive the blade into my heart—an instant before it could end my life like it had been trying to do for God knows how long—my abuela's words rang in my ears:

Evil has always drawn its power from fear, from anger. So don't hold on to any and it won't have any power over you.

I knew what I had to do. And it was easy, because just the memory of my abuela's words was enough to drive every scrap of the fear out of my heart. All I had to do was force the hate out with it so that's exactly what I did, and already I could feel La Mano's hold on the sword weakening. So I just kept thinking about my family, my abuelita, my parents, about Violet, about my friends, Alvin and Sam—basically everyone who loved me and cared about me, and I tried to let as much love into my heart as possible, because I knew that love always—always—chases out fear and hate. And when I saw the sword begin to shudder, I gritted my teeth, muscled the pointy end back over the La Mano's hairy, upraised fingers, and whispered, "My abuelita told me not to fear you. Not to hate you. So I won't. But I will *end* you."

Then, in one Ninja Turtle–like move, I swung my legs up over my head, doing a sort of handstand on the hilt of the dagger, and gave my wings a great, big *flap*.

For a moment nothing happened. Which, honestly, got me a *tad bit* worried.

But then, it *did*.

La Mano's hold finally broke. The dark, smoky tendrils first merged into a single boiling, roiling cloud, then scattered, shrieking, as the sword slammed down, piercing the hand and burying itself into the windowsill like a stake. In that same instant, the shrillest, awfullest, most *earsplitting* cry I'd ever heard ripped through the castle, and a wall of inky blackness exploded out of the hand with the force of dynamite. I went hurtling sideways, smashed against the bony wall, banging my head, my back, my shoulders, then hit the ground in a tangled, twisted heap. I'm not gonna lie—I was hurting pretty bad right now. Not to mention I was bleeding, teetering on the verge of unconsciousness, and really couldn't feel either one of my wings.

But the most important thing? I was smiling.

Smiling even as the world faded around me.

CHAPTER ONE HUNDRED TEN

When I woke up, I was lying on a comfy pew inside a large, beautiful church. The floors were white marble. A huge glittering chandelier hung overhead. Sunshine was streaming in through one of the high windows, painting the entire room in a gauzy, yellow light. I realized someone was sitting next to me—a woman, tanned, with dark reddish hair held up in a loose bun. As I rolled onto my back, she turned to look at me—and I froze. "*Mom?* Mom, what are you doing here . . . ?"

My mom, who looked like she hadn't slept in a day or two (or maybe three, to be exact), slitted her eyes at me the way she does when she's really, really—*really, really, really*—mad, and I knew I was pretty much done for. "*Carlito Ernesto Hernández,* do you have *any idea* what you've put us through? How *dare* you sneak out of the house in the middle of the night? You disobeyed me. You disobeyed your father. You put yourself in *unthinkable* danger, and before you say anything—even a *single word*—I just want you to know that I am just so, *soooo . . . proud of you.*"

"Mom, I'm sorry. I—" *Huh . . . ?*

I sat up, rubbing my eyes, and she threw her arms around me, squeezing so tight it hurt. "Joanna told me everything," she said. "You did so much good here today, Charlie; you saved many, *many* lives."

I could feel her crying now, her whole body shaking, and that was enough to make me tear up too. "Mom, I'm sorry . . . about everything."

"No, mi vida. Don't be. You know what's most important to me, right? What is that?"

I drew a total blank. And that was probably due to a mild concussion. "That I . . . *help people?*" Total shot in the dark.

"No. That's *a bit* further down on my list. The *most* important thing to me is that you're okay. And you are. So *I'm* okay." She looked at me, her eyes swimming with tears. "Now, are you still grounded for the rest of your *natural-born life?* Absolutely. And I'd ground you for even longer if I could."

Another tear rolled down her face as she gave me a lopsided smile, and I couldn't help but smile back, even though I had a sneaking suspicion that she wasn't kidding about that whole grounded-for-the-rest-of-your-natural-born-life thing. I was just so happy to see her, I honestly didn't even care. "But—how did you know where to find me?"

She held up her cell phone. "The app's called Where'sDoggy. You can thank Alvin."

I realized I was still wearing the stupid dog collar Alvin had given me and had to laugh.

A moment later, as my mom ran her fingers through my damp, messy hair, still smiling at me, I said, "Mom, I saw her. . . ."

She shook her head. "You saw who?"

"Abuelita. . . . We talked. She's . . . She says she's always watching over me."

More tears tumbled down my mother's cheeks as she leaned forward to kiss the top of my head. "She loved you so much . . . so, *so* much."

The door at the other end of the church opened. A thick column of sunshine slanted in, and someone poked their head inside for a moment before shutting the door again.

My mom was staring in that direction. "Where's your father?" she said, frowning. "I told him to get you something to eat; I don't know what's taking him so long. I'll be right back."

She had barely reached the doors and opened them when a voice spoke up behind me. "How are you feeling, Charlie?"

I turned to see Queen Joanna, El Justo Juez, El Cadejo, and Juan the basajaun all standing there, the four of them looking *a wee bit* more scruffy than usual, but still pretty good—all things considered, anyway.

"I've felt better," I said with a smile, and they all smiled back. (Except for Justo Juez, of course; though I'm pretty sure he was smiling on the inside.) "So what happened after I stabbed the hand?" I asked.

"Well, without their puppeteer," Joanna said, "the walking corpses returned to their natural state—*dead*. The Okpes and the rest of La Mano Peluda's followers fled the moment they realized you'd stabbed it. Wasn't much of a fight after that."

El Cadejo nuzzled my cheek with his big furry head; then he dragged his tongue across my face in his usual friendly greeting while he spoke directly into my mind: *Charlie, we all want to apologize for using you the way we did. For putting you in such a dangerous position—and for doing it without your knowledge. But when we learned El Dark Brujo's hand had once again been resurrected, we had to act swiftly; we had to draw it out into the open, and this was the only way. If there had been any other, pequeño, I promise you we would have chosen it.*

"I know," I said, stroking his thick, soft fur, and it was true. I knew they all cared about me—cared *a lot*—and from everything I'd seen and heard over the last few days, what they'd done really did seem like the only way. But there *was* something I was curious about. . . .

"So where were you guys the whole time?" I said, looking between El Cadejo and Justo Juez. "I mean, before we ran into you in El Salvador. . . ."

"All over Central America," Juez replied, his voice crackling like burning logs.

It was all part of the show, El Cadejo explained. *La Mano Peluda was trying to lead us away from you to make sure we couldn't interfere in their plans, so we had to pretend to be fools—to be fooled. But we didn't leave you without protection, as I'm sure you know.*

"And he certainly didn't make it easy on me. . . ." Anahí— or did she go by Adriana now?—walked up beside them, no longer in tree form except for a little bit of moss showing on the back of one arm; beside her stood the witch Zarate with her peacock; all three of them smiled warmly at me (the peacock included—which was a little freaky, but also cool); then Adriana wrapped me up in a big hug, the palms of her hands still rough and a bit barky.

"Sorry about that," I said sheepishly.

Queen Joanna took my hand between both of hers. Her many emerald rings glittered like fish scales. Her butterfly pin, I noticed, was once again pinned to the front of her gown. And interestingly enough, its wings were beating faintly. "No, I'm the one who is sorry," she whispered. "This was all my scheming, and for that I beg your forgiveness. But if it makes you feel any better, I did not exactly take it easy on myself, either. . . ."

That made me grin. "Does make me feel a little better. . . . So, like, you knew what La Mano Peluda was planning from the very *beginning*?"

"Sí. Which is why we had to put on such an *elaborate* show, and why *certain* players had to be left in the dark until the very end."

"Like Los Embrujados?"

"Precisamente," she said, sounding like a teacher whose favorite student had just given a good answer. "And it was a shame that we had to because those lobisomem are, in fact, some of our fiercest allies. See, it was El Dark Brujo himself who, in their moment of greatest weakness, exploited their grief and turned them into lobisomem, hoping to add them to his numbers. They have been his sworn enemies since that day. So naturally, when they uncovered the necromancer's scheme, they moved to stop him, which meant that they first needed to first stop *you* from breaking the elemental bonds on his coffins. And it was that exact reaction that we required, because El Brujo would have expected nothing less. In fact, *anything* less would have aroused his suspicions. . . . Like I said, it was quite an elaborate show."

"And what about Madremonte?" I asked. "You knew about her, too?"

"We've had our suspicions for a while. . . ."

"But why did she do it? Why would she betray La Liga?"

"Each soul carries its own burdens; I find that it is always best not to judge others. However, I can tell you that her feelings about *me* have changed over time; she's begun to feel that I've grown too cautious, too calculated. But if I have indeed become overly deliberate, it is only because I have found hope, Charlie. Because I have found *you*."

Juan the basajaun gave me a huge toothy grin through that bushy blond beard of his and reached down—like way, *way* down (dude was almost ten feet tall)—to ruffle my hair. Then he patted me on the back with one ginormous hand and nearly sent me flying off the pew.

"She did, unfortunately, manage to escape," Joanna continued. "Madremonte is quite powerful. And even more than powerful, she's infinitely cunning. La Mano, however—gracias a ti—did not."

"So we did it, huh . . . ?" I smiled up at all of them. "We won. He's gone for good, right?"

The six of them exchanged uneasy looks, and there was a sinking feeling in the pit of my stomach. "What? What's wrong?" I asked.

The queen raised her hands, patting the air, as if to calm me down. "We've won *this* battle, Charlie . . . but I'm afraid to say the real war has only *just* begun."

"But don' theenk on deeth," Juan said, wagging a furry finger at me

"¡No, ni lo pienses!" Juez agreed. "Eat what your parents are bringing for you and try to relax. . . ."

Nodding, I took a deep breath, trying to take Juez's advice, but suddenly remembered something—or should I say, some*one*. "What about Saci?" I whispered, sort of mentally crossing my fingers—hoping against hope. "Did you find him?"

Joanna's expression was tight as she said, "We did."

"He helped us," I told her. "He might've started off on their side, but he ended up on ours."

"Sí, I know."

"Were you . . . able to do *anything*?" I could hear the anxiousness in my voice, and when the queen frowned, I felt my heart break all over again.

"He was too far gone. But we will honor his memory *and* his sacrifice. We will bury him in his own country, as he would have wished."

"I want to be there," I said, and meant it, too. It was the least I could do for a friend. Especially one that had given his life to save mine.

"And you will be," Joanna assured me. "But for now, relájate. Gather your strength. We have a little more to take care of here and then we'll be off." She started to turn, then stopped, her green eyes suddenly bright with curiosity. "Oh, and, Charlie, one question: When Madremonte stabbed you through the heart with the thorn, who was it that you called out to?"

Called out to? "Uh, no one . . ."

"But you were communicating with someone, ¿sí?"

Surprised, I sat up higher in the pew. "Yeah, my grandmother. How'd you know?"

Joanna's face wore a shocked look, but she said nothing.

"But—that's because I *died*, right . . . ? I mean, was *dead* . . . *no?*"

"Death has nothing to do with it," she said. "At that moment, you reached out across the worlds with your innermost being. You reached from this world into the other. Into La Tierra de los Muertos. And . . . somehow your abuelita must've been reaching out to *you* at the exact same moment. Quite a remarkable happening, if truth be told."

"But what . . . *exactly* happened?"

"Un abrazo del alma—*a soul embrace.* It's a spiritual connection between two individuals. Very, *very* brief, but very, *very* powerful. And in a location such as we were, especially given the season, such connections are easier made. But do not be fooled—they are still *incredibly* rare, conjured only by the most *powerful* sombras. You two must've shared a very strong bond to be able to have found each other that way."

"I loved her. I mean, I *love* her. . . . She helped raise me." I watched Joanna nod for a few moments and then a sudden thought struck me, one that had me grinning like a gator. "But—can I do it again . . . ? Like, if I wanted to just say hi or whatever?"

The queen's expression suddenly darkened, and she shook her head vigorously. "No, Charlie. Do not seek out contact with the dead, for those affairs are beset with sorrow and pain. You must not pursue them. I nearly went mad myself attempting to do exactly what you speak of."

"You mean like with King Philip?"

That stopped her. Those bright green eyes sharpened on me. "How did you know that?"

"Saci had one of your memory-painting thingies in his pipe, so I kinda *saw*. Why didn't you tell us you were Juana de Castilla . . . ?"

"There are things in my past, things my family has done that I am not proud of. I have been trying to atone for some sins for quite a while now." She paused before saying, "Oh, and despite what you might have heard about me, from Saci or otherwise, I was never *actually* crazy . . . crazy in love, perhaps—madly, even—but completely sound of mind. . . . Thought you should know."

"I kinda knew that already," I said, and smiled.

Behind us the door to the church opened again, and this time someone shouted my name. I turned and saw Violet, and the moment our eyes met, she came running toward me, her sneakers making sticky, smacking sounds on the tile.

Perhaps we should give them a moment, said El Cadejo, and the queen, trying to hide a smile, nodded her agreement. "Yes, perhaps we give them some *privacy*. . . ."

I felt my ears turn pink and gave Joanna a *ha-ha, very funny* sort of look as they all turned to go, Adriana waving at me over her shoulder, a beautiful red flower peeking out of her hair. I couldn't help but wonder if she'd plucked that flower or grown it herself. My money was on grown.

"Sleeping Beauty finally wakes up!" V said as she came up behind the pew. I felt my ears go from pink to chili-pepper read

I rubbed my head, which still felt a little woozy. "How long have I been out?"

"Almost veinte minutos."

That made me laugh. "You're getting pretty good at Spanish. . . ."

Violet brushed a curl of blond hair out of her eyes,

flashing me one of her million-megawatt smiles. "I have a really great teacher."

"Really? *Who?*" I said, and when she gave me a look that was all like, *HELLO?* I finally got it. "Oh, right . . . well, I told you I'd make a good teacher."

V grinned, smacked me on the side of the arm.

"El brazo . . . Watch el brazo," I said, teasing her. "You gotta be gentle with me. Been through a lot, you know."

"Right, right. And el brazo is the, um, head, right?" Giving it back to me. "Brazo . . . cabeza—I'm getting them all mixed up now."

"Maybe your Spanish isn't as good as I thought," I said with a smirk, and V, of course, smacked me again, that million-megawatt smile still crackling at full voltage.

"C'mon, your mom and dad are waiting for us at the little café down the street. . . . They ordered tamales, chile colorado, and these crispy rolled-up tortilla things called *flautas*, which are, like, *to die for*."

"You had me at tamales," I said.

As we started down the aisle toward the church door, I asked Violet if she wanted to hear a joke. She said sure, so I said, "There was this Spanish magician who claimed he could disappear. And the way he'd do it was pretty cool; he'd always start by counting, 'Uno, dos . . .'. And then— *poof!*—he'd vanish without a *tres*."

Violet burst out laughing. "That's a *terrible* joke, Charlie. . . . Got any more?"

I didn't. So in my best Porky Pig impression, I said: "Th-th-the, th-th-the, th-th-that's todo, folks!"

CHAPTER ONE HUNDRED ELEVEN

The sun was setting over the ring of grassy green hills that framed the horizon by the time we made it to Casa de Frutas, a huge banana plantation some-where in southeast Brazil. Joanna said that Saci had been born not too far from here a couple thousand years ago—or so she'd heard—and she thought this was where he'd probably want us to bury him. So Juan handed Violet and me a couple of shovels, and all four of us went to work digging the grave where V and I would lay to rest our newest friend—a friend who'd showed us the mean-ing of friendship. It took only about ten or so minutes to dig the hole—thanks mostly to Juan's ability to move huge amounts of earth—and maybe five minutes after that we had Saci buried, with a large gray rock Joanna had brought over from Mexico to mark the spot. Joanna inscribed it with the words "Aqui jaz um Saci Pererê, verdadeiro filho da Pindorama, y um amigo leal até o fim," which in Portuguese means, "Here lies Saci Pererê, a true son of the Land of the Palms, and a loyal friend to the very end." Violet and I knelt beside his grave, and V opened her backpack and brought out Saci's little red cap and seashell pipe. She held the cap out to me, and I wiped my dirt-smudged hand across the front of my shirt before taking it. Then, gazing around at all the green banana leaves flapping in the cool November breeze, I breathed in the sweet smell of ripening fruit and found myself smiling—I knew Saci would love this place . . . even if there didn't seem to be anyone around for him to mess with.

Feeling tears burn behind my eyes, I placed the cap on the ground below the burial stone and whispered good-bye to the all-time king of pranksters as Violet did the same with the pipe. For what felt like a long time neither of us said anything. I listened to the wind blow between trees, to the steady rhythm of my heartbeat. I wondered how old Saci had been. I wondered what his childhood had been like. I wondered if he'd ever been to Miami and what he might've thought about it. I started to wonder something else and then stopped when I heard Violet give a weak laugh.

"You okay?" I said.

She nodded. "Yeah, I was just thinking about something Saci said . . ."

I smiled, imagining what it could be. Probably something completely off the wall. Actually, scratch that—more like, *definitely* something completely off the wall.

Violet wiped a hand across her cheek. "Remember when he told us how much Brazil loved him? How a witch had told him that Brazil herself would always look after him or whatever—that it would never ever let him die?"

"Sounds like typical Saci."

"Yes, exactly! That was *him*. Always making stuff up. Always having fun. Pretty much saying and doing whatever he wanted. That's what was so great about him!" Her smile faltered, turning regretful as she whispered, "I just—I wish it had been true, you know?"

I did know. Truth was, right now I wished it more than *anything*. "Yeah . . ."

A few seconds later, the wind picked up around us, gusting through the banana trees, and a few feet away I heard Juan whisper, "Debemos irnos. No debemos dejar La Provencia sin protección en estos tiempos."

I glanced back at Joanna. "Why do we have to go? Is something wrong?"

"No," she replied calmly. "Nothing's wrong. It's just that an enemigo is never more dangerous than when you've wounded him. And make no mistake, we've wounded him." The queen turned to stare out at the cloudless late-afternoon sky, her glowing eyes bright even in the column of sunshine illuminating her face. "But Juan is right," she said after a moment. "We should get going. A storm is coming—yes, is nearly here. It would be wise for all of us to prepare."

I couldn't say for sure, but something about the way she'd said that made me pretty confident she wasn't talking about the weather.

EPILOGUE

urelio Espenola, known by more than a few of his neighbors and friends—those who dared call themselves as such—as Aurelio El Curioso or Aurelio *the Nosy*, watched the odd group of strangers who had seemed to blow in with the wind itself with only mild curiosity. Aurelio had lived a long and rather remarkable eighty-seven years and had seen many peculiar sights in that time, and this group of strangers—even with their rather large, rather *hairy* blond-haired ape—didn't come close to making his top ten. Anyway, they stood well off his property, gathered in a little circle along the edge of the neighboring sugarcane field, a field Aurelio did not believe (nor did anyone else in this area) belonged to anyone in particular, so what did he care what they were up to?

At least that's what he told himself for the first handful of minutes as he busied himself yanking the dead and browning leaves off his favorite banana tree so his prized Prata bananas could grow big and strong. But once he was finished, Aurelio could no longer contain himself—and honestly, how could he be *expected* to? There was *clearly* something curious afoot; what *was* that strange woman with those two strange children and their enormous ape doing over there, anyway? They *obviously* weren't farmers, and they *obviously* weren't planting or reaping or tending the soil in any way he could tell. No, they surely were *not*. And this sort of odd behavior needed looking into—*required* it, in fact, and since there wasn't another soul out here, he decided that the burden had once again fallen upon him. In Aurelio's experience, it usually did.

Tossing aside a handful of dead leaves, the old farmer made his way slowly but purposefully across his three-acre banana farm, pruning a tree or two along the way so as not to waste the distance traveled (Aurelio had always been a correct, if not efficient, man)—and reached the spot where the strangers had been gathered just as they wandered off into the trees. To his surprise, he had come upon what appeared to be some kind of burial site, and at first he felt a pang of sorrow and shame, for he had thought ill of the woman and her children who had merely come here to bury some beloved pet—the family pig, perhaps. But when he read the inscription on the headstone, he had himself a great big laugh. *Saci Pererê?* Those bobos had come all the way out here to make a *grave* for that old and silly myth? Aurelio almost couldn't believe his eyes. Some people and the *ridiculous* things they did to pass the time . . .

The old man's left knee began to ache as it had after all these years of tilling the ground, and he cursed himself for his eternal, ceaseless curiosity (a curiosity which his mother, God rest her soul, had often told him would be the end of him), and then he cursed that wretched family and their oversize ape for giving him reason. As he turned to head back toward his prized tree—Mariana, as he'd named it, still required a bit more tending to, not to mention watering—something rather odd happened: In the blink of an eye the once-clear blue November sky darkened to the color of bruised bananas. Black clouds churned and boiled overhead. Lightning crackled. Rain began to lash down in violent, spitting waves.

Suddenly the ground below Aurelio's sandaled feet began to quake as he had never felt it quake before, and down from the dark, angry sky above snaked the largest whirlwind he had ever seen. It touched down on the grave with all the fury of a hurricane, uprooting banana trees and snatching up the cap and pipe in a swirl of howling wind and freezing rain.

To Aurelio it felt as if the entire field—no, the entire *earth*!—was now groaning.

His eyes flew back to the grave site, which had begun to throb like a living, beating heart.

And what he saw next did, in fact, make it onto Aurelio's top ten list of the most peculiar things he had ever seen. Made it all the way to number *one*.

GLOSSARY

alicanto: a race of mythical birds that feed on precious metals.

anchimayen: beings from Mapuche mythology that take the form of small children and can transform into fireballs.

bruja: a witch or sorceress.

brujo: a warlock or sorcerer.

castell: altars of resurrection magic.

chonchón: severed sorcerer heads with wings and talons; believed to be omens of impending danger.

chupacabra: a legendary creature known for drinking the blood of livestock. Its name literally translates to "goatsucker."

El Caballo Marino: a race of mythical seahorses native to Chiloé; these horse-fish hybrids are the main source of transportation for the sorcerers of Chiloé.

El Justo Juez: a legendary Salvadorian figure who prowls the night on horseback in search of evildoers. His name translates as "Righteous Judge," and it is said that the night belongs to him and him alone.

El Nguruvilu: part fox, part serpent, this river-dwelling creature unleashes powerful whirlpools to drown those who attempt to cross rivers.

La Mano Peluda: a cabal of evil sombras; also the name of the hand of El Dark Brujo, whose hand came back from the grave for revenge.

La Pisadeira: a powerful ancient hag who preys on those who go to bed with full stomachs. Her name translates to "She who steps."

lobisomem: a race of werewolves native to Brazil.

Los Embrujados: a clan of former priests who were turned into werewolves by El Dark Brujo.

Madremonte: the protector of the jungles and mountains of Colombia. "Mother Mountain" is considered by some to be the personification of nature itself and sometimes curses those who steal their neighbor's land or harm animals.

minairons: a species of tiny builder elves that live inside Saint-John's-wort.

Minhocão: a species of gigantic earthworms.

mukis: cave-dwelling goblinlike creatures found throughout South America. They possess the ability to transform rock into precious metals and are said to make pacts with miners—many times to the miners' harm.

nahual: a shape-shifting witch or sorcerer capable of transforming themselves into animals, most commonly large dogs, jaguars, or birds. Legends of the nahual first appear in Mesoamerican culture.

Okpe: a tribe of ogres with piglike features and impenetrable rocky armor.

Saci Pererê: legendary mythical prankster from Brazil known for his trademark red overalls and magical cap.

sombra: legendary or mythological being or creature.

ABOUT THE AUTHOR

Ryan Calejo was born and raised in South Florida. He graduated from the University of Miami with a BA. He's been invited to join both the National Society of Collegiate Scholars and the Golden Key International Honour Society. He teaches swimming to elementary school students, chess to middle school students, and writing to high school students. Having been born into a family of immigrants and growing up in the so-called Capital of Latin America, Ryan knows the importance of diversity in our communities and is passionate about writing books that children of all ethnicities can relate to. His first novel was *Charlie Hernández & the League of Shadows*.